Sam and Mike were lifelong friends, too wealthy and too sure of the future to let a Miami grand jury come between them. Sam had always covered the tracks of his investments. He was determined not to lose it all now. . . .

"Sam!" Mike called down the back corridor leading to the grand jury room. Sam quickly turned around. . . .

"The marshal ushers me in there, ushers me out. Got a personality like a funeral director," Sam said as he came up the hall to where Mike was standing. They walked into one of the waiting rooms.

"Are you here alone?" Sam asked, shuffling quarters between his fingers.

"Yes. You?"

"No. Liz is here." Sam looked around the room. He moved his head toward the air-conditioning duct, then sideways. Mike kept his blank expression, but he was thinking that Sam had seen too many spy movies. Maybe not. The government was certainly capable of bugging a room where witnesses waited before a grand jury.

"They didn't get anything out of me," Sam said. "I don't mind talking, but they're not getting anything for their fishing expedition. Fact or fiction. But," Sam went on, winking once, then winking again, "it didn't make any difference. I didn't know anything anyway."

Mike's expression didn't change. Sam *was* giving answers. . . . He'd said he "didn't mind talking." Sam was telling him he was testifying. *He was not refusing to answer*. He was *not* taking the Fifth Amendment. . . .

"Compelling enough to hold us to the last page. . . ."
—*The West Coast Review of Books*

ABOVE THE LAW

ROBERT ROBIN

POCKET **STAR** BOOKS

New York   London   Toronto   Sydney   Tokyo   Singapore

This book is a work of fiction. Names, characters, places and incidents are either products of the author's imagination or are used fictitiously. Any resemblance to actual events or locales or persons, living or dead, is entirely coincidental.

A Pocket Star Book published by
POCKET BOOKS, a division of Simon & Schuster Inc.
1230 Avenue of the Americas, New York, NY 10020

Copyright © 1992 by Robert Robin

ISBN: 0-671-74424-0

First Pocket Books printing July 1993

10 9 8 7 6 5 4 3 2 1

POCKET STAR BOOKS and colophon are registered
trademarks of Simon & Schuster Inc.

Cover art by Dru Blair

Printed in the U.S.A.

FOR ESTHER SHAPIRO

*with respect
and affection*

Acknowledgments

As much as writing depends on solitude, it also depends on people who care. First, *sine qua non,* to Loretta Barrett, who is beyond sufficient thanks; to Julie Rubenstein, an editor of patience and great craft; to Bill Grose, Editorial Director of Pocket Books; to Sandy Brychel, Marla Shlau, Morgan Barnes, Kerry Lehman, Rich Nelson, Alan Hergott, and Michelle Robin for their encouragement and support; to Jim Streicker, a sage and solid counsel, a specialist in crimes of white collars, the workings of grand juries and their managers; and last, but never least, to Chad Moore, who kept the balance in the boat.

ABOVE THE LAW

Prologue

BILLY, MY BROTHER, IS THE FIRST SON. I AM THE SECOND son. In the beginning, you either got it or you didn't. Frankly, a lot of people didn't get it.

Then, if I am the second son, not the first son, why am I here? Racing down a steaming black highway (the speedometer reads eighty) in the middle of a tropical rain in one of Dad's Lincolns, the windshield wet from torrents of gushing water.

Because Billy's dumb, Dad says. That's why.

Dad's car is midnight blue in daylight, looks black at night, and I am driving it down a narrow Florida two-laner, dark and inhospitable and, except for the air blowing past the windows, silent. The pine forest, close to the highway on both sides, is soaked. The rain is still pouring down, the ground cover buried in mud, and the animals, a squirrel, a rabbit, maybe a fox or two, are out there with wet fur.

I don't like Dad to say Billy's dumb. Billy's my brother.

There's soft wood inside those pines, "something you can sell, make money on," Dad told us. " 'Not worth much per cord,' they tell you. Goddamn lumber companies. Fuck you every time." Dad's words. "Horse and rabbit stew always tastes like the horse."

The windshield wipers try to wipe the rain from the glass,

which is flat; it doesn't curve back as it did in the old car, another old Lincoln, that old barge.

Billy didn't listen back then either.

"We're kikes to them," Dad said. "God doesn't grow trees for Hebes, they think," Dad said. "Dry goods, the jewelry store, okay, but not trees. They're wrong," Dad said. "God grows trees for me as well as them."

The red dirt is stained in streaks by rainwater, and tall, wet condos now tower behind the pine trees. White buildings. Trump's name on top of one. Dad hates Donald. "Let him have the Plaza. And the airline. He'll die with both of them," Dad said.

Billy still doesn't listen, even to this day. So it's me who must listen. Not my big brother. Me. I'm picked. I feel like the oldest man in the world, swimming like a fish in an aquarium.

"You don't win by getting A's at the Harvard Law School," Dad said to me.

I am the second son.

I am not listening either.

Then why am I here?

I don't want to hear what Dad tells me.

Mom doesn't want me to hear him either.

Or to be here.

"The Florida car will be in my spot at the Miami airport. You take it. They won't be expecting you."

So I make the car go faster. Two-laners twist. Whee! A wide turn between walls of trees Dad owns.

"In Israel, when they call you a 'dirty Jew' all they mean is that you need a bath," Dad said.

Dad's trees go by faster. I count not trees, but cords. Twenty cords per pine. Thirty. But the lumber company counts twelve when they count to determine our share. "I'll teach them," Dad said way back then. "No one fucks with me or mine."

Mom had squirmed at his choice of words, not at his determination.

"Be clear with them," Dad told me. My instructions for this trip.

2

"Your power is you are me."

At *that* I am listening.

Mom or no Mom.

"Forget what your mother says," Dad told me.

"Is that all, Dad?"

"You're going for me. Be me."

More rain.

Suddenly no wipers.

If I can only reach around . . .

. . . reach around and wipe the rain from the windshield. Did I keep my eyes and ears open? Did I do everything Dad asked?

. . . reach around and wipe the rain from the windshield . . .

. . . the car is shaking. Something's wrong . . .

And then, a parked ambulance, its blue lights rotating lazily, the driver and the policemen smoking in a group nearby.

PART ONE

1

BILLY SLIPPED ON THE SLICK PLASTIC RUNNERS LAID ACROSS the frosty ground and almost fell. He straightened up quickly and ignored the pain because he didn't want his father to touch him, though Sam had no interest in touching his first son. There was nothing to be afraid of on that account; there never was. Billy was turning twenty-eight, too old for a father to handle anyway, and he glanced around to look at his mother. She was following him away from his younger brother's grave, where Matt's classmates were shoveling in a few clods of dirt. They were surrounded by three hundred people, and they all stood in the oldest and shadiest part of the cemetery his father owned.

"You all right, Liz?" Sam asked. "He didn't trip you?"

Elizabeth Yones shook her head, saying nothing.

Billy didn't say anything either. He was used to the treatment. He kept looking down or to the side, avoiding by inches eye contact with his father.

Samuel B. "Two-Syllables" Yones was not surprised by being famous. He had always known he would be, and it was a long time since he had to personally tell anyone how to pronounce his name. He was a surprisingly small man, not like a dwarf but like a jockey, his body top-heavy with bulky shoulders and biceps, his face twisted by life as if lessons had been hammered into him since birth. He had a large round head, bright eyes like a bird, and jingled money in his pockets. A long key chain that went out of style years ago dazzled when he opened his jacket, and to this day he wore, clipped to his belt loop, a miniature gold photo album the size of a postage stamp that held bar mitzvah pictures of his boys engraved on gold pages. He walked with an athletic roll, as if he were aboard ship, never turned up except dressed too much, and a faint odor of Hermès cologne, even in a cemetery, heralded his approach.

It was cold, and the wind whipped at their hands and faces. No longer needing to turn pages in his prayer book, Sam decided to put on his gloves, first touching his wife's hand, feeling her skin. She was cold and also clammy, and he was concerned for her. "Liz, your hands," he said. "Did you bring gloves?" She shook her head, again saying nothing. "Then put your hands in your pockets, your hands are cold." She shook her head for the third time. "You, too," he said harshly to Billy, and Sam held his head high, forcing them all to look at him.

He was fifty-three years old, the general partner in more investment syndicates than most of these people could dream of, largely in timber, in land. People came to him with their money, paying him to invest their capital along with his. For his services, he received a larger share for his dollars than they received for theirs—he would put in twenty percent of the money and receive fifty percent of the investment—and those who wanted to be partners stood in line. Sam Yones controlled no public companies, made little disclosure through stock-exchange reports or federal agencies, but he would answer any question any partner asked, and he had an office door that was always open and his phone number was listed. He regarded himself available to his partners in a way that counted.

He did not change the American economy as Milken had, he wasn't that big, but those in his own world, the Steinbergs, the Icahns, and the Murdochs, knew him well. Sam liked being well known, but only by those who counted, and he loved to tell business-school audiences the lesson learned by the new millionaire who had just bought his first yacht. "Pa, look at this boat. Look at me with my hand on the wheel, the crest on my jacket, the scrambled eggs on my cap. Pa, look at me! Do I look like a captain?" "Son, to me you're a captain. But to a captain are you a captain?"

To the captains, Sam Yones was a captain.

He turned away from Billy, his remaining, his surviving son, and stepped back to take his wife's arm. The grass was a dense winter brown, and evergreen bushes marked the borders of the family plot. He began to steer Liz through the crowd away from Matt's grave. They headed toward the car on the far side of the pond, not the funeral director's car but another of his own Lincolns. Never a Mercedes. "You remember where you come from," he had told Matt and Billy he couldn't remember how many times. He didn't care what the others had or how much the press made fun of his little tics. Never that Nazi car.

Most people made way for them, but some pressed closer to hold a hand, kiss a cheek, touch, or say a few words. Liz was just about to turn fifty, slender, still with young skin although her hair had gone gray-blond. She was not wearing much makeup; her large, beautiful eyes were still clear, and she ignored any attempt to approach her. Every instinct in Sam made him want to halt, to please those who wanted to be near him, but he kept moving. He set a fast pace and she was glad to follow, to get away. Her thoughts were free now, and she could no longer control them. There was nothing to do but walk, no arrangements to make, no jobs to assign, nothing to be organized, nothing to look at but the gloomy winter sky.

Billy, still looking young from a distance, followed. Up close were the signs of his age: fine lines near his eyes, a slight loosening of the skin under his jaw. His eyes were old. He had already seen more of human nature than he could assimilate.

Among Matt's Harvard Law School classmates, his own Jewish Federation buddies, Liz's colleagues from the Guggenheim, where she sat on the board and gave tours, and the employees, lawyers, and accountants of his partnerships, Sam saw hundreds of people standing around, watching, but suddenly backing off, looking elsewhere when he looked at them.

Sam almost stopped to shake the hand of the reporter from the *Wall Street Journal*, the one who had written a two-part profile on him, not all of it bad. The article included two paragraphs on Billy, which was as much as anyone could manage. The younger son was a different story. Matt was a prince, a twenty-two-year-old to really write about. Promising, promising, promising, and on top of all that, accepted, as Sam never was, with a capital A, which pleased both Matt and Sam no end. He was the same reporter who had written that morning, for the Monday edition, that Matt was killed over the weekend driving back to law school from Fort Lauderdale, nothing about the plane trip, nothing about having sat in his father's seat, nothing about his return, his flight back through Miami to throw them off. The reporter made it look like a car accident over a winter break. He had written that Matt was driving a Lincoln, for he, like his father, wouldn't touch a German car. He had gone off the road. He had been alone. No other vehicle involved. He had just driven off the road.

Sam looked away from the reporter across what looked to be, for one short moment, nothing more than a huge winter field. Then his eyes fell on the headstones. So small, he thought, flat, a few inches off the ground, one headstone for each grave, spaced out in an even pattern, some in front and some behind a large family stone. They were all the color of the big stone that spelled Y-O-N-E-S, a painfully dark red granite with the five letters carved both in the front and on the back. The tiny flat markers told you who they were. Yetta Yones, in English and Hebrew. Beloved Wife and Mother. Jacob Yones in English and Hebrew. Beloved Husband and Father. Those were the ones he had moved from the old cemetery with the tilting cracked headstones to this, the new one. "So we can all be together," he had told Liz, who always understood that part of him.

Sam turned away from the headstones and markers. He

didn't want to think about the accident that should have been his accident, not Matt's, but it didn't work. "A cheering section, that's what a father should be," Sam had said the night of his Matt's bar mitzvah. From the podium, looking out over hundreds of people, his hand on Matt's young shoulder, he had said, "A father so blessed to have such a son." Tears began to form in his eyes, for Matt, and then for himself.

Someone said the cantor was going to sing again. Sam hoped he heard wrong. The chanting would make him cry again, more than he had cried already. It had taken him a year to cry for his father. For Matt he cried right away. No, dear God, Sam thought, heading for his car, don't let him sing. He guided Liz through the crowd. Without bothering to check, he knew Billy was there, tagging behind.

He tried to hold his feelings back, feel the cold air on his face, to regain control. Then through the crowd Sam caught sight of Mike Anker, and he felt the weight behind his eyes again, a genuine pull, a need for his oldest friend. "Friendship with Mike Anker was never a matter of growth or doubt. It was whole from the start," Sam had said in his speech saluting Mike on his fiftieth birthday, just two years ago. "We were friends before friendship became a matter of convenience or an instrument of greed or . . ." Suddenly, Sam couldn't remember the rest. He saw Mike standing too far away to touch. Mike was having as hard a time as he was. It was tough watching Mike trying not to cry but failing. Seeing Mike made Sam want to knock people over to reach him, to let go.

They had come so far together. No homework neglected for a pickup baseball game in the streets. No Mr. Moment-by-Moment for either of them. "It's not a question of being lucky and standing on the right street corner," Sam had said, his podium voice focused and well projected. "You take the street, bend it to *make* a corner, and you plant yourself there." He had said that at the first award ceremony the Jewish Federation of New York had held for him, and he had used the analogy several times since, from business dinners to Israel Bond drives to the night of the establishment of the Yones Internship, the named chair and lectureship at Columbia University. Like the Godkins at Harvard, or the Lehmans—they were at Columbia, too—a professor's chair and a lectureship on top of it. It was as if he had arrived twice. He had his name where the best had their names, not just the middle best, but the best best. Some kids at college dreamt of having a Cadillac; he dreamt of his name somehow at a university forever, tied to a subject for as long as it was taught. So much better than a building. He was looked upon differently by all of them now, even the hustlers who collected for the charities: not just taken, but taken seriously.

Mike was still out of reach, too far away, shoved back in the crowd, the one person in a life crowded with hangers-on that Sam wanted close to him.

Sam took a tighter hold on Liz's arm and they continued to walk slowly through the crowds to get to his car. Sam nodded to those who were attending their occasional Jewish funeral, who always managed to stand close together even though they might not know each other well. To two of his partners, one almost at the top at GM, another at Prudential, a figurehead with two feet on a banana peel, Sam smiled his big crooked smile, breaking through the sadness with the charm and intelligence that energized deals and brought people to him like a magnet. They lowered their heads but smiled back uncomfortably. Square, his driver, held the car door open and Sam put his hand on Square's shoulder.

Mike Anker watched the car door held open and saw Sam bring Liz, reluctantly, to a stop. A U.S. senator and his wife—his wife's presence a special honor—responded to Sam's acknowledgment. He saw Sam force Liz to allow herself to be kissed on the cheek by the politician who mangled her artists, curators, creators, the people in her world. But he, too, was a partner.

Mike had planned to wait, to be with Sam alone at the house, but he took Cheryl's hand and they moved again. He responded to the soft pressure of her fingers curling to the center of his palm, touching him. Her nails were short and well cared for and she wore an expensive watch and a Paloma Picasso ring, but not a wedding ring, which she wanted more than all Mike had given her. She had full, shining brown hair, thick enough to bury your head in, and she was only a few inches under his own height and he liked that. She no longer wore the angular Italian fashions she once did when she worked for Sam, and Mike liked that, too. She had been part of The Life, the sleek hallways, nights at this week's club, all night anywhere with anyone, lunches and dinners with crab salad and chanterelles. He was glad, as he hoped she was, that she was off Sam's payroll, away from him.

Mike disliked the push of shoulders, the touching of strangers, but finally, a few feet from the car, Mike and Sam faced each other for a moment. It seemed as if the crowds faded away, as if they were alone, just the two of them. Mike put his hand on Sam's shoulder, and they stood there, face-to-face. He took Sam's hand, not to shake it, but to hold it, and Sam Yones held on to Mike Anker's hand. He gave Mike a look of such thankfulness that it caused both men to swallow and let go of each other. Sam cut his eyes away, now full. But he forced himself to look back and take Mike's hand once again. Sam started to talk, but he stopped. Then he started again.

"Nothing goes away," Sam managed to say. "You live with it all."

He tried but could say nothing more. He dropped Mike's hand and reached for the rear door of the Lincoln and held it open as Liz stepped forward to enter the large backseat. Sam followed. For a moment, Billy stood alone outside, his fingers resting on the door handle, uncertain, wondering whether he should get in or if by some miracle he could stay on his own and avoid riding alone with his mother and father. But after a moment's hesitation, Billy's blue suit disappeared into the backseat of the long Lincoln.

Cheryl turned to Mike as they stood near Sam's car. She was careful not to touch him too much in public. He was a loving, gentle, warmhearted man with an uncanny gift of drawing people to him, and when he engaged you, he went through to your heart, but he was still shy and private about so many things. Two years and she had never seen him close to a tear until today. She knew he wasn't going to talk, but she loved that he let her see his eyes were full and didn't try to turn away. She liked so much the way he looked, so natural, nothing store-bought. His hair was almost completely gray now, his sideburns full and bristly, and his eyes pouched. There were still traces of youth in his face three years ago, when they first met when she was still working for Sam, but no longer. His looks had lost their consistency; they were attractive one day, haggard the next. Cheryl liked him that way; on such days he was attractive more to her kind of woman, so much younger than he was, than another. He had a face full of experience, with no apologies. He was real.

She saw Gordy's hand fall on Mike's overcoat and watched Mike turn around. Gordy Wiser was the middle man in the trio, and she loved the way they looked at each other. Gordy had children of his own. Mike had none, and she used to believe it was one thing to attend a funeral of a child if you had kids yourself and another to be there childless. But not if you felt about Matt and Billy as Mike did.

"Helen's at the house," Gordy said of his wife, "with the food."

Gordy held his skullcap on his bald head to keep the wind from blowing it away, trying to keep up a smile in that distant way of his. Gordy's father believed in Sam before anyone else. He had been the founder of one of the big retail clerks' unions in Minneapolis and Sam had gone to him when the banks turned him down. "If you're broke," Sam told him, "but you want to buy something big, there's only one thing you can buy, and that's real estate." The union pension fund made the mortgage, and with that, Sam bought the warehouse on Nicollet Avenue on his nineteenth birthday.

"Why did Matt go off the road?" Gordy asked.

He had inherited the union from his father, and of more importance to Sam, he had wrenched back control over the pension fund. And not without help. Gordy carried his wealth less well than Sam and differently than Mike, who had less money than either of them. Gordy was a man people talked about the minute he left the room. "One minute he's swimming along with a smile, then snap," someone once said. "There's blood in the water. Your head's gone. He has the balls of a Buick dealer," they used to say. He stared at Mike, attempting to coax answers, any answers, out of Mike, who had always been closer to Sam than he was.

"It doesn't make sense," Gordy said.

"I don't know what happened," Mike answered, not wanting to say more. He wanted no more questions.

It wasn't Gordy that Mike felt snapping away at his ankles. It was the questions. Anyone could be asking them. He had asked them himself. So had Liz. His Liz. No, Sam's Liz.

"You don't have the guts," he remembered Liz saying to him. That was when they were all back in college. Did she really say it as he remembered? "You don't know what you want. What you want is one thing at a time. First a place in life. Then a woman. Un-uh. It doesn't work that way. You want to know how it works? Ask Sam. Better yet, watch him." Yes, she really did say that.

Mike folded the mimeographed mourner's kaddish, typed in Hebrew and transliterated into English, which had been passed out at the funeral. Cheryl handed hers over and he put both of them into his pocket. You could have four thousand people at a Jewish funeral and there would never be one piece of paper lying around when it was over. Not one.

Sam's Lincoln had moved down the road no more than twenty feet. It had halted, the horn silent, waiting for the crowd to clear. Mike looked at Liz in the backseat. Even in black, her hair pulled back from her face, she was ready to be seen, on view for all to appreciate. Liz was the prize. He had lost the prize. Sam had won.

"Do you think Sam knows what happened?" Gordy persisted.

"Do you think anyone does?" Mike answered, looking away, then at Cheryl, then up at the sky, which was the color of a lead roof.

The hundreds of mourners had separated into groups, the Jewish Federation crowd over here, Mt. Sinai Hospital over there, Israel Bonds near the tent, careful not to step on the gravestones. Columbia University board members were on the knoll, the Guggenheim people near them, the employees of Sam's first partnership, Minneapolis Timber One, off on their own, the politicians and reporters off on their own, as Sam's long limousine, to the relief of those inside, started to inch forward.

Sam glanced out of the window. It wouldn't be long before Bayside Memorial Park, Orchid Section, would be quiet once again, silent in its winter stillness and suburban, just as he had designed it. He knew people wouldn't leave right away. It was as if hanging around a cemetery together would keep someone who had died with you. Of course it never worked.

He scanned the crowds and spotted his partners from GM, from Prudential, from the government, even the church. The highest of the "high gorum," a phrase he made up. "High" because they were the best, no one better; "gorum" because, unlike goyim, gorum was a word you could say in an elevator. He lowered the car window, raised his hand, and gestured toward them. The sign was for Gordy, who nodded, having picked up the signal, and Sam closed the car window.

"I see the high gorum showed up," Gordy said to Mike.

"How about the reporter?" Mike asked quietly. "The guy from the *Journal?* He'll put it all together."

"He's here, isn't he. To show up here . . ." Gordy said, shaking his head. "Let him go ask the U.S. Attorney if he wants to know anything."

"I wonder if he remembers me," Cheryl said.

"Who?" Mike asked.

"GM," she answered, referring to a high gorum partner by his company instead of his name, as they all did. "He's next to the bishop." She nodded across the dead lawn toward the tall, elegant white-haired man complete with Melton topcoat and folding umbrella. "We went to his granddaughter's wedding," Cheryl said proudly. "He was as courteous to me as if we were both in a play. He's not that bad."

"And so, obviously," Gordy said, trying for his smile again, "we have resolved the problem of who will welcome the partners."

"I like the old fart," Cheryl said.

For the first time in days, Mike's face took on the amused look she loved so much. "Do you eat with that mouth?" he asked. "Do you talk to your mother with that mouth?"

"And the beautiful princess kissed the old curmudgeon and he awakened a polite, even-tempered prince," she said, smiling, looking across Gordy's face into Mike's eyes. Some of his friends thought young chick—big bucks, but they knew none of it. Her own friends, younger, supposedly less rigid, weren't much different. They didn't know what it was all about either.

"GM is going to brag about switching his cheap raincoat for a Burberry at the Admiral's Club, and then he's going to carry on about pinochle games with Nixon and Bob Hope," Gordy said. "And then he'll say something about Sam being a fine Hebrew Gentleman. Not today. I don't want that now." Gordy turned away, angry. "Sam makes them the kind of money they couldn't make on their own if they stood on their heads. Hong Kong hotels that pay themselves off in three years, timber that pays off in less, and they're riding on God's green earth for the rest of their lives." Gordy's eyes swung from one end of the cemetery to the other. "Deals so good they can't be seen going into them, deals they don't know how to get into without Sam. Yet he's the one who's going to jail, and they're not. I can't take that," he said, walking off, dumping Sam's partners on Mike. Mike didn't try to hold Gordy back.

Maybe after thirty years of marriage Helen knew how to calm him down. He didn't know how anymore. Then Mike shrugged his shoulders and rotated his arms in their sockets, stretching, knowing that Helen could never bring quiet to Gordy's life. Only Ginger, the hidden one, who in reality was hidden from nobody, including Helen, could do that. Mike watched Gordy cross the narrow road that split the Orchid Section from the Lilac Section, walking west, toward the parking lot, which was camouflaged carefully with evergreens so no sight of a vehicle would spoil your view.

"I'll bet he still calls me Missy," Cheryl said, her voice cold. She nodded in GM's direction, her eyes evading Mike's. She could not bear to see the pain in his eyes.

"He calls all women under fifty Missy," Mike said, looking away. "I have trouble liking that man," Mike went on.

"It's his voice and the way he looks down on people you care for," she said, and Mike pulled her close to him. Cheryl had a hard, muscular body and right then Mike could feel her arms tense.

"They're Sam's partners, not yours."

"I know."

His place in life was assured. So was now the time for his woman? Was Liz really that right? Was he really not able to chew gum and walk down stairs at the same time? He smiled to himself, thinking of how people had described Gerry Ford.

Liz had lived in a dormitory out near the lake and you could see the water from her room. He remembered when she had scouted the way and he had followed her, both bent over like Indians, down the hallways of the third floor. No men allowed, the signs read, and that's the way it was in the women's residence halls back then. He would wait until her date dropped her off, he had told her, not knowing where the courage to say that had come from. Maybe he wanted to show her that he would risk everything, because that's what being caught after curfew upstairs in a woman's room had meant back then. She was the most beautiful girl he had ever met.

"I got my date angry," she whispered as she closed the door to her room. He didn't know what to say. He looked out across Lake Mendota and saw the ice at the shoreline and the clear lights of the houses several miles across the water. Mike thought of roommates and interruptions and losing it all, suspensions, incompletes, praying for readmission. She didn't seem to care about such things. She was beautiful.

But that was then. This was now.

Mike and Cheryl crossed behind the tent and walked toward Sam's partners, and as they walked they heard a chord, a whole ocean of chords. The cantor and his choir stood together singing, and suddenly Cheryl cried. Not for a Matt Yones she never really knew but for loss in general, brought on by song that forced her feelings out. Mike held her around the shoulders. He was relieved that Sam was not around to hear the singing. He was relieved as much for Liz as he was for Sam; there had been so much that had passed between them, those times before Sam had taken over her life.

2

BILLY RODE BACKWARD IN THE BIG LINCOLN, FACING HIS parents, trying not to look at either of them. Sam and Liz sat far apart, each at their corner of the backseat of the long limousine, so it was easy for Billy to look between them and avoid their eyes. Through the back window Billy saw the crowds receding as the car pulled away from the cemetery, and he knew he wanted to come back by himself to say good-bye in his own way. He was older, but uglier, Matt younger and handsome. "You look like your father," they had said to him. "You sound like your father." They had said that, too. He had everything but his brains. He had no brains, if you asked his father; but he had qualities more important than brains, if you asked his mother. He felt tears and he turned his head, not wanting his father to see weakness. Liz would treat him better, but never in front of her husband.

Their driver, Square Mercer, had been with them since the boys were children. On Sundays, when sleep for Sam was the household priority, Square would suit Billy up, put him in the backseat by himself, propped up on two cushions, and say, "Yes, sir, Mr. Billy, where to?" just as he used to say, "Yes, sir, Mr. Yones, where to?" Billy put his arm through the opening between the back compartment and the front seat, where Square sat, and touched his shoulder.

"Matt loved you, Square."

"Thank you, Billy, thank you."

And then Sam called out from the back of the car.

"Square, you mean a lot to us," Sam said, staring Billy down.

Billy turned. The scowl on his father's face was for him. Sam didn't like to be upstaged.

"Thank you, Mr. Yones."

Square drove slowly and they passed under the arch that led out from the cemetery to the main road. Sam had given the high sign to Gordy to take care of the partners, and now there was nothing for him to do. He focused on clouds through the skylight above the rear seat. He didn't look out the side windows until he felt the car rolling on the highway. He wanted his sight line to be free of tombstones and people staring at him. Once on the highway, he sat back, pleased the crowd was so large, larger than he expected. He looked up again at the clouds passing overhead and saw that they were moving fast. It would snow later in the day, he thought. His eyes were sad, and, thinking back, he could not believe that his son's coffin was so heavy.

It was not bronze, just plain wood, the kind he had picked out for his father. No metal screws either, as Orthodox tradition required. Only the locks were metal, and that was a state law requirement. He had instructed the rabbi to rotate the pallbearers so that they all might have the honor of feeling Matt's weight, the heft of a tall, husky, quick competitor, just as Sam needed to see himself. They should shoulder Matt proudly, all of them, those he wanted honored as pallbearers. All those who had come to him at the time of the death of his son. At a personal cost to them, at a price of saying to a U.S. Attorney that loyalty to Sam Yones meant something.

U.S. Attorneys, governments, military, need to know, no leaks, Sam thought. It's all nonsense. "The only way to keep a secret is when one person knows it and the other one is dead." That's what he had said earlier to Gordy, who had seemed almost afraid to bring him the news. "My people tell me the Justice Department is after you." Gordy's minions always knew. They were paid to know.

"Who do I shoot?"

"It's not funny, Sam. Nobody's written up a subpoena. It hasn't gone that far. There's no decision whether it will be handled out of the Attorney General's office or whether they'll give it to a U.S. Attorney."

"Which one?"

"Then you're not surprised."

"Which one?"

"It could be any of five."

"No, Gordy. Only one of three. New York. Chicago. Miami."

"You're ready? You're ready for all of this?"

Sam remembered looking away, staring off into the distance. The cossacks are coming, was what he had been thinking; always looking back over your shoulder to see who is out to get you. One day he would stop living like that. But not yet.

"It's not the government that's stirring the pot. It's always others. They'll make it look like taxes. They'll make it look like anything." Sam remembered a hollow feeling as he told even Gordy maybe too much.

"If you would have stayed small in scale," Gordy said, "then they would have let you be."

"But why should I have done that? Why should I not have had what they have?"

Gordy frowned and touched the black silk tie and then the grosgrain collar of his tuxedo. It was only then that Sam had realized that Gordy was dressed for a formal dinner, that Helen, or maybe it wasn't Helen, was waiting outside in the car, that real life was still continuing somewhere out there, that Gordy had come to him as soon as he could with all he had. At that moment, those few months ago, Sam had remained silent, his mind racing, until long after Gordy had left.

He reached across the backseat of the Lincoln, avoiding his son's eyes, and took his wife's coat and rearranged it across her shoulders. He could hear the sounds American cars make as they twist over uneven roads: a squeak here, a birdie there, but still, he would never have a Mercedes. Never.

Liz looked up and thought for a moment of taking his hand. She moved closer to him, but was unable to touch him. She would think of Matt and then follow the trail of some memory, wanting to smile to herself at the thought of a happy time, turn to Sam and tell him what she had remembered, but then the shock of realizing that Matt was dead would strike like physical pain. Then, in spite of how she felt, she put her fingers across his forehead. She watched Sam's eyes close as they always did when she touched his temples, only this time, for the first time in three days, she saw a tear-wet face. Billy saw the tears, too, and started to say something to his father. Liz gave Billy a look and he shut his mouth, turning again, tossing one arm up on the partition between the driver's compartment and their own, staring down the road in front of them as Square drove.

Behind his closed eyes, Sam saw Matt's dark head on the pillow, his face toward the hospital ceiling, eyes closed in the profound sleep that follows surgery. Sam had touched the sleeping face, resting his forefinger under Matt's nose. His fingertip felt warm skin, but there was no breath. Matt's face was young and clean-shaven, a longish face like his mother's, like the whole Eckland family, with Liz's slightly sardonic cast. Matt's chest had not moved. No lung stirred. Father and son alone. No heartbeat. Sam had thought of his father: Jacob, Itzchak, Jack, any of the three names would do. His face was not in Matt's face at all. It was the Yones face that appeared in Billy's, a face from a babble of immigrants. Sam had shifted his eyes and stared out of his late son's hospital window into the night. Then he had walked down the hospital hall to the waiting room to wake Liz and Billy and tell them Matt was gone. The hospital room seemed a long way away and a long time ago. Actually, it was only four days, just last Friday. He felt Liz's fingers on his forehead. Only four days ago, Friday to be exact. Saturday was the Sabbath, never a Jewish funeral then. Sunday the unions barred burial for anyone. So they waited. And they sat. And they waited, Friday, Saturday, Sunday, ignoring thoughts of Matt's body in a coffin, in an airplane, flown from Florida to New York, moved, bumped, inspected. Until today, Monday. Finally, their son at rest. He touched her hand. A hell of a way to start a week.

"The young die differently than the old," Sam said, his eyes open again, looking up to the clouds through the skylight of his car. Liz took his hand and he looked straight ahead at the road ahead, very still. "There was no coma, not like Dad." Sam went on, unfocused. "Or my mother, for that matter. Dad for three weeks, Mama two." He seemed to be talking to Square through the partition. "Even with all the oxygen and all the tubes, when Matt saw me he held out his arms to me." Then Sam fell silent again.

Billy started to turn around to face his father, to hold out his own arms to him, to bring what little he could to a man he saw in pain. He knew he was no substitute for his brother, and he let his hands fall in his pockets like weights.

"They came for you, Dad, all those people," he said.

Liz sat quietly, her hands now in her lap, no longer touching her husband.

"You went to them. They came to you," Billy said.

"To go to the bar mitzvah for Mike Milken's son?" Sam said. "They all saw it coming, but they went anyway, like ringside seats at a time bomb going off."

"But they came, Dad. They came to you. Even people who wouldn't go to Milken came to you."

"Their flag waves for any wind," Sam said. "They're whores."

Billy turned his back again on his father. He had two great women lined up, and all he wanted to do was get back to his apartment and bang them. No pretense. They loved it. Bang me, Billy. Bang me. He had three more hours with his family. Then it would be decent for him to go back to his apartment at the Dakota. Bang his brains out. Then he could tolerate another day in Sands Point sitting *shiva*.

"Only some were there for Mike Milken's kid," Sam said to Billy's back, as if he had not been heard the first time. "They were all here for Matt." Sam took off his gray kidskin gloves and ran his finger across the wood panel. It wasn't wood. He knew it. Lincoln knew it. A fake. Not like the old Cadillacs. He had taken his second son to his rest and all he thought of was fake wood. Sometimes he didn't understand himself. Liz had fought him and fought him and fought him. "Not Matt. Keep him out of it."

"And they indicted him and they got him and I'm next," Sam said.

"Who?" Billy said without turning around.

"Michael Milken, that's who, you dummy."

"Sam, stop it," Liz said.

Her skin burned when Sam did this. She remembered saying so many times, "Sam, Billy's not Matt. He's just average. He's not brilliant. But he's not dumb. He's just not Matt. It's hard for him. He compares himself to Matt. He asks himself all the time, 'How would Matt handle this? How would Matt handle that?' Sam, when a man like you beats up on a kid like that, it's awful." How many times had she said that? One way or another? In how many rooms? In how many places? Over how many years? And now Billy's real heartache was just beginning.

22

She had tried to appear in calm repose for four days, regal, if she could pull it off. She had turned out to be the kind of fifty-year-old who looked nowhere near it, but she was glad, even proud to tell you right off she was fifty, had a son as old as twenty-eight, and had to use glasses to read her menu. She had walked the inclined ramp of the Guggenheim with the best of them, and when Anselm Kiefer came, it was she they had selected to take the great artist through. IBM, GM, Prudential, and the others provided more than limited partners for her husband; they also provided customers for her. It had all been Sam's idea, her becoming an art curator to large companies, directing their purchases of fine art, keeping them out of the hands of the dealers unprotected. Like Sam, she received fees, and like Sam, she was trusted and tough. She adjusted her position in the back of Sam's limousine. Regal with juices. That's what Sam liked about her. That's what she liked about herself.

She felt the cold green leather of the seat. "I don't want to hear any more about time bombs. I don't want to hear you brag about the guest list at your son's funeral."

Suddenly all Sam's cockiness left him and he looked anxious.

"I don't know which way they're coming at me," he said.

"Sam . . ." Liz gestured at the open partition. Sam nodded and he reached forward to press a button on the armrest. Billy jumped as the glass inside the partition rose under his arm. He pulled his elbow out of the way as the back compartment was sealed off. Then he turned around and glared at his father, forcing him to look at his own face, only younger, his brother's face no longer around to please the old man.

"They're about to hit me and I don't know from where," Sam said.

He pulled his coat closer around him. It seemed to have turned colder suddenly. He had surrendered little for what he had achieved, only a little longer waiting time at urinals, normal for a man of fifty-three. That was the only price, in his own eyes, he had paid for the distance he had come. Until now. Until Matt. He did not want to rule, have twenty companies traded on the public market or give million-dollar birthday parties. He would leave that to those who had to have their names in the paper. Let them never forget that it was his timber that made their paper. But he could still be a target of a federal investigation just as public men were, and he knew it.

"Let's forget it, Sam," Liz said. "Let it go."

"You don't really want to know, hon, do you?"

"Did you see them?" Sam said, returning to the subject a third time. "They filed past Matt for close to an hour."

He took Liz's hand again and she tried not to think of either of her sons, but of her husband, obsessing about the size of the attendance at a funeral. It wasn't easy. She thought of how her handed-down tribal memories were different from Sam's. Her family had no history of beaver hats, long black coats, last-name changes to Shephard from Shapiro, or to Golan from Goldberg. There were no tales of shtetls, matchmakers, or fiddlers on roofs. Instead, there were stories of Ecklands and Andersons, of Scandinavian saints and legends of women, a grandmother named Elsa crying out "No bank will take this farm," a call to arms which, thank the Lord, was heeded. Liz liked coming from a string of strong women.

The car rolled on and Sam seemed to quiet down as the road started to run parallel to the Atlantic and they approached Sands Point.

Sam's hard eyes stared at Billy. "Let them think I'm going down. Let them think I'm through. Then I'll see who deserts and who stays." He looked down at his hands, drew in a long breath, held it, and then let go. "I'll clean house. The loyalists I'll save." His syntax was slipping, sounding the way he used to sound.

"How?" Billy asked, responding, trying so hard, still, to find a father.

"I don't know yet. I don't know what part of the government it will be. It could be Chicago. Or New York. Even Miami. I could confess to something not so bad and give them what they want by turning on everyone I can think of." It was one of the rare times his father seemed to be speaking to him. "And ten years later I can come out of obscurity with the millions they let me keep on the QT and reappear as the great humanitarian. No, not me. I'm not going anywhere. I've got a better idea."

In his mind's eye Billy could see his brother's face come back to him and with it, his own sadness. He knew he was the son his father had given up on. He was too eager to take his brother's place. He was ashamed of himself.

"Dad, you just buried Matt."

"You'll go with the rest of them if you're not careful."

"Sam," Liz said. "Stop."

"Don't worry about me. Like Hitler in the bunker, there's a lot of machinery set up in case you lose the war."

"You're copying Hitler?" Billy said.

Sam raised his hand high within striking distance of Billy.

"Stop it!" Liz called out, her hand landing swiftly on Sam's arm.

"Go ahead, Mom. Ask him. Ask him why Matt's dead. Ask him why Matt's dead and why he's still walking."

Sam felt himself shaking.

Billy pressed the button to lower the glass in the partition, and when it was down he had room to twist around away from them. He watched the road ahead curve toward the big house, getting a hard-on thinking of the two hookers he had waiting as soon as he could get out from under all these people.

"I can't tell you, Liz," Sam said. "I don't know. I don't even want to guess. I wish it would have been me." He shivered.

"Sam, are you scared?" Liz asked.

He shifted his weight, glanced out the window, and then back at his wife.

"All the time."

3

IF YOU HAD TOLD SPENCER PELCHECK SIX YEARS AGO WHEN he finished law school that he would end up an Assistant U.S. Attorney in Miami, he would have told you you were out of your fucking mind. Potsy Pelcheck, his father, would have had a stroke. A son of his, the kid he had to get out of one wild scrape after another. "I did everything so you should have respect," Potsy's voice had echoed across the fraternity living room, "and you get yourself tossed out of school. Nude pictures of a dumb broad. A broad with a boyfriend who happens to be a fucking cop," Potsy shouted in front of Spencer's fraternity brothers. "Dumbhead!" At that, Spencer, having the same temper as his father, walked out, found a job selling clothes at The Gap, and never took another dime again from his father. No one called him Dumbhead.

He rolled over on top of Becky and she let him do it again. Twice. Once at night. Once in the morning before they went to work. Nothing extraordinary. No harnesses like the cases he prosecuted for his first two years. No abuse. Just in and out. Once at night and once in the morning. She did more than not mind it. She was with him all the way. Latin temperament. He loved it. So did she. No fooling around with anyone else for either of them for the past two years. Becky was a doll about that. He was disciplined. There was a payoff. No condoms.

"Here's your reward," she said softly. She was thin and wiry and, somehow, her body reminded him of a guitar.

"It must be Friday," Spencer said, and he smiled his wicked smile.

26

He pulled the bottom half of his pajamas up to his waist, hiding his erection, pleased that it had returned so quickly. He threw both long, thick legs over his side of the bed at once and headed for the bathroom. She followed, throwing her arms around him, touching him where he liked it. Then she let go. She went into her shower, and he went into his, happy.

He liked what he did, prosecute. He liked the way he lived. With Becky. Rebecca Puig. "No relation," she always had to say as she gave her name at parties. Especially in Miami. He had not understood at first. But the name of a Latin author in a Latin city produced respect. And Miami was a Latin city. And Puig was a Latin author, and even if she was entitled to the respect, she didn't take it. He was her distant cousin. What was also true was that at one time Spencer had no idea who Puig was. Until he met Becky, who had told him on their first night together that he was ignorant not to know. That time he didn't walk out, as he had with Potsy. He stayed. He tried to learn. That was two years ago.

Breakfast was something you sat down and did. It was one of Spencer's rules. Becky liked the rule, but that meant early starts.

"Are we meeting at Coconut Grove this afternoon?" she asked, her black hair wet and with a sheen. "Remember? Our appointment's today, Friday." She tried to look casual, but she was checking out his eyes.

"We can't afford it." He didn't look at her. But then he did.

"We can afford it," she said, smiling. "Together."

"That is true."

"More coffee?" She poured it for him, something she'd never do if she didn't feel a need to pamper him today.

"The payments won't kill us provided the down payment is high enough," she said, "and we'll take a fifteen-year mortgage, not thirty."

"They won't give *us* the mortgage," he said. "They're giving it to you because you make more money than I do. Alone, I don't qualify. When we each qualify, then we'll

27

buy it." He picked up a piece of toast, took a bite, put the rest back on the plate, and stood up, killing breakfast.

Becky followed him from the table, but he wasn't ready to go to work yet. He walked over to their little balcony. Two folding outdoor card chairs, the kind that wouldn't get soggy when the rains came. Rains like the South Seas. In the movies. When it rained like that, he wondered why he ever left Ohio.

"It'll be bigger," she called after him.

"What will?" he said, looking out across Biscayne Bay.

"The new place. The terrace."

"And the living room. And the entry hall. And the dining room. And the library."

"They'll think you're on the take," she said.

"And the children's room?" he asked, trying to do a deal.

Becky moved toward the little balcony and then backed away. She took the headphones from the table near the stereo, plugged them in, and made sure the green diode was lit. She took the earphone on its long wire, handed it to him, but then decided to put them in his ears. She kissed him and he saw her lips move and he read them: "Two o'clock."

Spencer loved his boss's office. He was in there often; he was one of the young stars, so the invitation wasn't a big deal. He liked Byron, who had done a lot for him and was one of those hands-on U.S. Attorneys. He had a reputation for easily finding television cameras, but since the President withdrew his nomination for the last forseeable space on the federal bench in Miami, Byron laid off the phones to the networks and the local stations, sulking. Maybe it was the price of staying on as U.S. Attorney. No one was ever clear why Byron's nomination got pulled. Least of all he, if you believed what he supposedly told his wife, who had proceeded to tell everyone. By to By-By, the headlines could have screamed, but they didn't. The few who called By By-By to his face never called him that publicly. You had to go back at least thirty years to call Byron Varner,

U.S. Attorney for the Southern District of Florida, the double-B word. Few did. And besides, the implication was wrong, but that was another story.

Spencer wasn't the only one at the long end of Byron's T-shaped desk. There were six men altogether, one U.S. Attorney, one U.S. Marshal, and four agents from the International Operations Division of the Internal Revenue Service. Taxes. They couldn't get Sam Yones on anything else, but Spencer had yet to figure out why they really wanted him.

Byron, his skin fresh-colored and with pale eyes that could have been blue, stood behind his desk while everyone assembled. He looked out the window, waiting for their glances to follow his across the bay to Miami Beach. He wanted them to think about where they were, noting the corner position of his office and the height of his place in the pecking order, the fact that there were only two floors topping his, one for the federal courts and above, the highest, one for the chambers of federal judges of the U.S. District Court for the Southern District of Florida, and the men and one woman who ran those courts. One of those offices might still, maybe in this lifetime, be his, and he wanted them to think about that.

Byron was not as tall as he wished. No one was, Spencer thought, not even basketball players. Nor was he as thin, but his tailor did a great job. Were it not for his father, who taught him such things, the son of Potsy Pelcheck would have known nothing of buttonholes on sleeves that worked or shoulder pads without ropes so they would slope naturally, but not so much as to make you look like a wimp. Brooks was as far as he had progressed. He went to their New York store every two years to get suited up or picked up something in Washington if he got a freebie there. There was no Brooks in Miami. The Latin taste was not in that direction. Spencer had seen enough of Becky's family, the high-class ones, to know that.

"Gentlemen," Byron intoned, "Operation Angel Fish."

"Another one of those names?" Spencer blurted out.

Abner Parks, the black U.S. Marshal who liked Spencer,

didn't flick an eyebrow, but the revenuers turned heads, all at the same time, all in the same way, all at the same angle.

"You guys must be accountants," Spencer said.

"Gentlemen," Byron said, referring to Spencer, "if he weren't so bright, he wouldn't be here."

"Amen to that," Abner added.

Two IRS agents looked at each other, feeling left out.

"It's foreign bank accounts owned by U.S. citizens," the senior IRS representative named Davis announced. "They don't pay taxes on the interest. That's how we get them."

"No women on this team?" Spencer asked, knowing Becky would be proud of him.

"If we're not looking for any women, we don't have to have any women doing the looking," Byron said.

Spencer wanted to say something about having a good guess why the White House pulled him before the Senate got at him, but was smart enough to keep his mouth shut.

"Well, actually, sir," one of the IRS men said, "there is a woman."

Byron fumbled papers on his desk, as if he were a professor looking for a seating chart with pictures on it. "Mr. Davis?" he said.

"That's how we will get the list," Mr. Davis said.

Spencer had his bees-buzzing-around-his-head look, sensing a problem becoming his to solve.

"There will be no entrapment," the IRS agent named Davis said definitively.

"I want you to be right," Byron said, his tone flat, similar to Bogart saying "I stick my neck out for no one."

Dinks, Spencer thought, distracted. He scratched his ear, trying to stay with the conversation. D-i-n-k-s. Double Income No Kids. Spencer and Becky. Jewish Boy from Ohio, Cuban Girl from Havana, each one step removed. Dinks. Spencer shook his head slightly.

"Entrapment?" Spencer asked finally.

"There will be no entrapment," Davis of the IRS said again.

"What woman?" Spencer asked, persisting.

"Melanie Field. That's her professional name."

"What's her real name?"

"Something Polish," Mr. Davis said.

"Legal name change?" Spencer asked.

"Probably."

"Check it out," Byron said. "Better yet, ask her. You'll meet, I'm sure."

"I think not," Spencer said. "Where is this woman going to get these records? How is this going to happen? Here, on U.S. soil?"

"Are we going abroad?" Abner asked.

"Is there a pun in there somewhere?" Byron laughed a snide laugh, nailing his own coffin for any woman who might hear him. "Destroying their seed" was Becky's analysis. White men voted Republican and were antiabortion because no woman had the right to destroy her man's seed. That's what it was all about. She'd listen to this guy By-By for two minutes and then strangle him.

"We will have the records of the largest private bank in the Grand Caymans," Byron announced. "Is that right? And the links from there to Switzerland?"

"Not yet, sir," Mr. Davis said.

"I stand corrected. We have a way to get at the records. Is that accurate?"

"Yes, Mr. U.S. Attorney," said Mr. Davis. "It is."

"And what might that way be?" Spencer asked, furious that his voice spiked at exactly the wrong time, like a teen-aged kid.

Mr. Davis looked proudly across the room and then he answered. "If a man leaves a briefcase in his hotel room, and after he checks out, we find it, open it, and see that records we're looking for are in there, is there any entrapment?" Mr. Davis asked.

"How did he get into the hotel room?" Spencer wanted to know.

"He walked." There were smiles around the table.

"Under his own power?" Spencer asked.

"Of course. Into the Grand Bay Hotel, here in Miami."

"With anyone?"

"You'll meet her," Byron said.

31

Spencer moved in his chair. He'd let it pass. He knew things were going to go down that he would be better off not knowing. Nothing new.

"And what will be in that black briefcase?" Spencer asked.

"How did you know it will be black?" Davis asked.

"I didn't. I guessed." Davis stayed the sourpuss. He would be no fun.

"Foreign accounts. Held by U.S. citizens," Byron said. "Sam Yones and his gang." Spencer could hear *dirty Jews* in Byron's tone. But maybe he was too sensitive about such things, and he let it pass.

"How do you know he has an account there? And besides, nobody knows who he is. He's a connoisseur's criminal."

"Well, you've heard of him," Byron said.

Spencer went quiet, thinking of Potsy. Then he recovered, quickly.

"Why would someone be dumb enough to bring confidential Grand Cayman bank records, totally protected under their laws, into our jurisdiction, on our soil? It's nuts. It doesn't make any sense."

Davis, the IRS guy, put a cocky look on his face.

"Because, Counsel," and he snickered, "there's no direct flights from the Grand Caymans, that's why." He started to pack his briefcase. "If you want to go from the Grand Caymans to Switzerland, you change planes at Miami."

"And that's it? No change of planes in Jamaica? Bahamas? Even Mexico City?"

"Nothing convenient, Counsel," Davis said. "And you know how the British detest inconvenience."

Maybe he won't be so bad, Spencer thought. He watched Byron rise and the rest of them stand over him as he remained at the table. "And gentlemen," Byron said, "we thank you and the Internal Revenue Service very much. We will go for the limit. No tax deductible fines, no money left to bribe fellow inmates to do his laundry. Mr. Pelcheck will be in touch with you. Spencer, when will you be in touch?"

"This afternoon."

"At what time, Counsel?" Davis asked.

"Satisfactory, gentlemen?" Byron said, wanting to close the meeting.

"What time?" Mr. Davis of the IRS persisted. "Counsel, can you give us a more precise time?"

Spencer swiveled in his chair, reached out above his head as if he were plucking the time out of the air.

"At one twenty-seven."

Abner Parks laughed, and Spencer had no idea what being a smart aleck would set in motion.

"Spencer, will you wait a moment?" Byron asked. Spencer, who was about to stand and leave with the rest of them, stayed behind.

Byron ushered everyone else through the large double doors and closed them. Then he hesitated a moment, waiting to hear the outside door close as well before he turned back to his assistant.

"Spencer, don't fuck this up."

"Would I do a thing like that?"

"It's a test. I know it. Washington, IOD boys. International Operations Division. Everybody knows who this guy is. Yo-nes. So particular about his two syllables."

"Do they really know who he is?" Spencer asked, thinking of Potsy, his own father. "They guess. They think they know."

"Real estate. That's how he got started." Byron Varner wanted to say that's how all Jews get started, but he knew he had a Pelcheck in front of him. A cleared Pelcheck, that is true, traced and washed clean, but a Pelcheck nevertheless. "Mortgaged out a warehouse while he was still in school. Amazing." Spencer heard the admiration in his voice. "You folks do things the rest of us don't know how to do." Spencer tried not to let Byron see a reaction. "There's more there, I know it. It's a test to see if I know how to handle whatever it is we find."

"And how will you handle what we find?" Spencer

asked, ashamed that he hadn't said something to Byron, for his own sake, for Byron's, for everyone's.

"It depends what it is," Byron answered.

"What does that mean?"

Byron walked to his desk and sat down.

"This Sam Yones is a pivot. He's gotten too big to be on his own. There are others he's got to be fronting for. Probably all his close buddies, probably every raider, every fast buck marginal guy in New York."

Spencer averted his eyes. Byron would be on touchy ground in a moment, and he knew it.

"Who's Melanie Field?" Spencer asked, changing the subject, thinking of his own problems now, the potential entrapment issue.

"Beautiful. A model for *Interview*."

"You know that magazine?"

Byron adjusted his bow tie and the matching silk handkerchief peering out from his breast pocket. It could be eighty degrees outside and Byron would still wear his vest. He hated it when it crossed into the nineties. Then only, no vest. No remnant of the Professor Kingsfield look. It meant a lot to him. It had been real. Once.

As Spencer rode the elevator down to the lobby, he realized he couldn't have any long conversations with the IRS guys at one twenty-seven, or at one twenty-six or one thirty-four. He couldn't see them and meet Becky at the condo at two. He couldn't do both. The tax guys would have to wait. Four days, Friday to Monday. They'd survive. Fuck 'em. There would be no placating Becky. She cared as much about what went into her condo as she cared about what went into her body. Namely him. The elevator came to rest in the marble lobby of the New Federal Office Building in beautiful downtown Miami and Spencer Pelcheck smiled.

He made his call at one twenty-seven on the dot just to drive the IRS guy, Davis, nuts, and told him he couldn't get to him until Monday, but he would make it first thing in the morning. There was no complaint, no upset at all, just a simple, satisfied bureaucratic "fine," and five minutes later Spencer got in his car and pulled out of the underground garage below the old Post Office, where his own offices were, nowhere near Byron's tower, but close to his grand jury room, where Angel Fish and the search for Sam Yones would begin.

As he drove, he realized he hated lobbies with waterfalls or doormen who looked like colonels in Central American countries, but most of all, he hated living somewhere he couldn't afford on his own. A year is a year of living together, but what if Becky left. Where would he be? On the hook for a mortgage that left him enough to buy one sunnyside up egg full of cholesterol once a month? Or on the make with his big schlong for a rich babe to replace a departed Becky. He pulled over to the side and put the top down. Hell with the air-conditioning. How good would he be at finding a roommate with more bucks than he had? A gal to pay off his mortgage? Sure he was good-looking, muscular enough, especially where it counted, and he could play hot stud for a few more decades. But why should he place himself at risk? He would convince her the move was premature, talk her out of it if he could. Or, if not, he could procrastinate. Maybe somebody else would buy the goddamned apartment out from under them.

He wanted, in any event, to live in a house. Not a unit.

He pulled in front of the tall building and saw Becky's BMW in the driveway. He gave the doorman his Mustang and imagined a lifted eyebrow, but he knew there was none.

He walked in, and the place, to his surprise, was everything he always wanted, not everything he always hated. He could not make a cartoon out of it. No chance of that. He looked around, but Becky was nowhere in sight.

"Mr. Pelcheck, I'm Cynthia Koch, the agent for Palm Gardens." She said the last two words as if they were a prayer.

"Is Ms. Puig here?" he asked, letting her pump his hand.

The door opened and Becky came in. He always loved her in high heels. You'll be stunning in twenty years, he wanted to tell her. Maybe it was the surroundings, the marble, the paneling, the hush, that made him see her as elegant, older, chic, a prize. Maybe she was too much of a prize for him. Maybe that's what this fucking condo shopping was teaching him.

"Our elevators," Cynthia said, caressing the paneling as they rode up, "are, as you can see, larger than most." Ms. Koch rattled on through the entire apartment showing, and Spencer realized he felt so low he couldn't even perk up when they crossed the threshold of what was obviously a child's room. After the amenities tour of the building, the pool, Jacuzzi, tennis courts, sauna, the sun deck and the rest of it, they left, each with a set of gorgeous graphics, a pictorial take-home reminder of what their new life could be.

He was quiet as they left, and Becky let him be. They didn't talk about it until late Friday night.

Actually, it was somewhere around two in the morning when Becky turned over and saw, by the street light coming in through the window, that Spencer had his hand on his chest and that his eyes were wide open.

"A man provides," he said softly. "He doesn't take a woman's money."

Becky thought a minute about sitting up and debating him, but decided the upright posture would be dead wrong. So she allowed her head to lay still on the pillow.

"We share," she said, trying not to challenge him, but still trying to state a fact.

"I thought about that, too. You're right. We do share. But if I had to, I couldn't cover it all."

"In case something happens to us?" Becky asked.

"No. In case I want to make it mine to give."

"Spencer, that's control." She sat up, in spite of herself. "That's all that is. Control."

"Since when are gifts control?" He looked up to her.

"Ever hear of gilded cages?"

"Tin cages?" He smiled. She didn't. Then his own smile got lost.

"I guess that means you're always going to pay your way?" she said. "Is that what you're saying?"

Spencer felt his head heavy on the pillow, not wanting to answer, certain that any response would be the wrong one, would lead to trouble. Fucking apartment. Goddamn Palm Gardens *unit*.

"The condo is too expensive unless we're always together," Spencer said, "and who knows about always."

"I think that sucks," Becky said, lying down and rolling over on her side. Away from him.

4

THE WEEKEND DID NOT GO WELL. BY SUNDAY MORNING, Spencer wanted time off and so did Becky. She pleaded "family" and left. The first half hour of being alone wasn't so bad. A read through the papers, orange juice on the coffee table. No proper breakfast, there was no one to talk to, a rotten condition if you're used to voices. It seemed a good time to turn his attention to Sam Yones.

He read the IRS report, beginning with summaries of the man's tax returns. He scanned an explanation of how depletion allowance works for timber as well as oil with the result that Sam Yones had paid almost no taxes, not even on the profits on the sale of timber; depletion wiped out his tax bill. The report showed a profit, tax free, from the sale of a Minneapolis timber partnership: well over twenty million. That was five years ago. And the next year, a reinvestment of that money into a corporate general partner called Minneapolis Timber, giving him effective control of twenty-six partnerships, each on a twenty-million-dollar scale. Spencer read records of investigations tracing his property acquisitions and divestments all across the country, including Florida, California, Oregon, Washington, Alabama, and Georgia. Investigation after investigation. But they were all looking for the wrong things.

Then Spencer studied the second part of the IRS report: "Sources of funds. Investors." He read on. "Last year alone," the report said, "the money available to buy into private investment partnerships, including timber deals, grew over seventy percent. Close to $125 billion last year alone . . . And it doesn't just come from the insurance companies or the pension funds of America's largest companies and unions . . . also the largest and oldest universities in America. Double the figure of 125 billion dollars to 250 billion dollars, and that's *per year,* and you will have some idea of what this is all about."

How far this man had come, Spencer thought, this man's life evidenced in stacks of papers, reports of one regulatory agency after another, IRS returns going back over thirty years, the important transactions highlighted, beginning with the gain on the sale of some warehouse on Nicollet Avenue.

There was nothing steady about the man's material progress, dormant during college, even off course now and then afterward. But it never seemed as if he was floundering so long as he stuck to real estate. No one ever would have noticed him, no one in the government, at any rate, if his name hadn't popped up over and over again in timber deals. Sam had no money, but he had an idea. Oil in those days was good for wealthy people who wanted to save taxes. Invest one dollar in oil, you get six dollars' worth of deductions. It was all pretty complicated, involving the fancy tax law of depletion allowances coupled with bank leverage, but it worked. Sam applied it to timber—growing trees on tree farms—it was just that simple, and made it even better. Invest one dollar in Sam's tree farms and you get six dollars' worth of deductions. Even better was doing it overseas. Then you don't worry about depletion. You run the profits through some friendly bank in a tax haven and you don't worry about taxes at all. The rich stood in line, and because they were there, Sam could borrow money, sometimes even from them, to come up with his share, paying twenty cents to get one dollar's worth of the deal.

Then the tax audits started, not audits of Sam's deals, but of copycat deals. First an investor in New York. Then Palm Springs. Then Chicago. Then Sam changed tactics. He pulled his timber deals away from the Philippines; no more mahogany. It was back to America, Alabama, and Florida Panhandle pine. He cut back the ratio of deductions to cash invested to five to one. And his free-ride share? He cut that back, too. Cut back the greed, but not too much. Now he was rock solid.

The deals had come back to the states, but the structure was the same. Sam Yones was the pivot, the general partner in legal terms and the investors, the limited partners, put in the money, eighty percent of the money for fifty percent of the deal. God knows what the deals were in the days when they were overseas, God knows what profit went unreported for tax purposes. But when Sam brought his deals back home, it all looked clean. And the partners? My God, the partners!

Spencer turned the page: "Associates." There were two names. "Gordon Wiser. Father was founder of Retail Clerk's, Minnesota. Son succeeded. Funding of debt portions of Yones Investments supplied by union pension fund. Wiser also probably an equity partner." The second name was Michael Anker. "Holder of Yones chair. Extremely close personal relationship. No proven business relationships." He read twenty-six more pages. He skipped the charts and pro forma financial statements for now. It was Sunday.

Finally, a personal report on the man's family life: his wife, his shiksa prize; his two sons, the dummy and the chosen one; and Cheryl Stone, an early winner of one of his fellowships who ended up as his mistress for just over a year. Spencer decided to keep her in mind; she'd know plenty.

But why all this fuss? So he has an account overseas and failed to pay taxes on the interest it earns. Big fucking deal. Is he a drug dealer that they can't get any other way? Is he Noriega? Does he sell arms to Iraq? Why this guy? Destroy a life or three or four for *bubkes,* as his father, Potsy, would say? For nothing? Makes no sense. Except to get to the partners.

Then Spencer's ability to concentrate on Sam Yones gave out. He wanted Becky to talk to, to be with, to take to bed on a lazy Sunday morning. For fifteen minutes he paced the apartment and tried to make himself comfortable. He looked around the empty place, the living room floor littered with Yones papers and the sun streaming in from the east, low in the sky in the winter, reaching back from the window almost to the other end of the room. The apartment was like a solarium, and he loved it. If he wanted to take a walk, they were two blocks from the ocean and all the art deco hotels, now restored and once used as backdrops for shoots for *Miami Vice.* The *alter kockers* in South Miami Beach could tell their grandchildren about seeing Don Johnson whether they did or not and get an extra telephone call of attention out of it. The yuppies, guppies, and dinks bought in as fast as they could, sending up the prices, but he and Becky had been in on the ground floor. Maybe the increase in their equity due to the higher prices was burning a hole in her pocket. All well and good. It was not burning a hole in his pocket. He tried to convince himself that he liked sitting there alone in his shorts, surrounded by his papers, having nothing to do for a change.

He decided to go out. Their old building had kept the 1950's speckled mirrors, too many of them as far as Spencer was concerned, and there was no way you could get through the lobby without looking at yourself. His face was a little gray and there were bags under his eyes even though he was not quite thirty. In those pants he looked not so much like a clown as like certain old comics with faces like rubber from grimacing all their lives. Maybe that's precisely what he was.

Spencer walked the two blocks to Ocean Avenue, past the Cardozo Hotel on 13th Street and the Edison a block up, to Ocean Park. Maybe if he wanted that condo, all he had to do was peddle his knowledge of fraud to the other side. If you could prosecute it, you could defend it. You could even do more. You could sell something to those who wanted it and still stay on the safe side of the line. If anyone knew where the real line was, he did. Not the line they tell you about in law school. Not the line the big-firm litigators say to stay back of, but the real line, the line you stay behind and feel free to deal again and again, the line you cross and you're in a striped shirt. The Ed Meese–Dick Thornburgh line, he always called it.

Spencer picked out a bench at 9th Street on the ocean side of Ocean Boulevard. It was the middle of the day and he had neighbors, real people, men and women his and Becky's age, a young mom who pushed her pretty blond daughter along the ocean in a stroller and a tough young dad, maybe like him, who tossed his son on his shoulders and raced out to meet the water so he could teach his boy not to be afraid of too many things.

Spencer heard the horn but didn't turn around until it sounded off three short toots. It was Abner's way of greeting him. Abner Parks, U.S. Marshal, had the parking space next to his at work, and when they pulled in at the same time or ran into each other elsewhere, Abner greeted him with a toot-toot-toot.

Abner left his Toyota along the curb, right under the No Parking sign. Spencer knew that Ab normally was not that defiant. Here goes the rest of Sunday, Spencer decided, and maybe it was just as well. With Becky gone, there was nothing to do anyway except think about getting into trouble. He had never seen Ab in shorts before. Black bowlegs.

"It's started," Abner said, looking worried, heading for Spencer's bench.

"What's started?"

Abner looked around. No one sat nearby. There were just the Sunday strollers.

"Angel Fish."

"That's not possible."

Now it was Spencer's turn to look and then lower his voice. "We don't even have a grand jury yet."

The surf would muffle most of their conversation. The

41

strollers wouldn't catch enough unless they slowed down and he would keep an eye open for that. Half the *alter kockers* shuffling by in bell bottoms were more interested in overhearing Yiddish. This, the action, is what he loved.

"They got the documents Saturday night," Ab said. "The Grand Cayman bank documents. Just last night. Lifted a briefcase off a bank officer from his hotel room."

"How? They didn't clear anything with me."

"They did it anyway. The Davis guy."

"Where?" Spencer asked.

"The Grand Bay."

"Good taste." Then Spencer asked, "How'd they get the briefcase?"

"Melanie Field."

Spencer leaned back against the planks on the back of the bench.

"Don't you remember?" Abner asked. "Friday morning, in Byron's office. The IRS plant."

Spencer stretched his neck to get a kink out of it and at the same time checked the passersby again.

"She played hooker," Abner said. "Got the guy from the bank to pick her up in the Grand Bay bar and take her upstairs . . ."

Spencer's mind had started doing its Lexis, computerized legal research. The old-timers used to complain bitterly about computerized legal research. They didn't know how to do it, weren't taught in law school and didn't want to learn now. The smarter of the old-timers would go to the Index of Legal Periodicals and see if some terrific law student had done their research for them. They would look under "entrapment" and see if the *Harvard Law Review*, Yale, or even Michigan had done an article or a case note on the subject. If so, they would read it in the hope there would be something on "impersonation," or on a "free lancer" who sold the government something. The idea that these old-timers should step up to a keyboard, draw on some simple typing skills, and cut three days into three hours escapes them.

Spencer was a modern man. He would call the main computer bank in Ohio by inserting the proper commands and check for all federal cases containing the word "impersonation" used in a judge's legal opinion within twenty-five words of the word "entrapment." Maybe Lexis would spit out too many cases. Then he'd reprogram the requirements to search for cases that use the word "impersonation" within ten words of "entrapment," then within five words, then two.

"Is she really an IRS agent?"

"I don't know."

"Or," Spencer said, thinking fast, "with luck, is she a hooker who did it on her own and then sold it for an informer's fee?"

Spencer continued his legal research in his head, looking for an exception to the general rule that probably said, "Thou shalt not be an IRS agent whosoevereth engages in entrapment." Maybe if she wasn't an IRS agent but a free lancer making a buck, he could save the day. He stood up.

"What the fuck is the matter with these guys? It's one thing for me to run their goddamn grand jury. It's something else to start the whole mess wondering if anything I do will stick. Didn't they have the brains to talk to a lawyer?"

"They did. He called them at one twenty-seven and he told them to wait until Monday. That's tomorrow. They didn't wait."

For the first time in six years on this job, Spencer's mind stopped processing. Not a sound he heard, not a word he saw in print, not a memory of a moment on Friday came into his head. He couldn't concentrate. Then one twenty-seven, a number, came clear. The time he told the wise-ass IRS guy Davis he'd call. Becky and the fucking condo at two. Wait for me until Monday. "Fine" had been the response from Davis. Then he heard Abner Parks's words again. "They didn't wait."

"Can you give me a lift back to my place to get my car?"

"Where do you want to go? I'll take you."

"Is Byron home?"

"He sent me to find you."

Ab didn't push Spencer to talk as they drove north on Ocean Avenue and took the turn at 12th Street one block west to Collins Avenue, which was the only way to continue north. He tried to get Spencer to talk somewhere between Lincoln Road and 23rd Street but failed, so he gave up, and they continued in silence west to Pine Tree Drive and then up past 41st Street, now Arthur Godfrey Road, to Byron's house.

U.S. Attorney's and federal judges had to stay just this side of opulent in their choice of residence, especially in Miami. It would not do to live in Al Capone's old home on Palm Island, nor in Carl Fisher's old mansion two blocks from where they had stopped. Nor would it do for an Assistant U.S. Attorney to own an apartment at Palm Garden in Coconut Grove unless he wanted to explain himself over and over, Spencer decided. A signal of too much pleasure in possession, a question of how it all is paid for, precisely the way the revenuers brought down Al Capone. No, it would not do.

Before they reached the door, Byron had it open. He stood in an entrance hall, looking casual on Sunday: white slacks, reverse pleats, beautifully fitted; pale blue shirt buttoned at the throat. Too much opulence, Spencer decided.

"Byron, I won't run this grand jury."

"Yes you will."

"Can I come in or do I quit here on your doorstep?"

"If I wanted you to quit, I would have closed my door long ago." It wasn't the smile that took the wind out of Spencer's sails. It was Byron's voice, the pleading in it. There was something behind it that Spencer felt he could trust.

"Okay," Spencer said, "we'd like to come in."

Spencer knew what he was doing when he shifted pronouns and invited Ab to join him as he followed Byron down the cool tiled hallway. There would be no stage exits. He was sorry he had even hinted at one.

It was a long way out to the back of the house, which was really the front if you were lucky to have a house that had a lot of frontage on the water. Not the ocean in Byron's case, just Indian Creek, but that was no slouch. From the twenties to the fifties, on the hundred-foot-wide man-made waterway separating the strip of hotels and the residential islands of Miami Beach, Indian Creek is where you wanted your house, unless, of course, you were Harvey Firestone and had your house on 44th and the ocean and you could tear it down to make way for the Fontainebleau. Byron's house was stucco and had a tile roof, just one story and not too many rooms, but big ones, red tile floors, Indian rugs, sofas you could sink in, water you could look at from your huge living room windows that faced Indian Creek, windows that were really doors that rolled back to open up the whole room to the outdoors, and a lawn, even that lousy Florida crinkly grass that tickled your toes if you walked out your living room down to your polished mahogany boat that rode quietly at your dock on the creek. This was Florida, Spencer thought, not some fucking unit.

"Byron, they've fucked this grand jury, the whole thing." Then Spencer grimaced, wondering if Mrs. Varner or the girls could have heard him. He looked around but saw no one. "Sam Yones may have gotten off even before we get started."

"Spencer, you look like you're going to beat a spoon on your high chair. I wanted you to have time for your temperature to go up and then for it to come down. That's why I asked Ab to find you. Tomorrow you'll be back to normal, seeing the whole thing as a problem to be ruled on by some judge or some court of appeals years down the pike. But in the meantime, we've got the guy."

"Why all this concentration on Sam Yones? Why? He's not public, he's not headlines." There was a long pause.

"You mean nobody told you? Taxes, you dummy," Byron said.

Spencer winced. Dummy wasn't Dumbhead and Byron wasn't Potsy. Enough, he told himself.

"So I am right. Nobody told you."

Byron stopped for ice, liquor, mixes, iced tea, and a tray, and out of the corner of his eye he watched Spencer shuffle his dirty loafers on the floor, like a horse pawing the ground, getting ready to race. He was the best assistant in the office, Byron thought. God knows how I keep him. Byron had his plan for Spencer. If—when—he got on the bench. When that happened, he would send Spencer out, counsel him to specialize on the defense side of white-collar crime and then steer a big one to him and Spencer would make his mark. He couldn't do the steer right away. But within the first year. He wouldn't want to be the judge in the case, though. Too soon. Not illegal, so long as it wasn't pending before the U.S. Attorney's office before he took the bench or before Spencer went out on his own, but it wouldn't look good. No difference, Spencer would get the edge anyway.

"Come on, gentlemen," Byron said. "We'll sit out here."

Spencer was still burning but he tried to calm down.

Spencer and Abner followed Byron across the tiled terrace, outside to three of four cast-iron chairs painted white, facing the water in a semi-circle. They could smell the salt air, even though the ocean was on the other side of Indian Creek, a few blocks away. The ocean wetness in the air seemed to slow them all down more than a little bit. Byron put the tray down, took drink orders, and handed them around. Then the three of them took their seats out on the lawn.

"I want more than a whitewash here," Byron said. "Boesky's hundred million in fines was meaningless. He put up fifty million locked in a British trust that was really worth twelve. And he deducted half of it anyway. Milken did the same thing. The bigger the fine, the more you get to deduct."

"The government got fucked," Spencer said.

"They got what they wanted." Byron gave him the easiest look he could. "They got a scandal."

Byron folded one leg across the other, satisfied. He wanted to say they got the Jews, Spencer decided.

"But I want more."

"Byron," Spencer said, "what are we going to do with the IRS agents, Davis, Melanie Field."

"All right. It was a mistake. Tomorrow, Monday, you'll research it or have somebody run Lexis for you and get all the citations. You know as well as I know that there'll be cases all over the lot. Some for us; no entrapment. Some against us; yes there was entrapment. Of course there's an issue. But, Spencer, think. *When* will the issue come up? After it's all over. And by that time, if we've got something, some judge hearing a motion to quash the indictments on the grounds of entrapment will look for a way *not* to do it. Twenty-twenty hindsight."

"Angel Fish could go for a long time," Spencer said.

"And Sam Yones is out there on a string. So what."

Spencer saw Byron stare at him in that disconcerting deadpan as if he were very much aware of what you said and not at all of you as a person.

"I'm going into this knowing it could go down the drain," Spencer said, not thinking of Sam Yones any longer.

"Any deal can go down the drain," Byron said.

"What you're really telling me is that if I find something, using a whore to get it won't make any difference."

"Don't get moral on me."

Spencer could tell Byron was uncomfortable. It was something about the way his lower lip did a little dance.

"Davis told me he tried to get to you Friday," Byron said.

Now it was Spencer's turn to use his smile.

"I told him one twenty-seven. That's when I told him I'd call and that's when I called."

"But you didn't tell him you'd call to tell him you couldn't see him until Monday."

"And he didn't tell me what he planned to do if he *didn't* see me. Byron, he's sandbagging me. Not only me, but you."

They both noticed Abner twist in his seat. He wanted to leave, but Byron motioned him to stay put.

"How do you think it will look," Spencer went on, "if

it all fails because of entrapment? Because we can't introduce the list of those bank accounts pilfered out of that banker's briefcase into evidence at a trial because of entrapment." Spencer looked at Abner and then took a big breath. "Can you imagine the questions at your Senate judicial confirmation hearing?"

"Then get me something other than that list. Use it. Use it any way you want. Get me evidence that is independent of the list. If the list gets tossed, the indictments still stick anyway. It's like Ollie North and his Senate immunity. Get me something outside of the Senate testimony. Something outside of the list."

"How do you expect me to do that?"

"You'll find a way."

"Thanks."

"I won't forget you," Byron said, his words as pregnant with meaning as he could make them.

"I won't forget you either," Spencer answered.

Then there was one of those total silences in which no one moved.

"I suppose neither one of you saw the paper," Ab said into the silence. "Sam Yones's son was killed last Friday, right here in Florida."

"That was two days ago. How come nobody told me?" Byron asked.

"The kid didn't do anything. He was twenty-two years old, according to the paper," Ab said. "The funeral is tomorrow, up in New York. They do it fast. They don't wait."

"Any drinking?" Spencer asked.

"Didn't seem to be."

"Any drugs?" Spencer asked again.

"No. Just an accident."

"Sad," Byron said. "Isn't it."

"Do I ask you again why we want him?" Spencer said, upset. "One life is already gone."

"We didn't do it. We're not responsible," Byron said.

"The man has everything," Spencer said. "And now he has no son."

"Oh, he's all right," Byron said, swallowing his drink. "He's okay. He's got one left."

5

CREPES AND OMELETTES AFTER A FUNERAL. MIKE COULDN'T believe it, neither could Cheryl. Outside, on Sam's flagstone steps, Mike poured water over Cheryl's hands and then over his own to wash death away so they wouldn't bring it back into the house. Now they stood in the entrance hall on solemn green marble among fluted columns. Two extra maids had come out of nowhere to take their coats. From there, Mike looked through the gallery hung with brilliant paintings down to the dining room and saw the line to get your crepe and your choice of omelette with everything except bacon. There was a babble of conversation and gust of jazz from the stereo. Not right, Mike thought. Not right.

The sun had come out and filtered through most of the windows in the house, almost as if the sun shone on four sides of it. Sam was of a generation to have ashtrays everywhere, and cigar smoke sailed slowly up the stairs from the TV theater, where the men watched a ball game and talked business, having already separated themselves from their wives. Male voices, hooting a missed goal, came from below, and female voices from the living room, split as if separated in choir sections. Mike realized he was thinking of choral music, not Cheryl's rock and roll. He smiled and took Cheryl's hand, leading her forward through the crowd.

They made it to the gallery that led into the living room and found Gordy standing alone next to one of Liz's new paintings, quiet now after his outburst at the funeral, his recitation of Sam's deals done for the high gorum, a recitation that was only part of the story. He put it all out of his

49

mind and studied the canvas in front of him. Liz always tried the new ones out in her own home before she recommended a purchase by one of her corporate clients. This painting, of some subject Mike would never understand, would end up in some chairman's office; it looked that expensive. Gordy extended his hand in front of its shining surface and Mike shook it. Then an unusual thing happened: They had little to say.

Mike and Cheryl stayed upstairs in the living room, drifting from one group to another. Mike did not want to go downstairs and be bombarded by cheers and howls of men watching a ball game. He wanted to duck all that. Nor was he attracted to Liz's Guggenheim group or the crowd from Columbia, where he taught. Then he saw Liz, who stood alone.

She hesitated for a moment near the fireplace, her cheekbones highlighted by the sunlight. He had been gentle with her, Rabbi Aaron, a small man with almost no eyebrows. She was his first Eckland and he her first Aaron. His instruction was not aggressive. He had made conversion easier for her. Mike was surprised Sam had insisted, but he had.

Liz remained standing at the white marble mantelpiece in her black dress. People came and went, some saying the right things and some the wrong things, misled by the look in her eye, the press of her hand or the strength of her kisses, which signaled to them that their loss was her priority, not the other way around. It was her job. That's what she did.

She always looked tall to Mike, although she wasn't really. She had a toned body which could be imagined under her clothes, tiny ankles, a tiny waist, and well-shaped legs that disappeared so gracefully under her dress. A big part of him wanted to free his hand from Cheryl's and go to her. But he stayed where he was, caught her eye, and mouthed the words "I'm sorry," visible only to Liz across the room.

Liz's words from long ago echoed in his mind. "First a place in life, then a woman. One thing at a time. You don't have the guts. You're not man enough to do it, build a life

50

and share it at the same time." All those words, mashed together. Mike took a deep breath. They were back together in that small room in Madison, not in her room in the dormitory this time, but in his room, a room with one bed, one that had been theirs.

"I was just waiting for you to realize that I was still here," Liz had said, sitting quietly on the bed, dressed now and watching him. Her voice sounded so strange that Mike looked hard at her and saw that she looked almost fierce.

"I can't be possessed by somebody else," he said. "I don't even possess myself yet."

"Why did you take me this far if this is only as far as you were going to take me?"

He was suspended in time now, caught in this moment. He would never leave it.

Liz's eyes were still locked on Mike's. She knew she would have turned out to be someone else, someone cleaner, if she had married Mike instead of Sam. She knew that, and she wondered if somehow even now she could seek the help of someone who had flattered her by never marrying.

Finally, Mike reached for Cheryl's hand and set about moving her out through the smoke and the crowd. They passed the open door to the library and saw Sam sitting there, alone in the darkened room. Only one light was lit. Next to the desk lamp, Mike saw Sam put one cream-colored note card into an envelope, then pick up another one and get ready to write again.

Cheryl whispered, "Go to him, Mike. No one else will. Don't you see? There's no one else."

Mike nodded and walked into the room alone, closing the door behind him.

When Sam was sitting, Mike had noticed long ago, no one realized how short he was and his head didn't seem so large and out of proportion, nor his eyes as birdlike as they usually did. And when he sat he didn't jingle the change in his pocket.

"I'm getting rid of this bullshit right away. What do you think of this?" Sam began to read out loud what he had been writing on each cream-colored card. His voice was as focused and penetrating as if he were on one of his beloved public platforms. " 'Dear whoever'—and there I put in their name."

Just a short note to thank you for your thoughtfulness about Matt's untimely death. He was a terrific kid and his loss is felt by so many of us. Thanks again for your thoughts . . . whoever.

"And there I put in their name again. Signed, 'Sam.' Or 'Sam and Liz.' Depending."

Mike walked closer to the large desk, the sweep of Long Island Sound beyond the bay window. Sam looked like he had just come from the barber's.

Mike smiled faintly but said nothing. Then he sat down.

"Anything I can do, Sam?"

Mike looked for enlarged pupils, arteries puffing out too much, whatever signs he could think of. There were none.

"No, I'm fine."

Mike felt his head getting heavy at the top. He remembered seeing Sam like this before, fighting pain by ignoring it.

Mike had seen the same eyes, the same you'll-never-see-into-me hardness when they were eleven, crossing Penn Avenue, passing St. Olaf's on the way to Hebrew school, the goyim winning the fights because there were more of them. Mike could hear Sam's voice over the years. "Mike, don't cry. Don't show 'em."

"The rabbi come yet, Sam?" Mike asked.

"The service was too Reformed for me. Where was the Hebrew? Where is a good old-fashioned bare knuckles shul like where my father went, where the *alter kockers* see who can read the passage faster, slam the book shut, and quick look up to see who was still at it. They didn't understand Hebrew. They just read it fast." Sam looked across the room. "What's this bullshit rabbi supposed to do for me?"

"I don't know," Mike said, lost for a moment.

"What's he supposed to do for any of us?"

Normally, Sam's voice could cut through anything. If forty people were talking in a room, you heard Sam. Maybe because he was short, he spoke in a voice that would get him noticed immediately. Not so now. "Say, did you like my thank-you card? You think it's okay?"

"It's fine, Sam." Mike didn't know what to do next. "Let me get you a drink."

"You think a drink will get me to write better thank-you cards?"

Mike crossed the room and chose a crystal decanter from the lineup on the silver tray on the mahogany table behind the sofa. It had become a little darker and Mike switched on another lamp.

"Cognac?" Mike asked.

"Who gives a shit?"

Mike brought two snifters over and put one in front of Sam.

"Nice pen," Mike said.

Sam's eyes went flat. Then Mike remembered: The pen had been Matt's birthday present to Sam when he turned fifty-three. It was an old Parker Duo-fold, a real one, an original, made in the year Sam was born.

"Have a drink, Sam." Mike didn't know what else to say.

"Cry. Is that what all of you want to see? Sam Yones in tears? Well, fuck all of you."

"Come on, Sam. We'll take a walk."

"Bullshit."

"Let me go get Gordy, then. We'll sit around."

Without a word, Sam picked up another cream-colored card and resumed writing. Sam had not said no. That meant yes.

Mike closed the door behind him, not wanting anyone staring in at Sam, watching Sam do whatever it was he was doing to himself. Seeing Sam suffer would be a real kick for a lot of people, including many in this house. Mike knew that.

The noise of the crowd and the shuffle of people moving from room to room was a relief. It was life again, even the inane bits of conversation he overheard, the people pushing against others heading for the omelettes and the crepes as if they had just been let out of a DP camp. Gordy, Mike would find him.

How often he had heard the story from both Gordy and Sam. Both of them told the same version of the lunch at the old Gimel-Daled Club in Minneapolis, so it must have been true. "Why is he here?" Gordy had wanted to ask his father when Sam joined them. But he didn't. Gordy's father, old man Wiser, was almost eighty then, still the general secretary of the union, still vigorous. "I look good, but I'm not really," he told his son and Sam Yones in the noisy dining room of the only Jewish club in Minneapolis. "What do you mean?" Gordy had asked, and old man Wiser looked at Sam and said, "Help him, Sam. Take care of my Gordy." From that point on, the versions of lunch diverged. Gordy remembered his father's eyes, and Sam remembered instructions about elections, tips on where the government would look and where it wouldn't, methods to use and who to take care of to assure Gordy as his father's successor, not only as head of the union but also trustee of the pension fund. It wasn't three weeks after the funeral that Gordy sat in his father's chair, head of the union and the pension fund, the source of the money available for investments.

Mike spotted Helen. She usually stood together with Gordy whenever they went out, like twin totems, but not now. She was a beauty at one time, a face from the forties, full of angles. Mike asked Helen where Gordy was but got only a hurt look in reply. He mumbled something and moved on. He could explain about needing Gordy later.

Mike headed downstairs. Gordy might be in Sam's movie and TV projection room with the men cheering, booing, and smoking cigars, watching players on teams some of them owned. If not, he'd try the poolroom. If Gordy was there, it would not be to play pool but to take inventory of Sam's racquetball and tennis trophies that lined the shelves and to compare Sam's pictures of the famous to the collection he had. Gordy was in neither place. Mike turned to go upstairs and saw Gordy standing at the top landing, blocking out the light from the floor above.

"Helen said you're looking for me."

Mike moved up the stairs quickly.

"I think we should spend some time with Sam," Mike said.

"I've been ducking him. I know it."

"Why?"

"He should have been where Matt was. This has all gone too far."

Mike steered Gordy back into the library, closing the door behind them. Mike gestured to the desk, and Gordy saw what Mike had seen a few moments before. A tired man, looking older than he was, writing notes by rote to thank those who sent condolences on the death of a son. Gordy noticed the two brandy glasses.

"I'm going to get one, too," he said.

"One what?" Sam looked up.

"If you guys are drinking, I'm drinking."

"Suit yourself," Sam said.

Gordy put his cigar down in one of the industrial-strength ashtrays. He walked over to the window and opened it.

"I have a feeling you could use a few days off," Gordy said. Sam looked up and put down his pen, Matt's gift.

The dazed look had come back into Sam's eyes. Gordy looked over to the ashtray, watching Sam's cigar go out.

"I'm a known quantity," Sam said, "but what Matt might have become . . ."

You could see a hole right through Sam's eyes, a hole right through to the core of him, Mike thought, good and evil, just like the rest of us.

"Sam, you still have Billy."

"Billy? He's nothing but bullshit."

"Where's Liz?" Mike asked, trying to pull Sam back from whatever brink he had put himself on.

"With her father. He still sees me as the kike."

"Dammit, Sam!" Mike put his drink down. "Cut it out. It's sad. It's tragic." Mike found air. "But it's over."

Sam screwed up his lips and rolled his eyes. "You think it's over? Do you really think it's over?"

Mike closed his eyes, but when he opened them, Sam was still there.

"You never get to the top floor," Sam said. "No one knows where the top floor is."

"Sam," Gordy said, "by the way, is all the money in on the new partnership?" Gordy's voice was so calm and definite, his look so easy and businesslike that it seemed to jolt Sam for a moment.

Mike knew immediately what Gordy was trying to do.

"Yes, it came last week," Sam said. Gordy had tripped a wire in Sam's brain and he was coming back. "Well, not all. GM is in. Prudential is in. You could tell that. They were both there today . . ." Sam came rumbling back to life.

Mike walked to the window and looked out across Long Island Sound. Referring to their investors not by their names but by their business was something Sam had started the year the high gorum found him.

". . . the Church is late, and so is Defense."

"But that's it?" Gordy asked.

The high gorum appeared in Sam's life when he turned forty, almost on his birthday. Mike's memory was pretty good about such things, he realized. Indeed, it was on Sam's birthday. Liz didn't like it when he disappeared to take the call and they all sat at the table in the old house, waiting for Sam to get off the phone. The boys watched the ice cream melt, scoops of it piled high inside a crystal bowl, dribbling down the glass. "That was the finest birthday present any man could have," Sam said, walking back to his family, dismissing the silver cigar box Matt had saved for for over a year; Billy unaffected, used to it.

"That's it," Sam said. "But they'll all be in. The deal will net sixteen cords per tree, that's this year, up to twenty next year for acreage uncut if we want. We'll wait. We'll exceed reforestation requirements and in year three, the market for soft pine will be just right."

Mike turned to watch Sam predict the future. He had

been watching and listening to Sam predict the outcome of things since the first warehouse on Nicollet Avenue when Sam was nineteen, and assuring Gordy sixteen years later that the election was totally in compliance with all rules of the National Labor Relations Board and that there was no way the NLRB would find anything after their investigation.

"It'll make money," Sam Yones, a kid, had said to Gordy's father. "Trust me." And when he was still in his twenties and he first found timber, he said, "Trust me. It'll make money. A lot of it." How long had it taken Sam to perfect his ability to predict? Mike wondered, watching Sam's face now come alive talking business on the day of his son's funeral. When was it that Mike realized the fascination could prove costly? "We've made money, big money, in the Philippines on their mahogany. Why bring the profits back? Deductions are deductions, but why pay taxes at all? We're just going to reinvest the money over there again. It's legal. It's perfectly legal," Sam had said. And on that deal, back then, it was perfectly legal. If you didn't bring the money back, you didn't pay taxes on it. Then the law changed, and you had to pay taxes on profits earned overseas even if you left the money there and never brought it back here. To leave the money overseas without paying taxes on your profits became illegal. But the bank accounts were there, the tested telexes used to move funds from one account to the other were there, in place, beckoning. The move back to Florida, Alabama, Georgia, from mahogany to pine, made for bigger deals. The scale of the investments and the profits skyrocketed but the overseas accounts were still there, begging. Use all those foreign accounts. Make it look like foreigners owned those accounts. Keep the real owners secret. And, as Mike remembered Sam telling him over and over again, "If I didn't offer, the high gorum asked."

"You'll come out of it, Sam. You'll be all right," Mike said, but it came out in a whisper.

Sam stopped his conversation with Gordy instantly, and

touched Mike's shoulder. "Thanks. I'm lucky to have you."

Mike realized that other than those who had taken advantage of the accounts beckoning from overseas, no one outside of this room knew what they knew.

Sam had given Mike something unique, something no other man he knew had to give, something that was a passion, a skill, an art: the ability to construct instrumentalities of greed, to predict and arrange for the successful collection and storage of enormous wealth for the most powerful people in the country, secretly. The problem over the years was that Mike had become an addicted student, seeing the greatest of the great, the moral captains of America's industry, tuck a little away for a rainy day, cut the corner just a little as if they were sneaking an overweight bag on an airplane or exchanging a cheap raincoat for a better one without the owner's knowledge. He stayed silent so he could stay close. Or maybe his silence was based on something else. They went back so far. They were friends.

"Split up my piece the same way," Sam said to Gordy. "The A share for me, B for Liz, C for the boys' trust. That timber land is worth well past a billion this time. We're really trying to leapfrog with this one."

"What's for Liz?" Her voice came from the open door.

"We were just having a drink," Sam said, his voice focused, booming again.

"Sam, you haven't eaten," Liz said. She walked across the room, took her husband by the hand, and started to lead him out from behind his desk toward the door.

Watching, Mike could only think, He doesn't deserve her.

6

LIZ WALKED UPSTAIRS WITH SAM, BOTH CONSCIOUS OF being watched, but their guests would quickly turn away. On this day, even though the house was full of people, they could walk in their home as if it were empty. They took the turn of the broad main staircase and reached the second floor. By that time, the din was almost behind them, and Liz finally let her face fall.

Sam followed her into the large, airy bedroom with a view of the grounds which some, behind his back but to his pleasure, called Central Park East. There was a vase of freshly cut roses in the window, a four-poster deep in pillows, a Jasper Johns above the night table, and an adjoining bathroom where thick towels hung from English warming pipes and the cavernous tub had feet cast in the likeness of lions' paws.

He had come out of it and she found herself angry with him.

On her side of the bed there was an oval picture of her mother, an old black and white studio photograph taken when she was a very young girl, and a poem under the picture, beginning with the line, "As you softly sleep, dear mother . . ." and ending with the line, "We will join you one by one."

Liz went over to the window, sniffed the roses, and sat down in a large chair covered with a flower print, avoiding a glance at her mother's picture. She was still angry. She couldn't bear to see his eyes alive, talking business with his buddies. Not so soon.

She looked at the silk handkerchief in Sam's jacket

59

pocket. It was blue and indigo, almost black. She thought of the torn flag of black silk pinned to her own jacket. She carefully released the safety pin that held the symbol for rending of garments to her clothes, removed the little piece of material, and handed it to him.

"I don't mourn the way you do, Sam."

Liz picked up a magazine and started to turn the pages. Maybe that was what she wanted, to push him down, trample him, make him as alone as she was. She watched him lose his composure and saw his face crumple, but all Liz could think of was her own loss. She had heard that people who lost toes could no longer stand, and fell over constantly until they learned how to walk again. She felt like that, as if part of her had been amputated, and she could not get used to the idea that Matt was gone forever. But she had told Sam the truth. She did not mourn the way he did. She did not cure herself through business. Or maybe she did? Her own new, fresh, personal business. Maybe they did mourn alike? After all, this was the first time they had mourned together.

Sam walked over to the chair opposite hers. "When my father lost all his money in the hurricane in Florida . . ." She could finish the sentence for him: "He owned most of Coral Gables, you know . . . and then he was broke." She knew. "He said to Mama, 'Don't worry. We have each other and the baby.' "

That was Sam's way of telling her he needed her. Liz knew that. She also knew Sam had the story backward. It was Sam's mother who said, "We have each other and the baby." Not his father. His father thought the world had ended. His mother picked up the pieces and stood her husband up on his hind end and made Jacob Yones go on.

Liz looked around the room at the large bed loaded with pillows and her Jasper Johns and wished it were two beds, wished she could split it in half and take one half ten thousand miles from here. One big bathroom. She'd like to split that, too. A wife's anniversary toast to a husband from Sam's culture: "You should live one hundred and nineteen years, and I should live one hundred and twenty, so I can have one year of peace." She was telling herself Catskill comedian jokes. Her father would have killed her.

"Sam, let's go downstairs. It's better for us," she said, but he didn't move. He didn't have to say, "Give me a minute. What's the rush?" She saw from his face he needed time. What surprised her was that she felt no guilt for changing his mood, moving him back to sorrow. Suddenly, she felt the need to take care of him, to draw him closer to her, to be his wife again.

"I saw the Chanukah card you got from the Leningrad refusniks," Liz said. "It's nice they're in Santa Monica now."

"If I didn't get them out, they'd still be in that Italian town waiting for the visas. The same State Department that gave Jews to the Nazis in 1940 is drowning them now. You don't beg the powerful. You get the power to stop them from fucking you."

"She says . . . Sam, what's her name?"

"Marya."

Their maid had been thoughtful enough to leave cups and saucers and an English silver thermos of coffee upstairs for them. They remained untouched.

"That's it. Marya. She says they're getting ready . . ."

". . . for a normal life. Driving lessons for his daughter. A promotion at work." Sam's eyes lit up. "It's wonderful. Getting Jews out of Russia. The only place where a Jew can't help himself."

Sam smiled his wonderful, happy smile, the smile that revealed him at his best.

Aw-right! she wanted to yell out, seeing her Sam of years ago. So this is love, she remembered thinking to herself. It was Lake Lawn Lodge at the Wisconsin Dells. The spring formal, and Sam Yones, almost her height in white jacket, his cummerbund immaculate, holding her. She thought of opening her arms wide and saying, like Satan tempting Jesus in the desert, "All this will I give unto you if you will fall down and worship me." Yet she knew he wouldn't. That was why she was holding him so tightly.

"You know, Liz," Sam had said. "I'll belong here. I'll

belong anywhere I can take you." The dancing around the swimming pool was soft dancing, and it was good that the air was still a little cold for spring, because she was warm.

"It's our last spring here," she had said as they danced, listening to a white man who tried to sound like Nat King Cole.

"We'll go to Europe," he said, holding her. "You'll like that."

"Right after, huh?" she said.

"After we're married, we go where we want."

She smiled, and felt herself looking up to him even though it was actually the other way around.

"For how long?" she asked.

"The marriage or Europe?" He touched her cheek. "I was thinking of three or four months."

"Sam, we don't have any money."

"I have a little. And then we'll go to New York, just like we planned. You're not nervous anymore, are you? About that?"

Other couples, girls in pastel crinkly dresses, boys in tuxedos with white dinner jackets, swirled around them.

"Not one bit," she said. She liked matching his courage. She liked that a lot.

She thought of so many good times during that trip and afterward, Sam, sitting close to her on the couch when Gordy and Mike came over to their first apartment in New York on Sundays to watch football games; her pride in learning Sam never went back to her until he was sure it was over with Mike. How proud she was of his sense of honor, even though she felt Mike didn't deserve it. She remembered Sam coming home from days and days of meetings, trying so hard to make it, dejected but then flushed, excited to see her. Sam in bed, his quirky smile, his earnest, determined lovemaking. That had changed, too.

Sam reached over and touched the 1932 wedding picture of his parents. In spite of herself, she reached across the table and touched his hand as he held the frame. He had blood like tar but he hadn't always been that way, she thought. There had been sparkle in that man that no other man had, especially boys of her own kind with their blond hair and blue but dead eyes.

In her generation, if you wanted action you married it, even if your family was against it. Not so today. But she would have married Sam anyway, she knew that. Sam, with his fraternity laundry route, his deals selling cheap student flights to Europe, repping a rent-a-car company, even his poker games. He had his dreams that he shared with her, dreams that she knew even back then that he alone, without blond, blue-eyed looks, possessed the power to make come true.

She felt drained, overwhelmed, out of recriminations. It was like some days everyone has in a marriage: you just don't want to do it anymore. Her face became calm and delicate like the porcelain on the coffee cup. Soon, in May, she would be outdoors in the conservatory, having coffee in the afternoon on tiled floors, looking out at the Sound over sunlit windowsills. Somehow a cat went with those afternoons, but Sam was allergic so she never had one. Those days would come soon enough, but before that she had things to do.

She tested Sam's strength with a few more minutes of conversation about the allocations of Jewish Federation funds for his Save Soviet Jews campaign. She also gave him moments of silence in case he wanted to tell her more about Matt. Or anything. Even the government coming after him. Five or maybe as much as ten minutes went by. He had nothing more to say. As active as Sam was, he treasured his silent moments with her and Liz was fulfilled in so many ways knowing that she and she alone could provide this peace for him, for them. He had been with this woman and with that one; she knew all that, but it was to her that he came for his anchor. Maybe she was trained to expect worse from men. Jewish men make great husbands, a few had told her, but not all the time, not every moment, but on balance.

Then she stood up and he followed her out of the room, walking down the wide staircase to the still-crowded living room. The crowds were working on the mixed nuts in silver bowls. She decided to stay in the living room long enough to make sure that Sam was surrounded. Then she would go upstairs once again and wonder why she was deathly afraid. She could make a great effort to find evidence for her fears, her sense that somehow it was all going to sink with Matt now gone—because he was gone—but she didn't want to play sleuth. At least not yet.

Liz had left her father in Matt's room. She hadn't been able to move him. Not to the synagogue for the service. Not to Sam's cemetery for the burial. He had not been able to go to those places.

She walked down the long hall, past Billy's old room to the end of the wide corridor near the large window seat, where Matt's room was. Actually, it had been Billy's room until Matt took it over. It was a big room on the corner and Matt had liked the view from there, the forest and the water. She had done her best to stay out of Matt's bedroom, but now her father was there.

He turned to her, older, his blue eyes watery. Liz touched his shoulder and he stood up. He was in his midseventies, shorter, only as tall as she was. It hurt because she needed him to stand tall over her. She needed eyes to look up to, a shoulder higher than hers, a place for her head to rest, a protector. Oh, Dad! She wanted to cry out to him, wanted him to help her, to be her strong father now that her strong son was gone. Instead, she said, "Dad, we accept."

"No we don't." Liz took gentle hold of his hand. "Matt wanted me to take him to Norway. He wanted to see where your great-grandfather came from." Liz listened to her father and tried to calm herself down. She urged him to move out of Matt's reading chair, but it seemed the last thing he wanted to do, as if, somehow, being where Matt had been would bring him back.

"I would like to stay here," he said.

"There's nothing to do here anymore."

"He won't be here much longer."

She took his hand in hers, knowing that touching him

64

would make her cry, that her father should not see her tears, but she took his hand and held his fingers in hers because she needed him, because Matt would no longer bring to her his books and records, his ideas, his hopes and his secrets.

"You want to know why Matt really came to see me?" he asked.

Liz found it difficult to pull out Matt's desk chair and sit in it, but she did. She had been happy for Sam as Matt grew up, happy that Sam finally had someone, someone who was family that he might tell it all to. Not Mike. Not Gordy. But family. She had excluded herself. She knew that. She did not want to know. At least not all of it. But she was sad for Billy, her firstborn, who had committed the sin of being average, an unworthy successor, never a confidant, rarely a son. She nodded, yes, she did want to know why Matt had stopped to see his grandfather, an unscheduled stop.

"He was on the way overseas for Sam. He had some papers Sam had trusted him with." Liz raised an eyebrow. "He wanted to know what they meant, but he couldn't show them to me. He asked about his father," the old man said.

"He asked what?"

"I told him."

"You told him what?"

"What we all know."

Liz closed her eyes for a moment.

"Matt didn't know." She heard the weakness in her voice.

Her father's eyes were dark.

"I didn't know it all either. But maybe I knew enough." He turned away from her for a moment. Then back. "Matt's gone now and I can't clear it up. I can't take back what I said."

"What did you tell him?"

"I didn't know what to tell him. He never showed me the papers." The old man stared ahead for a moment, trying to remain calm. "I told Matt, 'That man will destroy you, father or not.' "

When somebody buys this place, Liz thought, they'll look at all the wrong things, the scale of it mainly, the high ceilings, public spaces, not the private corners.

"And me? Will Sam destroy me, too?"

" 'And when calamity or disgrace is coming, listen for his step.' That's Dickens," her father said.

Maybe Sam would outlive her. Maybe he would be the one to sell this place, not her. She thought of the job she had to do cleaning out Dad's big house after Mother died, and moving him to Sanibel. He didn't lift a finger. It was a daughter's job.

They stood in the center of Matt's room, not far from his bookcases, near his window looking out to Long Island Sound. Liz's eye fell first on her picture and then on the one of the two of them together, mother and son, that stood in a wooden frame on Matt's desk, not a silver frame, but a simple one he had made when he was eight years old in the woodshop at summer camp.

Liz kissed her father and watched his shoulders fall.

"I think I'll take a nap," the old man said. He sat on Matt's bed and untied his shoes. As she stood in the doorway, watching him adjust Matt's pillows and picking up one of his sports magazines, she saw that he was unwinding, at least a little. He looked at her, trying to smile.

"Do you mind if I keep the light on?"

"I wasn't going to turn it off," she said. "I know that feeling."

She went over and kissed his forehead.

For two days she had felt herself forced to pray for Matt in a voice that was not her own, in a language she had to struggle to pronounce and learn to read from the wrong side of the page. To lose her son and then say good-bye to him in a strange way, a convert's way, was not easy. She understood her father. She had trouble understanding herself. To stand before a rabbi who makes you speak to a God you suddenly find foreign made her heart ache. Sometimes, Liz thought, when we say we adhere to the faith of our fathers we mean the father we know.

Billy, looking so much like Sam when he was younger, stood under the basketball hoop on top of the garage door. Such an inconsistent ornament for this palace, Mike thought. The ball caught the side of Mike's leg and rolled past him. He picked it up and turned around. He could try for a basket or play safe, attempt two dribbles, and press the ball back to Billy. He played safe.

Billy had on his dark blue suit and tie, the suit jacket still buttoned, losing its shape. The kid with his father's face dribbled and sank one. No "all right!" No "good shot!" Just silence. Just the sound of the ball bouncing on the concrete, one bounce, two, then back to Mike, who couldn't avoid his turn to try. The shot wandered around the rim and then went in. Still no shouts. Just the sound of the ball and its bounces. Back to Billy. In. Back to Mike. In. To Billy. To Mike. Out. A miss. Mike said, "Shit." Billy stood next to him.

"Uncle Mike . . ." Billy hugged him. "Matt's gone."

Billy hadn't called him Uncle Mike in years.

"He always made a fool out of me," Billy said, pulling away. "Just like Dad." His brother jangled in his mind, dead, not dead; taller, better at basketball, better at women, better at all of it, making him feel smaller, shorter, like his look-alike father.

"Dad gave me nothing when I was twenty-one. Not that I expected him to. That was never what I wanted from him." Billy turned to look away, then found Mike's eyes again. "But when Matt was eighteen, Dad decided to make some transfers to Matt, and I guess there was no way for him to leave me out. There was a big powwow over who was to get what." Billy felt his face hurting. "We met in Dad's office. Matt sat. I couldn't sit. I had to stand. 'How would you like this?' Dad said. 'How would you like that?' Dad said. And then Matt said, 'Why don't you give Billy the apartment building on Amsterdam Avenue. Then he'll have something he can run on his own.' 'Good!' Dad said, 'and I'll give you a few shares in the timber business so you'll be equal,' and I could swear they winked at each other. I was out of Dad's real business. My own brother pushed me out. They gave me a sideshow."

Mike looked at Billy, thinking of the many times he thought of him as his own son, wondering what his own son would have been like had he married Liz, had he not hesitated. He wondered sometimes if he would ever be free of that missed chance thirty years ago and the son he would never have treated as Sam had. He grabbed hold of Billy's shoulder and hugged him again, knowing that his touching would confirm in Billy's mind the unfairness of Matt's and Sam's conspiracy to shunt him aside.

They let go of each other and watched the basketball roll slowly to the garage door. They walked toward the pier where Matt's boat would have been in the summer. There was a single bench out at the end, facing the sea, made for the telling of secrets. Neither led the other. It was just where they ended up.

"So you agree? My brother kept the many-colored coat?"

"It's not over yet, Billy. Sometimes it all evens out in the end."

"And sometimes it doesn't. Look at my poor father. Now all he's got left is me."

A waste of life, Mike thought. His heart could break over Billy, a kid who never had a chance because he looked too much like the father he was trying to please, a son who was shut out because he did not represent a Darwinian step forward. Mike yearned to reach out to Billy again. What difference does it make, Mike thought, the death of a child or the death of a man without a child? Both are a waste of life.

Mike heard Cheryl call him and turned around to find her standing on the terrace, looking cold in her thin dress. "Mike, the minyan," she called out to him.

"Come on, Billy, let's go in. The rabbi must be here to say kaddish for Matt."

"I don't want to go. I'll do it my own way."

Mike nodded. He had intended to put his hand only on Billy's shoulder, but it turned into a final hug. Watching, Cheryl knew they both needed it.

Downstairs, the living room was cleared of crepes and omelettes, and the men, only the men, began to form a semi-circle in front of Sam's marble fireplace. The rabbi stood at the mantel. He had stopped counting. He had his ten. The executives of GM and Prudential, their colleagues from the Century Association and the Racquet Club, removed themselves from the circle and stood as if at the edges of a primitive campfire at the perimeters of the room. The rabbi started to distribute *Yahrtzeit* books, handing a pile of the thin books of memorial prayers to the tall man who stood in his well-cut Savile Row suit nearest the fireplace.

This raider of corporations, whose picture had appeared on magazine covers, took a white silk cap out of a jacket pocket, and passed on the pile of prayer books to the man behind him, a friend and partner. He in turn took his book and handed the pile on, and as the books made their rounds and the pile became thinner, anyone in the know could look at the men in the minyan and see eyes feared by entrenched management from one end of the country to the other, management that had kept these men out of the mainstream for more than one reason.

Mike and Gordy put Sam between them and received their books from the hands of friends. The rabbi cleared his throat and twenty-two of the most powerful men in rebel finance began, in their suits of finest woolen, to bow their heads and bend their knees in the tradition of their fathers, for it was only the men who counted. Mike looked up, waiting for the rabbi to begin, and felt Cheryl's hand in his. She had pushed her way in and stood at his side, and suddenly he was prouder than he could recall.

They prayed for Matt and for their own sadness in a prayer that never mentioned death, that never mentioned Matt, that never mentioned men or women and equality or lack of it. They spoke a prayer that bore witness to nothing except the existence of their God.

" . . . *Yis-ca-dal v'yish-ca-dash* . . ."

On the broad balcony at the top of the staircase that led down to the living room, Liz watched America's captains stand in one corner and the men of Sam's world stand in a semi-circle in front of her fireplace, saying a prayer for her son. She saw Gordy, Mike, her Sam in between them, the trio who had come so far suddenly huddled in ancient ritual made public.

And Cheryl squeezed next to them, in a place not designed for a woman. She felt a heat inside herself, unexpected and powerful. Liz tried to block Cheryl from sight.

She felt the loss of Matt so deeply at this moment, thinking of other times when the trio stood together and when Matt had joined them, turning it into a quartet. Billy never, Matt always. At what cost to Matt had he been included. At what cost to Billy had he been left out. Liz thought of her summers with Matt, the boat, Tanglewood, Matt alone with her, then Matt with his girls, how proud she was they fell for him, how proud she was he saw women differently than Sam, differently than Billy. Matt was gone. A God— her God? Their God?—had taken him away. She couldn't connect with him anymore and she once again felt fear and at the same time a compulsion, a need to find out why he was gone. Maybe she knew already. Maybe that was what she was afraid of. There was no way she would stay in that house tonight. She knew that the promise she had just made to herself, to get to the bottom of this, carried as much weight as Sam's whole Torah put together.

7

MIKE'S TEN-YEAR-OLD MERCEDES ROLLED, HEAVY AND silent, immune to wind and traffic noise on the last leg of the ride home from Sam's house, across the Triborough Bridge, down the East Side Drive, off at 96th Street, to Fifth Avenue, to 74th Street and the garage.

Cheryl had been quiet most of the way home. Her hair was brushed high off her forehead and floated around her face. In spite of having been to a funeral, she had made herself up to get attention, and she wondered why she had done it. She had been performing until the time they dropped the partners off at Butler at LaGuardia, driving right out on the tarmac up to the Prudential plane. GM was proud of having known such a fine, devout family, hoping their suffering would be a light burden, and Prudential kept his yarmulke on all the way to the airport, Mike answering all his questions about funerals of the Hebrews.

"I didn't see the rabbi bless anybody," GM had shouted over the noise of a jet, this solicitous question coming from a man who saw Sam as a conniving small dick Hebe bastard, Mike knowing that was a quote. He was at the loading ramp, his hand on the stair rail. " 'Blessed art Thou, O Lord our God,' " Mike had called out. "God doesn't bless us. We bless Him."

Being a tour guide to Jewish rituals had begun to stink in Mike's nostrils. More to the point, Mike had thought, trying to concentrate on his driving, being a Jew was what was really on his mind and had been, on and off, since he turned fifty, two years before. Weddings and funerals were the times when it called to him, noisily, pulling at his gut from across the years. The yearning came not from his own upbringing, not his father's life, nor back to any generations he knew firsthand. It just came out from somewhere, a past beyond his reach. Process people. That's what we were, he told himself. No farms, no cattle, no machines, no land, no bricks, certainly no forests, no timber; it was not allowed. Just the process by which such matters of substance became useful. When he had been cross-examined about his heritage, standing next to their Learjet, Mike had wondered how GM with his Pat Robertson teeth would take to his Jewish process theory. Their appearance for Sam's sake at his son's funeral told him nothing except they had learned how to use each other.

When they were kids in Minneapolis, a Jew couldn't be on the streets of Edina at night. That's what kind of suburb that was. Today, it's a one-hundred-and-eighty-degree switch; it's almost like the street signs are in Hebrew. Maybe there would come a time, Mike thought, when no one would care who lived next door, but he knew he was wrong. People always cared. Tribal. It was all tribal, and Sam was an Indian who wanted to be a member of a different tribe. He had worked his way in. Originally, he needed the high gorum to front his acquisitions of timber property—no Jews there—and they needed him. They had never heard of the deals he could put them into. They knew about their big salaries, their bonuses and corporate perks. What they had no access to, what they hungered for, were big-buck Jew deals on the fringes. They teased Sam, their smart Jewish boy who did it to become one of them, because he'd make them money, but in the end they forced him to respect the limits they imposed upon him because he'd had no other choice. Until the next partnership opportunity when he would use them, when they would tease him and in the end blackball him from their world again. Until the next time. "I'll be with Yones nine-to-five, but not five-to-nine," the men he worshipped said about him. Sam used them quite consciously, but did he allow himself to see how they debased him?

Cheryl aimlessly looked out the window, then back to Mike, knowing he was off in some world of his own.

"What a pair, those two," she said. "You would think GM would have more sense than to show off a raincoat he had stolen."

Mike didn't answer.

"Does Prudential know he looks like Abraham Lincoln," Cheryl asked, "only two feet shorter? I love his white-on-white shirts, all twelve acres of them, and I love the way he uses the word *visit*. He's going to come up and *pay you a visit*, even if it means he's going to murder you."

"They're his partners," Mike said. "A few of Sam's partners. The big people. Sam's to-a-captain-are-you-a-captain people."

They pulled up in front of the Fifth Avenue entrance to the building and the doorman took charge of the car. Fifth Avenue. His Mercedes, even though it was old. Mike wondered about his own needs.

"Welcome home, Mr. Anker, Ms. Stone." The doorman knew who was married and who was not. Then into the elevator and finally, two tired, sagging people were home.

She watched as Mike leaned back in the sofa pillows and closed his eyes for a moment even before he had his jacket off. "Hug me," she said, joining him on the sofa. Mike moved toward her and kissed her. She kissed him back. Her lips opened, but he pulled away. She held on to his shoulders, but without pressure, just touching.

"Why is it," she said, trying to smile, "that I have the sneaking suspicion that something not nice happened to you today." He pulled her close to him again.

"It was okay," he said quietly.

"Mike," she said quietly, "it was a shit day. Even at funerals, you guys circle the wagons. That was the first time I had to elbow my way into a minyan."

"Cheryl, cut it out."

"Skin with no pores. Liz. I hate her, too."

He pulled her even closer to him, as if he were going to lose her. She must have felt it, because she emitted a small sound, a comfort noise of some kind. He leaned back farther, carrying her with him, and she felt herself a light-as-air pillow to him, conforming, soft. There was no need to talk. Sometimes the silence with another, new to Mike as it was, was what he wanted.

"I'm sorry, Mike. I think of Liz and I'm tired of being the little Jewish girl who's never pretty enough."

"It's a different kind of pretty," Mike said.

"Yeah, the kind that loses."

"Is getting me a loss?" Mike asked.

"Have I got you?"

The phone rang a short while after they had finished dinner and Cheryl picked it up. She moved her mouth silently so Mike could see she was saying: "It's Liz."

He decided he had had enough coffee and put his spoon down carefully in the saucer, next to the cup.

Then he watched and listened, but heard only one side of the conversation. He tried to guess, judging only from the facial expressions of Cheryl in front of him, what Liz might be saying. Liz must have been saying a lot because Cheryl was saying very little. Mike was able to deduce nothing from Cheryl's looks or her uh-huhs. She had been trained by the best, by Sam.

"It's Liz, Mike," Cheryl said finally, out loud. "She wants to talk to you." He wanted to get up and pace around the room as he did at work or at his small office at school, but instead he took the phone Cheryl handed him.

"Liz, how are you?" Mike said.

"Better now." There was noise in the background, cars, a highway. She was not home. Mike looked at Cheryl. He held on tightly to the phone, which suddenly felt hot in his hand.

"Good," he said. "I'm glad."

"I was just calling Cheryl. I needed her help," Liz said. Mike picked up his spoon and stirred his coffee. "I don't ask often, Mike. I hope it's okay."

"Anything. How can I help?"

Cheryl looked up.

"I don't know," Liz said. "Stay in touch, maybe . . ."

A truck passing drowned out her next few words. ". . . but I just left. I needed to get out."

Mike found his gut tighten.

"Where are you?"

Cheryl looked away, and then back. He could see her try to take on a confident look. "Ask Liz if she wants to come here," Cheryl said. Her brown eyes distracted him and he couldn't concentrate.

"Liz, would you like to come here?" Mike held his breath in a way he hoped Cheryl would not see.

"No, Mike," Liz said, her voice pitch totally changed. "I'm so glad you asked."

"Well," he said, "we're always here for all of you." Fences are fine to sit on, he thought, but they have spikes at the top. "You call us day or night," he went on as Cheryl came over and touched his shoulder. "I mean that," he added.

Cheryl leaned over, putting her ear to the phone.

"Thanks, Mike," Liz said. "You've always been there."

For a moment Cheryl disappeared in his mind.

"I guess you're right," Mike said.

"I love you, Mike. Good night."

He wondered if Cheryl had her head close enough to hear.

Mike took the phone away from his ear. And Cheryl's. He handed the instrument back to her. "She loves us," he said.

"I guess she does." Cheryl put the phone back on the cabinet and walked to the bedroom, both looking at their watches, both suddenly exhausted.

"What were you two talking about?" Mike asked, following her.

Cheryl scratched her ear. "It was a strange conversation. She started out by telling me that she assumed, since I was in the business world and she wasn't, that I knew all about computers, and then she rattled off a number of steps she wanted to perform to see if it made sense, and I told her that it all did make sense."

"Uh-huh," Mike said.

"She really didn't need any instruction from me," Cheryl said, feeling anxious now.

She took Mike's hand and felt him come to life and touch her as her lover. She felt the hair on his chest and let her head fall into the curve of his neck and shoulders, still corded with muscles. Cheryl told herself not to talk, just to press him to her, to lose herself in him, to embrace his age that he once thought was a barrier. He loved her over and over and she loved him back. They looked at each other, eyes open, and she wanted nothing more than to be with Mike forever. She had been around long enough at thirty-one to no longer want mentors. If only Mike could see that; that she had achieved in spades what women want most of a man's world, and that it wasn't enough.

When she stepped out of her shower and opened the doors, steam pulled away from layers of white towels, and she heard his voice from his shower say, "I love you," as he always did, and she answered back, "I love you, too." Then she waited, because, as always, he would come to her, a big bath sheet wrapped around his waist, and hug her, his still-wet body clinging to hers, and he would let the towel fall, and she would let herself be cared for as she never had been.

8

SAM HAD CHANGED HIS CLOTHES THE MINUTE ALL THE people left his house. They had gone through the catechisms of disbelief and sympathy, and he was annoyed, hearing it from some of them. He had picked out a pair of tan gabardine slacks and a deep red knit sport shirt which he buttoned up to the neck as if it were 1947. The last had left a few hours ago, at nine, more or less, and after the place had emptied out he could no longer pretend that Liz had not gone as well. For a while he wanted to believe that she might have been outside, walking around. She had done that on and off when the place filled with cigar smoke and it had become too much for her. Maybe a walk around the grounds, or over to the pier, where the boat would be a few months from now, or maybe she took a ride into town with Billy. He, too, had left, but had said good-bye. Liz had not.

Sam didn't know any of the extra servants, and he wasn't comfortable until they cleared out as well. He knew Liz had instructed them to clean the house within an inch of its life, free of drink stains, crumbs, filled ashtrays, and stray soiled silverware. Home was to look as if no one had been there, down to each fluffed-up pillow on each overstuffed sofa. *Pristine* was the term Liz always used. Or *virginal,* if she felt playful.

He stayed upstairs, attempting to read Monday's *Journal* until the sound of vacuum cleaners stopped, one at a time, and until Liz's own maid, Arlene, had knocked on his door to see if he wanted anything. Even though he said no, she went through the list of things she could get for him, apple juice, coffee, a sandwich, as Liz had instructed her to do a year ago when Liz began breaking away from the house from time to time. In one of his rare kindnesses, he never cut Arlene off. He always let her rattle on and on, and once in a while he'd relent and eat something when Liz was out. But usually not. Why did he allow Arlene that courtesy? Because he believed she disapproved of Liz disappearing on him as much as he did. Especially tonight. That was why.

He went downstairs to his library. Yes, he even read a book now and then; another of his habits that was nobody's business. They'd use it against him somehow if they knew. Someone would drop a title and without thinking he'd allow himself to be distracted and lose sight of a goal, and if you lose sight of a goal, you lose. So what he read, and how much he read, was his own business. Liz had been fasci-

nated with the quiet side of him. She had never suspected
it all those years ago when he led the pack and they all
followed him out of state to go to college at Madison. In
those days, in high school, girls like Liz were barred to
him. Their parents were there to guard them. The University of Wisconsin wasn't that far away from Minneapolis,
but it was *away*. He was on his own, they all were, Mike
and Gordy, and they could cross lines and date who they
wanted to, provided they could get a yes out of a Nordic
long-legged blond beauty. Yes, it was a cartoon: short Jewish guy, tall shiksa; he knew that, but it didn't bother him
because he had always prided himself on his ability to
learn. He was action. In his own way, he dazzled. And Liz
Eckland, too, one Saturday night, had crossed a line,
headed in his direction as he headed for hers. But not for
years now had they talked about a book. Or a play. Or a
movie.

Nine-thirty.

Okay, she's out. Big deal. She shouldn't be. Big fucking
deal.

There was still a stack of cream-colored note cards and
envelopes on his desk. He considered them but turned
away. You could rattle around from one room to the other
for days when the house was empty, and it felt very empty
now. He left the library, went downstairs to the TV room,
and began to open the doors which would expose his ten-
foot television screen. Maybe he'd watch a game. Something delayed from the coast. Too bad Gordy had to leave.
He should have stayed. Then Sam closed the TV doors.
He went to the refrigerator behind the bar and took a pil-
sner and a plate of mixed nuts. With a bottle in one hand
and a plate in the other, he walked up the stairs. He looked
out the front door and the only car in the driveway was
the '59 red and white Thunderbird he drove on the week-
ends when the weather was good and he could put the top
down. Later, Square would pull it into the garage with the
big Lincoln, where it belonged. He didn't want to call him
now. He put his drink down on a table near one of the
fluted columns the fruity decorator thought formalized the

place, and wondered what he was going to do next. He didn't know. Not a clue.

He looked across the living room, which had been filled with people not more than three hours ago, and thought of the times Matt had bounded down those stairs, happy to see him, taking his dad's hat and coat, beating the maid to it, reaching up on tiptoe to put the hat on the right shelf and carefully straightening a lapel on Daddy's cashmere coat after he hung it twisted on a hanger.

There is no love like the love of a child, he thought, and then he cried.

Out loud this time.

Because no one was there.

Sam touched his key chain and the little gold book with the boys' bar mitzvah pictures engraved inside, and then took out a handkerchief to wipe his eyes.

He walked back into his library, took a Davidoff out of his humidor, and took as long as he had ever taken to prepare his cigar. He rolled it, took the gold clipper to its end and cut it off so it would draw, ignored all the lighters in the room and took a wooden match from a Fabergé enameled box that supposedly was used by the czar who freed the serfs and let his people have some breathing room. Then he lit the match and with it, his cigar, a dark-wrappered handmade drug that was supposed to bring so much pleasure but did not.

Then the deflective techniques he had been using wouldn't work anymore, and the anger came up.

He moved faster when he was angry, and once the lid was off, it was useless to slow himself down or even try. Not a cigar, not liquor, not good sex cured anger. Good sex was wasted on anger. He reserved it for triumph.

He looked at the clock and found himself looking at it every ten minutes. Fucking whore. Then he remembered the voices of his friends from just several hours ago: "Where's Liz so we can say good-bye?" "Give our best to Liz," "Tell Liz if she needs anything to call." What's he supposed to say? "She always bails out like this." "Probably out fucking." Is that what he's supposed to say?

"Dad, does Uncle Gordy have as much money as you do?" He remembered Matt's voice as well.

"I don't know, Matt," he had said, looking at Matt, who was fourteen when he asked that question. "Why do you want to know?"

"Oh, I don't know. Dad, when do I learn to drive?"

Liz had listened and just smiled, a Minneapolis Mona Lisa.

Sam shook the memory out of his head and sat down at his desk, wanting to break something.

Instead, he looked at the pile of Crane's note cards and the stack of books containing the names and addresses of those who signed in at the temple for Matt. He drew a breath and started to finger the pages, and then, like air out of a tire, all of the spite went out of him. He put on his reading glasses and picked up his pen, put a card in front of him, and started. An hour later he glanced at the clock to see that it was now close to midnight, and began to write for the fortieth time:

Just a short note to thank you for your thoughtfulness about Matt's untimely death. He was a terrific kid . . .

And at that point, he heard a key in the door.

When he stood up, his gut had a pitchfork in it.

He heard footsteps on the marble in the front hall, and he could imagine her standing in front of the mirror, between the fluted columns, seeing if she looked all right. Then he heard the sound of her heels on the marble, heading his way. He didn't yell out, "Liz?" and she didn't call out, "Sam?" Instead, he sat down and waited. How did she think she was going to get up the stairs without passing the open door to his library? That he was just itching to see. He leaned back in his chair, waiting. He looked up as her figure glided past.

"Everybody wanted to know where you went," he called out.

There was no answer.

Just the sound of her footsteps continuing down the corridor and starting up the stairs, walking away from him.

"Liz!"

The footsteps continued, and then stopped. He heard her walking back down the stairs, approaching the hallway again.

He smiled. He had won. The footsteps stopped and he looked up. She was standing in his doorway.

"Yes?" she said.

"I don't give a fuck where you go."

She looked at him with a sudden downturn of her mouth.

"Would you like to try that in another language?"

She knew if she sought her release, he would only tighten the chain around her, so she stood there, strong as a steel statue.

He took a puff on his cigar, not for pleasure. For self-defense. Then he turned the cigar upside down so it wouldn't go out.

Sam looked down at the stack of condolence cards. "How about writing some?"

"I don't want to write any now."

"You'll do it tomorrow?" Sam asked.

"I'll do it tomorrow."

"Why not today? Why not now?"

"Because I don't want to do it now."

"They'll arrive late."

"I'll fax them," Liz said.

"Wasn't Matt worth it to you?" Sam suddenly shouted. "Can't you find the time to put pen and ink to paper and tell someone thanks, that you miss your son? Or did you have something important to do tonight that wore you out? So your son's condolence cards can wait until tomorrow?" He took a breath and the pitchforks, hoes, and rakes were at his insides again. "Here! Goddammit." And he threw them at her. "Write some fucking condolence cards for your son!"

The cream-colored cards fell all over her like rectangular fragments of snow.

"I'll miss him in a way you'll never understand," she

said. "And I'll write these cards . . ." she caught one in her hand as it fell off the top of Sam's crown-glass breakfront. ". . . tomorrow. When I want to. Not today."

Sam sat down again.

"How come you came home?" he asked. "Wasn't whoever you found good enough for you?"

"I couldn't find who I wanted to find."

"And I'm supposed to know who that is?"

"You bet you know who that is."

"I can buy Mike and sell him."

"No you can't."

Sam couldn't take his eyes off the note card she held in her hand, gently, as if the blank piece of paper were something delicate. He closed his eyes and he wanted more than anything to feel her fingers on his forehead, a signal that he meant something to her, something worthy of touching, someone to love, not just live off. Once he wore glasses that had clear plastic frames, and when he thought of switching them to tortoise shell she said she liked the clear ones better. They made him look vulnerable.

"You sent Matt over there," she said.

He could tell from the thunderous look on her face that she had to be stopped. He had to stop himself as well. Gordy's informers in Washington had delivered their tip-off. Sam knew he couldn't go. He couldn't deliver the list to safety. Away from here. Away from the government they could use at their whim. The list that matched the names of the high gorum with the numbers of their overseas accounts. He had to get that list, the matrix that tied it all together, safely out of the country. He would need that. That was his ace in the hole. He knew that. He wondered who else knew of the list, of Matt, holding it and carrying it. To visit the sins of the father on the son. He thought of that biblical injunction also.

"Go ahead," he said quietly. "Write the cards tomorrow. Write them when you want to write them. No one will notice if they get them Thursday instead of Wednesday. The days of the week don't count anymore."

"Not much does."

She disappeared from the doorway to his library and all he saw was the Regency wallpaper on the opposite wall across the corridor where she had been standing.

Sam stayed at his desk, thinking. When he went upstairs fifteen minutes later the light was on in the large guest room and the door was closed. It would not be the first time. He went to their bedroom alone, exhausted. Maybe it was the heaviness of day or the night, he didn't know anymore, and he closed the door and turned off the lights.

Liz had always been a light sleeper. It was part of the job. Over the years, Liz had developed a way of looking at Sam, checking after his well-being without becoming too intrusive about it: a glance to check his mood, a brush of her fingers across his forehead to check his temperature. A touch of her fingers to his. Warm at night, warmer than most, although she had less experience than she had led him to believe. Not that Sam had needed a keeper, but there were things, even at this moment in the middle of the night, she felt responsible for. Some days she wanted to be far, far away, and some days she knew she wanted to continue to be there for him. Thirty years ago he had been there for her, opening up her horizons, expanding the possibilities of life like no one else could ever have done.

She rolled on her side to face the guest room windows. She was the one who had instructed the drapery people to layer fabric on fabric so it would be lightproof in all the bedrooms and all the guest rooms, and now she was paying the price. She was no longer sure what time it was. She thought of Sam down the hall. It could be noon outside with the sun blazing, and in there he wouldn't know it. But light never woke Sam anyway; he was a heavy sleeper, a fact that would have surprised most people who knew his darting eyes that took in everything, ears that caught all sounds, nuances that others missed. She was the light sleeper, the one who needed every trick in the book to get more than three hours sleep in a row. There was one way to tell the time if she was with him. She could turn over and read the time on his watch. He always went to bed with his watch on. He never put it on the night table. She knew why. It was a Cricket alarm watch with a light-up-in-the-dark radium dial, his bar mitzvah watch from his grandfather. Someone must have figured out early that Sam would always want to know what time it was.

By the time Liz realized how silent the house was, she was fully awake. She had not expected the house to turn this quiet this fast. Especially tonight.

Sam had sent Matt to Switzerland on a plane out of Miami. Not New York. Not Boston. And told him to come back through Miami, using Sam's tickets, Sam's reservations, Sam's Florida car. In short, be Sam. He had made it there and he had come back. She knew that. That much Sam had told her, anxiously, in the hospital corridor, but he had told her no more. For whatever reasons, Sam had not wanted her to know; but the fact that he had prevailed, that Matt had gone over her objections, her pleading, was a win he relished. "There are no cheap wins," Sam had said in his one-of-a-kind voice, from podium after podium, in speech after speech. "There are only wins."

Was she a win all those years ago? Of course she was. She could still see Arlo Shields, the tall, bony aristocrat from Miami, standing on the white front steps of the Kappa house in Madison, introducing Sam to her. He was in Miami now at the Law School, almost renowned. She always wondered how, back then, that late spring day, Arlo had let himself be induced to bring sweaty Sam Yones to her, nervous, trying to put himself at ease.

"Liz, this is Sam Yones," Arlo said, making sure that he sounded the two syllables. "Sam, Liz Eckland."

Liz remembered that she wore her blond hair pulled back that year, that it was a weekday afternoon, stifling hot for April, and that she wore shorts and a workshirt tied at her midriff. She remembered all that because she remembered the power she felt over Sam as he stared at her. She had no memory of what he wore.

"We're in class together," Sam said, "but I wanted to be properly introduced." He had a voice that was deeper than the other boys and a smile that she had noticed before

across a large room in Bascom Hall, where they heard
Edgar Lacy talk about American literature. His mask fell
and for a moment he seemed edgy, as if he had done something wrong. She looked down at Sam's feet, and they
seemed to be hammering at the porch boards. To him, she
was sort of awesome. She liked that. This wasn't what she
had expected when Arlo, who was dating her roommate,
called to say he had someone for her to meet. She knew
why she wouldn't have met him on her own at a Kappa
party, or maybe something they did with the Betas, the
Humerology Show or Homecoming. Lines weren't crossed
then. But Sam Yones, smiling at her, sparkling, was doing
just that, crossing lines. Guts. The guy had guts. She liked
that. She saw him try to hide an exhale in relief as she said
simply, "Hi, Sam."

Liz was moving now, finding it hard to stay in bed without kicking her leg or straightening her arm, doing something to ease tension.

She had signed Sam's tax returns where it said
"spouse." She had never been asked to read what she had
signed. Documents requiring her signature were handled
the same way. She must have put her signature on hundreds of papers over the years. Never, never was she given
a copy to keep or a draft to read in advance. "Liz, here,
this is this year's tax return. Our personal 1040. The partnership returns for the buildings on Forty-eighth Street are in
this pile, and the Bayside deal" . . . his way of referring
to the cemetery, ". . . are there, too. You sign just above
where Gordy has signed. And then again on the schedule
above Gordy's signature." Only once above Mike's signature. Only once. That's the way she did it. She signed
where she was supposed to sign. She never did it any other
way.

Billy never did it any other way either.

But she wanted to learn. Billy didn't.

Billy had moved out six years ago. Actually, he had
never come back since quitting business school. But she
had counted on having a few more years of summers, at
the least, with Matt back home, not to mention school vaca-

tions, his room as noisy as he liked it, the volume of his music skyrocketing, making the sound disappear by using his earphones so as not to keep the folks up. His *New Yorker* would have still been delivered to the house, likewise, his *Economist,* his *Interview.* He would be here, under her roof, at her table in the attic for a computer lesson on Sam's computer, with her for walks and a sail, keeping her company when Sam was away on business trips.

If it were not for the night-light in the guest bathroom, she would have bumped a toe on something, but that's where an extra bathrobe hung and that's where she headed. She thought for a moment that maybe, subconsciously, she was headed to take another look at Matt's room, but she knew better. What she wanted wasn't there. What she wanted was upstairs. The answers to why Matt was sent on this errand. What he was carrying. Why Sam didn't go himself. Why that car crashed. Why it killed no matter who was in it. Somewhere in the program inside Sam's computer. In his private office on the third floor.

Matt had been a hard-eyed instructor, and boredom and pride had gotten her through the private computer course Matt had lavished on her. Sam had learned because it made sense. So had she. Basic. Nothing advanced. She had her choice of Apple, Compaq or IBM. She had taken IBM because Sam had IBM. An off-brand guy himself, when it came to his purchases he had chosen nothing but mainstream. His Lincolns. His IBM. He had just bought Lotus Agenda, and had laughed when she asked him why he bought the new program as if she knew what she was talking about, which she did. He just laughed. That was all. No explanation. Just a laugh. Just sign the papers. Liz felt herself getting angry. Maybe that's why she was on her way upstairs, almost daring him to discover her. But he wouldn't at this hour because when he was asleep, his eyes weren't darting, his ears weren't hearing, and he was dead to the world.

She felt herself thinking of Sam through the eyes of an attacker. For the first time, she sensed his need for the kill in one of his deals, the drive to win, to prevail, to figure it all out and conquer. But pulling the other way were her images of Matt, the crushing fear that Sam had somehow sent his son, her son, to his death. She felt her chest cramp and her eyes fill for all of them as she continued up the stairs.

Agenda was supposed to let you work the way you think and, most important, allowed you to get into files free-form. God knows what Sam's codes might be. God knows what he had behind the codes even if you knew them. Her stomach churned with fear again, but she kept going. "Put the information in the places where you'd expect to find them," proclaimed the literature. Liz sat down at Sam's desk, turned several power switches, and waited for the screen to light up. Let's hope the system lives up to its advertising, she thought.

The monitor came to life and she sat there, feeling like her grandmother saving the farm. Her father would be proud. Then her shoulders fell. Faced with the maze of machinery all at her command, she had no idea what to key in. Putting in the word "papers" or "documents" would provide her with a menu that would go on for pages. She could scroll from here to Christmas and she'd get nothing. Too broad. Answer? Be direct. She keyed in: Yones, Matthew.

A two-page report came up. Amazing. Matt's school grades, club memberships at Choate, Yale, and Harvard. Activities. Summer jobs. Sam keeps all of this? Liz wondered. It looked like everything you might need to prepare job applications. Liz nodded her head. Indeed. That's just what it was. Raw data for Matt's next step. What was to have been Matt's next step? Scroll a page. Matt's trusts. She inputted appropriate instructions and the investments in several of Matt's trusts popped up. Numbers. Names of partnerships. That wouldn't be it.

Liz stared at the columns of names and numbers and wondered if she should key in her own name. She keyed in: Yones, Elizabeth, to see what the menu would give her. Then she shook her head no. She was at this machinery

87

for Matt. Not for herself. She hit the revise button and the
screen went blank, but not before she saw that there were
eighteen pages under her name. Well, maybe, she thought,
someday.

The screen glowed green, empty. Direct hadn't worked.
Now she was stymied. She tried to think how Sam's mind
would work. Directly, according to function. It was the
system of his mother's telephone book. If you were sick,
you called the doctor. So where in the telephone directory
would you put the names of the doctors? Under S, of
course. "S" for "sick." Uncle Joe, Cousin Helen, Aunt
Sophie, all the rest. Where would you put their names?
Easy. Under F for "family." That's how his mother
thought. That's how Sam would think. Under S for "secrets." Liz keyed it in. Nothing. No menu. That's okay,
she thought. Then she tried: "Matt, personal." Again nothing. Two more attempts and Liz began to lose heart. Then
she tried not simply "papers," which was what she started
with and rejected because it was too broad, but instead
"papers, private."

This time a menu did appear.

She got "Refer to File Code Word BEHAVE ME . . . PLUS,"
and then the instruction, "INSERT SPECIAL ACCESS CODE."

"Behave me." Liz closed her eyes for a moment. So he
never forgot.

Behave me. She had told Sam that story only once. Late
at night. A long time ago, not at a good time for them. She
saw in her mind's eye Sam's 1953 Studebaker and she
smelled the mohair seats and remembered all of them being
packed in that car on her twentieth birthday. Sam had her
next to him, but then as other couples piled in she found
herself on Mike's lap, brushing his ear, seeing him, it
seemed to her, almost for the first time. She remembered
feeling the rest of Mike's body, thinking, Don't let me get
in trouble. You're attractive. You're sexy. Don't let me do
something crazy. She remembered whispering to him,
under the laughs and shouts of the others, "Will you behave me?" She remembered seeing in Mike's eyes that he
was afraid she would feel his erection.

She felt ashamed because it led to so much and she felt like a traitor now, feeling it all again with such freshness. She had accepted all Sam had given her and now she found him memorializing her harm to him in his computer.

Behave me, she thought, staring at the screen. She needed another word, some code word she didn't know, the magic word after dot-dot-dot that had to follow "behave me." You didn't need to be a computer whiz to know that that "dot . . . dot . . . dot," was Sam's way to say access denied. No merry-go-round. Just a clear end of the road.

Liz slouched and let the back of the swivel chair give. She put her hands behind her head, stretching, her robe pulling open. Then she sighed. But it wasn't a waste of effort, she finally realized. She knew more than she knew before. At least there was such a file. Cheryl's advice had paid off. There were private papers under Matt's name. For sure for Sam and Billy. And for Yones, Liz, as well, no doubt. Now the question was, where were they? She had that predatory-attacker look on her face again, and she could feel it.

She stood up, let the desk chair swing back to its normal position, and started turning computer switches off. Then the lights in Sam's attic office. Then the switches for the staircase lights as she went downstairs.

Mike could help, but there was a real downside going in that direction. The other member of the trio was Gordy. They were different people, Gordy and Mike. All three of them, including Sam, were different from each other, for that matter. Gordy, the kid who made good better in the union business, bought everything he ever wanted. Mike and Sam, skirmishers as kids in the alley, on the floor, under the table. One got up. The other not quite as far because he was not quite the killer.

Liz headed back to bed to be with her husband because it was smarter if you had a goal in mind. He acknowledged her presence with a smile she wasn't supposed to see. Nothing more.

9

"LADIES AND GENTLEMEN, MY NAME IS SPENCER PELCHECK and I am an Assistant United States Attorney. Mr. Yankus here is one of the clerks of the United States District Court for the Southern District of Miami, and he is in charge of the grand juries and will supervise the issuance of our subpoenas." He buried his son yesterday, Spencer thought, thinking of Sam Yones, whose name appeared on the subpoena at the top of the pile. "Mr. Abner Parks, that handsome fellow sitting over there" Spencer gave Ab a big smile, "is a U.S. Marshal who is assigned to us and who will supervise the serving of those subpoenas, both here and out of town."

Now, Spencer, making sure that he looked as calm as he could on opening day, giving no hint of bees circling around his head, checked to see that his suitcoat was buttoned and turned his "trust-me" face to the grand jury.

"There are twenty-three of you, and you have been selected as members of this grand jury." No puffed-up or pinched faces. This was going to be like teaching a dumb class. "There are two kinds of grand juries, a regular grand jury and a special. Yours is a special grand jury. Yours is an investigative grand jury. You will serve for more than a week or two . . ."

At this, Spencer heard a few muffled moans in the back of the room, but he decided to ignore them.

". . . but for only a day or so a week . . ."

He waited, but there were no sounds.

Spencer wore his dark blue first-day-with-the-grand-jury suit, and he was giving his first-day-with-the-grand-jury speech. He knew he was supposed to be bored, sick of the repetition, not at all looking forward to the gazing-out-the-window-nitwit questions he would have to endure as the months wore on, but somehow, each time he began, he hoped for more. He wore his blue suit because the opening day of a new grand jury was supposed to be an occasion. For them and for him. The man on the street may have a brush with the law once in his life. Let us look good. Let us all feel the weight of trying to do the right thing. Let us wear blue suits.

"As grand jury members, you will ordinarily not hear both sides of a criminal case and you will not determine guilt or innocence. Instead, you will hear only evidence tending to show the commission of a crime, and it is from this evidence, and usually without hearing evidence from the defense, that you will have to determine whether a person should go through the agony of being put on public trial for a serious federal crime."

Now began the bullshit.

"This is your grand jury. You will select your own foreman and your own deputy foreman. I will not run this grand jury. You will. I will merely be your lawyer.

"That means you will elect, by secret ballot, a foreman and deputy foreman, which may be any man or woman among you, and at the coffee break you may talk among yourselves to become better acquainted with each other so that your choice will be informed."

This, his fourth special grand jury, would do what the rest of them had done, pick a white man with a tie as foreman and a black woman as deputy. He had learned, from his four specials and God knows how many regulars, that they'd take as long as you gave them. If you gave them an hour, they'd take an hour, if you gave them a week, they'd take a week. So he gave them forty-five minutes. They never caught on that their first democratic act was subject to his control.

Spencer continued.

"You know you will be an investigative grand jury, but

you also need to know what you will be investigating. Notice that I didn't say who? I said what." More bullshit.

Spencer watched their eyes as he talked for close to twenty minutes. Some eyes stayed at half-mast, some nodded as if they understood, some stayed mostly open, hoping for a cross between *Miami Vice* and *People's Court*. And that was fine. These twenty-three people didn't count anyway, but they didn't know that. They don't know that some guy named Tuttle got out of seat 2B on Grand Cayman Air, went to the Grand Bay Hotel, stopped for a drink, got picked up by a babe, got his ashes hauled, his brain fried, and his list lost, and the babe was from IRS. They don't need to know that.

The lady sitting two over from the guy who looked like Beethoven smiled. He must have been smiling at her.

"When we begin next week, however, hearing our first witnesses, there will not be a television set in the front of the room as there is today." He gave them a big smile as he pointed to the Sony 27-inch set, and got a few smiles back in return. "Today we have a tape to show you which is shown all over the country to all federal grand juries. After all, John Houseman, who played Professor Kingsfield"—a few nods—"will be more interesting to listen to."

Houseman will sit in a leather wing chair and play Professor Kingsfield, speaking the same way to brand new grand jurors as he would speak to a class at the Harvard Law School. He'll teach them about *The People's Panel*, the title of the film, show them shots of Perry Mason, and tell them that this is not a trial jury but a grand jury and that their duty is not to decide guilt or innocence, but to decide if there is probable cause to believe that a crime was committed and that this person or persons committed it. The film shows the progress of a suburban lady, first trying to get out of jury duty, then becoming imbued with national spirit as she runs, breathlessly, to assume her responsibilities. They know their audience.

"This tape will run about thirty minutes. I will be here to answer your questions. And tomorrow we will begin by presenting to you a list of persons you may want to subpoena."

The lights went down and the tape started, the light reflecting off the set turning the faces of twenty-three people funny colors. He couldn't just sit there. He had to do something. It was a shit performance. He was in the room and he wasn't in the room. He had to call her.

Spencer left the grand jury room as quietly as he could, leaving Dan Yankus and Ab Parks with the jurors. He noticed the black guy who looked like Beethoven look away from the TV and stare at Ab, wondering maybe what a black U.S. Marshal was all about. Then Beethoven looked at him as he left the room. He had twenty-seven minutes, but he had never been on the phone that long with Becky in his life.

She was trading yen for the bank, and he could hear the noises of the trading room behind her. "Don't call me here unless you really have to," she had said, "but if you have to, do." So he had his opening line.

"I have to," he said into the phone.

"Have to what?" she responded.

"I have to talk to you."

"Go." That was all she had to say to him.

"How would you feel if I told you I was having dinner with a woman who wanted to get into my pants, but don't worry, she's just a friend?"

"Can I get back to work now?" Becky asked. "The phones are ringing all over the place."

"My folks," Spencer said, "for all the craziness of their lives, are married going on thirty-four years. I don't want anything less."

"Then let's move where we can live."

"Will I see you tonight?" he asked.

"Did you miss me last night?" was her answer.

He tried to put an enthusiastic spin on her words, but it didn't work.

"I'll be out of here early. It's their first day. The subpoenas go out tomorrow."

"Then hell breaks loose in about a week?" she said.

"Less than that," he said, thinking of visiting a subpoena on a man who had just buried his son. Sam Yones had to be waiting, though. It wouldn't be a surprise. Then his thoughts turned back to himself. To Becky. He had just hung up. Where would they be in a week? Beyond that he couldn't guess.

Spencer stood at the phone. Fortunately, no one else wandered the hall, listening to him or waiting for him to get off, or giving him the once-over because he had said good-bye and was still standing at the public telephone as if it had just electrocuted him.

What a case this will make, Spencer thought. White British bankers. Graceful accents. Snappy. Elegant. Four buttons on the sleeve that button and unbutton. And then there was Sam Yones. He was forcing himself to think harshly of this man.

There were other names on those Caymans bank records, names in code, names that meant nothing to him, cross-references to other accounts. The IRS had given the U.S. Attorney's office what they had stolen, but it wasn't enough. That figures, Spencer thought. One goddamn list of numbers opposite another list of numbers. No names opposite any of the numbers. Clever, Spencer decided. Numbers leading to numbers. But how about numbers leading to names? Where were these papers being carried? Certainly not to Sam Yones. If he was behind all of this, why would he need what he already had? Where were the second set of accounts? Bahamas, Liechtenstein? Switzerland? One country's secrecy laws weren't enough protection, apparently. One secret account screened another. Maybe there was a matrix somewhere, a list that tied the codes to the names. Of course, each bank could match up its customers with its codes, but was there a master list somewhere? A master list that tied all these accounts all over the world together? He could only hope. Hope he could find names of U.S. citizens who had accounts they hadn't reported as controlled by them, accounts that earn interest that these citizens hadn't reported as having earned. Naughty. That's a no-no. You go to jail for that. Don't even need twenty-three yokels for that one. Bring in Davis, the IRS guy, give him twenty minutes on the stand, sock the twenty-three geniuses with a true bill and, next day off, time to cigarette-boat it to Bimini.

If he had a cigarette boat and if he knew where Bimini was and if he didn't get seasick. But what more? Where else would this lead? Connections. Linkages. He smiled. Relationships. He knew they were there somewhere but didn't know just where they were. Yet. Hence an investigative grand jury. A special grand jury. A fishing expedition. Only not to Bimini.

PART TWO

10

MIKE PUT BOTH ELBOWS ON THE LECTERN IN FRONT OF HIM and leaned into his class, hoping they wouldn't sense that all he wanted to do was finish the hour and get out. He pushed the microphone aside and put his watch down so he could see how much time he had to go.

"I really do enjoy fraud. I like putting puzzles together, and I like, in an abstract way, seeing how people create various artifices. I mean there are some *great* schemes out there." He managed to force out the opener of his course in business ethics for which he was famous and they applauded as they always had. This year, however, all he could think about was Sam Yones.

There was still some shuffling around in the auditorium, boots being deposited in the back of the room, snow shaken off parkas, but no one was late. One by one, several hundred students quickly settled down, opened their notebooks, took out their pens, and canted slightly forward in their chairs, gazing up at the podium.

"The thing about fraud is that there are no limits to innovation. It's like reading a new novel every day." His voice carried without the microphone. He had to struggle to stay on top of it all, to make sure he didn't seem hollow. He felt like an actor starring in a long run. He knew the lines that got the laughs, but he had to force it to keep up his end.

"I don't do this full-time, and since somebody has to pay for me . . ."—the class went up in laughter—"the funding for these lectures is the gift of the Elizabeth and Samuel B. Yones Lecture Trust Fund." Mike paused, trying to forget that they had buried Matt a week ago, that Sam's call had come that morning. He lifted his voice again. "Sam is also a friend of mine, and if we're going to start clean, you should know that."

"Excuse me, sir. Is there always fraud? Is that what you're telling us?"

Mike thought about what he knew, wondered about what Cheryl knew, because he had never asked.

The piles of parkas on the floor, the falling snow visible through the big windows, the early morning phone call from Sam, receded. Mike now focused wholly on the class. Bright students always did that for him. Maybe he would be for the best of them the kind of teacher he had had, one who helped him realize that he was more talented than the average student and freed him from the fear of being a nobody.

"Well, Mr." . . . Mike glanced at his seating chart, ". . . Witz, what do you think?"

"Whether there's fraud or not? I suppose you ought to wonder."

"Don't be so tentative," Mike said, forcing a smile. "That's absolutely right. Now, how do you test your suspicions?"

"Ah . . ."

"You do due diligence," Mike said, cutting him off, "and that means getting your nose in under the tent." Mike jettisoned the Socratic Method. He was nervous, impatient. "You want the knowledge no one else has, you want what the insiders know." It was their turn to lean close to him.

Mike's thoughts kept returning to Sam, the phone call at six-thirty that morning, but he managed to pull his attention back to his class.

"Now, how do you get inside?" Questions and answers took too long. "You get in because you agree to keep quiet about what they tell you." He thought of how Sam had let him in. "You agree to tell no one." He wondered again what Cheryl knew, what she had agreed to, about her vulnerability along with his own. His mind was seesawing.

"I'm sorry to get you up," Sam had said, "but Mike, I had to get to you before anyone else did."

"I'm up. I teach this morning. Sam, what is it?"

Cheryl had turned over, touching him.

"They didn't have the decency to wait a whole week," Sam said. Mike could tell from the ambient noise that he wasn't calling from home. He wasn't calling from the car. Not secure. He was using a pay phone.

"Sam, what are you talking about?"

"The time bomb. It went off."

Cheryl had propped her head up on her elbow. She had watched Mike silently listen to Sam. When Mike hung up the phone she looked at him expectantly. He could tell her nothing. She was the best thing to come out of all of this. He had to keep her out of it.

"After you've signed the keep confidential agreement giving you the right to get inside, to get your nose in under the tent, you look for artifice and scheme. What you're looking for is bound to be there." Mike wanted to freeze his face so the fear wouldn't show. "The men will find it. The boys won't."

He knew if he looked around he could see any woman in his class ready to punch him. Take the blonde. He glanced down at his chart. Ms. Oken. She'd order Stolichnaya on the rocks, wear an oversized watch, and walk on the balls of her feet. She would try to be one of the men. Cheryl said the world had changed, that he was wrong, frozen in the pay-your-dues fellowship of his generation. Mike didn't agree. Not one bit.

"What do you do when you find the fraud? How about,

as my good friend Sam Yones might say, 'You cut out their *kishkas*.' " The classroom laughed and Mike waited for the oil portraits across the back of the room to twist like Dorian Gray's. "You know what Sam means when he says cut out their *kishkas?* He means pay them less, lower the price. He's telling you that business isn't for priests."

There was silence in the lecture hall.

"You don't like that answer, huh?" Mike waited. "Too rough?"

He looked out over his class. "Anybody have any better ideas?"

No hands shot up.

"No one?"

"Too bloodthirsty? Too much pleasure in it?"

Mike paused, finding as always the eyes of his students easy to look into. "Let's change the subject and talk about your jitters." They put down their pens and looked up at him. Then he asked them the questions he was asking himself. "Should you be rewarded for the fraud you find? Should you benefit by allowing others to keep what they steal?"

His voice carried. It rolled, it was warm, masculine, and full of authority like the radio voices he used to hear as a kid in the 1940s, and people said it was impossible not to listen to him.

The young man sitting three seats away from Mr. Witz took his ski cap off and leaned back. Ms. Oken stopped writing. She was listening, learning. That was why Mike taught. That was why they came here on snowy mornings.

He tried to recreate the full text of the telephone call from Sam, but he couldn't get past "Byron Varner's sending out grand jury subpoenas. I've got mine. Billy has his. Rumor is you're on the list." He remembered clamping down and biting his tongue. He remembered seeing stars and hoping there was no blood. He remembered feeling Cheryl stiffen in the bed next to him. "Why, Sam?" he remembered speaking into the phone as calmly as he could, ignoring the ache in his tongue. "What do they want of you?" "Nothing," Sam said, and Mike remembered feeling

Cheryl touch his shoulder. "It's you I'm worried about," he remembered Sam saying.

Mike rested an elbow on the lectern and cleaned his reading glasses. He started telling a Carl Icahn story. For a while his delivery was smooth, but then came the stops and starts and uncomfortable pauses.

He had a vision of Sam, head tossed back, saying in triumph, "The fucking high gorum. They're greedier than all of us."

"But, sir, the Icahn deal didn't fly."

Mike stepped back from the podium and began to button his blazer but realized he had already buttoned it a moment before. It seemed an odd time in his life to get stage fright, but that was what he felt. It was almost as if he were reliving each story Sam had told him over the years. Mike began to sense what a grand jury could wring out of him. The frauds discovered. The schemes perpetrated. The new novel every day. He could feel his heart beat. Mike tried to swallow his fear of what it meant to know what he knew. To be a teacher you must be a student, and maybe he had studied too dark a subject. But the man was his friend. They went back so far. It had all begun so long ago, so simply, so unthreatening, in such small steps. Mike propped himself up, drawing on the last bit of energy he could muster. Like so much in life, teaching was theater. His students were entitled to his show.

Mike used his hands as Sam might have, tossed his head back when he laughed, like Ike used to do in the fifties. He took his glasses off and put them back on, like Adlai, stepped back from the podium and leaned forward into it again, like Kennedy. He ignored his souring state of mind, and changed the pitch of his voice. He would carry off his seduction on the first day of class, no matter what. For the next twenty minutes, he gave one of the greatest lectures of his life.

Finally, after the bell, Mike lost himself in the crowded hallways. He nodded to students from last year, whose faces he always remembered, and he walked to the faculty lounge on the first floor to deposit his seating chart in the box assigned to him. Then, when he was alone, he approached the faculty service desk. His face gave away nothing.

"You're sure there's no message for me? Michael Anker. A-N-K-E-R." It was the second time he had asked, but it was a different clerk, and sometimes they had trouble with his name. A faculty phone was available for the asking, but Mike wanted a pay phone, a booth enclosed on three sides with a door he could slam tight and a fan overhead that would muffle his words. There was one just below the stairs, in the basement. He had used it twice before class. He would try his call to Minneapolis for the third time.

"We've found him, Mike." Gordy's secretary had worked for him for sixteen years. "He's in the Los Angeles office. He needed to get away after Matt. I guess you all did."

"Can I reach him?" Mike asked.

"Of course. He asks that you call in about an hour."

When the U.K. tobacco companies and the other foreign investors started making chains out of American retail department stores, Sam told Gordy to follow the smart money. "Go where they go," Sam had said. "What do you think, Mike?" Gordy had asked. "You're the professor. Is Sam right?" Mike remembered his exact words. "Of course he's right. If they bring the stores under common ownership, you bring the clerks under a common union." "Okay. We'll do it," Gordy had said, looking strangely at that moment like his father, old man Wiser, and out he had gone, first to Los Angeles, and then Miami, when Burdine's went the way of Dayton's. He told everyone he was going to split his time, but the balance fell in favor of the West Coast. Especially after Ginger.

Mike wasn't smiling anymore. He was eager to talk to Gordy now.

"Did you pass on my message? All of it?"

"Yes, sir."

"Does he know that I had a phone call from Sam?"

"Yes, sir, I told him. He's had one, too."

Mike sighed and tried not to be so tough with her. "Edna, I'm sorry."

"Thanks, Mike."

"How long will Gordy be in Los Angeles?"

"His usual schedule. There or in Miami until late April. Then he comes home."

It didn't take Mike a moment to decide. "Tell him I'm coming."

"He'll be delighted."

"Tomorrow," Mike said.

"Shall we send a car?"

"No, Edna. I don't need a car. I like to drive," Mike thought of the snow outside, "at least in Los Angeles."

Mike hung up the phone and sat inside the booth for a moment. Then he pushed open the sweating glass door to let in fresh air.

He walked up the stairs, heading toward the cloak room. He looked at his watch and went downstairs again to call his own secretary. He told her, "I'll be leaving school now, but I'm not going right to the office. I feel like walking."

"In this weather? It's snowing."

"Not a long walk, but I may be a few minutes late for Sam."

11

INSTEAD OF BEING DROPPED OFF AT THE DOOR OF THE SEA-gram Building, Mike left the cab at 59th Street at the bottom of Central Park. The weather was still cold, but by the time the Plaza hotel came into view, the snow stopped and the sun came out. The cab stopped in front of the entrance to the Oak Bar, and Mike let himself be carried along with the crowds pushing toward the subway entrance.

Rather than make his way directly down Fifth Avenue, he walked down a few blocks, then crossed back, zigzagging in and out of the side streets. He had forgotten the sensation of being freezing cold, being young and scared, walking the street, talking to brick walls, rehearsing his pitch so wealthy men would buy the stocks he had to sell. He remembered narrow buildings with shoe repair shops and delicatessens on the ground floor and one-man offices upstairs overlooking air shafts where a guy who had a lot of money sat behind a desk and sometimes bought stock or picked up a piece of a deal. He rode one rickety elevator after another to undistinguished holes with torn and dirty window shades more times than he wanted to remember and waited for the old guys to take him aside and tell him lies, but that was Edgar Stern's way of teaching him the business.

Edgar Stern was Mike's first boss, and even in those early years in New York was a living legend smoking Havana cigars. Edgar did what no one else did. He quizzed Mike closely on the reasons behind the full year gap in his college attendance, and when Mike, with shame all over his face, told Edgar about the bankruptcy and no money and quitting to bail his dad out, he left out the part about his father trying so hard so many times but getting nowhere; his mother, too far away from her own family, sweet but of no help to anyone, even herself; his revulsion at their place among his father's brothers as the poor relatives and of being taken in by Sam, by Gordy's family. He left out the part about never having, from early on, what other kids had. All he mentioned, with shame, was the bankruptcy, leaving school, paying off his dad's debts. Edgar smiled and said, "Good. You were a man earlier than most."

Edgar told him he was smart to get his master's degree in business even though he went into debt to do it. He insisted that Mike, while he was still young, meet men who looked like bums, men who had come from nowhere, men who had made a fortune but didn't look it, men who in a tradition older than either of them always wanted to appear poor and operate out of junk shops. Mike had learned his lessons from these men.

The wind had come up and Mike rebuttoned his coat, pulled his scarf tighter and headed for Park Avenue. He started to feel better, thinking how far he had come since the days of those dirty brown buildings on the streets between the avenues and how Edgar had taught him values. Maybe that's why he himself taught, to pass on the lessons that had meant so much to him, to be a teacher whose advice was sought and who gave it honestly.

As he headed for 53rd Street, he wondered again about the question he put to himself but never to his students: Can a person commit a fraud against himself? It was no trick question, and indeed, one didn't have to be a genius to answer it. We all do it every day, Mike thought. We do it when we give ourselves the wrong answers. We also commit fraud against ourselves when we ask ourselves the wrong questions.

Mike's thoughts shifted to Cheryl, and he felt terribly cold all of a sudden. You don't spend two years on a Yones Fellowship working with Sam and come out without being loaded with inside information a U.S. Attorney would kill to have. Suddenly, as he had been on and off since Sam's call, he was afraid, more for her than for himself. There was no subpoena for her. His job was to make sure there never was one.

He crossed over to Park Avenue and could see himself in the reflection of the windows of the travel agency next to the Racquet Club. With his taut face of an industrialist under his gray Gorbachev fedora, he looked like a piece of Park Avenue. How Sam had longed to become a member here, how many members he had buttonholed, how little good it had done him. Sam had no Edgar, never appeared to want or need a mentor who could help in such ways. Sam skipped the years of walking side streets, never hustled for anybody except himself.

No matter how preoccupied Mike might be, looking up toward his offices gave him a lift. Stern, Anker, and Company, all two floors of it, was one of the most highly regarded investment boutiques on the street. Although Mike did take the leading oar in the design of the offices, and although many thought oil portraits of both him and Edgar Stern should hang in the reception area as the architects had proposed, Mike thought Edgar alone should be there and that's the way it was. They didn't take fees anymore. They did their own due diligence and invested their own money, and the fanciest universities, most stalwart insurance companies, and most conservative pension plan managers stood in line to be their partners. In line just like Sam's partners, only they were different people attracted to different opportunities. It always had been that way.

Mike stopped for a moment before going through the revolving doors on the 53rd Street side of the Seagram Building. In 1954, Sam Yones had bet money that Kahn & Jacobs would never be the architects for that building and he shifted an investment away from a contractor that was affiliated with them. He knew people who knew the daughter of the chairman of Seagram's. He knew she saw herself as a supporter of Bauhaus architecture and so Sam knew, the minute she got home from Europe, she would end up in charge of picking the architect for her father. It was a surprise to everyone except Sam when she substituted Mies van der Rohe. It was one of the few times Mike had seen Sam so sure about something that would never net him big money.

People detoured around Mike as he stood at the entrance. He looked at his watch. His timing was just right. Sam would be waiting for him upstairs, in the building built by the architect that Sam and no one else had bet on.

12

NO HELLO FROM SAM AS HE WALKED INTO MIKE'S PRIVATE office. No how are you? Instead, cracks about Billy were the first words out of Sam's mouth.

"He lives in some goddamn fairy tale. Even with my money he can't make it. He sends me memos. The handwriting tilts up toward the top of the page like a ten-year-old writes. He tells me how this is going, how that is going. No truth; full of bullshit."

Mike didn't like what he heard or what he saw, but despite how he felt, he pulled a chair near to the sofa so he and Sam could sit close together. He could have taken refuge behind his desk, but that would be transparent; they would see that he was on the defensive. Mike kept his eye on Sam, not looking at the young woman Sam had brought with him. Unannounced, no permission requested, Sam had brought a lawyer.

Mike watched Sam's eyes. Clever, they always looked clever, but today, with his oldest friend, Sam's eyes were not at rest. His fingers, too, were very nervous. Sam was the kind of guy who told you stories that won him admiration, but never respect. He told you how he cashed out this deal or had a triple on Alabama acreage in four months. They always smelled of heat or smoke, and they were the kind of stories that discredit a person almost equally whether they are believed or not. For thirty years and more, that side of Sam never bothered Mike. It took him places he himself would never go, let him see things he would never see, and hear what few hear. But today was different.

Sam cleared his throat and lit his cigar. "You want one?"

Sam cleared his throat and lit his cigar. "You want one?" Sam held out a silver case with a single Davidoff left. Mike shook his head, but then decided to take it.

"I asked my lawyer to come along. Jenifer can help."

Mike looked at the young woman with hair that didn't move. He said nothing. He wanted to be left out of it, like a piece of furniture, but there would be little hope of that.

"I suppose it had to happen. You can't ride this long—thirty years a winner, too big a winner—without making enemies. The high gorum need to deflect notice from themselves, the S&L bailout . . ." Sam looked at his lawyer and stopped short. He smiled the smile that made rich men his partners. "Mike, they're after me for chicken shit, not paying interest on an overseas account. That's *bubkes*. It means nothing. Goddammit. It shows you. They dig all over the place and that's all they can find. And they don't even know why they're digging." Sam kept eyeing his lawyer and Mike sensed a tension between the two. "It's not that the subpoena is unexpected. But now, so soon . . . why now?" Sam turned away with a sad and knowing smile. "They've got to keep someone around to throw to the public, or whoever might come nosing around for a scapegoat." Mike looked up. Sam hadn't gone away. He still sat across from him.

"Billy should have realized that was a nothing deal. But he didn't. He treated it like a big thing." The animation had gone out of Sam for a second and he stared at the carpet blankly, like a fish. Then he looked up at Mike. "You can have a rich father, but when you're poor in your head, you're so fucking scared you panic."

In spite of himself, Mike turned to the young woman to see if there was a reaction to Sam's language. There wasn't.

Billy had found himself in his hallway shaking hands with three men, trying to smile, jumping nervously from one foot to the other.

"Hi! I'm Billy Yones. How ya doing," he said to each IRS agent in turn. Then he thought to himself: Why did I say Billy? Why didn't I say William? Or at least Bill? He was scared, as if in the night the window in his bedroom had suddenly blown open and the rain and wind had shocked him, making him wake up when he didn't want to, his heart pounding. "You guys want a drink? Or some coffee?" he babbled as he led them inside his apartment.

The tall man introduced the two others, said his name was Davis and that, no thank you, they didn't want a drink or coffee, but they would like to talk.

"Hey, that's okay. That's fine." Billy still felt himself dancing from one foot to the other. "That's cool. How can I help?" Maybe if he sat down it would help, he thought. His stomach turned. This can only be about Dad, he thought. I'm not smart enough to do anything wrong on my own.

"It's late," the tall man named Davis said, "so we'll come right to the . . ."

"No it's not. I'm always up at this hour."

". . . point."

There were papers being spread out across Billy's cocktail table by the second IRS agent, a messy fat man. When there wasn't enough room, Davis moved the bronze Arp sculpture his mother had given him off to one side and that made Billy mad. He wanted to say, Hey, wait a minute. Don't touch that, but he sat there, dumb. The third man appeared completely uninterested. He kept looking impatiently down the main hall toward the rest of the apartment. Billy felt his heels digging into his carpet. There was no way they were getting any further into his life.

"These are lists of numbered accounts," Davis said, halting, scrutinizing Billy, "representing money on deposit in the Standard-British Bank in the Grand Caymans. That mean anything to you?"

Billy shrugged his shoulders. "No," he said. Then he wondered if he said it right. It wasn't that he was dimwitted, he tried to tell himself. He was just afraid.

"Well, you're right, Billy," Davis said. "They shouldn't. They're just a bunch of numbers."

Billy smiled. How unusual it was for anyone to say he had done something right. "These accounts, we believe, belong to U.S. citizens. The trick," Davis went on, "is to find out who. That's why the numbers are there, to make sure that only the person whose account it is, and the bank, know." Billy nodded. "But we lucked out," Davis went on. "We found . . ."

And while Davis went off into a long explanation of secret accounts and code numbers, Billy withdrew into his own world, just as he always did when his father spoke of complexities, wondering why he had to be born a plain person, why he had to have Sam Yones as a father, why he couldn't have someone else who would just let him be.

"Some of these accounts," Davis went on, "led us nowhere, just to other numbers, other codes in other foreign banks, but some of them led us to actual names, names of U.S. citizens, and we have found out that your name . . ." Billy's heart started to pound, not out of guilt because he knew nothing, but out of fear . . . "that your name is listed as a beneficiary of one of those accounts." Billy felt his heart pumping, like he was tumbling down in the dark.

"It is not," Billy said. "It's a hoax."

"Billy didn't tell the truth." Sam put down his cigar and was now jiggling the change in his pocket. "If he had, we'd all be better off."

Mike could never figure out how Sam could jingle change sitting down.

"The IRS guy asks do we have an account in the Caymans, any kind of account. All Billy had to do was say 'Yes, of course,' but he doesn't. He could have said 'I don't know.' He could have said 'I don't remember.' He could even say 'Everybody does.' Instead he says no. Boom. Just like that. He doesn't say 'Ask the accountant.' " Sam was talking faster now, looking to the side at the young woman. "He doesn't say 'That's a long time ago.' He says no when he knows the goddamn answer is yes. If he would have told the truth, the tax guy would have gone away. The IRS knew it was there anyway."

Sam became distracted. No one said anything. He started again.

"They didn't come to me first. They went to my son. The one they knew wouldn't know how to answer. They did it just a week ago, just after Matt . . ." Sam swallowed.

Mike calmed himself by observing, waiting, as he had done for too much of his life. But maybe this time being out of the fray, being on a perch, would save him. He watched Sam's mood grow darker, and he could see him rolling the events over and over in his mind. Mike felt like saying "What do you come to me for?" but he didn't. He knew the answer. It was the subpoena Sam was worried about. Not so much his own as the one directed to one Michael Anker.

"Billy tells them—three IRS agents, no less, the head honcho, some guy named Davis—that he has no account there. The IRS takes out a microfilm of accounts with the boys' names on it and puts it in front of Billy's face. Did the dummy say 'Guys, I made a mistake. I was scared.' No, the dummy doesn't say that. Instead, he says the microfilm must be a hoax. Can you beat it? He uses the word 'hoax.' "

Sam put his hand wildly to his head. Then he did his fish-eye look toward Jenifer and then into the floor again. "Did you ever notice that people never answer what you say? They answer what they think you mean."

Jenifer, Sam's lawyer, cleared her throat. "Sam has been subpoenaed to appear before the grand jury in Miami, Mr. Anker," the lawyer said. "He is not—I repeat, not—a target," she continued.

"Or at least so we at this moment believe," Sam said, correcting her, looking straight at Mike. Mike looked back at Sam just as directly.

"That's correct," Jenifer said. "That is subject to change."

Sam would not let her lie, Mike thought. Whatever Sam might be or do to others, he would not harm him. Whatever secrets they had would stay with them.

"Sam has been asked to appear in Miami on the twenty-second. Next month. Billy will appear that morning, too. We don't want any delays. We might even push it up."

"No we won't," Sam said. "We'll do exactly what they want."

Sam tossed his head, looking to Mike as if he wanted him to supply a Jewish proverb that would protect them.

"Our guess, Mr. Anker, Mike, is that you will receive a subpoena as well."

For one second, no more, Mike felt fear. Then it passed, leaving him cold but perfectly clearheaded.

"Why would they want me?" Mike asked.

"They've seen the documentation."

"But there's no account overseas in my name," Mike said.

"No. Certainly not," Sam said. His voice had changed. A different pitch.

"But on the account for the boys' trust," Jenifer said, "your name does appear as a trustee."

"Trustee is different from the real owner," Sam said.

"I'm glad you said that," Mike cut in, too fast.

"We think," the lawyer said, "that they'll use that as a hook to get you in and . . . start asking questions."

"I don't know anything," Mike said in his best resonant voice.

Sam nodded, almost imperceptibly.

"Mike, I'm sorry you were brought in. I'm sorry for my Billy. I apologize for him," Sam said as if no one else were there, sounding like the old Sam. "I'm angry with myself more than anyone else. Maybe I never should have told Billy there was anything there for him. Then he wouldn't have had anything to hide." Sam turned his eyes away. "Matt was smarter."

"If I get the subpoena," Mike said, trying to keep his distance, "of course I'll let you know when I get it." Mike smiled an innocent's smile at the lawyer. "If I'm allowed to." He stood up. "Thank you for coming to me."

"Jenifer, you see? A gentleman," Sam said. "Mike Anker is a gentleman."

"Yes, he is," she answered. "Mike, let me leave my card with you. If I can do anything, let me know. You may want me to talk to your lawyer. I'll be glad to cooperate."

"My lawyer?"

"Who knows?" Sam said. "Maybe all of us should have lawyers."

"Miss . . . I'm sorry. Jenifer, I didn't get your last name." Mike took Sam's arm. "Excuse us, please."

"Mr. Yones, please . . ."

"Jenifer, it's fine. We go back thirty-five years."

"Forty," Mike said.

Mike led Sam through the reception room, where Mike's portrait could have hung alongside Edgar Stern's, across another hushed corridor, and into a huge empty circular conference room. A circular table, twenty feet in diameter, occupied the middle of it. Mike turned on the lights.

"I like this room," Sam said. "I've always liked this room. No sides."

"Pick a chair," Mike said as he sat down himself. Sam had a choice of fifteen swivel chairs, all high-backed, as if each belonged to a boss. He chose one next to Mike. When he sat, he didn't cross one leg over the other. No protective body language. Instead, he leaned back, as if to say, Here I am, wide open, no defenses.

"Sam, the truth. Are you a target?"

"They're waffling. Yes, I think I will be."

"This is not about a two-bit tax bill on unreported interest, right? It's not about me as a trustee, right? What's really going on here?"

"I told you."

"You wouldn't let her lie to me about being a target. That much I did catch. You told me Billy made a mistake. You told me there's a grand jury hearing, taxpayers who didn't pay taxes on interest in foreign accounts, my name is on an account, I'll be called as a witness, and have a good day. That's what you told me." Mike fixed on Sam. "Have you got anything else to tell me?"

"That's the thanks I get."

"And you come up here, not alone, but with a lawyer."

"I'm not supposed to have a conversation for the next sixty years without a lawyer." Sam tried a big smile. "I'm not supposed to talk to my wife without a lawyer."

Mike raised his eyebrows and said nothing. Sam looked blank.

"Sam, you're telling me Billy talked to the government without calling you first? That kid doesn't go to the bathroom without talking to you. I don't believe it."

Sam was silent a moment, and there was a nervous movement at his feet.

"He doesn't do a lot of things he should." Sam looked away. "You know that. I don't know who started this thing. I don't know who wants me, yet. But don't worry. I'll get out, and so will Billy and so will you. I have no Fifth Amendment to take. I have nothing to hide. They have nothing to ask. And you have nothing to hide. And they have nothing to ask you."

"They why were you worried about me at six o'clock in the morning?"

"I know it was early. They came to the house, my house . . ." Sam slapped the top of the round table with the flat of his hand. Mike kept his eyes focused on Sam. ". . . almost at eleven. Like the goddamn Nazis. Billy's phone call beat them by ten minutes." Sam folded his arms, rubbing the hand that slapped the table. "I almost called you then, but I waited. For Liz to come home." Mike gave him a small nod to hide his embarrassment. "Then we talked, and by that time it was the middle of the night. So I waited. I knew you had school today." Sam showed Mike another sad smile. "I knew you'd be up. I'm sorry if I bothered Cheryl." He didn't say, I know she sleeps late.

"What about Gordy?"

"They're wasting their time calling him. He'll claim his constitutional rights. Just like his father did. They won't even bother."

Mike swiveled around in his chair, but he was careful not to swing away too far. There wasn't a more beautiful conference room in New York, bubinga wood, soft seats, ease. There was no echo, even if only two people were there, even if one slapped the table.

"I'm here, Mike, because how would you feel if I

weren't here? How would you feel if anything threatened you because of me and I wasn't here?"

"That would be fine if you told me everything."

"Mike, we go back too far for this."

"Nobody brings a lawyer into my office without my permission."

"They're only lawyers. They hear you tell the story enough times and they believe it. Especially if you tell the story in front of people who can contradict you and don't. She was here for me to convince her, not to intimidate you."

Sam stood up and started to move around the table. He was a quarter way around it when he turned back.

"I'm sorry, Mike. So much of it is easy to remember. It's hard not to." For a moment Sam wavered, but he stopped himself. He had started what he had started. "That's what I'm worried about, your memory. Maybe we've made a mistake all these years."

All these years ago and all those places, Mike thought.

"So the guy from GM is not a complete asshole after all," he remembered Gordy saying some years before.

"He gave me a million one," Sam had said, a triumphant smile on his face. "He's got to have some smarts in that *goyishe kup* of his. That was Arlo Shields's guy, from the fancy club in Palm Beach. He really delivered." They had been at the Century Association which somehow Mike had managed to get himself into, where Sam loved to lunch and kept trying to get into himself.

"I can't get over it that they ask for the numbered accounts," Mike remembered saying.

"They're not that dumb," Sam had said. "In their own way, they're smarter than we are. They're smarter because they remember what we would never expect them to remember. They're soft and casual and they form beautiful sentences. 'Will we look forward to enjoying the benefits of the matrixed accounts?' " Sam smiled his smile again. "Have you ever heard a more elegant way to assure yourself of fraud for your benefit?"

"The guy's still an asshole," Gordy said.

Mike laughed, loving his place on the inside, watching the flames up close but keeping out of the fire. They were younger then, twelve, fourteen years ago. No gray hair, not even on their temples. None of them. It was a running joke, although Gordy said the gray hair on his chest was starting to pay off because young girls liked it. Mike had no sense that he was being poisoned. Willingly so. He remembered playing with a book of Century Association matches, folding them over one by one out of excitement.

"It's the double blind," Sam said, so confident he felt no need to turn to check out the room. "They love it. One numbered account leads only to another numbered account. The Caymans account leads to the Swiss account, and that, too, is a number."

"But only you have the names," Gordy said.

"I can't possibly give them the names." Sam smiled his smile again. "They're too dumb to remember."

That was before Sam became a member of the Century Association, Mike realized, before the Yones Chair at Columbia, before Liz at the Guggenheim, before Sam realized that graceful sentences did not mean vapid, unpowerful men.

"Is it really my memory you're worried about?" Mike asked, coming abruptly back to the present.

Sam caressed the surface of the conference table, his fingers following the sunburst pattern of finest wood.

"I'm just afraid somebody will get it out of you. All you know. All you've seen. You can put the names to the numbers. They're too dumb, but you're not." Sam's eyes narrowed. "I wonder sometimes why I let you guys see so much. Not Gordy. But you. I've given you an awful lot." Sam removed his hand from Mike's table and shook his fingers across the table toward Mike's face. "Watch your step. For your sake and mine."

"Don't do that, Sam. Don't ever order me around."

Was it there, that day in the Century, or was it somewhere else when Sam was telling secrets in corners that it dawned on Mike that maybe, someday, Sam's trust would turn to fear. Fear of a man who knew too much. They were almost brothers, the three of them. Better than brothers, although sometimes with a different kind of rivalry, the fun kind, not the destructive sort. The kind of rivalry that comes of making fun of the same people, getting ahead together, beyond those who thought themselves your betters, leapfrogging the idiots. Maybe it wasn't that day. Maybe it was even before that in some obscure restaurant or ice cream parlor somewhere on the edge of town in the middle of the day; a time when they were younger, much younger, when there was the excitement of sneaking off, cutting corners, winning, Sam and Gordy doing it, Mike watching, but feeling the same excitement, climbing over and beyond all the people in his life he needed to best.

"You're turning on me," Mike said.

"No, I'm afraid you'll turn on me."

"Why would I do that?"

When Mike was twenty, his father went bankrupt and Sam offered to lend him the money to go to graduate school. Then Sam lent him more money and all three of them took steerage class to Europe. Mike was fine until the *Queen Fredericka* slid into the open ocean and then started to pitch. Finally he was able to look over the stern. Years later he asked himself if he had realized that, like ships, people leave wakes behind, gurgles, debris, and waves. Did he also realize, in the grand scheme of things, that the wakes people leave behind last about as long as the wakes in the sea?

"So I'll see you on the tenth?" Sam asked, stopped at the doorway.

"The tenth? What about the tenth?"

"Passover. At your place."

"Yeah, my place," Mike said, still distracted.

He walked with Sam away from the round conference room, across quiet halls. They waited in the empty corridor for the elevator. No easy chatter of deals, Wall Street gossip, family, or pals. It seemed to take forever for the elevator bell to chime.

"You know, Mike," Sam said quietly, "you owe me one."

"I owe you one what?"

117

13

THE BIG GLASS DOOR AT THE 53RD STREET ENTRANCE always took more than two pulls, and when Mike finally yanked it open, the snow, which had started again, hit him in the face. It was after five, dark outside, and much colder than it was at midday. Cheryl had her old Dodge Dart out in front. Although she complained about not earning enough money, she had a bank account bigger than most, a little from what she saved when she worked for Sam, the bulk of it from her own consulting business, but buying fancy cars to be beaten up by New York potholes was not her idea of smart. The minute Mike yanked open the door, the sound of drums played by some rock and roll maniac blared out at him.

"Beethoven. Is that Beethoven?" he asked, trying to perk himself up.

Mike shut the door, shivered, and wrapped his arms across his coat.

Cheryl turned down the volume as he hugged his chest, swept his trousers. She wanted to do all that for him.

In the five hours between Sam's visit and the end of the day, true to Sam's prediction, the subpoena was served. Quietly, by a well-dressed young man who could have been an arbitrageur. Mike had it in his briefcase.

The subpoena listed only one account, the trust account, just as Sam had said. And legally, as his own lawyer had taken all afternoon to tell him, he had to testify only about that account and bring only those documents he had that pertained to that account. No more, no less. Again, Sam had been right.

Mike unbuttoned his overcoat, tried to sit back in the bumping Dart, and relax. He toyed with the heater, but reset it exactly where it was before he fussed with it. Then he lit Sam's cigar, using a strange-looking matchbook from London, dark red, with the name of some lord printed on it. It was her car, she hated the smoke, but she said nothing. He pulled another match out of the dark red book, then lit the cigar and opened the window wide to let the stink out.

"Where did you disappear to?" Cheryl asked, turning off the radio. "I've been waiting."

"I couldn't get out as fast as I wanted to." He closed the window and the snow started to fall against it, sticking this time.

Cheryl knew he was looking at her. She liked it when he did. Her eyes were wise and guarded except when they rested on him; her hair fine and straight as a string, and she knew he was glad she wasn't curling it anymore. She wanted to be blond instead of dark, more American-looking instead of having a solid piece of Jewish forehead, blue eyes instead of brown; in short, exchange herself for an opposite; if that's what it would take. How many men would she lose because she wasn't a shiksa? How many great Jewish guys end up with a blonde because they think that's the only place to get a blowjob?

"Mike, what did Sam want? Six-thirty in the morning the phone goes off. Even for him, that's the middle of the night. I went to work today and I didn't call you. I could have, but I wanted you to have time to come up with all kinds of reasons for keeping me out of it, none of which will be acceptable . . ." She smiled.

"I don't know how much to tell you. It's a legal matter."

"And I'm not a wife."

She took one hand off the wheel and searched for his hand. His fingers were strong and she touched the hair on his wrist. "We can fix that, you know," she said, searching again.

He pressed Cheryl's hand, holding her back.

"Sam was served with a subpoena to appear before a

grand jury in Miami. They want to know about foreign accounts. He's not a target."

"And that's it?" she asked, and then bit her tongue.

"Billy was served and I was served this afternoon as well."

She knew the right time for silence and he was thankful for that. She gave him time alone, even when they were together. Outsiders would never understand, but that's what their relationship was all about. He felt honored, respected, looked up to. It was corny, he knew, but he remembered the way Franklyn McCormick used to open his radio show back in the fifties: "I love you not only for what you are, but for what I am when I am with you."

"Sam says I'm not at risk and I've been with lawyers all afternoon who confirm that. I am a trustee for the boys' . . . for Billy's . . . trust, and that trust, instead of being at a bank here in New York, is at a bank in the Grand Caymans for tax reasons. It's perfectly legal."

"That much of it may be legal. What if there's more?"

"Cheryl"—and this time it was Mike who reached for her hand—"you worked there. It's you I'm worried about. Not me. You're out of it. At least so far. Stay out of it."

He was glad they had the privacy of the car surrounding them. They had been together over two years, and not once had they discussed Sam's business, what Mike had learned watching, and what Cheryl had learned working for him, being his mistress, a word Mike couldn't bear even to think about. He stole a look at the attractive crinkles at the corners of her eyes and he felt great love for her, protective love, needing love, but he hated it that she had come from Sam.

"Yes, I know some things," she said, holding on to the wheel. "There were the landfill waste disposal deals, the leisure hotels in Costa Rica, the casinos where an exit strategy meant selling to the syndicate, all the deals where the patina was wrong, class B office buildings, strings of old-age homes, all of it. The breakthrough was the tree farms, the timber." Cheryl had a way of staring intently at things, and she watched the road as if their lives depended on it.

"Not illegal. Not unsavory. Just quick." She stopped, unsure whether to say more. Maybe she didn't know, Mike thought, about the double blind Sam had come up with. One secret account screening another, a coded account in one bank that led to a coded account in another bank, no one with both codes and the names except Sam.

Then, interrupting his thoughts, Cheryl said, "It's funny, Mike. What you observed over thirty years, I was taught in two." She smiled the smile of an innocent and surprised herself. "When you let guys use you, make sure they're smart guys."

Mike touched her, a brushing, loving touch.

"Mike, what if they call me?"

"They're stumbling down there in Miami," Mike said, holding her hand. He did some deep breathing. "They don't know what they're after. It's a fishing expedition. They're not calling you."

"Who tells you that?" Cheryl asked, her voice clotted.

"Sam and the lawyers. The subpoenas are that narrow."

"Do you believe them?"

"My lawyers? Yes. I believe them."

"It starts with trust," Cheryl said, "then it turns into warnings, then it's who destroys who."

"Cheryl, don't talk like that. You'll be all right."

"You will be, too," she said. She smiled, praying inside for both of them.

The snow had done its usual job on midtown traffic, and Cheryl, like everyone else, had a hard time driving as they slid up Madison Avenue. The cars backed up at 72nd Street. There, it all stopped, and when they finally got through the traffic light, it was just as she suspected. Some goddamn camel driver had wrapped a hack around a lamppost. An hour it had taken them. A whole hour, silent, but they were together.

"Should I put the car in your space or in mine?" she asked as she brought the car to a stop in front of the building.

"Makes no difference."

"Are you upset?"

121

He was thinking of Sam. Sam was not fourteen and he was not twelve any longer, and the times should have been over when he broke up like glass whenever Sam came after him. Maybe he had yet to figure it out that adult friendships weren't continuations of childhood playmates, that you have to move on. You had to commit to an adult you trusted and cared for, such as this woman who saw good in him that he didn't, who hoped to marry him.

"No, not at all. I've got so much on my mind . . ."

"How about me? Am I on your mind?"

"More than you know." He squeezed her hand. "You must be terrific in bed when someone young enough lets you be," he said.

"I've been written up."

Mike walked through the lobby while Cheryl parked her car. He took the elevator to their floor, and just as he was walking in he heard what he was waiting for, the ring of his private phone, glad the call would be behind him before Cheryl came upstairs.

"So I'm going to see you tomorrow," Gordy said, the connection clear enough so he sounded as if he were next door.

"In the morning."

Mike touched Cheryl's picture which stood on his desk in a silver frame. She looked like her photo and yet she didn't. The nose was the same and so were the eyes, but not as cool as they appeared in the picture. She no longer parted her hair in the middle with the broad white line of scalp showing; now there was no part and no curls and he liked her hair straight. Most of all, the picture missed her lips.

"You know," Gordy said, "these fiber optics are so good, we could talk over the phone."

"Hooray for fiber optics," Mike said.

"I know you talked to Sam."

"The subpoena was served," Mike went on, "just as Sam said it would be. It covered the trust account for Billy and Matt, just as Sam told me. But I don't know enough."

"Sam's the guy to talk to, not me." Blood drummed in Mike's ears. He had never been refused before, and he tried to think as fast as he could. He could never keep up with these guys, never.

"You know, you're right," Mike said. "I'd like very much to talk with him alone, but he didn't let that happen." Mike smiled now, suddenly pleased with himself, not feeling weak anymore. He was doing what they do, shading things a bit. "He didn't come to see me alone. He marched into my office with a lawyer." Mike enjoyed the silence. He had told Gordy something he hadn't known. Sam was holding back on both of them.

"I'll see you tomorrow," Gordy said. "What plane?"

Mike pulled a pocket airline guide out of his desk drawer and chose a flight. "You sure you want to see me? Sam may not like it," Mike said, a clear edge in his voice.

"What plane?" Gordy repeated.

Mike turned the pages, finding the columns of flights from JFK, LaGuardia, and Newark to Los Angeles, eliminating LaGuardia, looking only for the nonstops.

"You have no subpoena, do you?" Mike asked.

"What plane?"

Mike gave him the information, hung up the phone, and stood up next to his desk. He touched Cheryl's picture frame again.

Then he heard her voice.

"Everything okay, Mike?"

"Sure. Fine," he said. Alone was very nineties, he had heard some nut say at one of the few parties they went to, very now, happening. How foolish, Mike thought as Cheryl walked into the library and kissed him. "Actually, I feel a lot better," he said.

Lovingly, she touched his graying hair and Mike said, "Quite a natural history museum."

"A lot of women think gray hair's attractive," she said, smiling.

"So I'm told," he said.

"Maybe I'll take a shower. It's been a long day."

"You want company?" Mike asked.

Their bathroom overlooked Central Park. They could see it all through huge windows, surrounded by marble, with a shower stall large enough to double as a steam room, which he had installed before he met her. Every time they went in there, she tried to banish the thought of other women in there with him, holding him as she was doing, adjusting the water temperature and the water flow so that it would not spray but just ooze out of the shower head, covering them with warmth and making their skin slip, the water falling slowly, without force, looking at him, touching the long gray hairs on his chest.

Mike's eyes closed as she wanted them to. She touched his temples and ran her fingers through the wet matted curls of gray and black on his head, and his eyes flickered open as she ran her hands once again down his chest, across his legs, down and then up and then down again so she could take him between her lips.

She stood up and Mike took over, his arms on her wet shoulders, and the atmosphere changed from feminine to masculine. Cheryl loved her men this way, this man in particular, this one who had learned how to put powerful and slow together. Cheryl heated to the boiling point as they finished together inside her. The only thing she could not do was holler. It had happened once and Mike lost it. She would have to work him into that.

Mike opened his eyes and they turned up the water to washing force and took their shower.

"I'll bet you once knew a shiksa who could undo shirt buttons with her teeth," Cheryl said under the water flow.

"You taught her." And Cheryl was satisfied beyond belief.

They ate dinner in, watched television without talking much, and after the news walked into the bedroom, where he wrapped his arms around her shoulders, pressing her to him. Cheryl knew a few things about herself, and one was that she liked a winner. It wasn't that Mike's wealth made him a winner, because he never needed that much. He was so watchable, she thought. It was the way he moved and the way he would suddenly become still the moment she touched him, still and quiet, almost like an entranced child. He was wary of the world. He was stern on the outside, but that all went away when he was with her. It gave her power. More than once she had watched him metamorphose at the will of her fingertips.

"Wait a minute," she said, "the drapes are open."

"Leave them that way."

"I thought you liked the room dark."

"How do you like it?" he asked.

"I don't care."

"I want you to care." His voice had changed again; it was a different voice now, soft and dreamy, with that childlike concentration that acknowledges no other interest in the world. "We can do things your way," Mike said.

"Now and then?"

"Right." He laughed. "Now and then."

She took his hand, and they lay together.

For a year now, she had had as many drawers and as many lineal feet of closet space as Mike, yet no matter how many times he had referred to it as "our" home, she hadn't felt that way. She had many times when she was alone sneaked into what she thought of as his bathroom and opened his medicine chest and taken inventory, excited by the prospect of the secrets she might find as well as the response she might feel if he had stormed in and found her. She had a great fantasy on the subject. He would say he was angry and he hated her. She would say, "Hate is a very exciting emotion," and then "I hate you, too." She would pull him on top of her and he would take his anger out inside of her.

Cheryl suddenly, once again, wished for him completely, for she had never felt so close to him, so eager to help him.

"I need you to make another life for me," he said. Then he stopped, wishing the glow of the city were not in their bedroom, on her skin, on his words.

Cheryl remained still, not moving a muscle.

He turned to face her, and she could feel that he was ready to make love to her again.

"If we keep this up," he whispered, "I'm going to get used to it."

"It's very low in calories and cholesterol."

Mike laughed and then he turned over and switched on the light.

Cheryl got up and turned it off.

"I'm going to California tomorrow," Mike said softly in the dark.

"To see Gordy?"

"Yes."

She propped up her pillow and pushed herself higher up on it.

"Do you have to go to him?" Now it was her turn to switch on the light. "Okay. I'll buy it. That's the only way you'll know what you have to do . . ." she said. She debated the next two words, and then she let fly, ". . . for yourself."

"Let's not get into that."

"You're stuck somewhere back with D'Artagnan. One for all and all for one. The Three Musketeers in Hebrew."

"Cheryl, it's not *all* about me."

"Maybe it should be. You're always turning the other cheek. You've got the wrong testament."

"Cheryl. Please."

"To you, the old days are real. To them, they're memories. They've moved on." She ran her hands along the night table and the objects on it. "To have Sam Yones return your greeting in a certain way was to be someone. I know, I was there, too." Her voice was agitated. "But, Mike, move on, like they did"—and she had a lot of trouble, even in the dark, finishing her sentence ". . . to a wife, to a family. Your own, not theirs."

He felt paralyzed, his perceptions, thoughts, and movements were slow, distant, sluggish. His thoughts were somewhere out of the room, downtown in some trendy place he would have heard of but never gone to, picturing Cheryl being powerful. There was no way he could expect her to do nothing. Her generation of women were able to create their own action; they did not live their lives through others. No matter what protection he offered, she had to do things for herself. You must respect this, you must tolerate this; you could only try to minimize the collisions.

Mike pushed the light switch. Cheryl made no attempt to turn it on again.

14

AT TEN THE NEXT MORNING, MIKE LANDED IN LOS ANGELES. It was like acrylic paints and watercolors to one who had just left New York in March. He took I-405 north to the Santa Monica Freeway, and then east to downtown, using the Seventh Street off-ramp which would bring him close to the Union Station district near the old City Hall, famous from *Dragnet* days. Gordy always liked to own the buildings he was in, and Los Angeles was no exception. Here it was a low rise, a 1923 six-story white stucco building with huge windows, Moorish-style architraves, and a water tank with no name on it mounted high over the roof.

There was always something old-fashioned about Gordy's private offices, all of them, from the earliest days when the retail clerks' union was on the fourth floor of a walkup a block from the Foshay Tower in Minneapolis to the one in Miami to the latest one in Los Angeles. A visitor could only wonder what era he had walked into. He would see the brown and cream colors, the polished mahogany furniture, and the square leather sofas; but what made the time warp real were the old-fashioned venetian blinds, the ones with the wide tapes and the broad dark wood slats; the light they let in was always sepia. Three of the original Oriental rugs they had bought together in Istanbul during their college trip still lined the floor. There were others, laid end-to-end, that Gordy had accumulated on his own, worth fifty times what the first ones cost, but Mike was glad the old ones were still there, treasured.

Gordy had moved eight years ago, when he bought homes both here and in Miami, although he kept the original office in Minneapolis, not only because they still had members there and because that was where it all started, but also because his secretary, Edna, wanted to stay to be near her grandchildren. He missed the Twin Cities sometimes, oddly enough, more in the winter, but business was business, and when there were more retail clerks out west, and in Florida, Gordy followed to keep his position of control.

He motioned Mike to take the wing chair angled to look out over downtown Los Angeles, and then he perched on the windowsill and regarded Mike silently for what seemed a long time.

Gordy's chart of the company he owned with Sam, Minneapolis Timber, stood on an easel off to one side. From the green arrows drawn in grease pen, Mike could tell two more huge timber deals were on the way. There were boxes drawn in black, initials scribbled inside them in red felt marker, and lines in bright colors drawn up to the holding company level, marked with a big red dollar sign. This was the key to the deal, the source of the money: equity from Sam's limited partnerships, money borrowed from Gordy's union's pension funds, and high gorum banks.

"What does Sam think you should do?" Gordy asked, wasting no time.

"Get a lawyer. His lawyer."

"Don't."

Mike pulled himself out of the wing chair. He walked over to the window and joined Gordy on the wide sill. One of Gordy's many idiosyncracies was living and working in rooms on low floors with windows that opened. Now the two of them looked up at downtown Los Angeles.

"Why not?"

"Forty guys a week get subpoenas," Gordy said, turning to face Mike. "You know it and so do I. You'll do what they do. You'll go there. You'll give them fifteen minutes. You'll tell them what they want to know, and you'll go home. Look at your subpoena. There's no questions in there that mean anything. No one's asking you to point a finger at anyone. They're not even after you. They're fishing, that's all. But listen to me. Don't roll into Miami with a New York white-collar-criminal lawyer. Use a local, someone from down there if you can find a good one."

Mike left the window and walked back into the room.

"Who?"

"How about Arlo Shields? The Beta Theta Pi from Langdon Street who could spot a lay from forty yards. Eagle Eye."

"The tall guy. Sure, I remember him. He's the one who brought Sam over to the Kappa house to meet Liz." Mike was frowning.

"That's him." Gordy followed Mike back into the center of the large room and moved to his desk. "He practices in Miami. You'll call him. If you don't like him, you won't use him. If you do, you will. You'd never believe it, but Eagle Eye wrote the book! The evidence book."

"You're selling," Mike said evenly, not responding to Gordy's smile.

"You're right, I am." He, too, went serious.

"Since when do you tell me what lawyer to hire?"

"Since when does Sam?"

The room seemed suddenly quiet and they heard a truck horn blast from the freeway several blocks away. Mike felt a little easier.

"Have you checked him out?" Mike asked. "I haven't kept up with him for a long time." Mike forced himself to keep a picture of Arlo, who had brought Liz into their lives, out of his mind. There was too much at stake for anything but calm.

"He ran for judge for the State Appellate Court but lost. Ran as a Republican," Gordy said, rocking in his desk chair.

"As I remember, he was smarter than that."

"He's been thought of for the federal bench more than once, but he doesn't want it."

"Why?"

"He's afraid of the phone call, someone wanting something back."

"It's a lifetime appointment. Why would he worry?"

Gordy stopped and blew air out of his mouth.

Mike looked at the autographed pictures on Gordy's walls, thinking of the range and power of the men there. Gordy walked toward the windowsill again and sat down.

"You're in it, too, Gordy, aren't you, both of you guys."

"I've seen the subpoena," Gordy said.

Mike knew the eyes of others as well as his own. His own were very quick, and he knew he had to slow them down if they were not to give him away.

"Sam's subpoena or mine?"

"All of them. Billy's, too."

Mike said nothing, but the alarm bell was on, ringing. When that happened he stayed quiet. He threw one leg over the arm of his wing chair, pretending not to give a damn.

"How did you see all the subpoenas? I didn't show you mine."

"I see what I see. I've got people who make sure I see what I should see. And that includes matters that matter to you." Gordy cleared his throat. "And don't worry about me. Me they don't give subpoenas to anymore. I take the Fifth Amendment. They know I take the Fifth Amendment. They know I don't give a fuck."

Gordy stood up again, restless, and walked to the other end of his office, the light seeping in through the old-fashioned venetian blinds.

"Mike, you're not a target."

Mike turned, watching, following him.

"That's the first point. Second, your subpoena asks only about the kids' trust accounts. The subpoena is narrowly drawn. You're not asked about anything except the trusts. It's true they're not supposed to ask you questions beyond the scope of the subpoena or the documents they ask you to bring, but suppose they do? What do you do? Get up and run? You tip them off like that and they'll never let you go."

"My lawyers tell me otherwise."

"What do they know? Have they been there?"

Mike felt half sick.

"I don't have any overseas bank accounts, this one or any other ones. And if I did, the government could see them. And they can see any papers about any deal I've been in."

"No, they can't."

"Gordy, what are you talking about?"

"Nothing. Just fishing. Doing what they'll do."

Mike glanced at an autographed Harry Truman, a Prime Minister Pindling from the Bahamas, and a Menachem Begin in the gardens of Jerusalem with the big King David Hotel sign in the background. He thought of a summer camp in Eagle River, Wisconsin, far from home for lonely eight-year-old boys, and how they had stuck together like glue. If anybody had called Gordy the "Admiral" because he wet his bed, Mike, although younger, would wind up his little fists and slug the hell out of the transgressor. As a result, when visitors' day came around, Gordy's dad would treat him as a son, letting him drive the mahogany-planked Chris-Craft across Catfish Lake, just like Gordy, getting the Hershey bars Gordy got, plus the ration stamps for the saddle shoes he coveted, always equal for each of them. Being better than a brother didn't stop at summer camp. At Christmas, Gordy's father always took the two of them to Dayton's in downtown Minneapolis, and when Gordy got a cap gun, Gordy's dad saw his son look down at his cap gun and over to Mike standing alone, at the other end of the counter, empty-handed, and then Mike got a cap gun, too. He still had it somewhere.

"Listen to me, Gordy. A guy with a subpoena walks into my office. The whole damn thing, not the money, Gordy, but my name, my name is out the window. And Cheryl. She's the best thing that ever happened to me." Gordy saw the shine in Mike's eyes. "He's pulling my name down where it never was."

"Who's 'he'?"

"Sam."

"Wrong."

Mike started to move an ashtray in small circles.

"Don't fence with me, Gordy. He's stringing me along and now you're tap-dancing. You're pushing me at a particular lawyer, you're predicting the course of a grand jury investigation based on your reading of a subpoena, my subpoena, which I never gave you, which you're not supposed to have, but which you have anyway, and you're telling me the government can't see any deal I've ever been in. I didn't come out here for this. I came out here for help. Don't fuck with me. If this thing blows, it'll blow so high you'll pick the Milky Way out of your ears."

While he had been talking, Mike had started walking around Gordy's desk, his father's old, heavy, dark desk from the union, and now he sat down again. In the meantime, Gordy hadn't budged. He remained perched on the window ledge in front of one of the few still remaining open windows in downtown Los Angeles. The room could easily hold meetings of ten or twenty people and sometimes did, but now, to Mike, this office seemed cramped one minute and cavernlike the next.

Both Mike and Gordy had the same photograph in their offices and their homes. Sam, the oldest, stood next to the wagon and held up a sign that said Kool-Aid for Sale. The younger ones, Mike and Gordy, sat in the wagon, Mike, with his little legs hanging over the edge, giving the camera a super knockout special big smile in imitation of his friend Sam. They were selling their Kool-Aid during the Second World War to men who were playing baseball on Sunday mornings in the school yard. It was a partnership. Gordy supplied the wagon, Sam the water and the ice cubes, and Mike supplied the Kool-Aid mix. It was their first deal together, and they made money, but Gordy's father made them give it to the USO because, after all, there was a war on. Gordy looked at the picture and Mike saw him doing it.

"Gordy, you're telling me not to be so sure who my enemy is," Mike said, calmer now.

"Don't worry about it. There's always time for enemies. Come on. It's hot in here. Let's get outdoors and have lunch."

When Gordy said "lunch" to most people he meant just what he said: You put on your coat, walked down the street, sat down at a table in a restaurant, and ate. However, when he said "lunch" to Mike, it meant he wanted to leave the office. Listening devices had become so sophisticated that leaving a closed room offered little protection. His words could be picked up off a noisy street if someone cared that much, but for Gordy it had become more a matter of comfort than security.

They headed toward the pedestrian bridge that crossed over the freeway. It was as loud as a subway station and the fumes were murder. Mike yelled above the traffic, "Where are we going?" Gordy pointed across the interchange of the Pasadena and Hollywood freeways to a point a few blocks away. Mike didn't get it at first, but then it was obvious and his shoulders eased.

They walked down to Union Station, through the restored waiting room and to the gate marked Passengers Only. The guard said a few words to Gordy and waved them through. They climbed up the long, sloping concrete ramp to track level. The passengers had long departed the recently arrived *Southwest Limited*, but the equipment had not been backed out and stood there, empty and quiet, like the ancient artifact it really was.

"It looks like a normal grand jury," Gordy said now that they were alone, "but it's not. Those clowns in Miami, they don't even know what they're looking for. My guys in Washington don't know either. But somebody wants to get him. They mean to get him this time," Gordy said, repeating himself, "and they'll use you, me, anyone they can find, anyone whose testimony isn't barred by one legal doctrine or another to do it. That's why they hit Billy. There's no father-son privilege. But he's no risk. They'll squeeze him dry and get nothing. Liz is out. Then there's me" . . . Gordy looked up to the top of the diner, his eye following the horizontal antenna strung taut from one end of the car to the other. ". . . and then there's you."

Mike stiffened.

"You're the guy he bragged to, the guy who never wanted anything or took anything, the clean confidant. You're the guy it was safe to impress. I'm worthless to them. I'll take the Fifth and it won't be the first time."

"As long as it's me and not Cheryl."

"And don't worry about Sam. He's not your enemy. They are. They'll come up with any cockamamie story they can to get you to talk. They're on a fishing expedition. They'll bait the hook with anything to tease you, trick you, even bribe you. You're a small fish. They'll put you on the hook to get a big one."

It wasn't just the light and his own reflection in the railroad car windows. Mike thought he actually did look older. Not much, just a little. There was a yellowish cast to the whites of his eyes and his lashes flicked a lot. Whatever had happened left him wise in a way that sometimes made the world no longer very useful to him.

"I guess we didn't grow up the way we promised each other we would," Gordy said. His face was no longer that of a good actor, and Mike had seen the change before most.

"That's all right," Mike said quietly.

"No it's not. Maybe it will all come down on us. I don't know what shocks anybody anymore. We're all so deadened to what we do. I don't need the politicians to stand next to me anymore, to have my picture taken with them, to have the political hustlers sell me a picture with the President for five thousand bucks or work me up to dinner in the family quarters for fifty." He pushed what little hair he had left off his forehead, almost in the old way. "But Sam? He needs his approving minions. The tall, thin tennis players with Bushlike faces and ancestors named Vanevar and Prescott, and women like Liz. They tell him who he wants to be, and without even knowing it he'll cut any corner to have even the least of them pat him on the head. It wasn't always that way. It didn't have to turn out like this."

Mike sat down on a trackside bench and put his feet on a baggage cart which he wheeled into place in front of him. Gordy decided to sit next to him and use the same baggage cart as a footrest.

"I'm glad you care about Cheryl, Mike."

"Is Ginger still . . ."

"Sure she is." Gordy smiled. "If anyone would know that Ginger would still be with me, it would be you."

They sat, one perched on a baggage cart next to the train, the other on a bench with his feet up on the wheels of the cart, across from each other, saying nothing.

"Mike, look, there's a private car at the end of the train, an old Hiawatha Bob-Tail observation car. Some guy must have spent a fortune fixing it up." Gordy stood and Mike followed. They walked together down the track to the end of the *Southwest Chief*.

"And I suppose you want one of those, too," Mike said.

"The old car just reminded me of when we took that old train up to Duluth one winter to see your aunt with the drugstore . . ."

". . . and how she wouldn't let us eat bologna without a note from my mother because it was 'dog meat.' "

Mike felt warm inside, and he realized that as life goes on, the list of people you know for forty years gets shorter.

They walked together to get a better look at the Hiawatha car named *St. Anthony Falls*, and as they stood a few yards back of it, Mike broke the silence.

"I'm afraid of Sam," Mike said, too clear, too truthful, too undefended. "He's given me the experience of a lifetime, but all of a sudden he doesn't tell me what he's thinking. He doesn't give a pulse. I don't trust him anymore."

Gordy reached into his inside pocket for his pen and started to play with it.

In the silence that followed, Mike remembered a weekend of skiing with Gordy's father when the three of them were still kids. Gordy was starting to become husky and more filled-out than Mike, and Mike, who was younger, wasn't wanted and he knew it. Gordy had gone off, and to Mike's surprise it was Sam who took him off to ski, just the two of them, alone. Sam offered him a cigarette, and stolen rum in his coffee at the top of the ridge. In five minutes they swept down the hill it had taken them all morning to climb. They followed ground that was uneven with dips and curves. They both fell several times, but in that not unpleasant, bouncing way which brings you to your feet again almost at once. Mike felt he was flying, and saw Sam as a terrific guy, not a bit intimidating, in spite of being older and rather a hero.

Could they have come so far—from jumping back up on skis to becoming two criminal schemers plus one licensed observer—and still be the same people? Probably not, he thought. You change along the way, somehow. Had he changed any less than Gordy? Or more than Sam? Who knows? Guys do things for each other.

In silence they walked to the front of the train, where Gordy stopped to look up into the cab of the leading locomotive. Then they walked back past the four power units and the baggage car and stopped in front of the lowered stairs of the single-decked Pullman with the good springs. During the walk, Gordy decided to say no more, and Mike had from time to time clasped his hands behind his back, Prince Philip style, as they walked along the train.

He thought of drugstores like his Aunt Sophie's drugstore and what bright places they were, having bologna sandwiches there with Mike, and sneaking a look at the pretty girls in *Esquire*. They knew then nothing too bad was going to happen to either of them, ever.

They walked down the ramp back through the gate, Gordy once again waving to the guard, across the vast nave of the waiting room and into the hazy sunlight. They talked of other things—Minneapolis, the old train, Gordy's cars from the fifties, whether he would move to Malibu. They stopped at a drugstore with a tile lunch counter for a dog meat sandwich and a Coke like they used to have years ago when they sat next to each other on high round stools and their legs had not yet grown long enough for their feet to reach the floor.

15

THE MORNING MIKE LEFT FOR LOS ANGELES, CHERYL dressed in a real dress, nothing Brooks Brothers. If you're going to be a woman, be one, she thought. She stopped at the candy counter near the 58th Street entrance for Reese's Pieces. Seeing Sam required extra energy.

The elevator door opened directly into Minneapolis Timber Holdings, and the hallways, sofas, receptionists, and busts of Roman emperors on pedestals hadn't changed since the first day she walked in there as a candidate for a Yones Internship six years before. She was nervous then. She was nervous now, but for different reasons.

Cheryl nodded to the receptionists. As she crossed the hallway, she spotted a new piece of ancient sculpture, a gift from the government of Israel, thanking Sam for his sponsorship of the Samuel Yones Expedition financing the Jerusalem Wall Excavations. No one else could have gotten that piece of Canaanite sculpture out of the country except the government itself; it was indeed thankful to Sam.

She knew Sam had probably timed his call to ask her back, "only on a consultant basis, nothing full-time," when he knew she would be alone at the apartment during the day. It was certainly no secret that even though she was with Mike, she had continued to work, advising on real estate workouts and bankruptcy valuations. She had a razor-sharp mind, and her opinion was worth a pretty penny. She had tried to mute the excitement in her voice when he made the proposition on the Marley estate, adding "Name your fee." "Why me?" she had asked. "You know Bob Marley's music and I know you," Sam had replied.

When she first started to work for Sam six years ago, she learned what it meant for three guys to go back forty years, how it really was all for one and one for all, and that it took a bigger shoehorn than God could dream of for a woman to get in with them. Sleep with them? Yes. Do deals with them? Of course. But really get inside? No. Or break one of them out away from the other two, no matter how essential it might prove to be? Never. That was the problem. And if that problem was not settled for Mike, it would never be settled for her.

"You're a terrific gal," Sam had said when it was all over, when he had broken her heart. "Why don't you give Mike a try. At least he's not married."

Mean feelings were easier for him than caring ones. She knew that as he spoke, yet she was deeply hurt. Shame, go directly to Shame, do not pass Go. That's what her parents had taught her.

Did she know who Mike was? How could she not. Did she find him handsome, attractive, seductive? More so physically than Sam? Certainly. Did she find him as determined, as hypnotic? No. Not right away. Maybe never. Did she find other qualities? Yes, as time went on, she told herself. Were those qualities more important? We all learn as we grow up, she told herself.

At the time, she had keenly felt the humiliation of having been dismissed by Sam and been shunted onto Mike, having to try to deal with her disappointment and constant questioning of Mike's place in her life, and Mike's place in the world as one stands next to a Sam Yones. Evaluating. She was good at it once. Who knew whether there will be yet another moment in life when the world would change forever for her, when all that Mike is would tower conclusively over all that Sam ever was.

"Why now for Bob Marley?" she had asked Sam.

"Why is 'now' the right time for any deal? I say 'now,' Gordy says 'now.' It's 'now.' You can ask Mike when he gets back from California."

"You think he's there?" Cheryl asked, knowing the answer.

"Yes, I do. Gordy told me. I also think, seriously, Cheryl . . ." his voice softened, almost turned warm, ". . . you ought to talk to him about coming back here. Especially now."

"Thanks, Sam. It's thoughtful of you to think of us."

"It sounds like there's an edge in your voice."

"No. Not at all. It's okay to be thoughtful."

"Don't spread it around," he said.

Cheryl glanced into her old office, but settling down to work was not the reason she had returned. She had returned to get back on the inside to help Mike.

She walked down the hall toward Sam's private staircase, its treads suspended on the thinnest stainless steel rods, designed by Mies van der Rohe and originally intended for installation in Edgar Bronfman's office in the Seagram Building. Instead, Sam got it.

She wondered, with all she in her short career had seen, who goes over the line easier, the Jew or the WASP? Whose law is it? Whose line is it? Who draws the line? The system or the guy with the pencil? Then she thought about all the bright lines that were still ahead for the crossing. She was going to have to push, to shove, use the New York elbows she had been born with. If she died, at least they could say she was loud up to the very end.

Sam's private office was on the top floor, his own private conference room adjacent through double doors. You could see all across Manhattan, and below was the Plaza hotel which Sam had lost to Trump. "Let Donald have it. He'll die with it," Sam had said more than once.

Sam sat behind a great glass-surfaced desk, the city of New York behind him. She saw more artifacts from Jerusalem and new ones from Ashkelon propped up on pedestals, and the mourner's strip of black silk still pinned on his lapel.

"Sam . . ."

He looked up, saw who it was, and smiled.

". . . take that thing off." He liked his women hard, smart, and abrasive. "You're wearing it too long."

Sam was in front of her, taking her hand, obviously expecting her to hug him, which she did. Why not? She hadn't seen him since the funeral ten days ago.

"Mike told you about Miami, I suppose," Sam said.

"Of course he told me." Sam sat down and motioned her to the guest chair.

"Cheryl, Cheryl, Cheryl. A subpoena. That he should get a subpoena because of my dumb kid." Sam shook his head. "It makes me sick." He shook his head again. "And over nothing."

"Sam, Sam, Sam," Cheryl said. "You're overdoing it."

Cheryl smiled, playing the hard, smart broad Sam expected her to be, the Jewish Queen of the Business School. "Sam, never kid a kidder."

He looked up across his glass desk. He crossed one leg over the other. Cheryl made it her business not to cross her legs, but to keep them open. But not too wide. Sam controlled his eyes. He was good at that, but Cheryl knew what she was doing and she knew what erotic thoughts he was thinking. Most important for her purposes, he was distracted.

"So where's Mike's risk?" she asked.

"That's what Mike's thinking, huh?"

"Isn't that what he should be thinking?"

He started to rock back and forth in his desk chair, holding it at the top of the arc for a fraction too long, looking between her legs.

"It isn't his risk," Cheryl said carefully. "Ultimately, it's someone else's risk." She paused. "They can want him for only two reasons. Either for something he did or because he can tell them about things other people did. And he hasn't done anything. So, ultimately, it's somebody else's risk."

Sam smiled his magical smile, but he felt the cold seeping under his collar and up his pant leg. He turned to her full face and said, "I don't know what they want of me. How am I supposed to know what they want of him? Or anybody else."

Cheryl shook her head, marveling at his amazing performance. "So all you guys are going down to Miami, is that it?"

"Not Gordy."

She knew enough not to be surprised, but asked anyway. "Just the two of you?"

"And Billy."

She nodded. "So as I said, Sam, where's the risk?" She repeated her words, trying to throw him off once again if she could. "Mike has no risk."

"You're right. So where's the risk?" Sam said, answering a question with a question. "Well, tell me . . ." Now it was all business. "Are you still avid for excitement?" His eyes were full of calculation and now, two years later, she could see that clearly. She felt a sense of rejoicing, realizing how far she had come, how acutely she could now see into Sam, how she would use her new skills. She would not quiz him on why he wanted her here but use his offer for her purposes to help Mike. In class, Mike used to call it doing due diligence.

Cheryl stayed at the office until seven, digging into the data on the Bob Marley estate deal, planning a presentation for the Boston Bank and Standard British in the Grand Caymans. Sam had told her nothing except Gordy was out of it, and that meant that only one member of the trio was left for the government to squeeze: her Mike. That kind of "nothing" was information she could use. Mike had told her less.

Billy might know something, but it was way past five, and when five came around, Billy was usually out the door. She went upstairs anyway to see if he might be with Sam or in his own office, although it was late and they were both probably gone.

The Mies staircase was dark and Sam's office should have been dark as well. But his desk lamp was lit and the office and the staircase were in a yellow shadow. Cheryl started up the steps two at a time. She didn't see all of her at once, first her legs and then Liz's face appeared through the open risers. Cheryl stopped, hoping she hadn't been seen, not wanting to embarrass either of them.

"Cheryl." It was Liz's voice. "Don't tell him."

Cheryl headed up the staircase once again, and by the time she reached the landing she saw that Liz had moved away from the computer behind Sam's desk, but not in time to avoid being seen turning it off.

"Who don't you want me to tell?"

"You're too bright to ask that question," Liz answered.

Liz had known. She had known all the time Sam and Cheryl were together. Cheryl was not surprised by the harshness in Liz's voice which she reserved for the rare times when the two of them were together alone. Half-unconsciously, Cheryl looked at her watch. She thought of Sam's rule. "Never go into a meeting with anything important to do after it's over." Do what's good for the deal, Cheryl thought. The eleventh commandment.

"You look like you have somewhere to go," Liz said.

Tell the truth. Cheryl's own commandment. "No, not right away."

Cheryl looked at the screen, tiny green blips fading away in the center. She tipped her head in the direction of the computer. "Is this why you wanted to know about computers?"

Liz had thought about pretending for a moment, and then she thought she saw something in Cheryl's eyes that gave her the go-ahead. "Yes. There's an access code. I know the first two words, 'behave me,' but not the last one."

The computer keyboard was on its own glass credenza behind Sam's desk, and they both looked at it for another moment. Then Cheryl made a decision.

"It's not what I do, but I'll try. How do you know a password is necessary to access the file you want?" Cheryl asked.

"I'll show you. It's the same program he has at home."

Liz sat in Sam's swivel chair and then spun around to face the computer. She lifted her fingers above the keyboard, pausing for a moment, as if to form her fingers as she might have done forty years before for her piano teacher.

"I could go through the whole process, but let me take you right to where I got stuck," Liz said. "If you press 'papers, private' " . . . and she typed in the words, ". . . then you get a menu. See?"

It popped up green on the screen, REFER TO FILE. CODE WORD BEHAVE ME. PLUS SPECIAL ACCESS CODE.

"Behave me?" Cheryl asked.

Liz knew she had no choice.

Cheryl had a tight look on her face as if she knew what might be coming. "Something private between you and Sam?"

"No. Not initially." The sudden hush was to Cheryl like going deaf. "It was something I said to Mike once a long time ago. Then Sam picked it up. I told him. Mike didn't. But it happened when . . . a long time ago. It was at my birthday party, and I asked Mike if he would always behave me."

"What was his answer?"

"The truth is I don't remember, exactly."

"Sure you do, but it's okay."

Cheryl leaned over Liz's shoulder. She stared at the two words, "behave me" printed in bold letters, flashing on Sam's computer screen. She looked past the screen for a moment and caught the rigging lights sparkling on the World War II aircraft carrier in its permanent dock on the Hudson River.

"It's all so incestuous, isn't it?" Liz said, staring into the screen as if something she was looking for would appear there.

The last thing Cheryl wanted to do was look at Liz. She must have had blond curls back then, the blue eyes must have seemed even bigger, and had Cheryl been there then, a prayer for bad looks as Liz grew older would have been appropriate. But the youthful looks had matured into beauty beyond any reasonable expectation. The voice as well, which made it twice as thrilling: It hadn't gone harsh and crackly, like a woman of fifty who had smoked cigarettes, but instead had turned even warmer than the high and happy voice of a young girl.

Cheryl imagined Mike and Liz standing together in the cold at Matt's funeral, and later at the house, looking at each other as only people who have once loved each other, and still might, could do. Not that it was the first time she had seen them look at each other that way, and maybe it wouldn't be the last. The closer she became to both of them over the past three years, the more likely she was, unless the wisdom of Solomon and the patience of Job were hers, to make a mistake. Any crack, any criticism, any unimaginable error could ignite the spark and make Mike turn to Liz and love her. Self-command and balance are not what Jewish girls are born with, but she would succeed. She had to.

"The demon won't go back in the bottle," Liz said, abruptly changing the mood in the room. She was thinking of Sam's misuse of Billy first and then Matt, the "if onlys" that were possible in her own mind because she knew, down deep, that no one had the power to control Sam. "Maybe I could have done more. I don't know. Kids always move in a larger world than their parents. The Puritans' kids knew the Indians' tracks. Billy and Matt could have been the same way."

Now Cheryl touched her shoulder.

Liz leaned forward in her chair, and swiveled around slowly as Cheryl stepped back to watch her looking to the west side of Manhattan spread out below them, where the rich people used to venture "only to get the boat."

"I won't tell him," Cheryl said.

Each caught the other's eye in the same instant.

"When we'd come home from college, I'd sneak over to Sam's house," Liz said, "when his parents were still alive. He was proud to have me there, not embarrassed. He was defiant and his mother, who was not supposed to like me, liked me." Liz began to smile. "I remember being warned one Saturday how religious they were, but Sam took me anyway and his mother, Yetta, on their Sabbath had the radio on, the *Texaco Opera Theater*. I'll never forget what she said, looking as if she were caught doing something impure. 'Next week is *shabbes*. Today is *Aida*.' Well," Liz said in her strong voice, "enough of that."

Cheryl had never been on one of Liz's Guggenheim tours or seen her in action at corporate board meetings curating art acquisitions by Philistines, but she could imagine the lady with no pores, with the silvery blond hair, the great features, and a voice to match, embellishing the culture of a generation. It crossed Cheryl's mind that Liz might actually be a very shy woman and more alone than any human being deserves to be. She watched Liz's face. It had acquired a remote quality, as if she were already anticipating an ordeal that would cut into her as deeply as the burial of her son.

"I'm supposed to pick Mike up at the airport," Cheryl said. "I'm sorry to cut this short." Cheryl felt rotten, but she couldn't show this woman how vulnerable she was. "I can't help you with that," she said, putting her hand on the monitor.

"I thought you were looking at your watch for some reason. Sorry. I didn't mean to hold you up."

"You didn't at all." Cheryl looked for a purse to pick up, and then realized she didn't have one; her briefcase was downstairs. She wondered whether she should kiss Liz good-bye on the cheek as she had done dozens of times over the last two years. Of course. So Cheryl tipped her head up because Liz was taller, as all blondes seem to be to all black-haired Jewish girls, and kissed Liz on the cheek, the one with less powder on it.

16

DESPITE THE PROTESTS SHE KNEW SHE WOULD HEAR FROM Mike, Cheryl took her Dodge Dart and drove out to Kennedy to meet the plane from Los Angeles. Mike frowned when he saw her, but then hugged her extra hard.

Mike liked her to take the wheel when it was just the two of them in the car. He opened the driver's door for her and locked the button before he closed the door to make sure she was safe inside. When he walked around to the passenger side of the car, he realized that he had locked himself out. Cheryl, who knew it all along, waited for him to knock on the window before she smiled and opened the door for him.

"Very funny. Very funny," Mike said, and laughed because he felt safe laughing at himself in front of her.

Her style of driving was tough, not because she preferred it that way, but because she liked less ending up behind taxi drivers or three-hundred-pound limo jockeys who thought it was their right to cut off all ladies in Dodge Darts. Out through the maze of roads taking them away from JFK, through the highways, almost until they were between La-Guardia and the Brooklyn-Queens Expressway, they made small talk or were silent. But as Cheryl swung over away from the BQE, Mike asked, "So what did you do today?"

"I went to the office. He offered me a free-lance, one-shot opportunity. Ten points, free, on all Bob Marley material provided we can buy the rights."

That meant Sam, and all Mike could manage after three thousand miles by plane and twenty-two by car was "God almighty, how could you do that?"

It took her until the approach to the Triborough Bridge to say, "Mike, I can't be left out of this."

Mike turned to her, and took her hand. "I don't want you in it." She was glad she needed only one hand for the wheel, and glad the other one was always available for him.

"Sam's told me all about your subpoena," she said.

She watched his shoulders fall.

The lights of Manhattan were visible through the windshield, the sky dark, the air clear. Cheryl had picked her time to talk. He could look at the scenery in the darkened car and she had no need to see his displeasure, but it was in his voice.

"How much did he tell you?"

"That he got one. That you got one and that Billy did. But that Gordy did not."

"He told you that?"

"Yes. Mike, how come Gordy didn't get one?"

"He can protect himself."

"You mean he won't testify?"

"That's right."

Neither one mentioned self-incrimination or the Fifth Amendment.

"So Gordy can't lead them to Sam," Cheryl said. Mike nodded, and Cheryl did her best to keep her eyes on the road. "Only you can."

"I don't want you in this."

"How slick he was. How concerned that poor little Mikey should be involved."

"What do you think pulling you back there is all about? Don't you think that's slick?"

"He probed all over the place, wanting to know if you were calm, if you were sure there was no risk to you. Mike, he wants you relaxed."

"Sure he does. And I'd want him relaxed. Under the circumstances."

Cheryl gave him a quick look.

"Why?"

It sounded like a question, but it was a demand.

"Because a grand jury is no fun, I would guess."

"You want him relaxed for his sake, not for yours?" she asked, incredulous.

She took the exit ramp off the FDR and 96th Street. "Mike, what's going on?"

They headed south on Fifth Avenue.

"I'm holding back. That's right. You have no privilege. They can call you. If they do, I want there to be nothing for you to say."

"I hate being protected like this."

"You want a subpoena, too?"

"It'd be better than this."

"You said a lot happened while I've been away. What else?"

She took the turn at 74th Street a bit too fast.

"I saw Liz in Sam's office."

"And?" Mike said, unable to keep the impatience from his voice.

"Her interest in computers is burgeoning," Cheryl said. "She seems to use one wherever she can." Cheryl turned to look at him, and just before the car tipped gently forward down the garage ramp, she said, "What do you know about the password BEHAVE ME?"

17

FINDING PASSOVER HAGADAHS FOR A HOUSE WHERE A Passover service had never been held was no mean trick, but Mike had done it within the week since his return from Los Angeles. He did not have the nerve to tell Cheryl that he had the books flown in from Minneapolis, from the old Temple Beth-El they used to go to on Penn Avenue. Old books, the old style, none of the newfangled humanism, just the traditional books with wine spots from red Mogen David staining the covers, telling the story of the Exodus the traditional way. He had one for each place at the table, and as he walked around, setting each book down himself, he was so proud of Cheryl and the way she had set it all up.

The table was long and shining, covered with starched white linen, sparkling china and silver, glistening crystal wineglasses on tall stems, and a big oversized goblet in the middle to welcome the spirit of Elijah. There were silk purses for the *afakamin,* the special matzos the kids are supposed to find, and silver candlesticks, three arms radiating out, white candles in each one ready to be lit. It was almost as if Cheryl had somehow found a picture of his grandmother's seder table and reproduced everything on it, the food, the ritual, the love, the whiteness, the sparkle, the family. Mike put the Hagadah that had been marked up for the leader of the service on his own plate, and he found himself swallowing quickly. He was the first son of a first son and he had no sons, and it was the first seder he was to lead.

He heard Cheryl answer the door almost the minute the bell rang. They were all coming, even Gordy and Helen from Los Angeles. Maybe three in help was too much, Mike thought, suddenly anxious.

What were those people doing in his house, anyway? he wondered.

He turned around and walked back to the dining room to check the table again. Cheryl saw him and wondered what he was up to. When he had a chance, he would tell her: Maybe the table empty meant more to him than it would full, the memory of the past meaning more than the present. He took one last look at Cheryl's setting in its pristine form, and then retraced his steps so he could stand with Cheryl at the front door when the people he had known the longest in his life and who were now a threat to him would join with him to celebrate the Exodus from slavery to freedom.

Liz, standing in the doorway, kissing Cheryl, looked

more dazzlingly beautiful than ever. Mike, at that moment, realized one thing about Liz that had escaped him for close to thirty years: Liz always presumed an audience. She must love to think of those watching turn to each other and say, "Who is she? Who is that beautifully groomed woman with the blond hair?"

Mike shifted his glance to Sam and felt a squeeze in his chest. It didn't last long and there was no pain. But it had never happened before and he waited a moment to see if he was going to be stricken. He was not. Instead, he felt Sam's hand in his, pumping it up and down, muttering something about how glad he was to be here. Not too soft and not too loud. Unusual for the old Sam. Perfect for signaling that he was relieved, after all the years, not to be excluded.

Mike nodded and free of Sam's handshake he put his arm around Cheryl's shoulders, greeting Gordy and Helen and Billy and still trying to understand what Sam's eyes had just conveyed. Sam, who had it all, was afraid to be left out, isolated, even with all he had. That an invitation to a seder should mean so much to him. A vulnerability.

Billy broke in with his own handshake, seeming like a young Richie Daley, bumbling, good-hearted, the son of a dynamic father whose lineage was in his face, a kid pushed into something he'd just as soon not do, but making the most of it when he got there. What would Billy have done had he been free? What would any of them do had they been free?

"Well, Uncle Mike? When do we eat?"

"You haven't heard the story yet. You've got to hear the story of the flight from Egypt before you eat. You've got to ask the Four Questions."

Billy's face fell. For a moment, Mike thought he had been too overbearing, but then, in a flash, Mike knew why. He had not thought to invite someone younger than Billy, because it was the youngest who had to ask the leader the Four Questions. It was the answers to those questions that formed the heart of the service. There was no Matt. The younger son was gone.

"Well, if we're going to start, let's start," Mike said, trying to figure out what to do. "Then we can eat."

"I'm not ready yet," Cheryl said, and Mike was relieved.

"Well, then, how about a drink?" he asked, leading the way to a uniformed waiter who smiled as he stood over a silver drinks tray filled with shining decanters. The sounds of ice and the pouring of the finest whiskeys filled the room, then laughter and talk. Five minutes passed, maybe ten, and as had been the case for decades, the trio gravitated together as if the room had tilted. There had been a time when they could gaze out together over the city at a world patterned in light and know themselves unwatched, inviolate, secure, and private. Mike had a feeling that those days were about to be gone forever. Behind him, Mike heard a steady hum of female voices and thought again about Billy, isolated, never to be included. Included in what?

"You think they'll ask us what we said at our seder?" Sam asked, his voice too loud, too quick, too nervous.

"Not here," Mike said. "Not tonight." Gordy tried not to listen.

Mike stopped to fight the forbidden urge to pretend that he never knew these men, especially the short one, making the change in his pocket into a noisemaker, never had been told what they had done, how they had done it, pretend that he had heard nothing, seen nothing. Off behind him, he heard a large round laugh. It was Gordy. He was free. He had his Fifth Amendment and no shame in his world to take it. At least he was having a good time.

"What I want you to do," Sam said, putting his arm around Mike, "is wrong by every standard except one. I want you to help me. I want you to save one of your own." Sam's lack of shame caught Mike by surprise. Just like a two-bit politician. Race before right. Mike said nothing, feeling the loneliness of the silent room settle on him. He thought even the chattering waiter went suddenly quiet.

"Okay," Cheryl called out. "We're ready now."

Mike ushered Liz, Sam, Gordy, and Helen into his dining room. Gordy's kids, Danny and Kate; he could have invited them. Gordy would have flown them in. They would have been younger. But he hadn't done that. Mike put one arm around Cheryl's shoulder, needing her and the free arm around Billy and they walked into the dining room, bringing up the rear. Each stood behind the places Cheryl had assigned to them, waiting. Then, unwilling to spoil tonight, Mike nodded, and Gordy, next to Cheryl, pulled out her chair, and Mike watched her assume her place opposite Mike's at the other end of the long table. Sam was on Mike's right and Liz on his left, Billy next to Liz and Helen, across from the matzos tray next to Gordy. There should have been kids, Mike thought. There should have been kids.

"Well, ladies and gentlemen," Mike said, "let us proceed. First, the prayer over the wine." He was still an actor. The show was not over yet. "Sam?"

Sam Yones looked up and Mike could not remember a face so grateful. The small man rose and for once the change did not jingle in his pocket.

"Blessed art Thou, O Lord, our God, who bringest forth the fruit of the vine."

"In Hebrew," Gordy called out from the far end of the white table.

"Absolutely right!" Mike chimed in. "Without you, we'd be in trouble. Sam, in Hebrew."

Was there a narrowing of Sam's eye? Mike couldn't tell. He saw Sam smile, tip his head, and then look at Liz.

"Baruch atoh . . ."

And before the prayer was over, the change started to jingle, not much; just a little.

"Fine, Sam," Mike said. "Just fine. And now, the prayer for the matzo, the unleavened bread, the dough that did not rise because we did not have time to let it bake because we ran from the pharaohs. The bread of poverty. Cheryl?"

Cheryl stood.

"May I join you?" Liz said quietly, looking at Cheryl.

She answered, a fraction too late. "Yes, Liz, of course."

To his left and across his table, the two women of his life spoke. "O Lord, our God, who gave us the unleavened bread, matzo."

"In Hebrew," Gordy called out again.

"Oh, I don't know if . . ." Cheryl said, smiling too much.

"That's okay," Liz answered. "I know it."

And Liz's voice was the one the company heard first, *"Baruch atoh . . ."*

Then Cheryl raced to catch up. *"Baruch atoh . . .*

". . . *al a che los matzos,"* Cheryl said, racing to finish on time.

"Nice, ladies," Sam said, "that was very nice," holding his head high. "How long ago did Rabbi Aaron teach you that?"

"How many years are we married?" Liz asked.

"It seems like yesterday," Sam said, beaming, proud of his prize.

"It was interesting," Liz said. "Our religion is the oldest continually practiced one in the world."

Sam nodded, proudly. "That's right."

No one picked up Sam's enthusiasm. Mike knew exactly what Cheryl wanted to do: drop a safe on the shiksa who stole the great Jewish guys and converted to make it stick. Billy looked away because Billy always looked away. Mike looked down at his Hagadah and moved to his next problem.

"The Four Questions," Mike announced. He could see Sam close his eyes and Liz pale.

Then it clicked.

"Why don't we change the rules, and why doesn't each of us take one question and read it?" Mike searched inside himself and found the best radio voice he had ever managed. "Any volunteers?"

Cheryl looked across the expanse of the white linen cloth and holiday table she had worked so hard to get exactly right and knew she would do anything in the world for this man. She thought of the raiders' faces praying at Sam's house, at least ten of them lined up, their knees bending to Hebrew prayers, none of them sensitive enough to think about a first son being pushed into a role reserved for a favored younger brother. Respect wasn't what she felt.

Gratitude for his difference from the Sams and the Gordys was more like it.

"I'll do it," Helen said, "but no Hebrew."

"That's a deal."

"Why, on this night . . ."

"Why, on this night . . ." Gordy took over.

"Why, on this night . . ." Mike was surprised to hear Billy's voice.

"Why, on this night . . ." And Billy a second time, his eyes full, speaking for his brother.

"And the answer," Mike said, holding his voice steady. "The answer is, we were slaves in Egypt."

PART THREE

18

ARLO SHIELDS PICKED MIKE UP AT THE MIAMI AIRPORT wearing a crushed linen suit with a wide hand-painted tie, a soft straw hat, and tan penny loafers, his only concession to anything past World War II. Arlo carried a copy of the evidence casebook he had written, cover showing, as if he were meeting a stranger and needed to identify himself. It was close to ten Monday morning, three weeks and several telephone calls after Mike Anker had called to seek his counsel for an appearance before a Miami grand jury. His waxed mustache was impeccable, light gray to white at the tips, and his Panama hat made him look like a thin Sydney Greenstreet. No one who wrote the casebook used by one hundred and ten law schools in the country could be completely dumb, Mike thought the minute he saw Arlo carrying the book. Mike had renewed confidence in his ability to keep himself out of the hands of losers.

Arlo lived in Coral Gables and his ancestors had been there since the Seminoles. Few had called him Eagle Eye since college. His credentials were fine, but which law school you went to and the ability to spot a woman you could make at a hundred yards, like most accreditations of that ilk, meant little as your life went on. What counted now was how you handled things, and on that score, Mike had no personal knowledge. Instead, he had Gordy, who had told him that Arlo wrote the book, but that he didn't live by it. Mike liked that, under the circumstances. He was the man to use.

"Your business is too brutal for me," Arlo said to Mike after the hellos, together with a long southern laugh. Mike had no idea what he was talking about, so he didn't answer. Another question he couldn't answer. Mike frowned, but Arlo didn't see it. For several days after Passover Mike was able to ignore Sam's demand—do it for a brother. Save one of your own. Mike tried to put Sam's appeal out of his mind. Then he was persecuted by it, as if thousands of years of heritage, denials, and exclusions came to a pinpoint on the survival of the beady eyes and jingling change of Sam Yones. In the strangest way, Mike was glad to be here to begin the battle, as if he were looking forward to a prizefight where the other guy was bigger. At least the fight would be fought and finished.

They walked outside to the car, and the Miami air hit him, hot and damp as a greenhouse. It was not raining, but it had been and, looking up, Mike decided it probably would again. Arlo drove a white 1963 Lincoln convertible and he must be an optimist because the top was down.

"This car is huge," Mike said as Arlo piloted the Lincoln into traffic. "You could have a barbecue on the trunk."

"You like it, huh?" Another sleepy laugh.

"Love it."

They drove for five, maybe ten minutes, working their way out of the twists and turns of the airport access roads. Traffic was impossible. "The cruise-boat crowd comes in at this hour, just before lunch," Arlo said.

"Sorry to make you come to the airport," Mike answered.

"No way you would know. Besides, I wanted to come." It took them two light changes to get through the final intersection, but then finally they felt the rush of wind of the highway.

"I understand you want to see the grand jury room before we go in there tomorrow," Arlo said, coming to the point as the palm trees went by in a blur. "There isn't much wrong with that idea." Mike looked up, studying him. "Rooms that are new to you are old hat to any lawyer in town. I wouldn't be distracted by the dripping air conditioner in three-west, or the outdated flag with only forty-eight stars in the grand jury room, but you might be."

"I like to know what a room feels like." Mike knew he could concentrate better on what he had to say and, of more importance, on how what he had to say was understood. If he had the feel of the room behind him, he could watch the eyes of others, pay attention to notes being passed back and forth, and all the other details that would allow him to get through this. Know the road before you drive on it, he always told his students; the journey will go easier. "I like to do that kind of thing, take a look in advance. If I can."

Arlo maneuvered his big car down the Interstate heading south toward Coconut Grove. He could have taken the local streets, Lejune to Calle Ocho; it would have been faster, and, as Mike looked across the town from the elevated highway, he wished they had gone that way.

Instead, Arlo had taken him into town on what Arlo called the white man's route. They crossed the causeway in front of the cruise boats, and Mike saw two pelicans gliding just a few feet above the water. It looked like a postcard.

"It wasn't easy to get you in there," Arlo said, caressing the steering wheel.

As they drove, Arlo thought back to yesterday.

"Spencer, I know you don't like people dropping in, but . . ."

"Arlo, I'll give you ten minutes."

Arlo put his Panama down on Spencer's desk, looked at the failing telltale waving from the louvers near the top of the wall, glad that there was at least a little air-conditioning.

"No special treatment," Arlo said. "But I want to talk to you about my client who's coming in."

"Mike Anker?"

"I have only one. He wants to take a look at the grand jury room before he goes on. Empty."

"Why should he get a free look?"

"A stranger could walk in off the street, ask to see what it looks like, and you'd let him in. Students walk in. I took my whole class in there. What's wrong with Mike Anker?"

"He's not a student. He's not off the street. He's a witness."

"Give him a break. He's not tied up with these guys."

"Don't tell me he's not with these guys. He's known them forty years plus. Maybe he's just the right guy to squeeze."

"Squeeze him if you want. But let him see the room first."

"That's eight minutes used up."

"One more thing. Don't start on immunity with Mike. He won't need it. We're glad to help. We've got nothing to hide."

"Ten minutes is ten minutes."

"So it is."

Arlo left Spencer's office all smiles, but his right hand shaking a little bit as he put the quarter into the slot to get the dial tone.

Arlo, still caressing the steering wheel, turned to Mike. "The U.S. Attorney doesn't like to do it. He's worried about someone placing a bug."

Arlo's voice, even though he had raised it a bit so he would be heard above traffic, was more genial than his face which had always seemed grim to Mike, even at college. It was a typically legal face with angular jaws and, now, heavily grizzled eyebrows.

"But it's been cleared; you're expected. You can go in by yourself."

"Thanks, Arlo." Mike had to concentrate not to call him Eagle Eye. "Is there anyone else I'm supposed to thank?"

"Yes, the Assistant U.S. Attorney. You'll have your chance."

Mike looked across the chrome dash, past Arlo's Panama resting on the broad armrest, the white leather upholstery cracked just a bit, as the highway drew west of downtown Miami. The old pyramid-topped City Hall across from the railroad station Henry Flagler built for the Florida East Coast Line was still there, and behind the station was a wilderness of rails and switches which more than anything, so far, made Mike remember and yearn to see a streamliner glide in and men in white double-breasted suits and women in picture hats gather to board her. That part of town was right out of another time. Hot weather was the forties, Mike thought, the last era before air-conditioning, when hot made you live in another way.

"The town seems so much bigger now," Mike said as they rode along.

"Doesn't everyplace?" Arlo took a hand from the wheel and drove casually with one hand, giving Mike a drowsy smile, letting him change the subject, pretending it went unnoticed.

"I remember that old City Hall used to be the tallest building in town," Mike said. "We'd take the *Dixie Flagler* down here in the summer. We couldn't afford the winter. The fancy hotels were closed. The Roney Plaza was behind wooden gates. We couldn't afford it anyway. In the summer, all you saw were the poor from New York speaking Yiddish, three families from Chicago, and two from Minneapolis. We were it. And the alligators." Mike felt himself slipping into matters too personal. A little of that was fine. It warmed people up and relaxed them, letting them know you were a regular guy. But not too much. He checked himself. "The Miami News Building, the one on Biscayne Boulevard?" Mike asked as the car rolled on. "Old Man Knight used to own it, who also owned the *Chicago Daily News.*" Mike didn't add that he, with his investors, had tried to buy its successor, the *Sun-Times,* before the Field family sold it to Murdoch. "Is that still here?"

Arlo looked out his window and nodded with his chin in the direction of the MacArthur Causeway. "You mean what used to be the storage warehouse." Arlo knew there was no glass in the window frames, and that the building looked bombed out. He was glad they weren't closer to it.

"Yeah," Mike smiled, his voice softer. "I mean the storage warehouse." Then he forced a hollow laugh.

"It's not that Miami changes less," Arlo said. "It's just that there are more things left that remind you of the way it used to be." Arlo didn't get as far as he got without being sensitive to moods.

"Our grand jury hearing . . ." Arlo let the words hang. He glanced to the passenger side to see how Mike would react to the words. There was no move in Mike's facial muscles, hand to his hair, or change in his posture. He might not make a bad witness after all, Arlo decided, off on his own in a grand jury room with no lawyer to protect him. He had been mulling over that issue since Mike had first called him.

"It's different than what you see on TV. There is no judge in there, no one there to call foul. And you can't have a lawyer with you. A person is all on his own, whether he is a target or just a witness."

"I know that," Mike said, thinking of Sam's fate which he seemed to hold in his hands.

"And the members of a grand jury just don't sit back and listen."

"I see."

Arlo knew Mike didn't "see."

"They can ask questions if they want to. They can decide if they want to stay in session another hour or another day or another three months. They can tell the government to go find them more witnesses or get them more evidence. And most important, they can indict."

The look on Mike's face was calm, receptive, the look of learning.

"You can be hammered. Anyone can be hammered." Arlo watched Mike again.

"Arlo, I've been around lawyers my whole life. Are you through with the battering-ram technique?"

Mike heard another slow, southern laugh.

Arlo gave up trying to sting Mike into a response. He lowered his pitch, but continued to speak over the noise of the traffic so Mike could hear him. He realized he could take Mike's temperature from here to doomsday and that Mike's flat, frozen Greek-statue expression would stay put and, in a way, that was a good thing. It would help Mike when he was on his own, alone, before the grand jury.

"Your subpoena is simple. It's very clear what you're subpoenaed for. It's the trust account for William and Matthew Yones, now all William's, I presume." Mike looked up. "They'll ask you what you've done as a trustee and your answer will be nothing."

"There's got to be more. They know I haven't acted as a trustee. They didn't drag me down here to tell them that. By the way, is Sam in town yet?" Mike asked, almost offhand.

Arlo continued to drive as if he had not heard the question.

"Is Sam here yet?" Mike repeated, thinking maybe his words were lost in the road noise coming into the open car.

"Mike," Arlo finally answered. "You pay me for advice. You want some?"

"Sure," Mike said, the pleasantness in his voice gone.

"Don't worry about Sam. Worry about yourself."

"Why?"

"They're out to get him and they don't even know why or on what charge. At least not for sure. The talk is there's an overseas account with interest on it that he didn't report as taxable income, but that doesn't justify the digging, the effort they're putting in." Arlo's voice was loud enough to be heard in the rushing wind. He was used to talking with the top down. "They think you know something." Arlo took his eyes off the road for a moment and caught Mike's eye. "Do you? Do you know something?"

Mike watched him focus on the road again. "Arlo, you haven't kept up with us since school. Sam went to New York. So did Gordy. So did I. I went to graduate school. They didn't. I'm not in business with Sam. I never have been. Not that he isn't smart, don't get me wrong. We just do different things. But we've stayed friends. Close friends. You know, Arlo, the older you get, the fewer friends you're going to have that go back forty years."

Mike realized how many times he had said or thought that. How closely he looked at this man who thirty-odd years ago had introduced Sam to Liz, and without Arlo as the link, Sam never would have known her. Links, he thought. It's all links.

"Have you ever been one of his investors? In one of his partnerships?"

"Once."

"Did the money you put in match the piece you got? Did you get any premium, you know, one dollar in, one fifty's worth in equity? Like he does?"

"No, one dollar in, one dollar's worth of equity. No more."

"And you took your money out, took your profit and paid your taxes."

"Of course I did. I'm a schoolteacher just like you are. How would it look if we did anything else?" Mike couldn't decide why he was trying to lighten up the conversation.

"Then why does the U.S. Attorney think that you can fill in the pieces?" Arlo's tone was not light at all.

"I don't know why I got that subpoena. I told you that when I called you."

"Don't get mad. I don't know why they served you with it either. That was three weeks ago. I've been sniffing around here on and off since then and I don't know much more now than I did then. Anything new occur to you?"

Privilege or not, Mike knew clients never told their lawyers everything. He had never held back before, but there was always a first time. Lawyers, you use them. Just like Sam said, Mike thought, doing as Sam did, convincing his own lawyer of a story.

"No, nothing at all. I have no idea what blanks I can fill in."

"I'd like to know what you're mixed up in."

Mike summoned another lesson learned on the inside. "So would I."

"Okay, maybe it's not you. Then they do want to use you. Maybe they think you could lead them, if not to Sam, then to somebody else" . . . Mike held his breath. ". . .

someone who was on the inside with Sam, someone who's not there now, someone who might have bitched to you about Sam. A disgruntled employee?" Mike began to perspire heavily. "A lawyer he fired. An accountant. Someone they might find who they can pressure to turn on him."

"No. No one like that," Mike said to the wind.

"Even if you know nothing, they'll try every trick in the book short of threatening you with a crime because then they've got to tell you you're a target, but other than that, they'll come up with a million schemes just to squeeze you to get to him or to get to somebody else who can get to him."

"But they don't know why they're getting to him."

"That's what it looks like, a fishing expedition. That's all the more reason to worry."

Mike wanted to freeze his face so it wouldn't betray his fear. He wanted Cheryl out of this. He would keep her out no matter what.

"The key, the way you try to protect yourself, the only chance you have, is to stake out your ground before the whole thing starts."

Mike listened.

"The way you do that is also one hundred and eighty degrees away from what you see in the movies or on TV. I take you by the hand and expose you, almost naked if I have to, to the lawyer on the other side. I try to make sure that you make a favorable impression on the Assistant U.S. Attorney, because he's the only one in the room with you who counts. And to make that impression, you see him before it starts. So look, your appearance is scheduled at three-thirty tomorrow afternoon, Tuesday. Got that?"

"I got that."

"Depending on how things go, you could be in and out in an hour, or you might not start until the next day."

"So when do I see him, this Assistant U.S. Attorney?"

"Just before you go in for your scheduled appearance."

Arlo's angled legal face, at the moment, was full of goodwill, and Mike realized, after all these years, that old Eagle Eye would have been really good-looking except that his eyes were a little too wide apart, but that made him appear more trustworthy. Not a bad trade-off.

They drove another mile, past Ronald Reagan Avenue and the new high-rises that had changed the skyline, and then they started down the long easy grade that led them off the Interstate to the old Dixie Highway south of downtown. It was all so built-up, full of Beware of Dog signs and sliding gates with key-controlled electric locks, paranoia in Miami Mike had never seen before. In the summers when he was a kid, it all seemed like a palmetto swamp and mangrove shoots, and movies in the afternoon on 41st Street with Gordy and Sam, rhumba dances at night by the pool, his first taste of New York girls. He used to think nothing changes. Now it had all started to turn around. It had all changed.

"Tomorrow morning you can go look at the grand jury room. Then in the afternoon you see the Assistant U.S. Attorney. Then you testify. Then you go home."

Mike watched the palm trees and the motels on the old highway slide past him and felt the older, rougher asphalt.

"In the front you've got a long table for the foreman. Off to one side is . . ."

Mike tried to tune Arlo out, listening instead to the V-8 rumble down the road, trying to concentrate on the sound, its bubbling, but he kept fading in. Arlo's Evidence lectures must have been doozies. I'll bet he paced back and forth, Mike thought, and would love an overhead boom microphone to follow him, if he could get away with it. With this guy the ham had sure found its platter.

"You get blue-haired ladies from Hallendale who would rather do this than shop. You get blue-collar Cubans who are smart enough to know that their union agreement forces the *gringo el jefe* to foot the bill for jury duty, guys who don't mind taking off a day a week from the assembly line, putting on a tie and sitting in an air-conditioned grand jury room." Arlo cocked his head to one side, a gesture Mike remembered very well.

"I don't care what the books tell you. It's the U.S. Attorney whose show it is. In there, he's the law. It's not supposed to be that way, but that's the way it is." Proof of this man's ability and experience was something Mike no longer needed. "Running a grand jury, whether fair or not, came pretty close to making Thomas E. Dewey president of the United States. It made Jim Thompson governor of Illinois. They all use it to get one thing or another."

"Oh, by the way, did I tell you the government gets a lawyer? You don't."

"You said that, three different times. It's as if you don't trust me in there."

"But I'll be sitting outside if you need me."

The usual summer afternoon buildup off the Everglades was bringing the clouds over Miami. Mike knew there was going to be a dark sweat butterfly on the front of his shirt soon. He could feel it coming.

Old Eagle Eye pulled the white Lincoln convertible with the suicide doors into the driveway of the Grand Bay Hotel, running one tire over the grass. Arlo turned off the ignition, slid the thirty-year-old turbomatic into neutral, set the parking brake, and tapped the chrome shift knob with his finger, thinking it over, watching his finger as he tapped. "We knew each other thirty-five years ago, but now you have a life, I have a life, each of us knows nothing about." Mike watched him tapping out his Morse code on the shining knob, his eyes still lowered. "But I'm your lawyer, and I'm here to help." Mike put his hand on Arlo's arm, caught himself looking again at sunburned hands, and said, "I'm sorry. It's been a long trip. Thanks, Arlo. Thanks again."

Why the lecture in a car rolling down public streets? Mike wondered. Didn't Arlo have time to sit down? Have a cup of coffee? Didn't he have an office? It was as though Arlo needed to get rid of this information, get it off his chest, do his job, discharge his duties fast, get it over with. Mike started to wonder if he was gambling on a very weak reed.

19

As soon as he unpacked, Mike called Cheryl at home. What he would say to her when he got her, he didn't know. One ring. There was something not right with Arlo. Could he tell her that? Second ring. He was going to have a private meeting with the Assistant U.S. Attorney? Could he tell her that? Third ring. They're afraid of him being alone with the grand jury. He was scared to death and needed her. Fourth ring. She wasn't home. She was with Sam.

"Answering machines are a bore, but I'm not, so please leave a message."

He wondered why he had expected her to be home. "I don't have enough cards. I'm going back to the dealer" was what she had told him. He couldn't talk her out of it, not without telling her precisely those facts that could land her in the middle of all of this.

"I love you. That's my message," Mike said into the phone.

He hung up and walked outside to the balcony. Biscayne Bay was different now, all those cruise ships on Ford's Island, new causeways like white shining strips over the water. The air felt good, and the panic was passing.

A wedding ring would have kept the legal system away from Cheryl. "I'll buy one," she had said, "out of my own money." Liz would have only what money her husband gave her. How lucky he was. Cheryl had money of her own.

While the phone at the apartment was ringing that morning Cheryl was at Sam's offices, trying to work on the projections for a reissue of the first Bob Marley poster. He was the big reggae star, now dead, but she wasn't concentrating. Instead, she was recalling a meeting with Mike, the second time they were alone together. Mike was on his knees at Books and Company on Madison Avenue looking for a biography of Filippo Strozzi, the Medicis' banker who later became an outspoken defender of the last Florentine republic.

At first she had noticed Mike's name pop up now and then in Sam's files. It had meant nothing to her then, in the early days of her internship. He was a one-time investor in a timberlands partnership in Alabama, and a trustee for Sam's children, and the best friend. She had also met him once before at the investiture ceremony naming him as Yones professor at Columbia. She was a student then. He was out of her league. As was Gordy, indeed as was Sam, in those early days. The closeness began later, but only with Sam, and when she saw Mike or Gordy, she felt awkward, presuming each knew what had begun between her and Sam, embarrassed because she believed they knew it all, because Sam was telling them, day by day, night by night. Sam never presented her to his friends for who she was to him; she did not have the eye-level access to them that Gordy's Ginger had. Sam wasn't comfortable with that, he wouldn't do it. When the affair was over, she wondered so many times why she had never been allowed around Sam's pals, as Gordy's Ginger was, and she knew the reason had to do with Liz and Sam's steady love for her, even throughout their affair. If she knew it, which she did, why did she press on? So many reasons. She was young, she would push it; if she lost, she would try again, unhurt. Wrong. She was Sam, a young Sam, in a woman's body, and he would see that, leave Liz, and come to her. Wrong. So wrong on so many counts.

She felt the same awkwardness and embarrassment at the bookstore that day, wondering what Mike thought of her, if he knew she had lived in an apartment with Sam, or why she had been left behind, why she had lost. Mike hadn't known what to do either. Of course, they said hello, each insisting on eye contact, Mike losing her for a moment as he stood up. But she remembered the tone of his voice, the way it rolled, making her feel easier, his eyes, eventually his arms, willing not to see her as used merchandise. How respectful of him. How he brought her back to herself with his patience and his love. He was responsible for her newly found belief in extraordinary luck.

She learned later why Mike liked the Strozzi story. It was what he would have done had he lived back then. He would have worked at the Uffizi, and he probably would have had a corner office overlooking the Arno. He would lose himself in the book, transport himself to other times. And he also liked it because it gave him hopes for the rest of his life.

Two versions of the Marley poster were Scotch-taped to the wall across the room, one an exact reproduction of the original done in 1969, one a modification. She didn't give a shit which one they used. And they didn't either. It was not an aesthetic decision. It turned on numbers. That's all anyone cared about.

After Sam, for almost a year she had time to read again, time to walk, to be alone, to wonder how she had fallen in love with Sam Yones and to ask, honestly, whether she had fallen out of love with him just because he said it was over. She had sensed reluctance in Sam's voice, even sadness, and she wondered whether he had searched for a way for them to go on. She was sure he had. She knew him that well.

She looked around her office, thinking of the power there, the seduction of movers and shakers that inhabited, visited, and did deals in Sam's suite. She knew that inside she was still drawn to that power, that it was Sam who gave her up, not the other way around. Mike doesn't have what Sam has, never did, never will. But he doesn't have his sleaze either. Never did. Never will. How come she felt stirrings of revulsion now when she never did before when she was inside, welcomed, treated as a comer. She kept thinking of the action of the place, the grit, the power, the danger.

After the poster pro formas, Cheryl was able to concentrate on the Bob Marley distribution report for no more than a half hour. It told her how Marley records had been distributed around the world, how much money came in and from where, how the pattern could be improved, how much more money they could count on due to their own ability to innovate, and how they could use the greater profit to offset the premium price the estate was insisting on for long-term world rights. She regarded part of the report she was reading as accurate, but only part. She regarded the section on European forecasts as garbage, the Far East as probably able to produce more income than the report indicated. Provided being black in China helped rather than hurt. And that you never knew for sure. She knew the issues, if not the answers. That's why she was there. That's why she went to business school. That's how she got to be a Yones intern and found her way to Sam and Gordy in the first place, not to mention Mike.

She looked at her watch again. Maybe she'd go upstairs and tell Sam what she thought. She'd carry the Marley posters along in case he wanted to see them, which he wouldn't, but holding them would give her something to do with her hands. Maybe he had already been in Miami, testified, run into Mike, and returned with good news. Maybe she'd find out something.

Cheryl started climbing the stairs, and as soon as her right foot landed on the fifth riser, she was eye level with the floor in Sam's office and she realized she was scanning the carpet, looking for a woman's heels.

There was no Liz there. Not today. Nor was Sam. Nor was either of his secretaries. The place was deserted except for marble Roman emperors. No one was in the conference room either. Then she looked behind Sam's desk. The computer screen was on. Why? If he was out, why should it be on? Made no sense.

Access to Sam's private office was easy for insiders and she took advantage of it, checking around, careful not to touch anything. A few documents were stacked on the huge glass-topped desk in careful order. She read the top sheet of each.

Nothing. She slid a top sheet to one side, violating one of her rules, but all the second sheet disclosed was her own memo of the Marley deal. She smiled. It was nice to know her work went to the top.

Then, out of the corner of her eye, once again she caught the lit computer screen. "Do you think we own the electric company?" she imagined Sam saying, but she made no move to turn the monitor off.

She left Sam's suite and walked back to the elevator lobby. There she crossed into a different part of the executive office area, where the carpet changed to a lesser quality, the same color but noticeably tougher under foot. There were people here, the muffled sound of voices, the soft ring of phones, bells turned down as if they were under pillows. She found what she thought she would find: one more empty office. Billy's.

If Sam had his way, Billy's office would have been in some basement in Karachi, but he was a Yones, so he had to be near. Now he was the only Yones son left, Sam's unchosen legacy, but it was doubtful that he would draw closer to Sam. Or vice versa. But you could never tell. In thanks for being allowed to be on the same floor as his father, Billy permitted a large silver-framed picture of Sam to sit on the credenza behind his desk. That way, as long as Billy kept his eyes on the papers before him or the view out the window, he wouldn't have to look at Sam.

Then she remembered how and where she had picked up all this inside information about the Family Yones, and she was ashamed. There was one more office to be left quickly.

She had learned what she had set out to learn. She was there for a reason. To get more cards. Both Sam and Billy were out, in Miami, most likely. Still. With Mike. Who was there. Alone. Without her. And it hurt.

Cheryl walked back down one flight, once again using Sam's private staircase. She went to her office, put a pencil between her teeth, and sat back in her chair. What kind of slip, mistake, or inattentiveness would have allowed Sam or his staff to leave his computer screen on? For more than a day. For several days, in fact. Maybe over a weekend if he left for Miami early. It was a fair enough question, she decided. Cheryl sat, feet on the wastebasket, hands locked behind her head, thinking about it.

"Ms. Stone, I know it's lunchtime, but are you taking calls?" Cheryl's secretary's voice came through like a shot. They had an intercom system that went operational as soon as someone on the other end spoke. No phone on her end to pick up. No choice. When they wanted you, they wanted you.

"Yes?"

"The bank in Boston just called. It's not good news." Her secretary had a sixth sense about this. "Do you want me to try Standard-British now?" Good secretaries knew everything. Even the name of the next bank you had to call when the first one turned you down. "The Caymans are an hour ahead and maybe there's still someone there."

"Wait. I'll call you."

Now there would be no choice. Sam had wanted Standard-British all along, but he let her play her card first. "You want a U.S. bank on a Bob Marley deal? Try. See how far you get." She left her office once again, heading up the stairs. The mere fact that Sam wasn't physically present didn't mean he wasn't in. If the phones worked, he was in. During her Yones internship days he told her: "Deals move by the minute. I must know instantly what's going on. If not, you'll guarantee that I'll make a mistake. And it will be your fault." So before she made up her own mind she had to pass on bad news, even a hint of it. Cheryl looked for either of Sam's secretaries.

The senior secretary, Doris, was the first she found, and just as well. Pushing sixty, she was the tallest person on Sam's personal staff, dressing as a tall person should, accentuating her height, not ducking it. How she walked on those spike heels Cheryl was never able to figure out.

"Your face tells me Sam won't be happy," she said.

"Where is he?"

"To you?"

"To me."

"Somewhere south."

The two women looked at each other for a fraction of a second too long.

"Not good news, huh?" Doris said.

Cheryl gave up all pretense of a smile.

"Not fun," Cheryl answered.

"I didn't think so." Cheryl faked a distracted look and started to walk away. One step. Two. Three . . .

"Was there a message?" the tall woman called after her. It worked.

"I probably should talk to him."

Doris stood up to her full height as if looking down would enable her to see farther into Cheryl's head.

"You want to wait until he calls? Or do you want me to call him?"

"Whatever is best." Bring her inside, Cheryl thought. "The Boston bank is going to screw the Marley deal." Give her half the agenda. "I just feel it." It had taken Cheryl two years before she felt ready to use instinct in this business; that was when she realized instinct was what made it work. Sam had taught her that, and for all her life she would thank him.

"You'd better call him yourself. He's at the house in Miami." She didn't write the number down. Doris knew Cheryl had it. Secretaries know everything.

"Is he alone?"

"Billy went."

"And the missus?"

Doris didn't look up, but quickly found some paper to write a note on.

"She left this morning," Doris said absentmindedly. "She stopped here to get something out of his office and then drove to the airport."

"I see." Then Cheryl smiled. More cards picked up, Cheryl thought, proud of herself. They just keep rolling in. "If he calls, let him know I need to talk to him."

"Will you call him later?"

"I suppose I should."

Cheryl walked down to her office, put the pencil back between her teeth, and sat in her chair. Her feet went back up on the wastepaper basket, and her fingers, once again, started drumming on the top of the desk. So that's why the computer was on. The "missus," at the records for the second time, forgot to shut it off.

Mike's voice didn't resonate that night when they talked. It sounded crumpled to her, constricted, controlled. She questioned him this way and that, but Mike was as skillful at ducking questions as he was asking them. Finally, he said, "Cheryl, I can't tell you much more than you already know, and that's probably too much. I don't want you involved in this. If they get any idea, even an inkling, that I've told you anything I may know, they'll come after you. They'll put you where I'm at. If they can't get it out of me, they may come after you, just assuming I've told you." It hurt to say the next sentence. "Or they may assume you know on your own." They had rarely talked about her year with Sam. It hurt too much. But he had to get to her. "You had your own access to Sam."

"I remember," she said.

"Then get out of there. Please."

"What's that noise?" Cheryl asked.

"A bus went by."

"You're outside?"

"You're a small fish. They'll put you on a hook to get a big one."

"You're outside in a phone booth," she said, the alarm clear in her voice. "I'm coming down."

"Cheryl, no."

She heard the wail of a diesel horn coming from somewhere on his end of the line.

"You don't know what can unravel here. You can't even begin to guess."

"What makes you think so?"

Mike saw one flash picture of Sam and Cheryl. He didn't want to see any more. It felt like the ground was falling away.

"Get out of Sam's office. Don't come down here."

"Where are you?"

"There's an Interstate a few blocks west of the hotel."

"Sounds like you're in it."

"Cheryl, have you heard me? Stay in New York, but don't do anything more for Sam. Drop that Marley project right away. Sever the links."

"Mike, I can't. That's what I do. I earn a living. I can handle him. And Mike, since when are you the American legal system?" She tried to calm both of them, and tried not to attack. "The language in the subpoena is the beginning and the end of what they're going to ask you about. It limits . . ."

"How do you know that?" he cut in.

"You told me, in the car, on the way home from the airport. And I have friends who are lawyers."

"Maybe we both asked the wrong people." Then Mike's voice went flat and final. "I don't want to talk about it anymore," he said. She hesitated, but they went on to other things because Cheryl knew enough not to press, not when he was away, not when they couldn't hold each other.

20

AT TEN THE NEXT MORNING, TUESDAY, MIKE TOOK A CAB from his hotel in Coconut Grove to downtown Miami. He felt torn; he wanted Cheryl with him in spite of the danger. He asked the driver to let him off on the south side of the Miami River, just before downtown began. There wasn't much pep in the air, and Mike was afraid. He needed to walk, to do something, to look around.

He looked at his watch three times, but he still had a half hour to go. He crossed the bridge over the Miami River and watched it going from oily black to green, winding past the impounded drug boats, working its way north through downtown to somewhere past the railroad station. Then he walked up Biscayne Boulevard, past the bandshell, then north up Flagler Street in front of the old terminal of the S bus from Miami Beach, just where the magic shop used to be, but that was gone, too. Looking at the white paint and sun blinds made him think of the gauze the British wore over their sun helmets in Jerusalem, and the whole feeling was reinforced by the water and palm trees that were almost everywhere. The whole town had a look of having been built for hot, muggy weather, hot and muggy the way it used to be.

Finally, Mike stood across the street from the Post Office. Its pediments were newly painted, but some of the small iron balconies were rusted, someone having missed them completely. With the front doors propped open, the interior was losing whatever air-conditioning it had, and the refreshment truck parked outside was a magnet for those who worked inside. A garbage can clattered somewhere, but Mike kept his eyes straight ahead. He could hear occasional voices, talking or laughing, coming from the small park across the street, as some people finished coffee and walked back inside. Mike, as if looking for cover, went in with them.

He walked through the lobby past the mean faces of southern politicians reproduced in marble, and took the elevator to the second floor staff office of the U.S. Attorney. He gave his name to the receptionist. That was what Arlo had told him to do. "Give your name. That's all. If the girl behind the desk doesn't know what to do, she'll ask. Don't you say anything. It's all arranged."

Mike thought it was a little cloak-and-daggery, but he did as he was told, and fortunately, the right girl was behind the right desk at the right time and she said, "Oh, yes, Mr. uh . . . uh . . . Anker. Here is the key. It's on the third floor, second door from the end of the corridor. There are

175

two rows of windows. I hope we won't need too many yards of fabric." Mike smiled and thanked her. He thought of Sam repeating Saul Steinberg's Joe Levine story and wanted to laugh out loud. Saul was twenty-eight at the time and goes to see Joe after hours. Joe's all alone, can't imagine who this kid is, so instead of interrupting his phone call to the coast, all he says is "Fix the windows." Saul stands there. "Fix the windows." Same thing again. Finally, Joe hangs up. "Why aren't you fixing the windows?" "I'm not here to fix your windows. I'm here to buy your company."

Mike went up a floor and walked down a narrow hallway. He looked at linoleum floors, bulletin boards loaded with notices, and a big clock at the end of the hall, which clunked every time the minute hand moved. The corridor was empty for stretches, but near the center of the building there was a water fountain and a group of people standing around it, and Mike stepped around them. Those with briefcases, the lawyers, he guessed, made eye contact; the others looked at the floor and occasionally took a side glance to look for the exit signs.

He closed the door behind him and looked around the silent, low-ceilinged grand jury room. It was lit partially by sunlight, but mostly by humming overhead fluorescents. A judge's bench was nowhere in sight. Instead, there was the long table in front, the witness chair next to it, just as Arlo said, and two rows of twelve seats each, one row behind the other, the back row raised up. There were twenty-four chairs altogether, spread out, curving across the back of the room in a crescent.

He walked to the first row, heard the old floor creak under his step, and sat down in the first chair, pressing his body against it. It was wooden and it swiveled, contoured for the rump, but not effectively. By the end of the day, the jurors would be squirming. It would be worse after the stretch at lunchtime, so three-thirty would be just fine, Mike decided. They would want to get out and be quick with him.

Mike imagined voices; he conceived questions, the ones they would put to him:

"I take you back to the Nicollet Street warehouse, sir. Did Mr. Yones pay a bribe to receive a mortgage?

"After that, when the property was sold, did a percentage of the profit go back to the union official, the founder of the union, old man Wiser, who approved the mortgage?"

Mike moved slowly to the upper tier of chairs and sat in the third seat from the end. There were loud squeaks when he pulled up the paddle-shaped writing tray and flattened it across his lap. This wasn't the third grade and they wouldn't bang it up and down ten times a day. They would do it once and be through with it. He wouldn't have to listen to squeaks and bangs all day. He looked again across the witness chair to see if the sight lines changed much, and they didn't. He felt very warm.

He imagined the same voice, resonant, sounding almost like his own voice, coming up with more questions:

"After the Nicollet Avenue warehouse, and now I call your attention to 1960, did Mr. Yones . . ." And Mike thought of mahogany in the Philippines.

"And in 1964, did Mr. Yones . . ." And Mike thought of soft pine in the Panhandle of Florida, Arlo's introductions, Sam's click with the high gorum.

"And from 1972 on did Mr. Yones continue to offer foreign accounts to his investors so tax payments on timber profits, this time Florida timber, could be evaded? Taxes on hundreds of million dollars worth of taxable profits?"

Mike wasn't feeling well. He knew he could continue his study of the stage as long as he didn't picture himself in the witness chair.

He left the arc of jury chairs and moved over to try the prosecutor's seat, where this Spencer guy would sit, and then he walked up behind the long table in front and sat in the foreman's chair, just to get a bird's-eye view of the scene. Hmm, he thought, surveying the room from up front, I wouldn't mind being a judge, he said to himself, envying the power and sense of control he now needed so badly. But there wasn't a judge; just a layman with a title who took attendance.

Then Mike took the big step and sat alone, unprotected, in the witness chair. He imagined more questions.

"And isn't it true that if Mr. Yones didn't offer those secret accounts to his investors, they would ask for them?"

That question Mike would feel free to answer. Overjoyed to see those who disdain Sam Yones beg him to share the fruits of his evil. To watch, to see the process up close, the pleading smiles, the tightly grasped handshakes, to hear the words of secret gratitude, to see the whole play performed in the private theater. Maybe that was the flame that attracted the moth. Maybe it was the fascination of corrupting the self-righteous that propelled Sam; maybe it was the addiction to the show that made Mike, as Sam's innocent shadow, treat his own revulsion as uncertain. Maybe it was being inside, getting his nose in under the tent, seemingly risk-free, that induced his loyalty to a friend who had given him nothing so commonplace as food and shelter.

Mike realized, although he had thought of it before as the witness box, that there was no box around him at all. There was just a chair, exposed, placed on a raised platform a little broader than the chair itself, and no screen of any kind to hide the number of times a witness crossed and uncrossed his legs or a right knee jerked frantically up and down.

He looked toward the jurors' chairs, and in the empty room, as much to shut out the voices he was imagining as anything else, he said out loud, testing the sound of his voice, "Yes, that is correct."

The acoustics were lousy. Then he waited, judging the echo, and said, "No, it didn't happen that way at all." Then he said it again, "No, it didn't happen that way at all," trying to adjust the volume of his voice to compensate for three-thirty this afternoon, when the room would be full of people.

The Four Questions, Mike thought. On Passover they led up to freedom. These questions? Where would they lead?

Mike walked to the door, opened it, and turned out the light so that damn buzz went away, and realized that he was breathing hard.

21

DISHEVELED WAS THE KINDEST WORD MIKE COULD FIND FOR Spencer Pelcheck. He wore one of those putrid-green Brooks Brothers wash-and-wear suits, his tie was pulled down below his frayed collar, and he moved as if he had a swarm of bees circling his head. Papers poked out of the books he carried in his left hand, and he walked sort of pigeon-toed as he led them, at three-thirty sharp, into a small conference room, also on the third floor of the old Post Office building.

To call that cubicle a conference room was a joke. Tops, the conference room was no more than twelve feet square. It had no windows and was painted two tones of government green (one of which matched Spencer's suit), and in it was a desk with one chair behind it, another on the side, and a third in front. There was an air duct on the wall near the ceiling with a paper telltale waving from its grille, indicating that the system was on. It reminded Mike of grammar school, and somehow his memory jumping from there, Mike thought of two bells, recess; three bells, fire drill, and he had to make sure that he didn't smile.

Spencer's long hair blew in every which direction, and before he managed to arrange his armful of files, with place markers peeking out of Acco-bound documents, Mike thought the whole collection of papers was going to end up all over the floor. Spencer absentmindedly invited Mike and Arlo to sit down. He stacked his files before him, pushing his hair back from his forehead several times: It was obvious that he was hot, overheated, and harassed.

How did it happen that his future depended on a boy no older than Cheryl, Mike thought.

"You know," Arlo said, "we're here voluntarily."

Spencer shuffled his files, and then put his hand on a third. Without opening it, obviously knowing what was inside, the dumb-fumbler act faded quickly as he said, "I thought we sent you a subpoena."

Spencer turned his head toward Mike as he finished the sentence, but Mike was smart enough to say nothing.

"Spencer, a subpoena wasn't necessary." Arlo smiled. "We would have appeared without it."

"Yeah, you're probably right," Spencer said, hiding his sarcasm poorly.

"And we don't need immunity," Arlo said.

Mike sat back and watched and listened as Arlo and Spencer reeled each other out and reeled each other in. Small talk was the guise, but the testing and the temperature-taking couldn't be missed.

"We never asked for it, even on a limited basis."

Arlo wouldn't want him to have immunity. Sam wouldn't want him to have immunity. No inducement to tell all.

"Don't think that went unnoticed," Spencer said.

"There's something I should tell you," Arlo said.

Spencer gave him a cagey eye.

"There's some gossip on the street about your investigation and, of course, that will let us get to your informers. That'll dry you up."

". . . there's nothing on the street."

". . . there are leaks, but we're not complaining."

Mike wanted to turn a big trench coat collar up around his ears.

"Mike has had no notice that he's a target and you're not telling me that he's a target so we're the last guys in the world to go to Judge Hall and try to get the backup you used to get the judge to give you those subpoenas." Arlo took out a cigar and Spencer shook his head no. Arlo smiled and put the Davidoff back into its leather case. "We'll leave your sources alone."

Why and where were they digging? Mike wondered. And

how deep? Would Spencer's questions be the ones Mike had asked himself when he was alone in the grand jury room? That's what went through his mind: questions like daggers that could destroy.

"By the way," Spencer said, turning to Mike, "did I send you a Request to Produce Documents along with your subpoena?" Mike didn't move.

Arlo answered: "The document request had some ambiguities in it, but I asked Mike to bring everything he had anyway." He looked at Mike, rolling a pen cap in his mouth instead of a cigar. "You did do that for me, didn't you?"

"Yes, I did." He followed Arlo's signal.

"Do you have any objection to showing your documents to me now?" Spencer asked.

"None at all. That's why we're here," Arlo said.

They were working each other as experts, Mike realized, and for the first time he felt as others must have felt when he himself was doing a deal so fast they couldn't follow. He was as helpless as they must have been. If you ever wanted to see surgery outside of the operating room, here it was.

"Let me have that file, Mike, will you please?" Spencer said.

Mike caught on fast and smiled as Spencer called him by his first name. Good. That was good. He had an idea: Better to put the briefcase on the desk, open the flap, and let Spencer see everything rather than leave it on the floor and slyly reach down and pull out one file at a time. Mike pulled his briefcase up and placed it on Spencer's desk, although it took some maneuvering to find room among the clutter of papers already there. Arlo caught on to what Mike was doing and smiled. Mike made sure the flap was loose, and gently moved the entire briefcase, contents wide open, to Spencer's side of the table.

Spencer put his hand on the polished black case and took possession of it. Then he turned to Mike, knowing every second precisely what he was doing, and said, "You know what? I'd rather hear about it."

Yes, there was a trust in the Grand Cayman Islands, and yes, the Yones sons were the beneficiaries of that trust, and yes, Mike knew all of that and yes, he had disclosed it all (Mike tapped the briefcase at this point) and yes, Mike had favorable legal opinions from two major law firms who said what he was doing was okay (Mike tapped the briefcase again).

Spencer looked at this man, impressed. Mike Anker is smart, he decided, but he has no subtlety, no skill at evasion. If he is going to lie, he would lie, but the lie would be confined to the words. Approval was what Spencer felt, but that was not what he wanted to signal.

"Aren't you really saying," Spencer asked, "that money can magically find its way into the trust and you as trustee dole it out to the Yones family. Isn't that right? Sam Yones, your old buddy, stashes money overseas, then blows in your ear and out pops the cash. Isn't that what a man in your position, an old friend, normally does?"

"Hey, Spencer," Arlo said. "Lay off!"

Mike wanted to yell foul, but Spencer was also the judge. He played all the parts.

"You wanted your man to see me. I didn't ask to see you," Spencer said, looking at his watch. Mike knew exactly the meaning of the gesture: He would be in with the grand jury in less than twenty minutes.

"Okay. Maybe it was a mistake," Mike said. "Maybe I never should have done it." Mike began his answer without waiting for stage directions from Arlo. "Sam Yones and I go back a long way," Mike said, his heart pounding. "All we wanted to do was make good in New York. That's what we all wanted to do. We've known each other a long time. The years go on. We all change. I know I should have hit the brake pedal when he asked me to help for old times' sake, but I did it."

"Why?" Spencer asked, his tone completely altered, kinder, surprising Mike, easing his heartbeat. "You were the trustee for the sons of a best friend. Why are you so upset?"

Mike thought long and hard about Spencer's question,

which hung out there somewhere. Mike remembered Cheryl's words. "Since when are you the American legal system?"

"See what happens, Spencer—" Arlo interrupted, saving Mike, using the same drowsy laugh he used in the car on the way in from the airport, ". . . when I bring someone in to you unrehearsed? And without a thought of immunity?"

Mike snapped himself back to reality. He wondered why he hadn't been rehearsed. Worse, he wondered why he hadn't asked to be rehearsed. He wondered about immunity, why he hadn't jumped at it, no matter what he knew and what he didn't know, and why no one had sat him down and gone through a step-by-step primer on what immunity was, how it helped, and how he could get some. Instead, he got lectures on furniture, and the more he thought about what was going on, the less he liked it. In the meantime, the questioning went on.

"Did you ever get any money for what you did?"

"No."

"What did the Grand Caymans bank have?"

"I don't know. I was given a copy of the trust agreement. It's in there," Mike said, pointing to his opened briefcase.

"So you never got any money out of this deal at all?"

Mike felt a flush under his hair, and he knew it was something he shouldn't feel. He hadn't done anything wrong.

"No, that's not true," Mike said. "Sam gives a lot to the university, and my professorship is endowed by one of his foundations. I also received a loan from Sam when I went to graduate school" . . . his strong professor's voice was coming back. ". . . and then, for the trip we took to Europe in 1958 . . ."

"Do you remember how much that was?"

"No, but I checked it, and I put a sheet in the file"—Mike pointed to the briefcase—"showing the computation."

"I guess you were ready for me, huh?"

Mike shrugged.

"Do you remember how you were given the money for the trip?"

"What do you mean, how?" He looked to Arlo, who said nothing, and pointedly looked out the window.

"You know, cash? Check? Paper bag?"

Mike felt the flush come back and, goddammit, there was no reason for it. "No, I don't remember."

"Didn't you also check on how much money there was in the trust before you came down here? Or how it got there?"

"No, I didn't."

"Don't you think you should have?"

Mike looked once again at Arlo, who, despite the plea for intervention that Mike was silently sending, said nothing.

"I don't know. I guess I should have, but I didn't."

Spencer leaned back, knowing all faces were turned to him. "No, you shouldn't have. You had no need to."

Then Spencer looked as much to Arlo as he did to Mike. "It would not have looked good if you *had* checked."

It must be the route of fund flows that interested them. It wasn't so much what came through the pipe, it was where the pipe was and the fact that one existed. That was what Spencer wanted to get at. And that was fine. Mike had nothing to hide. There was nothing he knew. Directly. Of his own knowledge. All those other qualifiers.

Arlo scraped his chair on the linoleum floor as he pushed back from the table. The room seemed lighter to Mike, but that was an illusion. He had spent his career learning what the public rules were and then learning how people actually operated. That was how he got smart, on that day when he discovered the private rules, the guidelines jammed into the bottom drawers, the laws that weren't written anywhere but nevertheless were the ones everyone who became anyone lived by. Now he was in another world with its own set of invisible rules. He didn't know even the public rules here, much less the private ones. He didn't know even what questions to ask, or where or how or of whom to ask them. How ironic, he thought. Here he was, the consummate insider in his own world, good enough to even teach it. But he was totally at sea in the inside world of others. His freedom depended upon what they did, what they knew, which set of rules they operated under, and whether they were smart enough to know that there were at least two sets of those rules. In their world, he was a lost little boy. As a reminder of how lawyers could scare the hell out of any decent person, the last ten minutes would certainly do, Mike thought. He waited for the next salvo.

"Mike." Spencer Pelcheck turned to look directly at him. "If you had come down here with that same team of New York white-collar-crime lawyers that everyone else has been running in on me, I wouldn't have given you the time of day, much less this meeting. I know Arlo Shields, and I know you hired him because he was the only one you knew down here." Mike, down deep, now felt the tactic of keeping New York lawyers invisible was a good one, but that Arlo was still a question mark. "Just tell the grand jury what you told me. I would like them to see your files, also, if that's okay." Spencer looked to Arlo.

"Sure, that's fine."

"Is it okay if I keep your originals?" Spencer asked, tapping the briefcase that remained on the table. "I'll make copies for you in the next few days." Spencer's hand rested on Mike's briefcase with Mike's original documents inside which were about to disappear. Again Mike controlled himself and said nothing. He dared not. He was in the hands of strangers.

"Sure," Arlo said again, Mike thinking *sure* was his favorite word.

"Never mind. I've got enough to carry," Spencer said. "Mike, will you hang on to these and bring them into the grand jury room when you're called?" Spencer looked at his watch. Mike found himself wanting to say "sure," but he merely nodded his head.

"What will happen inside," Spencer continued, "and we'll start with you in a half hour or so, because we're running late and there's some things I have to do in there, is that I will ask you to take the witness stand, then the foreman will swear you in, and then I'll ask you if you brought any documents in response to my subpoena, and you'll give me your papers. You can keep the briefcase. It looks expensive," he said, smiling, and Mike laughed too hard. "Then I'll ask you pretty much what I just asked you, and then I'll ask the jury if they have any questions and you'll answer whatever questions they have. The whole thing shouldn't take ten minutes."

You could pour a tub full of salt on that one, Mike thought, his guard up again.

"Spencer, are you going to go into why he took on the job of trustee in the first place?" Arlo asked.

"You mean the why-would-a-man-in-his-position-do-such-a-dumb-thing question?"

"That's the question." Arlo toyed with his mustache, then abruptly took his hand away from his mouth. He wanted no body language that would tell Spencer he had anything to hide. "You know, Spencer, I didn't stop Mike on that one, and I didn't stop him when you asked him if he knew how the trust was funded. And I didn't rehearse him either."

"I could figure that much out on my own," Spencer said just as he turned to Mike. "It's okay, Mike. You can smile."

"At this moment," Mike said, smiling now, momentarily relieved, "I don't know what I can do."

"No, Professor," Spencer said, turning to Arlo. "I won't embarrass your man."

Arlo put his fountain pen cap back into his pocket, and Spencer nodded. Spencer stood up and Mike and Arlo pushed their chairs back and did the same. Spencer looked at his watch, and announced, "Well, we've got to go to work. Drop him off with the marshal. He can come out and get you if he needs you." Both Arlo and Mike nodded, and Spencer turned to Mike and said, "See you in a half hour or so," and Mike, as if he were leaving the baseball diamond in the school yard when he was ten, wanted to call back and say, See ya.

22

NO ONE HAD TAKEN THE TIME TO TELL MIKE THAT THERE was a back corridor leading to the grand jury room, and that there were numerous small waiting rooms off the narrow corridor so that witnesses could be kept in isolation. Nor did he pick up on the existence of a back door that led in and out of the grand jury room into the narrow hall. If he had not been unceremoniously dumped back there and left on his own, and he had spotted the extra door himself, he would not have become so unsettled when he saw Sam come out of it.

Mike saw him just at the moment they were through with him, with his fresh haircut, the same bright eyes like a bird and the same sharp, puckered mouth. The color of his flesh, however, not only his face, but his hands as well, was nearly white. Sam stood there, drained, in the center of the dark hall. There were no hands in the pockets and no jingling coins. He headed in the opposite direction, walking even farther away from Mike, and, as quickly as he had appeared, in another moment he would be gone.

If it weren't for Sam, Mike knew he would never have been there. Nor would he have finished school with an advanced degree, without which Edgar Stern never would have hired him. Nor would he have learned what he had learned, seen what he had seen, both the good and the evil. Nor, but for Sam first finding her, then breaking her heart, would he have Cheryl. There were reasons why Sam never made any friends, legions of stories about him, speeches of his pledging undying loyalty followed by spitting people out. Sam would take your eyeballs out before the sun set

187

on Friday night, but he would not so much as take a phone call on Yom Kippur even if it meant millions to him. He was dazzled by the kind of person he would never become, and it took only an accent like William Buckley's to get into his deals without an entrance fee. Guys rode him, made money off him, and you wondered as much about him as you did the elegant leeches he willingly let near him. Sam would cut any corner for them. Anything would be theirs for a few words sung in the right key. But you don't weigh the scales on friends.

"Sam!" Mike called out.

The beautifully tailored jacket was buttoned, his key chain concealed, and he looked more formal than usual, as if dressed for a school play. He quickly turned around, and then, seeing Mike, he looked as if the weight of the whole building were taken off his shoulders.

"The marshal ushers me in there, ushers me out. Got a personality like a funeral director." He walked toward Mike. "Stand at the door, look sad, and hand out yarmulkes . . ."

He tried his famous smile, but it came out all the wrong way.

He came up to where Mike was standing.

"Billy . . . he's downstairs. He's waiting . . ."

Sam held out his hand now, wanting to shake hands with Mike.

"I didn't want Billy to see me come out of there."

They shook hands and Sam wouldn't let go. Finally Mike put a hand on his shoulder in order to break his grip.

Mike walked him back through the labyrinth of corridors and waiting rooms and found them a corner of one of them.

"I don't know if you're supposed to be here with me," Mike said. "We're supposed to be isolated, but I wanted to—"

"I know. Thank you."

They sat and looked at each other. Then Sam took four quarters out of his pocket and started shuffling them around, between his fingers.

For the first big timber properties Sam had bought, Mike

had found equity money for him. Before there were any foreign accounts. And he found more at the last minute, making him a hero for having done so when American Financial backed out ten years ago. Mike didn't have to say no cute overseas accounts for his clients, don't even offer, they're not the type to ask. Sam knew that, and never allowed Mike's clients to be compromised. Trust was a big yet lovable burden to Mike. He let his students trust him. Sam too. Gordy as well. Cheryl got it all; others should start getting less.

"Are you here alone?" Sam asked, the coins silent now.

"Yes. You?"

"No. Liz is here."

"Cheryl wanted to come."

Sam took out a cigar. It shook in his hand, but he pretended it didn't.

"She's good for you, Mike."

"She's not my wife." Sam nodded.

But then the corners of Sam's mouth turned down. He looked around the room, sweeping it. He moved his head upward toward the air-conditioning duct, then sideways toward the lamp that sat on the table between them. Mike kept his blank expression, but he was thinking that Sam had seen too many spy movies. But maybe not. The government was certainly capable of bugging a room where witnesses waited to go before a grand jury.

"If I were only a lawyer or a doctor or a priest," Sam said, pointedly letting his words hang in the silent room.

Mike had referred to one kind of legal privilege with "she's not my wife" sending him a signal. Sam came back with three others: doctor, lawyer, priest. Their minds had touched: privilege. "I don't have any" was Mike's message. "Cheryl doesn't have any" was the message. "I understand" was the answer.

"They didn't get anything out of me," Sam said. He shook his head slowly. "I don't mind talking, but they're not getting anything for their fishing expedition. Fact or fiction."

Mike wanted a pen, a paper clip, or his own cigar to play with. Sam sounded casual, but his eyes were slits.

"But," Sam went on, winking once, then winking again, "it didn't make any difference. I didn't know anything anyway."

Sam *was* giving answers. "I don't mind talking." He was testifying, Sam was telling him. He was not withholding answers. *He was not refusing to answer.* He was *not* taking the Fifth Amendment. That was the first thing Sam was telling him. But there was more.

He was also telling him that when he did testify, he was telling the grand jury nothing. Words, maybe, but words that meant nothing. *Bubkes,* as Saul Steinberg might say. But now he wanted the same back. Testify, don't take the Fifth, but tell them nothing.

"How's Billy? How's Liz?" Mike asked.

"Fine. They're both fine." Sam nodded, his eyes opened fully again, gazing up at the light fixture. "I don't think I'm supposed to say what went on."

"I think you're right," Mike said.

"You going to stay down here long?" Sam asked.

"I don't know," Mike answered.

Strain. That's what had set in so suddenly. They sat not eighteen inches from each other, a table between their chairs, a lamp on it which Sam thought was bugged, and they sat in silence, concerned about discussing even airplane departure schedules. Neither one of them was used to this limitation in their freedom of speech. Mike studied Sam, hoping that his color would come back, wondering if he himself would look as pale when he finally finished.

Sam stood up, his jacket open, the key chain with the boys' golden pictures visible. "Mike, thanks for saying hello. I guess I ought to go. It's nice not to be tossed away."

Both for a moment had run out of lines.

Mike stood up and they shook hands, walking out of the minute waiting room together, surveying the empty back hall with all the doors opening off it. Mike watched Sam until he turned the corner and disappeared. Then he went back to the waiting room and picked up a magazine and tried to read but couldn't concentrate enough to get through a paragraph. He sat there as if he were waiting for a dentist who was running late, and wondered why he was so eager to get in.

Mike heard the door between the grand jury room and the corridor open, and then the door of his waiting room was flung open to its full width. Spencer Pelcheck stood there. "Mr. Witness, would you like to come in, please?" he said gently, motioning Mike through the passageway.

23

INSIDE, SPENCER TURNED HIMSELF INTO AN IMPOSING, fine-voiced Robert Stack.

"Ladies and gentlemen," he said, smiling, ushering Mike to the center of the room, "I have explained to you who our next witness is. I will ask our foreman to administer the oath and then ask our witness to take his chair." Spencer smiled again, too much.

Mike stood quietly, looking at the jury sitting in the swiveling classroom chairs. The older women must see Spencer as a son and the old guys see him as Eliot Ness. Fat chance any witness had that Spencer Pelcheck didn't like. In his putrid-green suit, he had them in the palm of his hand.

Spencer benevolently invited Mike to step forward, and Mike assumed his place on the witness stand. He did not sit. He looked around for a clerk or a bailiff or someone like that. But there was no official in the room except the foreman of the grand jury, a distinguished-looking forty-or-so-year-old wearing a too-tight double-breasted suit, probably from somewhere in South America. He now stood before Mike, a Bible in hand, inviting Mike to place his right hand on it and repeat, but without the Latin accent, "After me. 'I promise to tell the truth, the whole truth, and nothing but the truth.' " Mike said, "I do." Then there was only one other voice in the room; it was Spencer's, and it said, "Be seated."

Mike decided to concentrate on the juror at the end of the front row, the one who looked like Fats Waller and had his famous jumping eyebrows, and then work his way twelve chairs down and then back across nine chairs in the second row. He had the configuration of the room in mind; he would place the people quickly, and then concentrate on what was transpiring. But something was going wrong and he didn't know what it was. When he was young, like all boys, Mike expected to have an edge, to be a hero. Nothing was farther from his reach now.

Spencer asked him to state his occupation.

He noticed a woman in the back row with a furrowed, wrinkled face, her tiny eyes covered by puffy lids, scrutinizing him uneasily. Mike wondered if her eyes were always like that or if they were swollen from crying.

"Sir, will you tell us what you do? Your occupation?" Mike noticed, for some reason, that Spencer winced, then held his jaw. Poor guy has a toothache, Mike decided.

"I teach and I'm an investment banker," Mike answered, the silver in his hair gleaming under the fluorescent lights. Mike thought about the order in which he listed his professions and he realized which meant more to him.

The lady with the wrinkled face startled Mike by saying: "Will you speak up? I can't hear you."

"Of course, ma'am." Mike said investment banker louder this time.

This was like no courtroom he had ever seen before. No bailiffs, no clerks, no judge, no audience, no lawyer except the guy belonging to the other side, and jurors who talked. As and when they pleased.

The old lady mumbled something incomprehensible and then Mike saw that Spencer had walked to the other side of the room, away from him and away from the jury. He stood alone.

"A teacher," Spencer said. "Everybody knows what that is all about, but an investment banker?" Did he earn fees for introducing buyers to sellers? Did he earn fees for taking companies public? For taking them private? For raiding them? For finding them white knights to protect them from raiders? Mike meekly answered every question: yes, yes, yes. But he was never asked if he had ever worked with Sam Yones. Indeed, Spencer had not even mentioned Sam's name. Mike looked at him and no longer saw a tense young man with bees swarming around his head out to capture prey. Instead, he saw an easy, boyish face, using his innocent expression well, showing Mike great kindness. Too much kindness. Making it easy. Too easy.

"Oh," Spencer said, snapping his fingers, "I forgot to give my speech." The old lady with the puffy eyes laughed and Fats Waller rolled his eyes. Two serious-looking men in the back row, dressed for church, put their pens down and gave up their show of taking notes.

"The grand jury has been used since the time of Henry II in England, and . . ."

Mike watched a black man in the front row who looked like Beethoven. There were the same deep lines around his mouth and the same stern furrows in his forehead.

"So you see, Mr. Witness," Spencer said good-naturedly, "it is these citizens, here in front of you, who determine if there is probable cause for the government to make any citizen stand trial. It is not the government, but these citizens right here, who issue an indictment which is what starts a trial."

Mike didn't move, impressed by Spencer's deep-voiced history lesson which he probably copped from Arlo Shields's book.

Spencer stood quietly in front of the row of windows and the venetian blinds that covered them, some drawn up, some down. The sunlight coming through the slats flickered in the room. Then he left his place in front of the windows on the far side of the room and started to walk back toward the counsel table stacked with papers.

"Oh, yes, since no one here is accused of anything"—Spencer gave Mike a friendly look—"the history of the grand jury proceedings provides that neither you nor any other witness is in need of a lawyer, at least right here in the room." Spencer now moved closer to the jury. "Our witness's lawyer, Mr. Arlo Shields of Miami, Florida" . . . Spencer stopped long enough for Arlo's hometown to sink in, ". . . is outside should our guest feel the need to consult him."

Mike assumed the most benign expression he could manage, conscious of the break Spencer had just given him.

"Sir," Spencer said, focusing Mike's attention. "We know you are not a commercial banker, but perhaps you can help us understand how U.S. citizens open and operate bank accounts overseas."

Mike stiffened.

"I don't know that I can be of much help."

"Oh, by the way, do you have any accounts overseas that are in your name or are controlled by you?" It was the exact language printed on the IRS form. "Other than the trust account, that is?"

"No, sir, I do not."

"Actually, we didn't think so."

Mike fought to keep his jaw from dropping. He wanted to say something, but kept his mouth shut.

"I suppose," Spencer continued, "that the first thing you do if you want to open up an account overseas is call up a bank or go see them and ask them to do that for you." Mike was silent. "Does that make sense to you?"

"I really don't know. I've never done it."

Mike braced for the follow-up questions. They should have been, "You mean you have *no* idea how it's done? You mean you never asked? You mean Sam Yones never told you?" Mike knew those were the questions he would have asked if he were doing the asking.

But Spencer never asked those questions. Instead, he picked up his papers and put a large-hearted smile back on his face. Spencer was pushing him up to the edge, then intentionally letting him off, giving him a pass. Why? Mike wanted an answer fast, and he wasn't coming up with one.

"Well, if a person didn't know the name of a bank in a foreign country, could a person go to a phone book in New York, or here in Miami, and look up the local number of an overseas bank? Do you think you'd find local offices and phone numbers for the big ones? The ones in Panama? The ones in the Grand Caymans? The ones in Switzerland?"

Spencer addressed his questions more to the jury than to Mike. Mike looked at them. These people were more than awake. They were eager to know.

"The phone book is full of wonderful information," Spencer continued, "names which would bring profit to all of us." Beethoven laughed. Mike said nothing.

"If you open an account in Switzerland or one of those fancy places, don't they ask if you're an American citizen? And if you are, don't they insist that you sign a document pledging to comply with all the laws of the United States and report all deposits and income earned to the Internal Revenue Service?"

This time Spencer paused; he wasn't challenging; he seemed not to care if he got an answer.

Mike didn't want to say he didn't know. He'd have to think of another formulation. Then he found it.

"Mr. Pelcheck. Ladies and gentlemen, if I knew, I would be glad to tell you. It is true that as a teacher and an investment banker I have seen many unusual things, but, well—"

Spencer interrupted him.

"Sir, I believe you," he said.

Again Mike waited for the follow-up questions. The first one should have been "Was it ever done *for* you?" The second question should have been "Did you ever see anyone open a foreign bank account? Sam Yones, for example." But there were no such questions.

Spencer walked to the windows and looked out for a moment. Then he walked back toward his grand jury.

Another pass. Another hook not hung on.

"Ladies and gentlemen," Spencer said, "let me show you what one of those special IRS forms for reporting foreign bank accounts looks like."

Mike watched the young man with the messed hair in the putrid-green suit pass a blank IRS form around, letting each grand jury member glance at it, practically shoving it under the eyes of each of them, forcing them to concentrate where he wanted them to concentrate, not on him and, most important, not on Mike. He had focused them on something that meant nothing. Why? Mike wondered.

To show Mike something very clearly, that was why— to show that *he,* Spencer Pelcheck, had the power to hang Mike out over the edge and that he and he alone had the power to pull him back. Mike was impressed and afraid. He looked at Spencer, the court reporter pounding at her machine, the grand jury sitting in a broad arc across the room and then at the corners of the room in what was now the afternoon light.

"Well," Spencer said, looking at his watch, "I guess that's it for the day." He turned to Mike. "Thank you, sir, thank you very much. If we need you, we'll be in touch again. I'm sure you'll be in town for a day or so." Mike stood as Spencer walked toward the witness stand, and Spencer escorted him out as he had escorted him in. As they reached the door, Spencer put his arm around Mike's shoulder for the whole grand jury to see, all twenty-three of them, and said to Mike, "You see how easy it was? I promised you ten minutes and that's all it took. Talk to you later." And out of hearing of the jury, he said, "Thanks, Mike."

A sense of uneasiness came over him. He felt vulnerable, like a three-legged animal in the wild.

PART FOUR

24

SAM HAD GONE HOME EXHAUSTED. HE LEANED BACK IN HIS leather wing chair in the tower that rose above his home on Bay Road in Miami Beach. He knew sitting on leather in Miami heat would not be the most sensible thing to do, but he had to have that chair. It had belonged to J. P. Morgan, and putting his *tuchas* where J. P. had put his *tuchas* meant something. He would have bought his toilet if he could have found it.

He counted the windows of his study that looked out over the rooftops of the adjacent homes, and he could see all the way across Indian Creek to the Atlantic Ocean. His study was higher than any building for blocks around, probably for miles, because the city of Miami Beach no longer issued permits to build residential towers. His tower was five stories high, one room square, like the slim structure of a church in a Renaissance town, with large windows on top, slits lower down, and red tile on the small roof. Morgan himself might have been in this room at the top of this tower. Rockefeller was, for sure, because this home was built by Carl Graham Fisher, Rockefeller's partner in Standard Oil, the owner of the Indianapolis Speedway and the man who developed Miami Beach before World War I. Fisher was the man who brought in the machines that sucked up the sand and turned a swamp into "America's playground." Then he built this Italian-style villa with stucco walls, arcaded loggias, and interior courtyards, and put his study at the top of a bell tower you could reach only by taking an elevator, the ascent or descent of which only Carl Graham Fisher, and now only Sam, controlled. There were no stairs. When you got up there, you either did the deal each wanted you to do or you found your way out, through a window.

Sam knew Liz wasn't crazy about the place. Too many dark rooms with high ceilings and feeble light; too much dusk for her. She liked the sunlight, so he built her a solarium that looked out over Biscayne Bay on the ground floor adjacent to the pool, and there, with sliding glass walls to admit the sea breeze, is where she spent most of her time. He walked over to the windows on the side of his tower that faced the bay and looked down through the glass ceiling of the conservatory at Liz sitting below.

The unused phone was at her side, an unread book was in her lap, and she had no interest in the bowl of fruit one of the maids had brought out. She had opened the wall of French doors that led out to the pool and seemed to be just sitting there, staring out. She had not unpacked; the maids had. But she had brought her photographs with her, those of Sam, Billy and, more than ever now, Matt, and had placed them in their bedroom. There were other pictures of all of them around, but she always took her own, in her favorite frames. She never liked Sam's house in Miami. She liked her own in Sands Point. She never liked the weather here, too much humidity, and she didn't like the people.

Liz was not the kind of person to keep all this to herself, but, in the beginning, she had expressed her likes and dislikes to him in such a way that made him believe that anything he did was okay.

"What do you think about a house in Miami?" he had asked.

"Oh, that's fine," she had answered.

"What do you think about remodeling Sands Point?"

"Oh, that's fine," she had answered.

Her signal for disapproval was subtle. If she hated what you proposed, thought it was the worst idea she had ever heard, she would say quietly, "That's an idea," and leave it at that. Leave it to him.

Sam sat down again in the Morgan leather chair. Matt was raised in her way, he thought, but along with Matt's politeness went a Jewish peasant mind that crackled. He looked across his desk and the picture of Matt on it. Billy's picture was behind him, on the credenza, but Matt was in front of him, where he would always see into the eyes of the son who could not only have succeeded him but gone light-years beyond him. Billy would never achieve parity. Sam had that figured out since Billy was six. Not so Matt. And there was never an ounce of jealousy against him that Sam was conscious of feeling, not at all like it was with Billy. Just love for a father and pride. And now no more.

There was no need for things to have turned out like this, Sam thought. If only he had done this. If only he had not done that. So many "if onlys" had been going through his mind since he had received the call about Matt and they had raced down to the hospital in that dinky town near the tree farms, near Trump's big white buildings. It was all he had thought of as they flew down on the chartered plane, all he thought of as he stood alone with his son, the tubes going in and out of every part of him, watching Matt trying to breathe, touching his skin, feeling it grow colder, praying for his son's chest to move when it stopped.

It had always hurt him that it had taken him so long to cry for his own father. It had taken less time for his mother, but on both occasions, never in public. He looked again at the picture of his smiling son in a silver frame on a desk near a leather chair that J. P. Morgan sat on, and was thankful he was alone. He took the silver picture of his second son and held it to his chest. No, he would not cry, even though no one would surprise him at the top of his tower.

He put the picture back on his desk, walked to his window, and looked down once again through the glass ceiling of the conservatory below, but this time the chaise was empty. Liz had gone.

Suddenly, he felt tired, and he lay down on the white cotton sofa and put his feet up. Not a long nap, he thought. Just a short one, and when he woke up he would feel better, and his mind would be clearer and he would start to do what he needed to do about Mike's newfound ability to threaten.

Sam adjusted the pillows behind his head and under his shoulders and sighed loudly. Never make a decision until you have to, he thought, a rule he had taught himself years ago. Get the facts first.

Some facts were in. He did not need to figure out what Mike knew. Mike knew it all. It had felt good to let him know, and Mike's praise and attention had become almost addictive. That Mike would tell anyone what he knew was, until now, unthinkable. That was also a fact. Mike had known and loved him so well, he knew Mike could feel in his own flesh the pain any telling would bring. And it had been reciprocal, the affection, the respect. It had been Mike who had rescued his own father, pulling him out of bankruptcy, quitting school to manage that tragedy, and still earning A's when he came back. It had been Mike who earned honors instead of selling cheap air fares to Europe or running laundry routes, Mike whom he could top only by blindly buying a white elephant of a warehouse on Nicollet Avenue, back-dating documents to do it, getting lucky, not smarter. He knew another fact: Mike was the only one who could have taken Liz. He had told the to-a-captain-are-you-a-captain story too many times. Maybe, he thought, Mike was the captain to whom he needed to be a captain. Mike was his other self, his better self. He had never placed so much confidence in any one man. But that was then, before all this. That was the final fact. He just didn't want to come to terms with it. He thought again about a short nap to make him feel less sad, but he knew the sadness would not go away.

He'd start doing what he needed to do in fifteen minutes,

when he woke up. Not now. He set his mind and closed his eyes.

Like a Swiss railroad, fifteen minutes later he was up, wide awake. His father used to go in to his office on Saturday, "just to get the mail." He did the same thing every day he was away from New York with his fax, his modem, and his phone, all tied directly to the top floors of the Segram Building. Sometimes when he called the office he was easygoing, sometimes demanding. He was always intense. This time he sensed it was the end of an era.

"What's this I hear that the Boston bank turned us down?"

Sam's voice came through Cheryl's phone loud and clear. The projections for the Bob Marley poster reissue had been put to bed over an hour before, and she had waited for Sam to call the office from Miami, hoping he would say, Okay, switch me to Cheryl.

"Sam, how's the weather?" she asked, wanting him to talk. She hadn't heard enough yet to take his temperature, to find out if the irritation she detected in his voice was because he had been through the grand jury or because they had been through him.

"I'm not finished yet, if that's what you want to know." Cheryl smiled.

"That's what I want to know," she said.

"That's all?" Sam asked.

"No."

"Mike's not finished yet either," Sam said.

Cheryl bit her tongue and kept silent, asking no questions, making no sound, a technique Sam himself had taught her.

"He went in as I was going out."

She waited, still silent. Did Sam see him? Did they talk? How did he look?

"So Boston?" Sam asked.

She would get no more.

"Yes . . . ," she paused. ". . . Boston. Actually, they've said no."

He was pleased with Cheryl's work on the Marley deal. He had been pleased with her since he first saw her.

"Now what do you propose?"

"We'll go down to Standard-British in the Caymans. It's where you wanted to take this loan in the first place."

Sam smiled with satisfaction.

"The Grand Caymans is an hour ahead of Miami. You can call now," he said.

"You think someone is still at work?" She knew what he thought of British Colonial working hours.

"Try to get through. Now, is that all you need from me?" Sam asked pleasantly.

Caught off-guard, Cheryl didn't know how to answer.

"You don't have anything else to tell me?" He was pushing. "You're not missing anything?"

"Do you have anything more to tell me?"

Sam had taught her the value of silence, and she waited. She counted, a thousand and one, a thousand and two, prepared to outwait him. Finally he talked, but about the wrong subject.

"Look, about the Marley deal . . ." He went back over it, analyzed, and angled, summarizing the deal in a way that showed how he won his fortune. She became so engrossed that for a moment she forgot about Mike, and that frightened her. She saw herself six years before, young and proud to have been selected and jittery at meeting Sam Yones himself. He had been kind, offered her one of the Mies van der Rohe chairs, spoke softly and with pride of having come so far on his own, without family help, without sponsors, and he wanted her to take the same pride in whatever she became, for when it came right down to it, what you become is up to you.

And when a phone call had interrupted her first interview with him, he apologized but took the call because he said he had to. He talked for ten minutes and she learned so much just listening, she felt giddy. She could only dream how much the next year would teach her. She didn't know it then, but the rules the women of her people had learned to live by for five thousand years were going to fail her.

". . . So what you'll do is easy," Sam went on. "Boston wants out? Invite them out. Call the man back. Whatever he tells you, tell him you understand and you're glad to have had the chance to have him look at it. Talk goy to him."

Cheryl listened to a tired but excited man, harsh and warm at the same time, she thought, but always accurate.

"Then you'll bank the deal in the Caymans. Go there if you have to." He paused deliberately. "Now, Cheryl, did I let you have your try?"

"Yes, Sam."

"Did I stand in your way?"

"No."

"Good. Now do it my way."

She could imagine his smile, the lines of late middle age leaving his face, looking twenty again, his eyes beaming "winner."

"Sam, is Mike in trouble?"

"Anyone in front of a grand jury is in trouble. Even if they're not in trouble, they're in trouble."

"I didn't understand a word you said."

"You didn't ask if I was in trouble. You should ask that question first. It's only polite."

"You've got Liz to ask that."

Now the repartee stopped. There was a long silence.

"I know I have Liz," Sam said softly. "No, Cheryl. I'm not in trouble. Neither is Mike. These days the measure of your importance is how many grand jury subpoenas you get." His voice came across Cheryl's phone more brightly now. "They ask you a question. You give them an answer." Cheryl could almost hear Sam debate with himself, and then it was out in the open. "Didn't Mike tell you all about it?"

"Of course he did, before he went down there. But I'm asking now."

"Why are you asking me? Not him?"

"Because I'm talking to you first. I'm sure he'll tell me when he can."

"I'm sure he will."

There was a very short pause. Sam now knew something he hadn't known before. That was a plus. It was five o'clock in the afternoon and Mike had not called to ease her mind, which meant that he had been in the grand jury room since three-thirty. Or worse—maybe he had been excused to go into a private office to make a private deal.

"Let me know how he's doing," Sam said. "I know he's here, but I'm only protecting him if we don't talk. You know I care."

25

LIZ HAD LEFT THE HOUSE AS SOON AS SHE CAUGHT SIGHT of Sam staring down on her from his tower. She could barely deal with him. She could sit with him at a Passover table, imagining Matt's voice singing with the rest, celebrating the festivals of the people she had turned Matt over to, to be consumed by Sam. If Mike had not been there easing her pain, she could not have stayed. She was running and she knew it. She didn't want to know, yet she knew she had to know if Sam's doings and Matt's death had anything to do with each other.

It was early, but she left anyway, giving herself plenty of time to drive aimlessly around to calm down before she went over to pick up Billy. He wasn't staying at the house. He had not done so in years, and as much as she wanted him to this trip, she had not asked. The request would only have hurt them both. It was sunny and warm as she drove up Collins Avenue along the ocean almost up to Bal Harbor and back. It had seemed as though life had used up all its good news. She had not wanted to be here alone with Sam. Rage made her voice jump, made it sound uneven, and that he took to mean fear. But in a way, the fear was the other way around. He respected her, she knew, even feared her and certainly loved her. Of all of that she was sure. She felt again her anger toward him. It was the rage of childhood, hot, terrified, and aching with disappointment. Suddenly she found that she had driven herself halfway across town, that she was on a deserted street, somewhere on La Gorce Island, and it was time.

She picked up Billy and now stood near him at the check-in counter at Miami International Airport. First class line or not, the crowds were pushing and noisy, and neither Liz nor Billy was comfortable. Billy had just had his passport checked and his seat assigned, window, not on the bulkhead, Cayman Air, flight sixty-one, for the 480-mile flight due south to Georgetown, Grand Cayman. Sam always thought it was better to fly commercial. To do anything else would call attention. As a further safeguard, Billy had nothing in his briefcase that could mean anything to anyone. He had it all in his head.

"Mom, you could have dropped me off. For that matter, I could have taken a cab."

"There was nothing for me to do. I was just sitting around the house with your father staring down at me."

"Be glad that you weren't anywhere else, in that courthouse, for example."

"They won't even bother with me."

"I'm glad."

Liz smiled and took her son's hand. They stood still for a moment in the middle of the crowd. She remembered when she was expecting Billy, her first, when her eye was no longer drawn to babies in buggies; when she knew that her own child would be superior. With his first allowance, Billy, at six, bought her a bunch of violets which she held to her cheek before putting in the best vase in the house. She had that same look of love on her face now.

"You want to know why he wants me to go there, don't you." Liz looked away, down the long line of ticket counters. "He told me not to tell you."

"Billy, that's the same story I heard before. I don't want to hear that anymore."

"Mom, I can't tell you."

She looked back at Billy. "I'm a wife."

"But there's no mother-son privilege."

"There should be."

It was noisy, the airport was packed, but Billy was careful to look around and then keep his voice down.

"Mom, I have instructions to make transfers on our accounts down there."

She knew there were accounts—that much she never hid from herself.

"Billy, do you know enough not to hurt yourself?"

"Mom, don't. He tells me do it, you tell me don't."

How much did Billy talk to Matt? Did they talk at all? A lot? About Sam? His business? About her? What she knew? What she chose not to know? She had never asked those questions either.

Liz took Billy's hand, turned his wrist to look at his watch, and said, "We've got time." They walked together, Liz leading, to the door to the private club for VIPs, where Billy took over. He dropped her hand and took hold of her arm, pretending to steer her toward the reception desk, pretending to be a man. She liked it; he was still touching her, connected. They signed in, "William Yones and guest, one," and he guided his mother, who for an instant allowed herself to feel his strength as real, to a table circled by three comfortable chairs far away from the door, near the giant window, the planes, in their various sizes, visible across the horizon.

"It's the same accounts we've had for years, the same ones they're asking us about."

Her eyes avoided his, and she tried to be logical, to keep her emotions managed.

"Does Dad think you should change anything around in those accounts while they're asking you about them?"

"That's what I asked him."

"And what did he say?"

"What does he ever say to me?"

"Billy, I hate it when you're bitter."

"What did you do about it when Matt was around?"

Liz's eyes filled. "Billy, don't. If anyone has been on your side, it's been me."

"He hates it that I look like him." Billy straightened. "I want to leave him, Mom. There's a lot of places I can work. If he wants me under his thumb, I can work for Uncle Mike. They're almost the same thumb."

"No, Billy, they're not," Liz said, looking away.

"Then maybe I'd have a chance to make more of myself. I'm thirty in two years. Who will I ever be?"

"You don't have to work for a living, Billy. Your father has given you that gift." Liz looked out the window at a taxiing plane.

"As long as we do what he wants. He's not the same. I've never seen him like this before."

"I haven't either."

"I'm scared of him. Matt was never frightened of him, even when he was a kid. I'd cower when Dad walked in and Matt would run up to him. I'd hide behind you. I'm still doing it. What kind of pair do we make, Mom? Who are you hiding behind? I wish you had married Uncle Mike."

"Billy, stop it. I love your father."

"But you didn't always."

"In no marriage do people love each other always." Liz put her long fingers to her silvery-blond hair. "If it's most of the time, you're lucky. The bad times you get over because the past tells you there's more good to come."

"Do you believe that, Mom? Do you believe that still?"

Billy took his mother's arm, and together they walked toward the wall of windows with all the planes parked below, standing ready at the various gates.

They rode out to the satellite in the people-mover and watched as one of the three-car trains poked its nose out of the tunnel to cross the bridge from the main terminal to the international departure lounge, where they stood.

"Mom, do you like it that Dad keeps secrets from you?"

"Billy, he always has. There are some things I ask about, some things I don't."

"You paint yourself like the Japanese wife who saw her husband's butcher shop for the first time after forty-five years of marriage."

She was amazed that she had a laugh left in her.

Billy tried to look into his mother's eyes to see how she really felt. He could not remember this ever happening before, his mother talking to him like this. Maybe she talked to Matt this way. He wondered for a moment. No, he doubted that. It was true that Matt was more like her in some ways, physically for sure, almost too pretty. Billy had thought so many times that if you're pretty, you like your youth, you like to look good while you're young. But if you're just regular, or if you look like your father and that father happens to be Sam Yones, then no one notices you when you're young. There are no distractions then, no time wasted attempting to look good, because you can't. The only thing you want to do is get through your youth as fast as you can so you can get to a time where maybe it will be better. That is, Billy thought, if your own father doesn't prevent it.

"Billy, sweetheart, the last thing I am is a Japanese wife."

"They're calling the flight."

"I know. I heard it. Come on. I'll walk with you."

"Mom, I'm not going to Timbuktu. I'll be back tomorrow." He turned to kiss her, and then she asked, "It's about the trust, isn't it?"

"Mom . . ."

There was something in his mother's eyes that made him stop, want to tell the truth, but instead of telling the true purpose of his trip, he said, "Yes, it's about the trust."

"Your uncle Mike is the trustee."

"How do *you* know that?" They stood still in the strong light of the terminal.

"I'm learning a lot of things, sweetheart." She touched his arm gently. "In the car, on the way home from Matt's funeral, you wanted me to ask Dad why Matt had that accident."

"I was angry, Mom. I didn't mean anything . . ." Billy's mind tumbled.

Her hand on his arm tightened.

"I never wanted Matt to go. I begged your father."

"And me? It was okay for me? For me to do his work?"

"Oh, no, son," Liz said, hardly able to keep the tears from her voice. "I didn't want you to go either." It was like a dark shadow moving up and down in her life, and finally, she formed the words. "Somehow it's never been my place. It all meant so much to Dad, for him to know it all and for no one else to interfere." She remembered a day when they had all been happy.

She looked into Billy's eyes. " 'For what shall it profit a man, if he gain the whole world and lose his own soul,' " she said.

"That's the New Testament."

"You think I forgot it all?"

Liz watched the plane taxi on its way to the Grand Caymans until the tail became very small as it merged with all the others on the darkening runways. She boarded the people-mover, and when the train rose out of the tunnel onto the overhead stretch of track, the sun was just about gone and the sky was turning pink and the tall windows turned reflective. Scanning her face in the glass, she saw not the fine skin, the strong, well-spaced teeth, her blond hair tinged with silver which she had no intention of touching up, but instead she saw her secret possession, her body that men loved. Not many men had slept with her, but her body was part of what made her believe, at least in the company of men, that "I am the best." In that way, if not in others, she was Sam's match and mate, because he, too, with his imperfect body but with his extraordinary mind could also say "I am the best."

She still loved her shape, and remembered that when other girls drank vanilla malts, she contentedly did other things, such as wash her cashmere sweaters, which girls of the fifties treasured as billboards for breasts, if they had the right kind. She had the right kind. She knew she had. So did Mike, who was first of the few.

She couldn't say how or when Mike disappeared. He just wasn't there one day. Unable to take on two of life's tasks at one time, a career and a woman. Then she thought of Sam, who was there, who never left, and then she thought of Matt, who, like Mike, just wasn't there one day.

The narrow train, lightly loaded with a few people, went below ground again, heading into the terminal and as Liz lost her reflection against the sky, she realized that Billy was now over the ocean on some errand for Sam. This was too close a parallel; she couldn't lose another son. No, never. She would muster the strength of her grandmother who saved the family farm.

26

SPENCER WATCHED THE SAME SUNSET FROM BYRON'S OFFICE on the thirty-eighth floor of the Federal Building. The door was still ajar and the brass plate reading THE UNITED STATES ATTORNEY was still visible until Byron walked to the door and closed it. Spencer had just come from the grand jury room in the old Post Office building. He wouldn't have the whole transcript of Mike Anker's testimony for a day or two, but he couldn't wait to report. He was on a roll.

"Do you think he understands that you can drop him off the edge?" Byron asked, walking to his desk.

"I opened the subject of overseas accounts but gave him no follow-ups. You could see him waiting for the other shoe to drop, but I gave him nothing. I did it three times, just to make sure." Spencer handed him two pages of the transcript of Mike's grand jury appearance that he'd had the court reporter type up.

Bryon read the transcript excerpts slowly, knowing that it was only words, that he would have to imagine facial expressions, time gaps, jerking knees, to get the full picture.

"How about the Yones testimony?" Byron asked.

"You've seen that. There's nothing there."

"I know, but are you going to use it? The way I told you to use it?"

Spencer looked at him, feeling trapped. "I'll see Mike Anker tonight, but only with his lawyer present."

Byron nodded. "All right. I understand that. Then what?"

"He's been on the stand once. He's at risk. He's uncertain. He doesn't know what's next. He'll be worse by the ten o'clock news." There was some acting needed here, Spencer knew that. "He'll have a visit from me tonight. My strategy is to see if I can get him to perform. There's one other thing I want to do."

"And that is?"

Spencer wanted to back off, to buy time for himself to see what kind of person he was turning himself into. He felt surrounded by bloodthirsty crowds cheering him on. He didn't like himself.

"If you can get Mike Anker to break, you can get to Sam Yones. Plus, there's a second way to get to Sam Yones. One additional person will do the same thing, get you to Sam Yones, directly or indirectly."

"Stop selling."

"The girlfriend."

"Whose?"

"Both of them. First she was Sam's mistress. Now she's with Mike Anker. It was in the IRS personal report. Cheryl Stone."

"What do you want to do?" Byron asked.

"Nothing threatening. Just talk to her."

Spencer looked at the huge chart on rollers that took a big man to move. It was on an angle, a maze of boxes,

lines, and arrows in grease pen, the organizational chart of
Sam Yones' holding companies. Byron had this in his private office. He was paying attention, his hands-on U.S.
Attorney boss. Too hands-on.

"You want a subpoena? You'll have to go to Judge Hall
to get it," Byron said. "But, of course, I'll sign the request.
Now, if you want."

Spencer sat down, watching the planes criss-crossing the
darkening skies over Miami. "No, I'll wait on that. I'll hold
it back, but we'll let her know we can drop a subpoena on
her whenever we want. She's smart enough to know that
can leak. Wouldn't help her career much, would it?"

"Tough guy, huh?"

Spencer looked across the room at the chart. It wasn't
easy to follow because no one company owned one hundred percent of another. There were pieces of companies
owned by pieces of companies, and the boxes on the side,
outlined in red, controlled the controlling companies. It
looked like a printed circuit. Then he made sure he found
Byron's eyes, and locked in on them.

"That's right," Spencer said sadly. "Too tough sometimes." Did he have to be such a killer? For who? For
Potsy? So his father off in Ohio would be proud of him?
He was turning into the kind of person he used to hate.
"All I want to do is send the FBI up there to talk to her.
And then I'm going to squeeze him tighter. Are you happy
now?"

"I'm not suggesting you do anything illegal, and you
know it. Sam Yones did not assert his constitutional privilege against self-incrimination." Spencer nodded. "He did
testify that he knew how foreign accounts were opened,
that he had one in the Grand Caymans, and that he was
sorry that his son became so upset that he didn't tell us
right off when Davis asked him. He said the whole thing
was a mistake. Then he got cocky. It happens with all those
guys when you put a microphone in front of their face."

Spencer nodded. You could sense it from the transcript,
even though you weren't there.

"He went too far. He bragged. He said a lot of 'guys,'

his word, had accounts overseas. We're just asking if Mike Anker is one of those guys. You'll ask the question in a different way. It's just a different kind of probe."

"Yeah. Like backing an aircraft carrier up his ass."

"That's vivid. Look, just tell him Sam Yones testified to a secret account in his name. Shade it a little bit."

"I don't know." Spencer shook his head. "He'll never buy it. He'll never believe Sam dragged in his name."

"Try it. If it doesn't work, okay. Then we've got the other one, the girl. Spencer, you're doing quite a job."

"On who? On me?" He looked away. "Why am I doing all of this? To buy a condo?"

"Not at all. You're doing this because you're a lawyer, and a good one, and this is what the process permits. You're not a judge. You're an advocate."

"Never love your job. It'll never love you back."

"We'll send someone out from the New York office. We'll invite her to cooperate. Easy. Just come in to talk. But we'll send them to her home. You know where she lives?"

"It's Mike Anker's address."

Spencer saw Byron's eyes light up and he could see *judgeship* flash on and off.

27

AFTER SPENCER ESCORTED HIM FROM THE GRAND JURY ROOM, Mike felt drained. He had understood, even admired Spencer's technique of leading the witness to the edge, then pulling the punch. But as he made his way from the building, he could only wonder what was coming next.

The little breeze there was only ruffled the tops of the

palm trees and the air, although fresher than inside, still smelled like some old aunt's attic. He was in the taxi halfway back to the Grand Bay Hotel at Coconut Grove before he realized that Arlo had not been waiting for him. Mike called as soon as he reached the hotel, using the pay phone in the lobby before he picked up his key. The place was full of potted palms and smelled of fresh dirt. He didn't reach Arlo. He had not been at his office at the law school since yesterday.

Mike went back outside, sat on the terrace in a huge wicker chair, and made a monstrous effort to clear his mind of Miami. He thought of Cheryl, remembering her pretty face, her brave brown eyes, and the first time he saw her after it was over between Sam and her, that time at the bookstore. He couldn't figure out where she began and where that crazy coat she wore ended. She was so wrapped up in brown fur that he couldn't tell which was hair and which was fur. But the face, in the middle of all that brown, the face was shining. He remembered thinking back then how hard it was to be alone, and that it didn't get easier as you grew older. We don't let ourselves get older easily. We let ourselves get older in a tough way.

He wondered about Cheryl and Sam, how she ever got away. She never *would* have gotten away if Sam hadn't called it off. She would have stayed, intoxicated, just as he knew he had become intoxicated over the years. She got out because Sam said it was over. He had thought he needed Sam's blessing before he began seeing Cheryl, and he remembered Sam's surprise at being asked, "Do you mind? Don't say it's okay if it's not." He remembered his own surprise when Sam answered, "No two people, you and Cheryl, have ever been so kind to me. Love each other, it would make me happy."

A waiter came by to see if he wanted a drink. Mike shook his head, checked his watch, got to his feet, and headed for the reception desk. Maybe he would call Arlo again tonight. Maybe not until tomorrow. Hangovers, the few he had had in his life, felt better than this; his eyes were tender and he wanted to wear his sunglasses indoors.

He was exhausted and alone and he thought it best to stay that way.

There was only one message at the desk, and Mike unfolded it on the way up in the elevator. The message read:

Cheryl called. Just wanted you to know that she was with you. She's out now. She'll call again later. Taken by operator two at four-thirty.

Maybe it was the kind of day he'd had, or maybe it was because he was feeling alone, fighting an avalanche at every turn, but now his need for her increased. Mike walked into his room and took off his suitcoat and tie. Sometimes he felt this hole inside him and it hurt so much and he couldn't do anything to make it go away. He closed the doors leading out to the terrace, and the noise of traffic faded.

Mike liked the early memories of Cheryl best, the first fresh days with him when they walked together through the front garden of Sam's house in the country. He liked it when the summer smelled of bug spray and fresh mint in the gin. He liked it when they would pass the edge of the lawn and look out over Long Island Sound. He liked when they were in his prize convertible, with horn sounding, coming nearer and nearer, a pale green car of splendid speed, great elegance, a car that would sweep up Sam's drive like a bird and stand there throbbing. He could see Cheryl in her white cotton sundress from Haiti, hear the voices of other people's children coming and going, the boys racing down the slope to see the great green 1947 Roadmaster. He liked the way she held his hand all the time, then as now. He liked the way Cheryl had laughed as he made mouth noises that mimicked the engine and when, during the rush of fast driving, he had told her, "I think I was meant to be a burglar."

He got his shirt off before he fell back on the bed. The lights were on, the sun was still out, barely, and the drapes were still open, the airplanes heading this way and that. He was asleep in a few moments.

He was too tired to have any dreams, but if he did, they were gone the minute the phone woke him.

"Mike, it's Arlo. How did things go?"

"Yes . . . no . . . that's okay . . ." he said, sitting up, confused, searching for words. He shook his head. "Arlo, I was taking a nap."

"Spencer told me you did fine."

Mike got off the bed and tried to walk around a little, but the phone cord wasn't long enough. He sat on the edge of the bed. "Did he say anything else?"

"Well, I didn't see him. He just called me."

"He just called you?"

"Yes," Arlo said. "I missed you. My fault. I'm sorry about that. And then I missed Spencer. He called me here at the house." Arlo stopped and Mike said nothing, still forcing himself awake, his eyes now wide open. He knew there was no further explanation coming, and he didn't like it. "He said you were a great help to him, explaining things to his grand jury, and he wants to know if we'll help him some more. He wants to know if he can get together with us tonight."

"Tonight? What is this? What's wrong with tomorrow?"

"He's got a dentist appointment."

"Tonight?" Mike asked for the second time.

"Do you want to do it?" Arlo asked.

"What does he want?"

"It depends how long you want to stay in Miami. He just thought you might want to get back to New York, so he offered tonight," Arlo said, not giving him a direct answer.

"Is this normal?"

"Of course not."

Mike was still trying to wake himself up. His sleep had been too deep; he was still groggy. He opened the doors and watched a jet head out of Miami, its wing lights blinking, timing its beat to a channel marker in the bay. He shook his head again. "Arlo, what's this all about?"

"Tell me what went on there this afternoon and maybe I can help."

Now Mike was fully awake. If they're such buddies and they talked and I did so fine, why doesn't Arlo know what I did so fine at? Try the truth. See what he does.

"First Spencer asks me leading questions about overseas accounts and doesn't care whether I answer or not. He pushes me three times to the brink, but doesn't push me over. He could have made me point to Sam and look like a conspirator, or worse. But he didn't."

"Tell you what, Mike, I'm not too far from the hotel. I'll stop over and then we'll decide whether to see Spencer later."

Now Mike knew there was trouble.

"It's late. Is he going to see us at midnight?"

"Mike, where's your watch?"

"On the night table."

"Look at it."

It was only six-thirty.

Leaving the airport, Liz remembered that her mother used to parade her around without clothes when she was a child. What bothered her was that she liked it. She heard her grandmother's voice saying, "She's growing up. Don't let her do that."

She drove the Lincoln out of the airport, using the surface roads, not the expressway that would take her back into Miami Beach to Sam's tower on Bay Road. Instead, she drove out 36th Street to the Palmetto Expressway, which wasn't an expressway at all, just a wide four-lane highway with motels and car rental agencies on the margins. Sam liked Miami because it was serious business for him, the banking capital of Central and South America, yet she saw only the silly side, a glass wall at one end of the swimming pool at the Eden Roc so you could sit at the bar and watch women with varicose veins make fools of themselves underwater. Not her.

She looked out and reflected how Latin the city had become over the years. As many signs on 36th Street in Spanish as in English, the balance even more to the Spanish side as she turned into Palmetto. She would really be in the heart of it when she turned east down Calle Ocho, 8th Street, past the Dade County Auditorium, and in sight of the Orange Bowl on the way to Coconut Grove. She had only to make two phone calls to find Mike: the old Biltmore out in Coral Gables or the Grand Bay, which would have been his choice if all he wanted to do was get in and out fast.

After a lot of talking thirty-two years ago, what Mike had called an *assessment,* he stopped seeing her. After that he went back to spending most of his time in his room in the attic that he rented from Mrs. Fisher on Gilman Street, only three blocks from campus. He had filled his refrigerator and started, once again, to study with all his might and watch the eaves so he wouldn't bump his head as he took his underwear out of the dresser first thing in the morning. She had come to visit once, but it wasn't the same. The furniture, the bed, and the banged up dresser were the same, but she didn't feel the same way about him. As Sam had put it in a different context twenty years later, "The clock struck thirteen. You couldn't trust what came after and what came before."

That wasn't the way Mike had put it in his *assessment.* "I have to be somebody. I have to have a place to stand. If I have no place, how do I make a place for you?"

Not easy for him to say, Liz remembered thinking at the time, and the truth was she didn't want to go through life without a place to stand, a worthwhile place. Sam had the same worry but much more confidence, so that concern didn't cripple him, not with her. It was the energy in Sam, then and now, that she found electric. No one would tread on him and therefore not on her. And she was, well, "worshipped" would be too strong a word, but it was a little like watching the faces when her mother paraded her around nude.

She turned down Dixie Highway and had second thoughts, ready to make a U-turn two blocks from the hotel, but she decided that if she had come this far, she would go the whole distance.

It was all different now, ever since Matt died. The whole

world, that is. In his last moments he had wanted his father. Okay, that's the way it was. She didn't love him less. He was her Matt as well as Sam's, and if you asked the world who he belonged to, they would say Matt was Liz's son, just look. But "you had to start with where you're at," another of Sam's sayings. And Liz knew she could not lose Billy. If the world thought that Jewish mothers had a monopoly on how to do it, she thought, watch out.

Seeing Mike was linked to saving Billy. Was it really, she asked herself? Should she be ashamed of needing Mike? Or of recognizing that "people can be right for the wrong reasons," another of Sam's sayings, from more speeches before more microphones.

The doorman thought she was smiling at him, and as she passed through the revolving doors, she could feel her step was strong, as she liked it to be. She felt eyes turn in the lobby to look at her. "Who is that handsome woman crossing the lobby?" they were asking.

"Mr. Anker," Liz said, standing at the reception desk.

"Of course, ma'am," the young desk clerk said, smiling. He reached for his phone. "Mr. Anker's room, please." He smiled while he waited to be connected to announce her. Then the smile faded.

"Sorry, ma'am, they can't find it. But I know he's here. Let me just look through these." He pulled copies of messages kept at the desk, duplicates of those which were sent upstairs to the rooms, and started sorting through them. "Yes, ma'am, we have it here. The operator must have been spelling it wrong. I'll connect you now."

He left the message on the desk and Liz read it upside down, another trick Sam had taught her. "Cheryl called . . ." was all she picked up.

"May I have your name, please, ma'am?"

His voice seemed to come from far away.

"It's not important," she said.

"But, ma'am . . ."

28

SPENCER WAS AT THE DOOR OF MIKE'S HOTEL ROOM TEN MIN-
utes later. Arlo had arrived only minutes before him, and
something in Arlo's face gave Mike the clue that his just-
in-time no-time-to-talk arrival was intentional. Maybe it
was the way Arlo jumped up to answer a knock on a door
to a room that didn't belong to him. Arlo tried to talk about
Spencer's toothache but Spencer was having none of it. He
wanted to get down to business right away.

"Arlo, I'm going to break some rules because I like you
and because you don't bullshit me."

"That's right. I don't."

"Sam Yones went on just before Mike . . ."

Spencer looked at Mike to see if there was a reaction.
Mike knew enough to look like a piece of furniture. Someday, Mike thought, he would tell Spencer that two doors
to a grand jury room, plus an open corridor between them
and the witness waiting rooms was pretty dumb, but not
now.

Spencer couldn't figure out why Mike's face showed no
emotion. ". . . And he had very interesting things to say."
He continued to provoke, looking Mike in the eye. Puzzled,
he waited for Mike to react, but it was Arlo who
commented.

"Such as?" asked Arlo.

Spencer started to smile, but then he grabbed his jaw.
"This goddamned tooth." No one said anything and Spencer rubbed his jaw. Then Spencer decided to do his head-
scratching number. "First Sam Yones testifies that our
friend Mike here is one of his oldest and dearest friends."

Scratch. Scratch. Spencer smiled and patted Mike's shoulder. "Sam's telling me that you were a limited partner in one of his timber partnerships that was sold."

"That's true," Mike said, deciding to answer. "I bought my interest years ago, paid cash, received cash when we sold. I told you that."

"I'm not sure we understand," Arlo said, butting in. For once Mike was satisfied with Arlo's performance.

"But that part of what Sam said is not the important part," Spencer said, being as careful with the setup as he could.

Mike forced himself to sit still. His eyes roved and finally found a blue blinking marker light out in the channel.

"He says a lot of guys had secret accounts down there, that a lot of guys never paid taxes on those accounts. How about your profits? Your secret account? The one Sam talks about." Spencer had been careful, more so than Byron would have wanted him to be. He had chosen his words. But would that excuse him? In his own heart?

Mike looked at Arlo, and again there was no signal. Mike had no choice but to wing it.

"I don't believe it."

"You don't believe what?" Spencer said. "That you have a secret account or that he said it?"

Mike drew himself up. "Neither one." Center stage, and he hated it. "Who supposedly paid me money I never paid tax on? And where did I supposedly put it?"

"Let's take your last question first. Standard-British Bank, Grand Caymans."

"I don't have an account there," Mike said, waiting for no instructions from anyone. "I don't have an account overseas anywhere."

"Why not?" Spencer asked. "Sam says . . ."

"Why should I? I never needed one. I never made my money that way."

Arlo, finally finding his voice, asked Spencer, "Do you believe what Sam Yones tells you? If indeed he told you that? I'm not hearing an account number in this so-called Grand Caymans bank. I'm not hearing amounts. I'm not hearing you've changed your mind and my man here is a target."

"It depends," Spencer said, still watching Mike. "You want him to be a target? Keep this up."

Spencer walked over to the sofa, holding his jaw. He had gone too far. He pushed a few pillows over to the other side of the sofa, sat down, shoved a magazine over to the place on the glass table where he wanted to lay his feet, and then put his feet up.

"How do you make your money?"

"Mike, you don't have to answer that," Arlo said.

"How do you make your money?" Spencer asked again, shifting his body, but not much.

"I'll tell him," Mike said. Then he turned to Spencer. "I don't have any problem telling you."

Mike walked over to the sofa, pushed the pillows farther over, clearing a place for himself, and sat down next to Spencer, up close.

"I make a decent amount of money. I told you that this afternoon. And I'll tell you that on oath if you want."

"I know full well what you do," Spencer said, hardly ignoring how close he was to Mike, not needing space to provoke.

Mike went on, ignoring Spencer's needling. "Stern, Anker has its own money in each deal. If it is a buy, our money is in; if it's a sale, we bought in a long time ago. We're partners with a company, we're partners with the management."

"And who are *your* partners?" Spencer asked. "Who invests with Stern, Anker?"

"Banks, insurance companies, the finest universities in the United States of America."

"How about your other investors? The *individuals*, not the institutions. Are there any?"

"Sure," Mike said, wanting to get up and move to the other side of the room.

"And who are *they?*"

It was one of those questions that gathers in the slack and shoots the spear forward.

"You know I can't tell you that."

"So Sam was right," Spencer said, hating himself for being such a little prick.

"I wish I could tell you more," Mike began, eyeing Arlo, looking for him to jump in, "but Spencer . . ." It was the first time Mike called him by his first name, but no negative signals came from him. "I'm not a lawyer, but I know enough to know that since the names of our investors are not a matter of public record, I simply couldn't tell you who they are without their permission."

"Don't you at least have to register the names of the limited partners that invest with you? Just their names?" Spencer said, pressing.

"Of course we do. But the investors don't use their own names as the names registered as limited partners. They hold their investment in the names of nominees. There's nothing sinister about that. It's the same way that people who own stock hold it in the name of their brokers, in street name."

"Just the way a lot of accounts overseas are held, if you believe Sam Yones"—Spencer shot a look at Arlo—"which I do. Is there an account there for your man?" Spencer turned back to Mike. *"Is* there one there for *you?"*

"The trust account. I've told you that."

"But a personal one? 'Like all the rest of the guys.' The words came right out of Sam Yones's mouth, your old buddy."

Spencer was getting ready to cap his attack by dropping Cheryl's name, to threaten her involvement, but caught himself in time. "I don't want to hurt you. I need your help." His tone had changed completely.

"I think you'd better let us take time to talk privately, Spencer," Arlo said, finally opening up his mouth.

Spencer stood up. "Sure, take all the time you need. I'll be in my office tomorrow." Spencer looked directly at Mike. "Will you be in town?"

"You asked me to stay in town. You told me that this afternoon."

"I'll call you," Arlo said to Spencer. "What time will

you be in?" Arlo had moved Spencer to the doorway of Mike's room.

"As soon as I get back from the dentist. Probably before lunch. But there's no rush."

"You're right," Arlo said. "There's no rush."

Cheryl had watched the ten o'clock news and now walked aimlessly around Mike's apartment, looking now and then across Central Park, doubting she'd ever get Mike to move to the west side, even to the Dakota, so they could start fresh together, have a home that belonged to both of them.

Jewish-mother instinct number one: Get on a plane and go down there.

The kid isn't doing well in school. Get out of that apron, put on your coat, and storm down to the schoolhouse, grab that teacher by the throat and scream, "What do you mean my Mike got an A-minus?"

Sit on that instinct for a while, Cheryl told herself. She went to the bedroom, the one room she felt she shared. Not always, but in the last year she had finally come to believe it was truly theirs.

She had promised herself a year ago to give him two more weeks or she'd move out. And he had met her deadline, just under the wire, telling her one night: "Cher, I'm not going to fight you anymore. I want you and I want you here. There'll be two steps forward and one step back, then three forward and two back. Nothing is ever an even trajectory," he had said. "It doesn't make any difference that we want it smooth. Nothing is that way." But she still wanted to get married. He did, too. She felt that.

Jewish-mother instinct number two: Think of what he needs, not what you need.

Devotion didn't mean giving up your rights, she told herself. It didn't mean being a second-class citizen. Cheryl kicked off her shoes and lay down on their bed. It didn't mean giving any less than he would give if the situation were reversed. She felt herself smiling for the first time in an hour. Maybe the best Jewish mothers are men.

Then the smile faded.

The reverse of the Jewish mother was Liz. Her rule: Leave those you love alone. Then they come to you. No wonder Mike stayed single for her all those years. No wonder Liz liked it that he did. It was the first time she had let herself understand that Liz had as much at stake in Mike remaining single as she used to have. Cheryl turned to the window and shivered. They both needed to keep the option of each other open. Even if it was a low-likelihood option, Cheryl told herself as she sat on the edge of the bed, her feet dangling.

How hard it had been for her that first year. The permanent guest in a home, there on sufferance. She'd feel settled some days, on a tightrope on others, depending not on her but on his moods, thoughts that crossed his mind that had nothing to do with her. Sometimes she thought she would have been better off if Liz and Mike had actually carried on up until last Tuesday. Then they would have gotten it out of their systems and would have seen each other grow older firsthand. None of this out-of-the-clouds fantasy from thirty years ago. That was harder to fight, especially with the two of them in Miami.

Cheryl realized she had violated her last Jewish-mother edict. She had been thinking of herself, not Mike. But she wanted Mike and she was best for Mike, and that made his interests and hers the same. If their interests were the same, why weren't they together? Cheryl pushed herself off the edge of their bed and walked to the window.

She thought she heard a buzz on the intercom in the front of the apartment, but she wasn't sure.

And then she felt the cold again. It would be so easy to battle Liz if she were a superficial opposite, and that's all, a tall, blond, hot-bodied, not-too-swift shiksa. But the contrast was more subtle than that, and sometimes Cheryl didn't think there was a contrast at all, just a difference in age. Liz is loyal and standing by, something Cheryl was not doing because she wasn't there in Miami. With Mike.

The intercom buzzed clearly this time, and Cheryl walked to the front of the apartment.

She'd have to strike a balance. Get down to Miami but give Mike a choice. Make it seem like it was on her way to or back from somewhere. Cheryl had decided it a long time ago. Long-distance romances suck.

"Ms. Stone?" came the doorman's voice through the intercom phone.

"Yes?"

"Two gentlemen to see you. They're from the FBI. Excuse me for ringing, but they showed me their identification and said it was important."

"It's the middle of the night!"

"I'm sorry, ma'am. They told me to ring."

"It's all right, Dwayne," Cheryl said, suddenly very tired, knowing she had no choice. "I understand. Tell them to come up."

Arlo closed the door to Mike's hotel room, and when he turned around, Mike was about to pick up the phone.

"Who are you calling?"

"Cheryl."

"Don't. That's just what he wants you to do. I haven't seen Sam Yones' testimony. I won't even be allowed to see it. I don't know how they're shading it. Or even misrepresenting it, just to see what you'll do. Who you'll go to. Who you'll implicate. And then they'll go there, too. This is an investigative grand jury. Is that what you want?"

Mike still had the phone in his hand.

"You want something to eat?" Mike asked. "I'm ordering eggs and bacon. I didn't have any dinner."

"A drink's all I feel like. I won't be staying much longer."

"Change your mind." It was an order.

Mike called the order down to room service. Then he turned off the air conditioner, saying he hated that thing, and suggested they talk on the terrace.

Arlo followed Mike outside and they sat across from each other. The sounds of the traffic on Brickell Avenue beat up into the terrace. Mike leaned over the railing to examine the street, then turned back to the lawyer.

"Arlo, what the fuck is going on here?"

Arlo hesitated. "Mike, I told you."

"What was that man doing over here tonight?"

"I told you."

"You told me?" Mike's eyes became clouded.

"Let me be more accurate," Arlo said.

"Yes, do be more accurate."

"It's not that I don't know, Mike. I'm not sure."

"What's your guess?"

Mike put a hard edge in his voice as much to provoke Arlo as to camouflage his own fears.

"They wanted you to bite, to believe Sam had pulled you into this."

"Why would he do that? Why would he throw forty years out the window like that?"

"It sounds like part of you believes he might. May I ask you why?"

Mike slowed down. "These whys are coming across like a broken record. I don't know. Maybe to deflect the attack away from him, to send them scurrying after a new target. Maybe that's why he'd say I had a personal account."

"Mike, it makes no sense. If you were hurt by him, you'd have nothing to lose. But he depends on your friendship."

"How do you know that?"

Mike crossed his leg, hitting the top of the table with his knee. It might have stunned him, but it didn't throw his thoughts off.

Mike watched Arlo and listened to the slightest change in the wind moving palms outside on the terrace. From habit, he had taken to watching Arlo's hands, thin, with veins showing, but tan, too tan, and now appearing just a bit nervous. Men are afraid of intuition, Mike believed. They think that only women should intuit, but that's the most important factor in any deal, how you feel about someone. He remembered the time when he was much younger. Edgar had yanked him out of a meeting and asked him if he wasn't being too personal about a deal. "You bet I am," Mike had said. "I don't like that guy and I like his lawyer less." Edgar had smiled, and said he agreed. Mike had learned.

"And I'll tell you something else," Arlo said without answering the question. "I don't think Spencer knows what he's fishing for." Mike looked warily at Arlo.

"What am I supposed to do about that?"

At that point the doorbell rang and the room service waiter wheeled in a cart. "Where would you gentlemen like to eat?"

"Out here is fine," Mike answered, and they sat silently while the waiter set up the table, looking at the lights of the MacArthur Causeway which connected Miami to the south end of Miami Beach. Mike counted the islands strung along the MacArthur Causeway and when he came to island number six, he knew that was Palm Island and he spotted the house, still lit up after all these years, that was once the winter home of Al Capone.

"Is that all, gentlemen?"

"Yes, thank you," Mike said, signing the check.

"Thank you, sir." The waiter left. They watched the door close, and then they turned back to each other.

"Tell me, Arlo, how long has it been since you've seen Sam Yones?" Mike had carefully designed the question, hoping for a telltale response.

"At the reunion in Washington," Arlo answered, looking at Mike directly. There was no hesitation or hint of concealment. "Don't you remember?"

Sure he remembered. Mike took Cheryl to the White House. To introduce her to the President in the Oval Office, to have the President call him Mike and then turn to Cheryl and say, "He's a fine man," and to hear Cheryl say "Yes, Mr. President. I know." He remembered the smile spreading across her face as she said that.

He tried hard to get his mind back on the track. He was not trained to cross-examine, and if he thought he could outwit the trial-practice professor who had written the book, he knew he was nuts. So he got off the scent. He had one regret. He had been wrong to ask about Sam. He had telegraphed his thinking.

"Didn't they do the eggs right?" Arlo asked.

"They're fine," Mike answered. "Sure you won't change your mind?"

"No, Mike, I'm okay."

"So what do you think?" Arlo asked, almost too eager. "Do you think you're being set up? Do you think it's the government? Or do you really think, after all these years, that it's Sam?"

Mike paused to look at his watch, not answering.

"I guess you ought to stay here a few more days," Arlo said. "I don't know when we'll get this over with, but I think being willing to stay will help. You won't look rushed. Never go into a meeting when you have to look at your watch."

Mike recognized the Sam Yones adage. He walked Arlo to the door and thanked him for his time as he left. No more lawyers, Mike thought. He was better off on his own.

"Gentlemen," Cheryl said to the two men who sat opposite her in Mike's living room, "I don't know if I can talk to you people or not." They looked like FBI agents were supposed to look, she thought, cookie-cutter neat, small ties, just back from the barber.

"The FBI is assisting in a grand jury investigation involving Samuel Yones. Do you know him?"

"Yes."

"He is a target of the investigation and we would like to make an appointment to talk with you about him, or if you like we would be glad to put some questions to you now. We are not here under any court order. There has been, as of yet, no subpoena issued for your appearance before the grand jury in Miami and frankly, we're not from there but they have asked us to help out. They think you can help, as a voluntary matter, if you'd be willing to do so. Of course, you can have a lawyer with you if you like, and we will be available at any time in the very near future to meet with you, alone or with counsel. Which would probably be much easier than a subpoena. Or if you like, as long as we're here, we can talk now. It won't take long, and we'd be grateful.''

"I haven't worked for Mr. Yones in years, although I'm an independent consultant on a particular transaction right now. Everybody knows that."

"May I put my coat down here? Ms. Stone?"

The tall one looked like he was getting comfortable. Cheryl didn't want that, but she couldn't force him to keep his overcoat on his lap. She wasn't going to offer to hang it up or get them coffee. That would be worse.

He put his coat aside and looked at her appraisingly. "We have received instructions from Miami to interview Mr. Yones's former mistresses, and to start with you before we go on to the others." Their eyes met, and they stared at each other as if they were alone in the room.

Mike undressed, leaving on his shorts. He went back out to the terrace, sat down, and put his bare feet up on the table. He looked out past Miami Beach, toward where he thought Cuba would be. He had never been there, but had always wanted to go.

He sat outside for over an hour, simply staring out to sea. Just doing nothing. If this was what happened when your life was about to fall apart, maybe it wasn't all bad.

He thought of Sam with his flat hair and his uneasy eyes. Spencer would not have lied about Sam's testimony. The stenographic record would surely back Spencer up. What, by contrast, backed Sam up? Forty years. That was all.

There was no way Mike could make the stories agree, or even slide by each other. No way. No passings in the night.

It's nothing new to lie, Mike thought. We all do it. That's how he had talked himself out of Liz. He had to wait until he was wealthy enough, on his feet, worthy. A lie. The truth? He was afraid he would never be any of those things. He just didn't have the balls to say to himself, "I'm the best" and take her. Sam had the balls and he took her. He was the winner.

Mike decided to wait up for another half hour or so, still wanting so much to hear Cheryl's voice. He was thankful he had the self-control to stay away from the phone, to keep her out of their reach, away from all that was going on down here. Then he went to bed thinking that Cheryl was safe, a thousand miles away.

29

"GENTLEMEN . . ." CHERYL SAID TO THE FBI MEN SITTING on her sofa in the middle of the night. She stood up, and, well mannered as they were, they followed suit. "I will have to consult with my lawyer. I'm sure you understand that this is no indication that I intend to be anything but cooperative, but, under the circumstances . . ."

"We certainly understand," the tall one said. "We're sorry to have disturbed you."

"Just doing your job," Cheryl said, walking them toward the door, keeping it ajar until she saw the elevator door close with them behind it.

Cheryl listened as the phone rang twice before Ruth Seigel, counselor at law, picked up her receiver.

"What the hell is going on in this country?" Cheryl was almost shouting. "In the middle of the night . . ." And she told the story. "Ruth, what do I do?"

"You do nothing. You let them serve you with a subpoena."

"I have their cards." She gave Ruth the names and numbers.

"Oh sure, they want to talk to you, but they're much more interested in something else."

"What's that?"

"They want you to get on the phone and call Mike, tell

him what happened. Scare the shit out of him. Get him to give them whatever it is they want of him in order to protect you."

"So they're betting on my doing what I have to do?" Cheryl said, resignation heavy in her voice.

"You can always not tell him," Counselor Ruth Seigel suggested.

30

SAM HAD SPENT THE LAST HALF HOUR, FROM NINE TO NINE-thirty, going through the evening papers, hoping no news of the grand jury had hit the street. He finished the *Miami Herald,* then handed it to Liz, just to make sure he hadn't missed anything. The *Miami News* and the *Miami Law Bulletin* followed. Dutifully, after he finished each section, without looking he passed it to her. She read it, folded it, and added it to the pile on the floor next to the sofa. All in silence. Once, Liz cleared her throat and Sam looked up, startled, fearful she had found something. She realized she enjoyed having this power over him: the ability to frighten him by announcing his exposure in the newspapers. He read every line, every page, as if his name might be hidden in a Toyota ad. She had stopped rereading after him some time back.

They sat in the living room overlooking the sea on one side, the inner courtyard on the other. The television set was on, but no one was watching and the sound was so low neither was aware of it. They had eaten dinner outside and used the sunset as a reason not to talk.

"All right," he said with a sigh. "Nothing so far. Not

today anyway. I don't understand politicians. Why no leak? What does Byron Varner want?''

"Who?"

"The U.S. Attorney."

"That kid you're complaining about?"

"His boss. He was halfway on the federal bench but the president pulled his name."

"If anyone can put his name back on again, you can," Liz said.

He looked at her. "I've never heard you say that before. I mean quite that blunt."

"You've never been before a grand jury before," she said.

Billy's prayer, I wish you had married Uncle Mike, rang in her ears. But of course things had not gone that way. Sam knew about Mike, even back then. He was across the street in his Studebaker all night, parked within sight of Mike's room on Gilman Street the night she stayed there.

She could see him, squatting down in the driver's seat, trying not to be seen, thinking that if he were invisible, his car, painted four different colors of yellow, would be invisible also.

"Didn't you think I'd see you there?" she had said to him. They were in a back booth at Rennebohm's Drugstore, a block from campus. Nat King Cole was singing "Unforgettable" and she remembered playing with the jukebox control unit, flipping the small metal-trimmed selector boards, trying to find something to do with her hands.

"If you wanted to be there with Mike," Sam said, "then that's where you should have been. That's your choice. I wouldn't have done that. I wouldn't have done something else, either. I wouldn't have made a move on a woman my best friend was in love with. Never."

"In love with?" Liz asked.

"That's a surprise to you?"

"I guess not."

Sam brushed his crew cut, and his eyes were hard. "You guess? Let me tell you something. You either know what you want in this life or you don't. If you don't know, you don't even have a chance."

"In love with?" Liz said, proud that she could ignore his determination, but impressed by it beyond belief.

"Yes, in love with. And I'll tell you again. I would never make a move on a girl Mike was dating, much less in love with."

"You have an advantage, Sam," Liz said. "I love the way you press it."

That was the only time she remembered Sam being the slightest bit jealous of Mike, ever speaking ill of him, comparing himself to Mike, painting Mike as the lesser person. He made comparisons only later, when he was rich and forty and should no longer have cared. Not comparisons with Mike, but with others. It started when people beyond his reach came into his life, needing him. Only then did he compare himself and set out to equal them, to reach what he saw as the heights. And she? Did she stop him? Slow him down? Ask him to look beyond the dulled patina he coveted? Help him see how they saw him? No. None of it. Leaving him, Matt, Billy, and even herself to benefit. But at what price?

"Put me down for the Miami newspapers tomorrow," she said.

"You like doing this?"

"It's easy to spot your name. It's my name, too," she said.

"You're on edge again," he said. "I've been watching you since you came home."

Mike was here in Miami, just across the water, and if she looked carefully and counted the buildings south from downtown she could spot the Grand Bay Hotel. Palm trees, soft air. They were like the couple on the balcony in *Private Lives,* listening to "Someday I'll Find You," loving each other again after marrying the wrong person.

She looked once again at Sam, and realized she was glad that she had dutifully signed the tax returns where it said "spouse" and kept her questions to herself. To start interfering in his business was to assail the image that she had of him, and she had nothing to put in its place. But her boys, her sons. What had her willingness to stay out of it cost them? She would pay her own price for the sins of silence, of acquiescence. She had read his newspapers, eaten his dinner, and controlled her body throughout all of it. To make sure that he would see no movement, receive no clue to how hard it had become, being in a room with him.

The first week after Matt died, even while looking at Sam it was Matt she kept seeing, and she wanted to keep seeing him instead of Sam's face, his voice. It was hard during that time to see even Billy, God help her, because he looked so much like Sam. Awake was when she had the problem being with Sam, not asleep in bed, which is what she thought she would have been afraid of. Maybe because it was dark in there and she didn't have to see him. Or hear him. His voice and his face in the light in the confines of handcrafted stucco walls, tile floors, and coffered ceilings comprised the trap. She would do what she could do to pretend the trap was not there. She had heard of people with cancer who attacked it by studying it, reading the medical books, looking at diagrams. Her way of attacking her own cancer was to involve herself in computers and programs and passwords. But the quest had not paid off. Not yet. But it still might, because Sam had brought his laptop and his modem, and before it was over she would tap into the secrets he thought he had hidden from her.

"I'm trying to see you in a different light," she said, telling him the truth for the first time in days, smiling as she spoke.

He put his feet up on the coffee table. "Why?"

Then she realized that his face was shiny from shaving. When had he shaved? Just before dinner, while she was at the airport? More important, why? Was he going out?

"Why what?"

"Why are you seeing me in a new light?" He tried to sound jaunty.

She smiled again, but in a different way now, all feeling

gone. "Because you've shaved so smoothly," she said. "It makes you look younger."

"I gather you took it in your head to make a lightning trip to the airport this afternoon."

"I gave Billy a lift. Didn't I tell you? I can't remember."

He had the sharpest face alive when he was deciding whether to believe someone.

"Did you come straight home?"

"Where would I go, Sam? To visit all the friends I've made in this town?"

She looked inside herself for just one safe room. In the midst of the castles Sam had built for them in two cities, suddenly, at this time of her life, she felt not a square inch belonged to her that didn't belong also to him, that he gave her, that he paid for.

"But if you're going out, I might as well go for a drive, too," she said.

"I had no intention of going out. I just thought I'd feel better if I cleaned up and shaved." The television set was still on, the sound barely audible. She had nothing more to say anyway.

"You think it hurts any less because we're in Miami?" he asked, not moving.

He reached out and turned the television off, leaving the room dead silent.

"I'm only going out for a ride," she said.

Then she took a gamble.

"Come along if you like."

She watched his face color, and then he closed his eyes and she saw tears come out from between the lids.

"To do what?" he said quietly. "Watch?"

Where did she ever get this screwball notion of a 1940s marriage, perfect down to the Servel refrigerator, where two people wanted to be with each other only and never left each other for long, never for the night. Who started it? She wondered, looking at Sam, the newspapers in his lap and on the floor. Who was the first one to say "It's not my place to impose curfews." Sophisticated? Yes. Smart? No.

236

She wished his tower could protect him, wished it with all her heart. She wondered why she just sat there; on the other few occasions over the last thirty years when she had seen her husband cry, she had gone over to wherever he was to be close to him, to hug him and love him. She seesawed between believing what she told Billy, that the bad times you get over because the past tells there's more good to come, and taking a clear look at a madman whose business might put his son in harm's way, where *he* should have been.

31

THIS TIME THERE WAS NO HESITATION AS LIZ APPROACHED the front desk of the Grand Bay Hotel. There were no mistakes in spelling as the desk clerk, a different one this time, immediately found the right Anker and called upstairs to announce her. "Suite eighteen A, ma'am," the young man said politely, and Liz nodded because she didn't trust her voice the closer she got.

"Here I am with the usual erratic attention I show to you," Liz said to Mike, feeling old in the hotel corridor.

Mike had draped around his shoulders the white terry-cloth robe good hotels provide, and she could see that he had hastily combed his hair.

"I hope it's not too late," she said, suddenly ashamed of herself.

Mike's eyes looked puffier than usual. In twenty years, she thought, he would have lines like W. H. Auden. She could see the beginnings of them now around his eyes.

His expression was nerveless and remote. For a moment she thought she saw fright.

"Come on in," he said. She followed him and listened to him try to make her welcome. She kept noticing the remoteness of him, the deadness of his eyes and the way he confined himself inside his learned courtesy. He opened the minibar in the living room to offer her a drink, and as he bent down his robe opened slightly and she looked at his legs.

"I'm having a tomato juice. But the hell with it. Vodka won't pollute it, do you think? Liz, how about you?"

In the other room behind him the bed was unmade, as well it should be at this hour, she decided. A king-size bed, twice the size of the one they slept in the last time.

"That's fine for me," she said, "but, you know, if you have" . . . she changed her mind. ". . . some good Scotch, no, make it gin and tonic, that would be fine." She wanted something that required a mixer, a bottle that with luck would be in the back of the refrigerator, something that would keep him there with his robe pulled open just a little longer.

She thought he might be feeling some resentment and tried to clear up any possible misunderstanding.

"I didn't come here for him. I hope you know that," she said.

The rings under his eyes were a little more prominent, a little sadder, as he stood up, the gin in one hand, the tonic in the other.

"You didn't have to say that." Which meant that she did.

The robe was a size or so too small, and he looked older late at night by a few years, the way we all do, she thought. She needed to find a mirror to check herself, her face, her body, her stock-in-trade, as she saw it.

He mixed the gin and the tonic in a double highball glass and brought the drink, fizzing, to her, belting his robe before he started to move. Then he greeted her with a kiss, and Liz no longer felt she had been warned to stay away.

She brushed some loose strands of hair away from her forehead and looked for a place to sit.

"Is it too warm in here?" he asked.

"No. Not at all, but why don't we sit outside," she said, noticing the big terrace, the lounges out there, and the strings of lights of the cruise ships on Biscayne Bay waiting for their romantic midnight departures.

"Sure, why not," he said. He stepped aside to let her lead the way, and there was something in the stiff way he stood when they were out there that made her sure of his uneasiness.

"I'm not going to push you, you know," she said.

"In what ways, Liz, are you not going to push me?" he said quietly.

"Mike, did I ever push you?"

Now he smiled, a real smile, and she heard what she had wanted to hear for years, "No, but who knows what would have happened if you had?"

"It's not what a woman's supposed to do."

She took a sip of her drink and felt its cold track all the way down her throat.

There was still a ring of chairs around the glass coffee table, arranged as they were several hours ago, when Arlo, Spencer and Mike had met. Liz and Mike sat in two of them.

"You have all the virtues, Liz. You always did."

He tried not to sit stiffly, tried not to fold his arms across his chest.

"Sam can look after himself," she said.

"He can? Can he really?"

". . . I'm not here for him."

"You don't have to say it again, Liz."

Mike looked down at his glass, surprised that it was empty, and decided he wanted a refill. He called back from the minibar, bending down to fish out another tonic, and turning quickly to ask Liz about her refill, he caught her staring at him, almost feeling the touch of her fingers on the insides of his thighs.

"You know," he said, "one of us, one of the many of us, is likely not to come out of this."

"Why the common sense, Mike?" she said as he brought the drinks back. "Why now? Or, really, why not now? You were always so good at common sense." She made no attempt to disguise her sarcasm.

He stood over her, his arm extended with her drink. She reached up and took it. He stood there and she continued to look up at him.

"What do you think happens when your child is gone?" she said. "I mean, if it didn't have to happen."

Mike took her drink from her, set it on the table, and held her hand.

Mike remembered Liz, when she was younger, walks with Billy before Matt was born, and Sam, presiding at Passover in the small apartment in those early years, with Gordy and Helen there, too, at the long table that stuck out into the hallway, all of them celebrating an exodus, a relief from bondage. He would bury their memory as deep as possible inside himself. There wasn't any other way.

"Emerge gently, Liz."

She looked up at him, her eyes starting to fill.

He raised her slowly and they stood together before he put his own drink down and wrapped his arms around her.

"Oh, Mike," she said in a voice with no doubt in it.

She was standing still and looking young. A small wind whispered on Mike's thighs, below his shorts, under the Grand Bay's terry-cloth robe. He watched her face. Her eyes were closed and she appeared to be smiling, God only knew about what.

He could never describe making love. Never in his own mind did he articulate his own moves. "First I touched this, and then I caressed that." Never would he think such things.

But when her mouth was responding to his, he heard words of thrilled purpose and felt a technique still as sweet but learned compared to the last time, a time he found embedded in his memory more accurately than he had realized, with enough precision to note the variations. Which is the way it must always be, he thought, holding her, when, at the end young lovers come together again, given the odds against it.

And she made love to him again and again, holding, needing, receiving him with joy the way she had the first time, so long ago.

"I wonder . . ." she started to say when it was over, staring at the ceiling, yet still holding Mike. "I wonder why I'm still with him."

He pulled away. Not far, but away, and she knew that Mike was still Mike, a man of honor, living by some strange code, in bed with her, wanting her body but not her thoughts. But her thoughts were still hers and she had her questions—I wonder why I'm still with him—even if she wouldn't voice them. Maybe her father was right. Maybe she did marry beneath her. Maybe she did sell out. But that was back then, when there was such joy and drive in Sam, such vision. Back then he was adventurous, ingenious, quick to act and single-minded when he chose to be. And to be with a man like that? Is that a sellout? He ran everything out of his hat, but his hat, in those days, was all he had, and look what he did with it. What other men dreamed about, he did. Sam did so much more, even more than the man in bed next to her. And then she wondered again, and she heard herself say it. "I wonder why I'm still with him."

She felt Mike's fingers tighten around hers. "None of us just sat back and watched it happen."

She thought of Billy and Matt, what she had done, what more she could have done. "You don't get away scot-free," she said.

"That's right. We were all players."

They said no more, and a silence settled between them, bringing them closer than words ever could.

He looked at her watch. He would never have given her a Rolex with diamonds. A Patek, maybe, but certainly not that. He wondered if she was asleep and if she was, should he wake her. But she was awake, and she told him about Billy, taking him to the airport, and where he was going, fearing that like Matt he was on a horrible errand for Sam. "Because if he can do what he did to Matt . . ." She stopped.

"Don't do that to yourself, Liz." Mike took her hand.

"You, me, all of us. We're so tied in to him. Some things are just too hard to uproot."

"Get yourself out," Liz said. The room was dead quiet. "Put him away, Mike," she said harshly. "Drop him down a hole."

She made sure the lights were out as she dressed to leave.

32

BILLY HAD BEEN GIVEN THE SEAT HE WANTED, 2A, NOT ON the bulkhead. His plane taxied to the Georgetown terminal. Especially in the early evening, the whole complex looked like old pictures his father had of the L.A. airport in 1931, except the planes were slightly newer. It had been a hassle to get on a flight in Miami because of the crowds, the checking and double-checking. "May I ask your occupation, sir? Are you carrying more than fifteen thousand U.S. dollars in cash or bank credits of any kind? Would you open your briefcase, please, sir?" It was easy to get off in Georgetown. Welcomes, ease of entry, swift baggage claim, cab drivers who smiled, twenty minutes to downtown, past the Government House where he used to stop to see the insurance commissioner when Greater Minnesota set up its own captive offshore insurance company for timber risks, and ten minutes past there, out Harbour Drive, tall trees on the right, lit in the soft night from below, the view on the left to the villa his dad kept in another name, also on Seven Mile Beach.

On the way out, Billy saw new buildings and new cars everywhere, evidence that the Cayman Islands offered the highest standard of living in the Caribbean. The small British crown colony had come a long way from the original settlement by shipwrecked sailors, marooned mariners, and a different kind of buccaneer. The ride was a nice one, easy. The hotels were new but not overpowering; treetop height was the limit. The tourists came to deep-sea fish and scuba-dive to a living coral wall that plunges six thousand feet below sea level, or they came for the Queen's birthday celebration in June. Those activities were for the tourists (passports not necessary; just proof of citizenship and a return ticket). The real business was for others, those with briefcases and memorized messages.

The action used to be in the Bahamas, in Bermuda, the Netherland Antilles, the Channel Islands, even Hong Kong. Pindling took over in the Bahamas, the ownership of BATCO, Bahamas American Trust Company, changed because a partner got scared and pulled out and there was an opening. The shores of the Caymans were littered with bankers, technicians, the whole shot. A few smart lawyers got together, bought a desk, hired some back-room banking types and a few typewriters, sold themselves as on-island directors and officers so "names" could be put on papers. "You want an account? You got an account. You want an insurance company? You got a charter. You want names? You got names." To top it off, the Caymans passed a law that says no person on-island can answer any questions about a bank account, and to take it full circle, the law also says that anyone, that's *anyone,* who comes on-island and even *asks* a question is in violation of the law. Nice trick, huh. You go to jail even for asking!

What helped as much as anything else was that the Caymans are one hour ahead of the U.S. time zone and the language is English and before you know it you've got offices of the Big Eight accounting firms opening up down there and you can even get the bank to let Peat, Marwick; Arthur Andersen; or any one of the others audit your account to keep the bank honest without the accountants telling the IRS one single solitary number unless they want to join you in jail. It's a bonanza. And a legal one.

Once at the villa, Billy would unpack and have use of

his own car, ready for an all-nighter with two women he would round up somehow. But not yet. The bankers were waiting for dinner at the Grand Old House, a table reserved on the screened porch, away from the crowd. There was no need for them to meet at the bank. There were no papers that anyone needed.

The restaurant was in what used to be Plantation House and dated from 1900, old on this island. The fresh white paint and bright trim couldn't quite hide the rust stains from the tin roof that showed through like old wallpaper. There were green plants and bright red bougainvillaea hanging from pots hooked to the ceiling across the large room leading out to the screened-in porch. When he walked in, Billy heard music that sounded like it came from a muffled marimba near the bar on the other side of the main room.

Billy, dressed in easy white trousers and a silk shirt with a Versace jacket, checked himself out in the mirror in the lobby, feeling a little like Don Johnson. They would wear ties, the bankers. He, the client, would not. A full Hollywood moon was frosting the ocean with light. Billy liked this place. It felt old and refined with an air of grace from another time.

The bankers, however, were not from another time. The older man, older meaning fifty or so, was quintessentially British, tall, white mustache, wavy hair, Savile Row summer suit in light blue, and one of those silly shirts with a striped body and a white collar with a tie around his neck that would be better off on a bathrobe. His presence was a courtesy to Billy; his rank was clearly evidenced by the battered dark red Hermès briefcase, the word *Depose* engraved on the large brass lock.

"Billy, my regards to your father. How nice to see you."

Billy wanted to say something about the priority, always his father first, even if he wasn't there, but he had learned long ago to accept Sam's primacy, even in his absence. Did he want his father to die so he, the surviving prince, could take over? Or did he just want out? What did he want? Two women to fuck? That he had to pay for? He hated admitting that to himself, that it was money that brought him what he wanted. Such an admission socked him twice: It made his father right and it made him realize that he was ugly.

"Dad was sorry he couldn't come himself, Sir Victor, but he sends his best regards."

"Well, thank you. Billy, you know Paul Flavian, our general manager, and his aide, Susan Derry."

"Miss Derry." Billy smiled at the beautiful mulatto woman. "Paul. Good evening." Billy, too, could set priorities.

Now it was proper for Billy to take his seat, and as he moved toward his chair, Paul Flavian, general manager of the Standard-British Bank of the Grand Caymans, pulled it out to ease Billy's effort. How clear a signal, Billy thought. How well the British could ignore the secondary status of a representative if they chose to do so, or, to put it another way, how well they could regard Family, no matter who its representative. It must be all those years with second or third sons of earls, lords, and baronets. Billy sat back in his chair. Refined. He liked it there. He liked being somebody. It made him feel expansive.

They talked, mostly Sir Victor talked, that is, and more important, they let him talk. Billy looked occasionally at the shadowy girl, this Susan Derry, and he knew why they had brought her. For now, however, he took his enjoyment in other ways, sitting at the head of the table, being listened to, being his father. Time swept by, not as slowly as Billy had feared. Every time he looked at his watch he was amazed to notice that another half hour had gone by.

Then the warning signal went off. He could hear his father's voice. "You're a Yones. They'll use you, try to get to me through you. Make you feel like a bigshot, get you to talk. It happens to everybody's kids, Rodman Rockefeller, the Pritzker kids, all of them." It was the one bit of advice Sam gave designed to help him. Of course it helped Sam, too. Billy held his hand flat across the top of his wineglass as the waiter offered more.

Billy discovered that he was good at describing the places people had lived in all their lives and thus ignored, and he loved to watch them perk up when he complimented them on surroundings they had taken for granted. In this, Billy was a quick study.

"I've always loved this place, right here, this porch, this table near the water," Billy said. "Robert Louis Stevenson went to Samoa right after *Dr. Jekyll and Mr. Hyde,* and being here always reminds me of what the South Pacific must have been like then, while it was still real."

"Oh, come now, Billy, we're not the stuff of legends."

"Of course you are, Sir Victor. Your island here is like the Gilberts in Micronesia, and this place, the Plantation House, looks like Aggie Gray's Hotel in Samoa." Billy had traveled. He could compare. He liked himself now. He was doing something real. "And the singing. They take Sundays seriously. I'll bet you have that here."

"Perhaps Susan can show you."

"That would be very nice, Sir Victor." Billy smiled at the young woman brought so clearly for his use. "Of course, Susan, if it would not be an imposition."

"No, not at all," she said in a voice darker than her skin.

No one gave any thought to the fact that they were nowhere near Sunday and that it was unlikely that Susan would find a church service full of big-breasted singing natives in the middle of the night. But that was not the point. The contact had been made, the deal done.

"Well, Billy, shall we talk here?" Sir Victor gave him a kindly smile, but he was really indifferent except for the business they were about to do.

"Wherever you wish, Sir Victor."

"If you'll excuse us for a moment," Paul Flavian said, rising to pull out Susan's chair. That she was black never bothered the Caribbean British and excited Billy. It was not his first, but it had been a long time and he liked the memories. He shook hands with the general manager, whose function was to pull out chairs, and Susan, who held his hand just a little too long and pressed a little too hard.

Sir Victor waited until his colleagues had left the porch, and Billy noted they were now alone. The other tables which had been full for the first seating were empty now even though in the main room just up a short flight of stairs diners were laughing and talking their way through the nine-thirty serving and others were waiting. Obviously, Grand Old House had seen fit, in a most discreet British way, to save the screened-in porch, all of it, for the privacy of Sir Victor Hewitt, Bart., Chairman, Standard-British Bank, Worldwide.

"Billy, I have been instructed by your father to discuss various accounts which you may or may not know about."

Billy looked up.

"Sir Victor, please let me take care of my assigned business first."

"Of course, Billy."

"On the special list, Dad wants . . ."

Billy hung his head for just a moment.

". . . Dad wants one million eight, cash, put into account number four. Show one million two as the capital deposit. Show seven hundred as interest. Show the capital deposit as having taken place on June 8, 1985."

"Are those to be book entries only? Does he want actual funds moved?"

"Yes, that's what Dad wants. The actual funds are to be moved, the date on which they were actually moved, according to your records, will be June 8, 1985. Is that understood?"

"There is a special charge for that service," Sir Victor said elegantly.

"That is acceptable, provided the charge is the usual charge."

"It is the usual charge."

It was just like Switzerland, as Billy learned a long time ago. You deal with the man whose name is on the building and he knows you and does what you ask. The first few times were fun, acting as honored representative of Sam Yones on his own, eschewing titles in offshore corporations because he knew better and because the lawyers down here offered themselves as "names" for one to use. Names as directors of companies. Names as officers of companies. Names to use to instruct banks on the opening of accounts, the receipt of funds, the investment of funds, the dispatch of funds, all by names which were rented, or numbers if you were a traditionalist.

"Are we to charge the usual account to provide funds for that transfer?"

"Dad says yes, the usual account."

Sir Victor bent down and extracted a small orange pad, Block Rhodia No. 11, two by about three inches, put on his gold-framed reading glasses, and made the appropriate notes.

That's all there was. That's all there ever was. A few words and a few notes, and money moved. It could have been done by phone, but that would require special authorization from the holder of the accounts and the bankers did not like to do it unless they knew the client well enough to recognize his voice. Or a tested telex could have been used, but that left a paper trail that no one wanted. Bankers had to assure the authenticity of their instructions; they had to make good if they made a mistake. Voices were acceptable. Faces were better.

Sir Victor glanced up from his small orange pad and tilted his head to one side as if he had just thought of something.

"Your father wants you to know that your brother's accounts have been transferred to you."

It was hard for Billy to hold back the tears. He didn't know if he could manage.

"Sir Victor, account number four, the June eight account. Was that Matt's, too."

Billy would try to make his mind work like his father's. Like his brother's. He really would. He was finally in Matt's shoes, Billy realized. He was doing what Matt would have done. He was the trusted son by default. But was he smart enough? There was a time when it was the other way, when it was Matt who needed him, like the time when Matt was fourteen and wanted a motor scooter. A green Cushman, history on wheels. "Not a chance, Dad told me," Matt had said. "Mom? She wouldn't even listen to the end of the sentence. Billy," Matt said, his eyes pleading, "just come take a look. Dad won't even know you were there with me." And so they went.

"You want it, Matt? Do you really want it?"

Billy loved being looked up to by his little brother.

"Would you? Would you really?"

"Give the kid the keys," Billy said, putting his arm around Matt's shoulder.

"You're lucky to have such a brother," the salesman said, and Billy got the kind of hug from Matt he always loved.

The first few payments were on time, two in person, when Billy happened to be home, one mailed to Billy at college. Then the money came late, and then none at all for two months before Christmas vacation.

"Dad told me I didn't have to pay you," Matt said, polishing the blue-green scooter in the garage.

"And why is that?" Billy asked, standing over him.

"I don't know. Ask him."

Billy walked to the other side of the cars parked in there, not wanting Billy to see his hurt face, and he smelled the garage smells, wondering what to do next. Then he came back to his brother. "Why did you bring him into this?"

"I didn't. He brought himself in," Matt said, misting the windshield, then polishing it. "After all, he knew I had the bike and wanted to know where the money came from."

"Why didn't you tell him that was between you and me?"

Matt looked up, his father's smile on his face. "Then I'd have to pay you."

Billy closed his eyes. Then he left the garage, Matt and his Cushman.

"Billy, I . . ." Billy refocused on Sir Victor and account number four, the June eight account.

"Is it some special account?" Billy tried to strengthen his voice.

"Your father . . ."

". . . has instructed you to discuss accounts with me." Billy's voice hardened.

"Michael Anker," Sir Victor said.

A horrible thought entered Billy's mind, one he would not allow to take root.

"He is the owner of account number four. It was opened in his name, by him."

"By him?"

Billy, for once, took full advantage of the face his father said was the face of a dummy.

"It was never closed," Sir Victor said.

"He never closed it?"

"No, Billy."

"He never put money in it?"

"Never. The account has been empty, without funds, until your instruction today."

"Then why was it kept open?"

Sir Victor looked uncomfortable, and Billy tried as best he could to turn his eyes into slits as he had seen his father do so many times. "Why, Sir Victor, why was an empty account in Mike's name kept open?"

"At your father's instruction, Billy."

"Thank you, Sir Victor," Billy said, covering his fears, his crashing disappointment. He waited for more, but from the look on the face of Sir Victor Hewitt, Bart., there would be no more.

As soon as he saw Paul drive away, leaving Susan waiting for him in a 1950 open MG-TD, Billy tried to perk up, knowing the evening was not over. Her old car was British racing green, and she had the front windshield folded down so the wind rushed into their faces, and he forgot his brother's face and Uncle Mike's face as she took the Harbour Drive all the way into town, across Georgetown to south Church Street to the Atlantis Submarine Dock. The sub was fifty feet long, thirteen foot beam, forty-nine tons, went one and a half knots submerged, and you could go down to a depth of one hundred and fifty feet and look out through two-foot-diameter portholes, eight on each side, with a huge fifty-inch porthole in front. There was a big sign on the dock that said DAY AND NIGHT DIVES OFF THE FAMOUS CAYMAN WALL. NORMAL NAVIGATIONAL LIGHTS PLUS TWELVE FLOODLIGHTS FOR NIGHT DIVES. As soon as he boarded, he saw seats for twenty-eight passengers but no one there. The latch clanked behind them, and Billy knew what his experience was to be. There would indeed be a night dive off the Cayman Wall.

33

WALKING INTO A HOUSE, LIZ THOUGHT, EVEN YOUR OWN house, in the middle of the night was never easy. When the house was empty, the uneasiness came from knowing you would be alone, wandering around, longing for another voice. When just the two of you were there, the problem became bigger, one you could solve only by getting away, even for a little while at a time. But then you had to come back. For the first time, Liz had the feeling that she wasn't going to have to face this feeling forever.

As Liz turned her key in the door, she immediately thought of Sam, upstairs. He had always been able to shut down her contacts with others, cut off a friendship, imprison her in his life, do all of it without raising a hand, or, in many cases, opening his mouth. All it took, most times, was a special look at those who came too close to her. He was not a man to be challenged, not a man to be piqued or offended. The only persons she got close to were those he approved or those he didn't know and who didn't know him. Except Mike.

Sam was in bed, reading. She wasn't sure what, but it was a book, not a report, not something in loose-leaf binding with pull-out spreadsheets with pro formas on them. He looked deeply and completely at peace, and so defenseless in his blue pajamas that he looked innocent. His face, for some strange reason, looked handsome, his eyes at rest, absorbed; watching him, she could feel again a little of the seduction of his power over men and events that had first attracted her. He smiled, and Liz caught herself in the act of smiling back.

She looked more closely at their bed. Usually, there were four pillows, two for Sam and two for her on her side of the bed. Tonight there were only two, and both were propped up behind Sam's head. She checked around the room and saw that they were not on her chair, not on the bench at the foot of their bed. Her two pillows were gone and there was, blatantly, no place for her next to Sam.

"You want me to go somewhere else? Is that what you want?"

Sam stopped smiling and flung his left arm over on her pillowless side of the bed, claiming it as his territory.

"Mike had a big day. You should have let him get some sleep," he said, regarding her with an eerie calm over his reading glasses. "I figured I'd have somebody watch you this time."

"He'll sleep better because of me."

It seemed like minutes passed, but it was probably only a moment, no more, before his hard face disappeared and he crossed his arms over his body, protecting it.

"I'm not good at this," he said, his tone no longer tough. Now he seemed to be asking for help, help to make him stop. His book rested across his chest. "Gordy asked me just the other day, 'Do I have to win every argument?' I told him . . ."

"What did you tell him?"

"I told him yes."

Sam extended his arm across her side of the bed again, and the icy cold returned to his voice. "Three's an unstable number," he said.

"Sam, do you want me in the house tonight or not?" She planted her feet on her carpet on her floor. "I'm asking you, but I'm still going to do what I want to do."

"Then why are you asking?"

"Because my father taught me to be polite."

"Was that why he called me 'that little kike'? Because he was polite?"

"Is that what it comes down to, Sam, after all these years?"

"Liz, he's my oldest friend." For the first time, she heard the pleading in his voice.

"He's my oldest friend, too."

Her expression grew softer. And Sam's smile, signaling the beginning of triumph, was almost imperceptible.

PART
FIVE

34

SAM YONES HAD ALWAYS BELIEVED IN CELEBRATING IN THE middle of adversity. It showed the world that there was no adversity, that you were not afraid, even of a grand jury hearing that was to start again the next morning, and that if push came to shove, you could organize cheering crowds on the steps of the Federal Court Building when you came out after having pleaded not guilty.

Liz had not wanted a party. Sam had called it "having a few people over" but thirty-two years of marriage had made her an expert translator of his vocabulary and "few" could mean anything from twenty to two hundred. And this house could easily hold that many. She looked at the huge Francis Bacon he had bought her, now hanging on their most important Florida wall. She looked at his colors, his images, men discarded like rotting meat behind what was presumably bulletproof glass. Curating corporate collections had made her feel important, but now she felt it was a charade, because in a way, her success depended on him. Hire his wife, he'll do you a favor. She struggled to remind herself she had talent. It wasn't easy.

She walked into the bedroom. Sam had gone for his run, leaving the party arrangements in her hands. She was angry about that, thinking of the phone calls she would have to make, the coordination of service people she would have to manage, all the time she would have to invest in his behalf. The room was empty now, filled with morning sunlight, but she still saw his conqueror's smile in the night, more threatening than she had ever seen him direct toward a stranger. The windows were open, and she listened to the wind a moment. She replaced her pillows on her side of the bed, now rumpled from sleep, and she shivered even though the air was warm, remembering the horror of finding them gone. She pictured him as he must have been, moving around their bedroom the night before, setting the stage for her return, putting on his blue pajamas, selecting his book to read, setting his face to look innocent for her first view of him, smiling, watching her smile back, waiting for her to notice her dismissal, no pillows on her side of the bed. Her shame, her anger at his having her watched, her stupidity in allowing him to win.

Cheryl had been sneezing so much that she excused herself from her morning negotiation session at the Standard-British Bank, but not for more than ten minutes. She had arrived that Wednesday morning with her team of accountants. Maybe it was the scented soap at the souvenir shop, that big table heaped with it, ready for the tourists off the boats.

It takes a lot of effort to be charming. She had learned that lesson from Sam, in precisely those words, and she was close to exhausted by the time they had finished. Marley Schmarley, as Sam would say. At more than one point in the negotiation she didn't give a shit anymore. "You want to do the deal? Do the deal. You don't? Don't," she wanted to tell them. But that was not the way you dealt with bankers. "Yes, we'd be delighted to be your senior lender." That was what she wanted and, finally, that was what she got. Not talk of compensating balances or points. She had learned that they had enough of Sam's money down here one way or another to make them feel secure.

What if the FBI asked her about that fact, the existence of Sam's money in an off-shore bank. She wouldn't remember, and as long as she wasn't under oath, big deal. But what if they smelled the lost memory as a fake, got mad, and subpoenaed her? *All the mistresses,* the tall FBI guy had said. She sat across the table from the bankers and covered her anger by sneezing.

She recovered in time for "the lunch." More like an audience, she thought. Sir Victor Hewitt himself presided, parked at the head of the table in his private dining room like a pasha, eating with rough hands, a rim of black under one nail. They make such a fuss over him, she thought. He's just more of the flotsam that had rolled onto this atoll in the last twenty years. Big fucking deal.

She had spent at least a year learning not to look at her watch during meals. But when the sun started to creep past the top window in Sir Victor's dining room, and when the cream in the coffee cups on the polished mahogany table started to curdle, she knew if she was going to get to Miami and be with Mike tonight she had better do something to wind things up.

"Well, Sir Victor," she said, "what is your decision?" Pose a direct question to a Brit and they run for cover.

"I . . . I . . . think we need a bit more time to consider this proposal, don't you, Paul?" Paul Flavian nodded.

"May we give you transport to the airport?"

"No, thank you, Sir Victor, we have a car."

"Fine. Then we'll be back to you?"

Don't let him weasel out. Punch him again.

"When may we look forward to your answer?"

"Paul, do you think the end of the week will give you enough time?"

"Of course, Sir Victor," Paul said.

"Well, young lady . . ." Sir Victor said as he stood.

She had gotten them out of there, a dear young lady, and extracted a definite date from a Brit. As it turned out, her accountants wanted more shopping time on the island and she decided to fly back commercial.

FBI, FBI, FBI. That's all she could think of. Ruth Seigel, counselor at law, could hold them off since her client was out of the country. But what if they asked "Where is Ms.

Stone?'' What if they had a hunch and checked passports? Assume they know she's in the Grand Caymans. They'll come after her like salivating dogs.

Cheryl stood near the check-in counter and looked down the short flight of stairs leading to the main lobby of the airport. The line was long, too long. She looked at her watch. There was a phone outside, and there was time.

The sun was over the top of the building and it warmed the right side of her face and cast her shadow against the sidewalk as she waited for an overseas operator. Trying to steer clear of Mike, to leave him free, shiksa style, was hard, much too hard for her. "Be careful down there. Please." She remembered his words. "I know what I'm talking about." From the phone her view was to the waterfront out to the piers and past them to the white cruise boats. The strong sun made them seem even more brilliant. "You may be at the only pay phone in the western hemisphere that's tapped," he would say to her. "Not on this island," she would answer. "In this place it's even a crime to ask. We heard it four times since the plane landed. From two bankers, one lawyer, and even the taxi driver."

"Tell Mr. Anker," she told the Grand Bay operator, "that I tried to reach him. I'm Cheryl Stone. S-T-O-N-E. Yes, that's right. And that I should be there" . . . she looked at her watch again ". . . in four to five hours. That's right. Four to five." I love you. I want to be nearby, she wanted to add.

She looked at the boats a long moment before she walked back inside the terminal building which seemed to have become hotter and more humid. She started to approach the ticket counter, then stopped in her tracks.

She knew the young man at the far end of the lobby was Billy Yones just by looking at the back of his head. It was Sam's head, but he, unlike Sam, still had a full head of hair and on his arm one of the most beautiful black women she had ever seen.

He had spotted her instantly and walked up the stairs into the lobby toward her. For some reason, maybe it was his resemblance to Sam, she felt she could not take one step toward him, that she had to hold her ground. When he reached her, she held out her hand, but he kissed her instead.

"Cheryl, this is Susan Derry."

"Ms. Derry," Cheryl said.

"Susan," she answered in a lilting Caribbean voice.

Seeing Billy, especially here, brought back all kinds of memories that pulled her in several directions; the early days with Sam, her belief in his loving her well beyond just those first months, his feelings for her. The things he could share with her, never Liz. Her pride in that. Her sense of who she believed herself to be because he believed in her. The ending that broke her heart. And Sam's, too, in some ways, she knew that.

Whatever else Billy did not have, he had a great smile, Sam's smile. Like Gatsby's, the kind you come across maybe four or five times in your life. Being with him made her feel close to him, and his insistence that they sit together on the flight to Miami made her feel taken care of. She thought of Mike's commitment to this kid who startled his father by looking so much like him but who was shoved to the bottom because he didn't have the brains to match the profile. She felt more than ever her respect for Mike, so glad he was there for her so soon after Sam. From Mike she had learned what respect was, how long a love could last, how blessed she was.

As the plane rose, they watched the water and then the clouds as they obscured the Atlantic below.

"Did Dad tell you why I was here?" Billy asked, turning to her.

"No." Cheryl pulled off her scarf. The air-conditioning was still not working right. It was still warm.

"And you?" Billy asked her. "You came on his say-so?"

She saw longing in his eyes. He wanted her to be Sam's servant. The steward served one drink and then another.

"I guess you were the one he sent to do important things," Billy said.

A shrug and a shake of the head told him that was not

the case. He wanted her to know that *he* had been in the Caymans as a principal, not as an agent but someone who could act on his own, for himself. A brick lay on his tongue. All he could do was ask, not tell. It would only get back to his father, he thought. At least he had Susan's phone number. Maybe he'd fly her up to New York. Soon. He had that suddenly simplified gaze that could make him seem a boy, as if he had just remembered something pleasant.

"When you first met me," Billy said, "I'll bet you thought you were meeting this big New York hotshot. Now you must see me as a real chump."

"No, I never look at you like that."

"You were always so deferential," he said.

"I know," she laughed, embarrassed.

"You're down here doing the heavy stuff. Being deferential obviously didn't hurt you."

Cheryl wondered what sort of stories Sam had told him about her? To his son. Certainly not to his son. She felt her head shaking from side to side, as if she were saying no, no.

"You're the one doing the heavy stuff," Cheryl said. "Not me."

She was probing, tossing out the words just to see what Billy did with them. Maybe she had learned one too many of Sam's lessons, and that thought upset her. She watched Billy out of the corner of her eye and tried to recover her composure.

"Do you know Sir Victor Hewitt?" Billy asked.

"I know who he is," Cheryl answered. She had learned the ropes and was creating a few of her own.

"I had dinner with him last night," Billy said, his eyes suddenly tired. "I hate the fucking son of a bitch. Steward, a refill?" She saw that his eyes were red-rimmed now.

"You know, we were closer than they gave us credit for, Matt and me. I did all the big-brother things," Billy bowed his head as if he were praying. Then he sat up straight in his seat. "Even more than my share because Dad was so busy. Riding the bike. Driving the car. Fucking. All of it," he said, his eyes glued to hers. "Dad thinks Sir Victor fuckoff is ace high. No way. A flushed-out has-been. You blow into his ear and he moves money. That's his calling in life. He's a whore." Years worth of held-back opinions. She knew what she was hearing. "And I hate being there, doing Dad's shit. What do you think Dad does with me? What do you think he did with my brother? Let Dad do his own shit. Let Dad go down there and move his own fucking money. If he wants Mike to have almost two million dollars, real money, let him move it." Then out it came. " 'Lie down with dogs, get up with fleas.' "

Cheryl picked up Billy's napkin which had fallen, brushed it off, and handed it to him. She understood. Some account was a fake and it was worth two million dollars to Sam to make it look real. That fucking son of a bitch. Who was running this goddamn grand jury? She had plenty to trade.

Billy looked up. "Steward, do I have time for another martini?"

"Your uncle Mike used to say that about people, too. 'Lie down with dogs . . .' "

"Fuck Uncle Mike."

"Is that the way you really feel about him?"

"Sometimes, yes." No liquor voice anymore. "That's the way I feel."

"Why?"

"Because he doesn't have to protect Dad, but he still does it. He still protects Dad."

"They go back a long way," Cheryl said, hating herself for standing on the wrong side.

"So do a lot of people."

Five minutes later the captain made the first approach announcement. They were twenty minutes out. There would be two more sets of landing instructions, one when the seat belt sign came on and the second when the no smoking sign was lit, signaling final approach and accompanied by the whir of motors under the wings extending the flaps to give the Cayman Air 727 more lift as it slowed down for its landing.

At the second announcement, the steward came by to

remove all glasses, and to Cheryl's relief Billy didn't start an argument with him.

As they pulled closer to the gate, Billy searched the faces of the people behind the broad expanse of glass as if he were expecting someone to meet him.

"You know Mike's first love was my mother. Don't hate me for telling you that."

"I don't hate you. It's not news."

"Maybe that's why I run hot and cold on Uncle Mike. He might have been my father and he wasn't. I guess he chose not to be."

"I suppose you're right," Cheryl said. "He chose not to be. It's hard on you. I know that, but I'm glad for me."

It was late afternoon now, and Liz, one leg folded under the other, huddled in the corner of the sofa, alone, in the conservatory on the first floor. Sam stood in the doorway, wearing his dark blue linen slacks, jingling the coins in his pocket. "Liz, it's getting late."

She wished she could manage an expressionless face, all the way down to the eyes, but she had no hope of that. *Do you know what your life will be like with Sam's people?* her father had asked her. "They'll tear you down. They'll use words you won't understand. They'll answer a question with a question. Ultimately, you'll be an outsider, you'll always be the gentile." From her first real knowledge of Sam, behind his poor clothes, the clumsiness in the beginning, Liz had thought, *I can make you better.* She now put on her shoes and stood. She watched as Sam walked up the stairs. Mike had held her, she had felt him inside her. Was she still that beautiful, pulsing woman? She thought of three people holding hands on skates: the one on the outside being whipped around, the safer one in the center.

She put her drink down on the glass top of the wicker table. She looked at Matt's picture across the room on the table with all the others, opposite the Francis Bacon, and she felt tears in her eyes for Matt, for herself, for Mike, for Billy, for all of them.

She rubbed her eyes dry, drew herself up, and left the conservatory.

Sam was dressing, too. There was something buoyant about him. He was humming and it worried her. Something was going on. For years she had never cared. Now she did. For years she had known he was a tough guy, a son of a bitch, but her son of a bitch, her protector, her champion. Maybe his ship was finally sinking. Did she want him to sink? If he went under, where was her proper place? On the deck with him? Or swimming away, fighting the undertow, trying not to get sucked under, pulling her simple, sweet, and last son behind her. She went upstairs to dress for Sam's party, but she wanted to be alone again, or at least with Mike, not in the midst of all this turbulence.

35

THE EVENING WAS CALLED FOR FIVE, ANOTHER "SUNSET party," as Sam called them, a time which under normal circumstances Liz loved also, one of the few reasons she liked being in this town at this house. It was beautiful at that time of day. The air was softer and the light, especially in the spring, was still strong enough at that hour to turn Sam's tower a pale yellow, softening its harshness, for she saw it now as a tower for a prisoner, not a tower for the deals he loved.

The evening would not be a complete loss for her. She knew that. "Who is that stunning woman standing in the doorway?" Or next to the sofa. Or near the end of the white planked pier, just toward the stern of the Chris-Craft.

The house filled fast because they all knew Sam liked punctuality. She had seen to the caterers, seen to the oranges, the bar, the buffet, the lights, white and in colors, for sparkle after twilight. The vice president of GM, who went back as far as Nixon and his pinochle games, was there. So was Will Slater, Mr. Prudential, the man who looked like a short Abraham Lincoln. Sir Victor Hewitt was not there, but Sam told her he knew where Sir Victor was and what he was doing. Also not there were Gordy and Helen. Or Gordy and Ginger. Liz took Sam's arm and he walked with his prize toward the lawns crowded with people, stepping down the broad terrace steps. It was the kind of entrance he loved, the murmurs, the partings to create a path, the resumption of conversation at the signal of his smile.

Mike was there, too, somewhere in the crowd, probably standing alone on the fringe. Calling to invite him was Sam's way of finding out that Mike was still in town, that the grand jury was not through with him and that the government wanted more. She didn't have to be a genius to understand that Mike's continued presence was a worry to him, what with Sam constantly on the phone, pacing. He had sounded more like his immigrant father with every call, reaching back to his heritage to help him keep his head above water, help him survive.

Arm in arm, they looked like the couple on the top of the cake, older, getting married for the second time. This Sam was nothing like the man his guests had seen sitting *shiva* for his son, and why should he be? she thought. He was gracious, charming, smiling his rare smile; he loved the background of the strolling violins. A party at sunset in Miami in the soft air with fiddles was the perfect setting to display his confidence in the future.

He worked the crowd, or, rather, the crowd worked him, so many were there just to make sure they could say they met him. Liz had learned to watch and to participate at the same time. She knew so well what he was going through; if it were in her power, she would have given him an Academy Award. She touched her hair. And maybe one for herself.

A chamberlain, Sam had told her. One day he would hire

one of those guys with a wig and pantaloons and a big stick, like a shepherd's staff from the Bible, who would shout out the names of people and bang the staff on the ground as the guests entered the receiving line.

"So I'm standing there, in this military club in Paris down the block from Hermès. The wedding was two blocks away at the big church, the Madeleine, and we went back for the reception." Sam told the story every chance he got. He stood on the terrace, outside the door to the living room, full of Giacometti tables. "So there's this big room and this line of wedding guests and this fruit dressed up like Louis the Fourteenth, banging a stick up and down while he yells out the name of the couple that's next. I told Liz 'I want one of those.' Didn't I, honey? I told you. Right?"

He had an audience, he was onstage. The ham had found its platter.

"Sam, you want it all," Liz said, sure to have a big smile on her face.

"We all do," GM said. "If you don't want it all, you don't get any of it."

The crowd of people around Sam laughed. There were somewhere between six and ten people surrounding them, Liz thought, two of the women in summer white, pushing it too soon, their bare shoulders goose-bumped.

"Now, sir," Sam said, rising on tiptoe to slap GM's back, "that's wisdom. You hear that? You all hear that?" Liz smiled at GM. She could be adorable and malleable and was well trained.

Double-breasted suits were back in, Liz noted, looking around. She liked them. Sleek. But she had talked Sam out of wearing one. He was too short. Or one of those shirts with a white collar on a striped body. Too top heavy for a short man, but she couldn't quite put it that way. "Dress gray," she had told him. "Understate." He needed reminders now and then, especially before a party when the ebullient side of his nature, the spirited side that had first attracted her, came out full force. It was a time when he played Broadway show albums, when he sang out loud and bounced around, a would-be tap-dancer, belting out "Everything's Coming Up Roses." He was a dynamo, and some of his energy, years ago, went into private life, not just his partnerships. She had loved that side of him, and if there was one big plus to a party, it was seeing Sam like that again. Even if only for a short time she could see what had been lost and get a sense of what life might have been like if the heaviness and the sorrow were gone.

She took Sam's hand, and she must have pressed it too hard because Sam stopped in the middle of a sentence to look at her.

Then she noticed that the crowd around her had changed. Sam had been walking arm in arm with her, among his guests. She turned her attention once again to the guests on the lawn, picking drinks off silver trays carried among them, standing in line for sushi or pasta or ratatouille at a half dozen umbrella-covered carts spotted across the grounds. How he enjoyed millionaires standing in line for food at his house. How he loved it.

How he also loved the music. There was never a party at a Sam Yones house without live music. A piano at small dinner parties, more instruments when there were more people.

"So, do you believe it, at this wedding in Paris," Sam was telling a new crowd, "the violinists went around in the middle of all the French aristocracy playing 'If I Were a Rich Man.' They didn't even get it!" The truth was, and Liz alone knew it, that Sam had copied everything he could from that party in Paris he made fun of. It was safe for him to copy. He was the only American to have been asked. Not Malcolm Forbes. Not Carl. Not Saul. Only Sam. He arrived on time at four at the Church of the Madeleine and stayed for the whole wedding Mass, unlike the Parisians, who arrived for the last five minutes and stood at the aisle so the family could see them and assume they had been there the whole time. A fuss was made over him. And he met Catherine Deneuve.

The more Sam talked about Paris, the better he felt at his own home, at his own party with hundreds of people milling about, listening to his own violinists, feeling on top again, making them realize that he was on top and always would be. No one would bring him down. No one.

Mike was one man who could wear a double-breasted suit beautifully. Liz had known that for thirty years. Today she felt a sense of loss more keenly than ever before as she watched Mike walk toward her. The man who might have been hers and was not; the man who would have had a different life with her and she with him. She could have made him better, too, just as she had made Sam better, but not, as was the case with Sam, at such a price to herself.

Maybe, Liz thought, maybe if Mike can only get out of this. Maybe if he's free when it's all over.

"Liz, you look wonderful," Mike said as if he were seeing her for the first time. "It's good to see you." As always, he kissed her. She took his hand and held on tight. "It's good to see you at a party again." He tried to let go but felt her fingers tighten; she didn't want to let go.

"Sam, you look great." Mike put an arm around Sam's shoulder. He was careful not to stoop to do it.

For a moment, Mike felt the old love for Sam, seeing him so happy and relaxed, away from the terror of the government, free, smiling, as certain of the future as he used to be. As they all used to be.

"Where's Cheryl?" Sam asked. Both Liz and Mike stiffened and Sam, overjoyed, noticed it.

And then Sam answered his own question. "She's probably on her way back. She's been in the Caymans for the day at Standard-British, doing a great job."

He gave them a take-no-prisoners smile. She had seen Matt, as a child, try to copy it. By the time he was bar mitzvahed, he could. Billy never.

Mike could barely hold still. My God, in the Caymans, he thought. Cheryl was under Sam's control. That was the message.

"When does she come back?" It hurt him in his gut to ask.

"She'll miss the party," Sam said. "She'll hate that. Didn't she call?"

"Yes."

"Well, good. Then there's no change."

Liz understood the signals as well as anyone else, maybe better. Not only did Sam think he owned Cheryl, he also thought he owned Mike. He thought he owned many people. She hated that in him. She sided with the underdogs, the people he thought he owned. That very large crowd of people, many of whom were now in this house. The gathering of those who in his eyes he owned. Including, Liz thought, herself.

She mixed among the several hundred guests for what seemed like at least an hour, talking animatedly about art, which show was up, which show was down. She knew she could sleepwalk her way through that subject, keeping an eye on Mike as he moved from the lawn to the pier and back again. She suddenly realized that Mike had the power to determine where they would be come next Saturday when they changed the clocks. In Miami. In New York. Free or falling.

Twilight came, and subtly, not all at once, the lights in blue, pale yellow, and clear lit the grounds. The violins no longer strolled but had settled at one end of the deck surrounding the swimming pool, where white flowers floated. She would hold up. She had always held up. "Who is that stunning woman standing . . ." Even the extra servants would ask. Liz tried for a second wind and got it. Another hour of this and it would be over.

36

AND THE BAND PLAYED ON, LIZ THOUGHT, LISTENING TO Sam's violins, settled, playing Rodgers and Hammerstein. She kept seeking glimpses of Mike, and when she saw him she had to be careful not to smile, not to head his way. He looked so grand in his double-breasted suit. No one had to tell him what to wear, Liz thought. No one ever had to.

When she was unable to spot him for a space of fifteen minutes, she left Sam.

There were a few people outside of the family who felt at ease on the upper floors of any of Sam's homes, friends close enough to walk upstairs during a party to use a family bathroom or call a long time-out from the performance required on the main floor. In the old days they came upstairs to talk to one of the boys, or use the phone in an upstairs bedroom because it was quieter there. Upstairs, she found Mike, sitting on her side of the bed, the phone in his hand.

"Just calling the office," he said.

She had often seen Mike in bedrooms. They had all taken trips together, crossed in a split-level suite on the *QE2*, and sailed in Sam's boat often enough for that not to be unusual. But now it was different. She imagined him as she had last seen him, in Jockey shorts, not boxers like Sam, bare-chested and then naked, his legs separated, open. She saw him ready for her, straining as he was last night when she ran her hand across the thick hair on his leg up to the inside of his thigh. She felt Mike looking her over. Was her hair in place? Did he notice the blush she felt? Her eyes jumped around. She would not turn toward the window. She would force herself to remain looking straight at him.

As Liz sat down at the edge of the bed she was conscious that no eyebrow had been raised, nor was there any indication she had cheapened herself in his eyes the night before. That was important to her, especially since sitting on the bed together was no longer without voltage. She knew it and so did he, but he did not move away.

He hung up the phone.

"Do my eyes look tired?" she asked.

"Not when you look at me like that."

When she first met Mike, she had forgotten Sam completely and saw her world with Mike as a golden cloud. But she sought to push that aside so she could see Mike as he really was and not a character in her play. Now, on the bed, she curled up, feeling like a mole, or some other perfectly happy blind animal, burrowing deeper and deeper, coming at last to its true home.

"I don't know what to say to you," Liz said.

His arms hugged his chest. He would touch nothing, lean on nothing, be as little trouble as a brown paper bag.

"I think I'm going to make a joke of this," Mike said. "I think I'm going to say, 'We sure do pick up where we left off.' "

Liz, saddened, foresaw discussions between them about this stretching on into infinity in the Miami house, in New York, in all those boats, lasting for the rest of their lives.

"I'm not good at being unsettled either," she said.

"We sound like two people trying to talk ourselves out of something, don't we?"

Power, she thought. Maybe she and Sam had too much in common. Maybe Mike was a cleanser, a solvent, a way to ream Sam out of her system, to make her someone new. Maybe she would never be new, because to be new and fresh meant she would never be having thoughts like these.

He was not responsive and she stopped what she was doing.

"Maybe I don't need either of you," Liz said.

She watched a shadow move across her bedroom window. It was a low-flying helicopter, and without knowing what possessed her she walked to the outside terrace and waved. The helicopter banked, as if waving back, noticing her, and then it flew on, heading south across the water over the white causeways. It was dark now, and she came back inside.

She was wearing her "gorgeous-clothes uniform," fine white silk jersey that molded and draped. The armor it was supposed to provide wasn't working. She now felt weak, alone, and wondered if there was any way she could summon up the strength to deal with this relationship and all the other problems.

"I didn't mean to lash out," she said to Mike. "It's hardest for women like me who have never done anything but be wives. We don't know what we need. We don't know what we have. That's why we lash out."

"I'm not any better," Mike said. He stood up, and both of them were a bit unsteady.

"Maybe we'll have a chance someday to look inside ourselves, to look at all the wiring. I don't know," she said.

Then she looked at Mike, her young man who might have taught history had he not had Sam to keep up with. She wondered if she might have ended up a full professor's wife, a dean's wife, or even a college president's wife, and whether this would have made her happier. She wouldn't ask herself if she had made the wrong choice.

"Mike, do you think you can get us out of this? All of us?"

"You too?"

"Especially me."

Mike, always the gentleman, had said good night to Sam, and then he went back to his hotel.

37

DOWNSTAIRS, ATTRACTING AS MUCH IF NOT MORE ATTENTION than Sam, was Gordy. Coming down the stairs as Sam was giving him a hug, Liz was still shaken by her brief embrace with Mike just before he went downstairs to say good night to Sam. There was no way she could not go up to Gordy and hug him too.

"Sorry we're late," he said to Sam, both of them smiling broadly, glad to be together. "We took the train."

"It took us four days," Ginger said. Not Helen, Liz thought standing next to Gordy, but Ginger. She had sharp features that made her seem to be smiling when she wasn't. "We're not too late, are we?"

Liz had spent a very bad half hour with Helen not six months earlier. She didn't like hearing about Helen's continuing heartaches with Gordy because it underlined her own problems. "Putting yourself in the middle of everything," her father used to say, and probably, he was at least half right. "When he's gone, the house just dies," Helen would tell her when it first started with Gordy, and Liz would think of the silences in her own home when Sam was away, even sometimes when he was there.

Liz remembered being wedged into a table in the corner of The Ivy when they were last in Los Angeles together, looking out on the traffic on Robertson, wishing they had a table outside, where she wouldn't feel trapped. "Here's to the Ladies Who Lunch." She thought of the line from the Sondheim song. She was lost in thought, but did her best to listen to the questions Helen put to her. How do you and Sam handle this? How do you handle that?

272

"I don't know, Helen. It's all very personal. Different people . . ."

"Then Sam has someone else, too. Just like Gordy has," Helen said into the noise of the restaurant.

"No, Helen. He doesn't."

Liz thought about Cheryl, the affair which by then was long over.

They listened to the buzzing of other conversations, which was easy to do because it seemed to Liz that, to her relief, everyone at every nearby table was shouting. Helen asked the same questions every time they were together. She shouldn't be alone with her anymore, Liz knew that, realizing that Helen played victim for some reason of her own, especially with those who knew Gordy, those who, out of love for him, or for old times' sake, had accepted Ginger in their homes.

She should have realized twenty years ago that listening to Helen was bad for her. What else was she hiding from? A lifetime of glancing over the things Sam does? Denying all she's buried in her heart? Maybe Sam is just like Helen to her; she cares because she's supposed to, and when she faces up to it, she has no reason to care. Helen had sold herself to Gordy. Had she sold herself to Sam? Helen at least still has her two kids, Liz thought. Her husband didn't take one of them from her. Liz suddenly became frightened, and she wanted to leave all these people. If she let herself say *I no longer love Sam,* then what is her life about?

It was nighttime now. There was champagne and stars, and the food stands were restocked with ratatouille and sushi. Guests coming back from the end of the white planked pier, now lit by tiny lamps, for seconds. There were still flowers floating in the pool, violins playing, and the air was alive with laughter.

"No, you're never too late," Sam said, as if he were to be a free man forever.

Liz knew she had to leave, pretend she needed to make a phone call, check on something, go upstairs, be alone.

"The train went through our original acreage," Gordy

said, and then he turned to Ginger. "Sam and I came down to Defuniak Springs, Florida, and we bought trees. Acres of trees. Pine trees, soft wood inside. They use it to make paper. Sam, remember?" Sam nodded, suddenly far away. "We couldn't be here all year, so you made a deal with, who was it then? Alabama Pacific, to cut some timber and plant some more. You'd come down five times a year to see what they were up to, and it took you two years before you figured out how they were screwing you. But we hung on because it was *land*. Not a warehouse or a factory which you bought to sell, but land that had dirt on it that grew things, that would always grow things, season after season, generation after generation. Yours. Land." Sam touched Gordy's shoulder. "That was the beginning," Gordy said, "stumbling into a Florida backwater, meeting people who didn't care if our people for two thousand years couldn't own land."

Liz had heard it all, but certain words popped out this time: "*warehouse* or *factory* which you bought to sell . . . the first one." She had heard the story so many times, but now she was hearing it in a different context. *Behave me* and the first warehouse, which Sam bought to sell, both coming from the same time in their lives. *Nicollet Avenue.* The first warehouse was on Nicollet Avenue. She could see the letters spelled out on the computer screen.

Upstairs, finally, Liz heard the elevator door close behind her, and a moment later she looked out of the window of Sam's tower and saw Sam and Gordy surrounded by a large group near the diving board. She was high enough to see it all, and for a moment she seemed to be recording the sights and sounds as if for the last time. Then the memory of her mother's voice intruded. "They eat their children. All they think about is money. He'll never think of you. Our grandchildren will be Jews."

Liz did not expect the screen on Sam's laptop to be as clear as the monitors in Sam's office or the desktop at home, but once she had opened the lid she could make out the words easier than she thought possible, the white letters against the deep-red screen. She thought of blood and turned away for a moment. She sat in front of the instrument, picked up Sam's phone, connected it to the modem, and connected herself to his memory.

How much easier it was to do things with equipment, she thought.

"Booted up." When Matt had first used the term, she thought of football, watching Alan "The Horse" Ameche steamroll over the goal line, and the way the four of them—Sam, Gordy, Mike, herself—used to follow the band up University Avenue after a win, singing "On Wisconsin" at the top of their lungs.

The screen displayed BEHAVE ME, ENTER CODE KEY. She tried Defuniak Springs and Pinewood just to eliminate them and because she was afraid of the dead end she would feel trapped in if her best guess failed. But it didn't. Her third try, NICOLLET AVENUE, worked. Seeing ACCESS GRANTED produced no exhilaration. It just made her sad.

She went through Matt's name, Billy's, and her own, paying nowhere near the attention she thought she would. The letters glowed, the numbers in their accounts sang out, and Liz was having trouble focusing on any of it, suddenly not caring. Then she pressed A-n-k-e-r, M-i-k-e, and a life-long chronology came up, the first entry being:

1956 GRADUATE TUITION LOAN	$1500
1959 LOAN REPAID	-0-

And then more information followed:

1985 INVESTMENT FOR MIKE ANKER	$380,000
1985 MIKE ANKER INVESTMENT WITHDRAWN	-0-

She pressed Scroll Forward to the last entry. It was *this year, yesterday.*

FUNDS ($1,804,000) TRANSFERRED TO AC-COUNT NUMBER FOUR I.E., DELETE DESIGNA-

TION ACCOUNT NUMBER FOUR. INSERT A-N-
K-E-R CONFIRMATION HEWITT VIA BILLY

They found an account, filled it up, and put Mike's name
on it.

Not in 1985. They did it yesterday, pretending the
$380,000 was still Mike's and grew to almost two million.
They. Her husband. Her son. And she drove the car.

She steadied herself and looked at the collection of instruments on Sam's console: the phone, the speaker attach-
ment, the fax, the laptop, the modems. She turned around
in her chair until she saw the lights of Miami, and the lit
blue tower of the Grand Bay Hotel. Then she picked up
the phone.

She shivered, afraid, as if a stranger were in her house,
and she knew if she had to speak through her rage, her
words would come out in a stutter, distorted, malformed.

38

MIKE WAS SO EXHAUSTED HIS EYES HURT. HE HAD BEEN
going, it seemed, for days. Sam's party hadn't helped, but
he decided to stay up and wait for Cheryl. He sat back in
a lounge chair, pulled over a stool, and put his feet up. He
turned on the television, and God knew what he was watching; he didn't. The bay and the dark water and the stars
outside the open terrace doors did not have their usual
relaxing effect tonight. He looked at his watch and wished
for Cheryl.

The TV screen flickered and churned out one program
after the other and at each commercial break he checked
his watch. When he found he was checking more than eight

times an hour, he knew it was after eleven-thirty. Local, non-network programming had taken over the airwaves and the FCC allowed more commercial minutes per hour. He had learned that when the purchase of a group of TV stations was a case study in his class. That's what he knew about television: commercials per hour, dollars per day, rate cards. He knew such things about a lot of industries: railroad freight car loadings, how many rooms in the hotel were rented per night, vacancy factors in office buildings, production line utilization.

Then a knock on the door signaled a bellman followed by Cheryl. It unnerved him to see Cheryl and think of Liz. There was a time when he wanted nothing less of Liz than her standing up to Sam and saying "I never loved you." And now?

"It's a good thing I didn't promise to call you," Cheryl said, walking into his life again. Mike found it hard to believe she was real. "I didn't even know when I was getting off that island."

"Ma'am, where do you want me to set this bag?"

"Anywhere."

Mike stood, pulled money from his wallet, but Cheryl gave the boy a tip and saw him out.

"In any event, I made it," Cheryl said. "It's close to twelve. I'm sorry."

Mike went over to her as she said, "I'm sorry." He put his arms around her, and all he could think to say was "Thank God." He hugged her hard and wouldn't let her go. For some strange reason he remembered rearranging her pocketbook, telling her that was a great way to learn to know her. He had arranged the pens and the pencils, the hard candies, the little notebooks, and her *mezuzah*. He brushed all the loose tobacco out of the corners and told her to stop smoking. He could see her smile and feel her laugh.

"Mike, let me unpack!"

He let go. "Sure."

The hotel bedroom seemed so much more human now that there were two people in it instead of one, especially when it was her clothes, her small overnight case, combs, brushes, and toenail clippers that littered the place. He loved all of it.

He watched Cheryl unpack, moving from the dresser to the bathroom and back, wearing less and less as she went back and forth. In so many ways she seemed more an anchor for him, especially right now, than he had ever been for her. He thought of Liz again, her body, his ability to recall to a millimeter the moves of making love with her; better forgotten, better not to have experienced again.

The doors to the terrace were still open, and as Cheryl turned off the second-to-last light she asked, "Mike, you want them open?"

"Whatever you like." Had it been wrong? He and Liz, the two of them, together? He watched Cheryl move and she blurred with Liz, then separated again.

Cheryl left the terrace doors open and got into the same side, the right side of the bed, she had chosen from the first night they slept together. Mike reached over toward the bedside table only to find that there was no lamp where a lamp should be. He had forgotten. Spotlights in the ceiling. He found the switch and the last lights went out.

He could feel her body rise, swell, and then relax again. Then he became conscious of her breathing again.

"If you'd rather not talk, it's okay," he heard her say, and he realized he must have been quiet for a longer time than he thought. "I can always order up some whipped cream," she said, "and we can try that again. It's your mind I'm into. Sex is something I do only to maintain our relationship." The bed shook, and he knew Cheryl was laughing.

"You're laughing," he said. "I'm glad."

He turned toward her and held her as she caressed his temples and circled his bushy sideburns. She knew every detail of his face. She had told him he looked like no one else, and that she knew his looks by heart. When they were touching he felt a thickening between them. Cheryl did not stop her gentle pressing and circling of his temples, occasionally tracing the contours of his jaw, once touching the lobe of his ear to see if he would pull away or make some small sound. He turned to lie on his back, and as he did, Cheryl lifted her fingers from his temples. He knew she was waiting for him to talk, using considerable self-control. Still, he could say very little. He didn't know what he could say without endangering her.

The noise of the few cars below in the street was faint, and even the harbor at this hour was silent. The only sound was the breeze rustling the palm fronds on the terrace.

"The Lincoln Center Awards were on at ten tonight. George Burns got an award," Mike said. "They were the only couple in the history of television who didn't make fun of each other. My father smoked a cigar. Just like George Burns. Mom was like Gracie. We used to listen to them on Sunday nights on the radio." Cheryl took his hand. "They said their parents came to America so we would have a better life. They wanted that for us more than anything in the world. And what did we do with what they gave us?"

Cheryl clung to his hand tightly. The talking had started. It had to come out.

"There's an account in the Grand Caymans with almost two million in it," she said into the darkened room.

Cheryl turned over, the movement of the bed bringing them closer together. "It's got your name on it," she said.

She took a deep breath and tried to think how to continue, given his silence. "You think you can find one for me?" she said finally.

He touched her hair. He thought of what Cheryl had said about women not growing up the same way men did, wondering if one woman could leap-frog another, pass her by, leave her choking in the dust, the same way one man could surpass another man and still come together when it was all over.

"Your eyes are open," she said quietly.

"I find ceilings delightful places."

She could hear the anger in his voice. "I know you don't want to draw me in, but Mike . . ." He touched the down on her arms. They lay together silently for a moment.

"I'm getting some water," she said. "You want some?"

"Okay."

"Promise not to spill it in bed?"

He smiled. "I promise." She left the lights off.

She set the glass down on the night table on his side of the bed as he pushed himself up and lay back on the pillow. Cheryl sat next to him, her glass in her hand, her legs hanging over the edge of the bed. She looked out of the window. There were fewer lights burning across the bay, and now, as she saw the digital clock flashing almost one in the morning, fewer boats going back and forth. The door to the terrace was open, and the air, still warm at this hour, mixed with the cool from the air-conditioner. Mike knew this was her way of telling him that she was willing to stay up and talk as long as he liked.

"It's a plant by the government. They're out to squeeze me."

"No, Mike. It's not the government."

Mike shifted his weight suddenly.

"Who, then?" he asked, not wanting to hear.

"Mike, do you know where the account came from? And the money in it? Your buddy, Sam, that's where. He sent Billy down there to move almost two million, cash, that much money, into an account which he put your name on. He may even have back-dated it to make it look like it was done years ago, and by you. He doesn't even care if you keep all the money in it. He's going to hang you with that account unless you protect him. That's worth two million dollars to him. That's an expensive way of putting a clamp on your mouth."

"It isn't my account. I have no account."

She looked puzzled, but she went on.

"I know that. Sam created it for you."

Mike became conscious of a bubble in his chest.

"I sat next to Billy on the way back from the Grand Caymans. Billy had a few drinks, and let all the anger out. He's been used and he hates being used. I'm down there doing the Marley deal and he, the son and heir, is down there destroying the one man who paid attention to him. You."

"Cheryl, I don't want to hear this."

"You think I like telling you?"

"Who do you think you are?"

"Me? I'm just the messenger."

In the dark the phone rang. Mike had no need to fumble for it; his eyes had adjusted to the darkened room.

"Are you okay?" Cheryl heard Mike say. "Who is it?" she asked.

Mike held his hand over the mouthpiece. "It's Liz," he whispered.

"Why are you whispering?" Cheryl asked, hurt. "Am I not here?"

"Yes, Liz, what can I do?" he said out loud.

Cheryl heard Mike say many yeses and um-hmms. Then she heard Mike say "A chronology? From 1956? He kept what?"

Cheryl knew full well what a chronology meant to Sam Yones. "Why am I nobody's fool?" she murmured.

Mike shifted his attention for a moment, not understanding her words. Then he said to Cheryl, "Liz wants to send us a fax."

"Okay," Cheryl said, ice cold, "let her send it."

Mike checked the top of the night table. No hotel notepaper. Then he opened the night table drawer and found what he was looking for. "Liz, the fax number is . . ." He read it from a tiny book of matches he had found next to a candle all hotels put somewhere in case the fuses blow or the generators go out.

"Liz, are you all right?" Mike asked, his voice, to Cheryl's ears, painfully warm. Cheryl put her hands in her lap and squeezed them. She listened to Mike's thanks and his attempts to comfort Liz. He refused to look at her as he hung up the phone.

"Wait until you see what Sam's done," Cheryl said, her anger undimmed. "You have no idea what a chronology means to that man. If Nixon remembered every slight, Sam remembers every favor. Not what you did for him, but what he did for you. Just wait. Wait until you see what she sends you. Then yell at her. Just the way you yell at me. Ask her, 'Who do you think you are?' "

"That's the fax," Mike said, hearing a knock at the door. He sighed, blowing air like a beached whale, and threw both legs over the side of the bed.

Mike tipped the bellman and carried the fax into the bathroom, and Cheryl watched him read it in the hard fluorescent light. He walked back into the room, feeling the anchor to that whole part of his life with Sam Yones drop right at the end of the darkened pier outside, the pier that led to the sea. Cheryl walked over to him and took the paper out of his hands, and saw the listing of the account worth close to two million dollars. DELETE DESIGNATION ACCOUNT NUMBER FOUR. INSERT A-N-K-E-R.

"You need any more proof?" she said. "Or will that do it for you. After all, her fax is better than my word."

Cheryl stretched out her legs and smoothed them with her hands. It made her feel more comfortable as she waited to hear what Mike had to say.

The account was not his, he thought. But it had started out that way.

He had asked, demanded, to be backed out of the transaction. Sam had said of course, there was plenty of time. He'd do it. But now it was clear Sam had not done it at all. Sam was holding him hostage, just like the rest of them. It was Sam's plan to guarantee his own survival if he lost the war, just like Hitler in the bunker.

"Her evidence is written," Mike said. There was no sense of triumph in his voice.

He remembered his father's funeral, listening to Rabbi Aaron speak of his father's strivings, his yearnings to make his mark, and Mike recalled the rabbi's very words: "We are all destined for the grave, but truly blessed is he who leaves the earth with a good name." A good name Mike knew he had helped to sustain. Mike loved his heritage, but could he live up to its standards?

"You say one more thing about Sam or one more thing about Liz and you'll break my heart."

"I can't keep quiet, Mike. You've got to be clear about this. He'll use it on you if you don't use it on him first. Mike, it all has to stop somewhere."

"I know."

He was quiet as he got into bed. He touched Cheryl's hand, and for a while they both lay there, looking up at the ceiling.

"All I want is for this to be over," Mike said into the darkened room. "I just want us to be free of all of them." Cheryl turned and hugged him, knowing he must feel like a caged canary in a mine shaft, knowing that all he could do was wait. "For me," Mike went on. "For you. For Billy. For Liz, even for Sam."

"Why Liz? Why her? She did all right," Cheryl said, then bit her tongue.

Mike sat up on one elbow, and in the dark she could tell he was staring at her. Then he let himself down again. She knew his eyes were open, and that he was looking at the ceiling.

She turned and hugged him again.

"I'm sorry, Mike."

She felt the bed move and then the light over his night table went on. Her eyes had become used to the dark and she shielded them against the spotlight over her head. She heard him lift the phone.

"Telephone number of Spencer Pelcheck. P-e-l . . ." And she heard him spell the name, say thank you, and then press buttons.

"Is Spencer Pelcheck there? It's Michael Anker." Cheryl watched as he waited and heard him say yes a few times. "I understand. I respect that," Mike said. Then he said good night and hung up the phone.

"He doesn't think it's right to talk to me without my lawyer present."

"Well, what do you know," Cheryl said.

"He'll see me tomorrow morning in the grand jury room, early, at eight o'clock. He's not breaking any rules there, because once I'm in the grand jury room, I'm not entitled to a lawyer."

"What are you going to do?"

Mike remembered Sam saying a long time ago, "This is my best friend, Mike Anker." "Why, of course, Professor

Anker." This was a surprise, coming from the Assistant Secretary of Defense. From the chancellor of the Theological Seminary, he might have expected it, but not a politician. "Well, gentlemen," Sam went on, and Mike watched the famous faces and listened to the words coming out of their mouths, nothing matching the pictures the world had of them. Will-they-ever-find-out questions. How-will-it-work questions. Drooling. And Mike remembered Sam through the cigar smoke. He sat not at the head of the table, but in the center, as the president does at cabinet meetings, and Mike tried not to be dazzled. It was later, when each of them was alone with Sam, one walking in Rock Creek Park, another at Heathrow Airport, wherever and whenever each one saw Sam privately in a public place, that codes and accounts would be discussed. Mike had been the observer at a few of those clandestine meetings, fixing a flat on a bike path in Rock Creek Park, buying the *Tatler* at an airport kiosk, Sam and his client giddy as children, weaving their conspiracies.

"He's lied to me," Mike said to Cheryl. He was thinking of one lie, she another. "Enough."

"I guess now it's okay for me to tell you," she said, "now that you've made up your mind." But she hesitated.

"It's okay," he said softly, sensing her anguish as he had so often before. "Tell me."

"Mike, last night, the FBI . . ."

Mike listened and Cheryl told him. She saw the life go out of his face.

Small and cold, a shiver went down his back.

"They're trying to make us eat the peel," Mike said slowly. "No more."

She relaxed only when she felt him hug her back and her fingers play gently in the long gray hairs on his chest.

She could imagine him tomorrow morning, back in the grand jury room, doing his best, and she knew his best had been good enough for thirty years. Her head fell into her own pillow, but she still held his hand. She thought, "I know he's brilliant, but is he lucky?"

PART SIX

39

"LADIES AND GENTLEMEN, WE WILL PICK UP WHERE WE LEFT off two days ago." Spencer held the door open for Mike. "Our guest is back with us."

Mike followed Spencer into the grand jury room. He had told Arlo nothing and showed him nothing. They left Arlo in the waiting room, reading magazines. The door shut the rest of the world outside; Spencer, Mike, and the grand jury were together, on their own, behind closed doors.

Mike touched his jacket pocket again to check that the fax was still there and nodded the sweetest greeting he could muster to twenty-three jurors. He avoided the witness stand, and sat in a side chair near Spencer's table.

"Well, ladies and gentlemen, I'm sure you're wondering why I have asked you to reconvene on such short notice for the second time in the same week and, on top of that, at eight o'clock in the morning."

Spencer moved around the room, touching various pieces of furniture, sitting on the windowsill, leaning against the wall. He owned the place. It was his. He knew every inch of it as well as a pianist knows the keys of his piano. He left his perch on the windowsill, crossed in front of them, and sat down at his long table. He pushed the sign that read MR. PELCHECK off to one side so he could make room for two new stacks of papers that he extracted from his briefcase, and then went about rearranging the other papers at his counsel's table. It seemed to do little good; it looked just as messy as it had when he started.

The grand jury room looked exactly as it had two days ago. Beethoven, Fats Waller, Grandma Rosen, who wore a gold necklace that spelled E-s-t-e-l-l-e, and the twenty others were all there. Even though the time of day was different, morning now, late afternoon last Tuesday, oddly, the light coming in the window seemed the same. Maybe, Mike thought, that was because the light didn't come from a real outside; it just spilled down an air shaft. He touched his jacket for the second time to make sure Liz's fax was still there. It was his lifeline: documentary proof that Sam had set him up. His chest hurt from the weight of it.

Back in their seats, most of the faces that had once seemed strange to Mike became familiar again. For a minute it seemed like a boy-girl-boy-girl twelfth-birthday-party seating pattern, but there were two extra women, both in the top row. Mike started to feel for the fax again, but realized how foolish a gesture that was, like a gunslinger reaching for a Colt .45 he knew he could never use. To use it would lead to Liz. Corroboration and authentication. Questions would be put to her by Spencer, questions that had nothing to do with her conversations with Sam, questions not covered by the privilege that protects communications between husband and wife. These questions were, "Did this document come from his computer?" "Did you break a code to get it?" "Did you print it out yourself from that computer?" All that was fair game. The fax Liz had sent him was a lifeline for him only. It was not at all that for her.

"It has always been my policy to make full disclosure to you," Spencer was saying, using his Robert Stack voice again. "That way, if and when unorthodox proceedings occur in our investigation you, all of you, in your capacity as grand jurors, will know three things. First, you will know what we are doing. Second, you will know the legal authority which allows us to propose to you that we do what we do. And third, you will have the right to question what it is we propose."

The only thing new in the room was a huge tray of sweet rolls and doughnuts. It looked like fifty some odd, two for each, assuming Spencer took three for himself. There were two big urns steaming, maybe one for regular coffee and one for decaf, or maybe the other one was hot water for tea. Napkins were available on the windowsill.

"But first". . . . Spencer sure knew how to gesture and smile, Mike decided—"we certainly aren't going to leave all those rolls and coffee sitting there untouched, now, are we?"

Since no one wanted to make the first move, Spencer took a coconut glaze, and coffee tinkled out of the spigot into his cup. Finally, it dawned on the foreman of the grand jury that it might be part of his job to lead the troops to rolls and coffee. So he scraped his chair on the floor, which everyone tried to ignore, got up, and followed Spencer to the coffee urns. That did it. They all followed. The "ham sandwich thesis," Mike thought, the New York judge's notion that a grand jury would indict a ham sandwich if led to it.

At the end of the parade, Mike decided it was his turn. Coffee in hand and rolls balanced on napkins, no one returned to their seats but stood around in several groups. None of them gathered around Spencer.

Mike stood alone also, first in one place, then moved nervously to another. He overheard parts of several conversations, excluded from all of them. "It was the first time I missed Sunday Mass since I had use of my reason," Mike heard the old man say, calling Estelle "Mrs. Rosen," and she calling him "Manuel." Mike thought of Chanukah and being the oldest grandson, first in line to be handed a shiny quarter from his zayde's loving hand; Kol Nidre night wearing his blue suit, skullcap and *tallis* fresh from his bar mitzvah, standing next to his father and thinking, on that Day of Atonement, of his father's bar mitzvah and his grandfather before him and all the fathers and all the grandfathers and someday he'd be a father and a grandfather too. Then he thought of the Passovers with Sam and Liz at their apartment when they were first married, with all the single strays invited to seder, Gordy and himself included, Mike asking the four questions because he was the youngest. He watched Manuel put down his coffee and say, "But, Mrs. Rosen, God will understand."

Mike took a bite out of his powdered doughnut, trying to keep white flecks off his suit, and out of the corner of his eye he saw Spencer approaching from the left.

"Coffee okay?"

"Ever thought of business school? Running a big company?" His voice was cooler than he wanted it to be.

"My mother always told me it was the little people in life that count, that to be poor was to be sanitary." Spencer rocked backward on his heels. "Do you take cream or sugar?"

"Black is fine."

Spencer headed toward the window and Mike drifted behind him. There was a wide sill just under the windows, and Spencer parked his doughnut on it. The jurors had clustered on the other side of the room, gathered around their swivel chairs, using the flip-up writing surfaces as tables, improvising, just as Spencer and Mike were doing.

"You can put your coffee cup here," Spencer said loudly. "Your doughnut okay?" Spencer sang out. He checked again. No one had turned around.

Mike knew Spencer was testing sound levels, how loudly he could speak on this side of the room without being heard by the grand jurors on the other side. It was the same kind of experimenting Mike did before he lectured in a new auditorium, or testified as an honored expert before Congress in a room he hadn't used before.

"What do you want to do, Mike?" Spencer had dropped his voice to a whisper. "This coffee act is for you."

"I thought so."

"You called me last night. I'll do as much for you as I can."

"Only as much as you can?"

Spencer put his glasses in the steam rising from the cup,

clouding them on purpose. He pointed to a chair near the windows, but Mike wanted to stand.

"I want to talk to you about immunity," Mike said, the weight of a forty-year friendship pressing him down.

"I'll do more than talk about it. I'll give it to you."

"When?"

"Relax." Spencer looked down at Mike's tapping foot, and Mike stopped the movement.

"I don't want anyone to know about it. That would be as bad as . . ."

"I know. I have your immunity letter here." And while he was talking, Spencer took a letter out of his pocket and handed it to Mike.

"But it's addressed to Arlo, and Byron has signed it."

"Byron always signs it. He has the authority."

"So he knows?"

"Yes, he's usually awake in the morning."

Mike tried a smile, but there wasn't much humor behind it. "And Arlo?"

"No, he doesn't know. You can tell him if you like. Or you can tell no one . . ." Spencer watched him like a hawk and Mike watched him back. ". . . because the way we've done it, no one on the outside will know." Spencer took a swallow of his coffee but winced when the hot liquid hit his tooth.

"Why the special favor?"

Mike felt like a man afraid of his own shadow, and he knew that was precisely the wrong way to feel because Spencer would seize on it.

"I want what you've heard over the last thirty years."

"That's hearsay," Mike managed to say. "Even I know that."

"In a trial, you're absolutely right. That is hearsay, and it couldn't get within miles of a jury. But here," and Spencer gestured to the room, "you're wrong. Hearsay is admissable. Hearsay is what grand juries thrive on. Ask any lawyer."

Mike looked away, then he locked eyes with Spencer.

"No one will know it was you who testified. Sam in particular." Spencer paused. "There will be no trail to follow. We call this stand-by immunity. The fact that you have it is itself a secret. This is what you want, isn't it?"

"This has not been a perfect day."

Spencer smiled, but not too much. All at once, and Spencer didn't know why, he was beginning to feel for Mike.

Mike wanted more than ever to stretch, to change his glasses, to tap his foot again, do anything. But he knew not to do any of it.

"Spencer, I've already been in front of the grand jury. I sat in this room and testified in front of these people. They know who I am. They know my name."

"No, they don't know your name. Did you ever hear me call you by name when you were in front of the grand jury?" Mike stood quietly. "Don't stop to think about it. You won't remember. You were concentrating on other things. I called you 'sir' or 'our guest,' but never by name." The words did not seem to reach him at first. "They know who you are by category, but that's all; not by name."

"What the hell does that really mean?"

"It means that I can go to a grand jury and tell them that the next witness is so important and can help so much that we have to do everything in our power to convince that witness that it is safe to be forthcoming. And that includes protecting his identity when he appears before the grand jury. So . . . well, why should I tell you what I said to them? Here. Read the transcript. I said this just before you were called in. Remember the first day, Tuesday afternoon, when you sat out there waiting to be called? I'll bet you were wondering why it took me ten, fifteen minutes to get to you? Well, here's why. This is what I was saying to the grand jury. Read it."

Mike took the transcript Spencer handed him. He did what he was told. He turned the folded page back and read.

MR. PELCHECK: Ladies and gentlemen. What I am saying to you now is being taken down by our court reporter, Mrs. Lillian Rabinowitz, so there will be a record of what I am saying to you, which is required by law. This is a procedure I am now going to ask you to approve, because the grand jury proceedings are under your control, not mine. This procedure is permitted by law. It entails asking a person to appear before you as a witness, for you to take his testimony very seriously, but you will never know the name of that witness.

Who sells out? Mike wondered, walking over to the window to read the rest of the transcript standing in the sunlight. How much moral ground do you lose in exchange for getting your nose in under the tent? How much does Sam lose when he turns a friend into a hostage? Goddamn that man, Mike thought. He doesn't give a shit what he loses; only I think of the times gone by.

This procedure is for people whose presence before a grand jury could hurt them, people who are not targets, people whose help to us can be potentially so massive that we, your government, and me, as the representative of your government, ask you to allow him to help without knowing his name.

Ladies and gentlemen, this is a very sensitive witness. He has information that is quite relevant to our investigation. It may be that he will never be a witness at trial and we are very concerned that if someone is indicted as a result of what he tells us, that person's lawyer will come in and get transcripts of this hearing, know the identity of the witness and what he said, and we don't want that.

And what times they were. In the rooms where big men showed their souls. An attentive observer of the down side. Like having dinner with Hitler.

This is a person you will not know by sight, so identification that way is unlikely, and it may be a person you may not even know by name. However, if anonymity is what it will take to assure his help to us, that is what we shall give him, with your permission, and I hope you will agree.

MR. NOVAES (*FOREMAN*): Is this legal?

MR. PELCHECK: Yes, it is legal.

MRS. ROSEN: Are you sure?

MR. PELCHECK: Yes . . . *(unintelligible)* It is legal. I am sure.

MRS. ROSEN: Did you ask the judge?

MR. PELCHECK: This is not a matter that requires the approval of the judge.

MRS. ROSEN: Ah-ha. So you didn't see the judge.

MR. PELCHECK: It is not required. And as I have said, we should provide this witness with all the comfort he can receive, and if anonymity is what is required, we should provide it and I hope you will agree.

Mike finished reading and looked up at Spencer. "And, undoubtedly, they agreed."

"How did you guess?" Spencer pulled at his putrid-green suitcoat. Once more he was Lord of the World, having a rich man's destiny in his hands. "I don't know how else to tie the ribbon for you. You're safe in every way I know how to make you safe and still have your testimony under oath."

Spencer looked at his jurors finishing up their doughnuts.

"You need me almost too much," Mike said. "Why? Something must be wrong." He hesitated, then continued. "Is the rest of your evidence okay? Or is it tainted?"

Spencer looked surprised, and without thinking he said, "Who said anything about entrapment?"

Mike decided to study Spencer, who had slipped, who had just told him too much. He took notice of Spencer's loose-jointed style, the way he could stop on a dime, dart here, dart there, juggle so many ideas that sometimes he had to stop and clear his head to remind himself where he was headed. Mike caught himself smiling at Spencer's slips the way Edgar used to smile at him, and he remembered the afternoons he used to sit with Edgar in his grand corner office, looking out of the windows high over Manhattan, playing follow-the-money, each enjoying the thrust and parry, a game that was between friends, a game nobody lost. Mike realized that this game, the game with Sam, the game with Spencer, was not that kind of a game at all.

"Who said anything about the FBI and Cheryl?" Mike said, his voice tight, barely controlled. "Your fucking government bangs on our door in the middle of the night. You knew I was here. You knew she was there alone." Mike's jaw tightened. He was glad the sound levels had been tested. He turned around, just for an instant, to see if the grand jury had heard his fury. "What in the hell is this country coming to? No, it's not this country that's wrong. *You* sent the FBI out in the middle of the night to our home. *You're* the one who's wrong. *You*. All by yourself. What do you people turn yourselves into?"

"Make up your mind," Spencer said. "Now."

"You make up yours."

Mike caught his breath. Then he looked at Spencer and saw an empty face. The bees had started buzzing around Spencer's head, but he tried to pretend they weren't there.

"Listen, Mr. Anker, you called me at *my* home last night, and I said I wouldn't talk to you then; I would talk to you here. You walked in here and asked for immunity. I gave it to you. You see those people over there?" Spencer gestured to the empty chairs of twenty-three impatient people who were standing in groups, coffee cups drained, out of doughnuts, wanting to move on or go home. "Those people are known as an investigative grand jury. They hear testimony, and now they're going to hear you."

Mike tried to choke back rising panic for a moment to find some logical way to behave. He had no ideas as he stood with Spencer in what seemed like a darkening room. They were coming after him, he knew too much. He was the fish who swam too well. He was grasping, trying to find a way out. The room felt warm to Mike, and he felt the sweat dripping down his legs.

"Isn't there another way?"

Spencer took another drink of his coffee. Mike was silent. He wanted to be anywhere but where he was, even back in a raw hole of an office on a midtown cross-street where everything smelled of garlic and old clothes.

"You know," Spencer said, breaking his silence, sweat standing on his own forehead, "maybe there is another way."

Mike looked up, and neither of them was sure who should move first.

"What do you want?" Spencer asked.

"I want it to be over with."

"There's a choice, maybe. It's up to you."

Mike laughed, but it was a shaky, nervous laugh. "I don't know if I like all this power."

"You love it. Tell me what you know. Tell me privately. Me, just me," Spencer said, "and then you won't have to tell them." He didn't gesture this time toward the grand jury seats. He didn't have to.

Mike shivered in the air he felt as heat.

"You tell me what you would testify to before the grand jury. You tell me off the record. Not even under oath. Then I don't call you at all."

Mike begged some unknown God to prevent his toe from tapping or his forehead from sweating or his right eye from twitching.

"Why?"

"Because everyone else is asking for too much." Spencer looked at Mike directly now. "And the worst isn't over. Everyone's riding your ass. Everybody gets something by trading you."

"And you?"

"I hope so." Raoul started tapping his coffee cup, looking across to the window where Mike and Spencer stood. Spencer put on his glasses again, clean now, and his eyelids steadied.

"What more is there for me to tell you?"

"I don't know."

"Why will I tell you more?" Mike asked.

"Because you'll have nothing to fear."

Spencer felt the force of Mike's direct gaze, just as they all had.

Spencer stared him right back.

"From anyone. From any direction. And neither will Cheryl."

"No testimony under oath," Mike continued. "Nothing to lead back to me. No involvement for her. All in exchange for some private talks with you. No one, no one even in your office will know it's me. Is that my deal?"

"That's your deal."

"Since when are you the American legal system?"

"Since when am I not?"

They had rounded a corner and both of them knew it.

He thought about Cheryl and Liz, those who had given him honesty and love, but without the violation of federal statutes. The joke here, he thought to himself, after all these years, is that women turn out to be the best men.

"Mr. Pelcheck, sir . . ." It was the impatient voice of Mrs. Rosen.

"I called them in at eight o'clock in the morning," Spencer said, looking at his twenty-three people. "I've got to give them something."

40

"SIR, IT WILL NOT BE NECESSARY TO READMINISTER THE oath. I assume that is all right with you, Mr. Foreman."

Spencer looked at Mike with the same calm expression of thirty seconds ago, but now Mike didn't know how to read it.

"Yes, Mr. U.S. Attorney," Raoul responded.

The grand jury was back in session. The coffee cups, the doughnuts, and the informality were gone. The room was silent, the only sound being the catch-up clicks of the court reporter's steno machine. Mike had no idea what Spencer was up to, why Spencer had put him on the witness stand in the first place.

Spencer caught the expression on Mike's face and realized he had spooked him. He had made a mistake. He had not explained enough, that he simply couldn't let Mike waltz out of there, that he needed a record. Two minutes more to explain precisely what he was trying for would have helped. Dammit. It was all Mike would have needed. "Give them a half hour of innocent questions and answers; then they will have seen you twice and be through with you. What you had they got, and it's all in the transcript. Don't worry about answers. The questions will do the trick," he could have said. "Just follow my lead. It's what goes in the record that counts. It will look like a lot, but it will be nothing." Clear as a bell was how it could have been.

Spencer smiled, trying to get Mike to relax, but it didn't work. Now he had to do it the hard way. He would have to go through a series of questions with telegraphed answers, who's-buried-in-Grant's-Tomb questions.

"Tell me, sir, *if*, and I repeat, *if* anyone were interested, why would one invest in a timberlands partnership? Would you have a *speculation* on that?"

Mike tried to force himself to sit up straight, to take charge. The steno machine did not record the stress Spencer put on *if* and *speculation*.

"I'm sure, sir," Spencer said, "you have a *guess* or two." Spencer focused on the stenographer's machine. He wanted Mike to see the word *record* blinking on and off in five-foot-high red neon lights.

Mike caught on.

"If you can find proper management, timberlands investments produce important tax advantages. First of all . . ."

Mike began to get the knack of talking for the record. It was nowhere near easy. You had to think how everything you said would appear in print. And you had to do it as you spoke, actually a few seconds before you spoke. It was like walking around with your every word being taken down by six of the best reporters from *The New York Times*. He began to get a kick out of it because it stimulated him. But underneath the excitement he developed a new respect for free speech and he wanted the game to be over.

Spencer read Mike's eyes. They had the beginnings of their own language.

"Well, sir," Spencer said with maybe too much a sense of relief in his voice, "now that we have *that* settled . . . Now, sir, you spoke of management. Does that mean the general partner makes all the decisions, what land to buy, what to cut, when to replant, when to distribute profits?"

Mike carried on in a voice that was his alone. It was like the first day of each new semester. The stop-start hard labor would show up nowhere. If he just had a little more time to think about each response, he could do better, but for now, all he could do was hope the grand jury would never indict for twitchiness. He knew Spencer wanted the record as long as both Testaments put together. And just as detailed, layered, and acceptable; the gospel. He watched the court reporter click his words onto her paper and he thought of the fortune transcribers could have made during the Babylonian Captivity. The trick now was to avoid being cocky. There was a glint in Spencer's eye that Mike found dangerous. Maybe it was the upturned corners of Spencer's mouth that he flattened out in a flash so no one else could see that it made Mike uneasy. The glint became triumphant. Spencer would spike him with another question, and he would roll out another answer. It got to be like singing the National Anthem. You loved the drum roll and you knew the words.

Not once in any of Spencer's questions had Sam's name come up. Or Cheryl's. Or Gordy, Billy, Liz, or Matt's. Spencer had seen to that. Had any of those names surfaced, and had questions been put in the correct ways, Mike knew he would have had the choice put to him, perjury or the only family he'd ever known. But it hadn't happened. Mike knew the absence of names so close to him for his whole life was not an accident. It was his deal. Spencer was keeping his side of the bargain. Mike knew he would owe him for that. It was his vow. Spencer was entitled to a payback, but was he entitled to all he wanted? Mike knew the morning had knocked the wind out of him, but he had threaded his way through. The art of the ad lib was not dead.

Mike looked out of the window and thought of wonderful summers, year after year, hot, steady and brilliant, that they spent together for so many years. Each day was like the last, in the back end of Mount Desert Island, near Southwest Harbor, where professors summered. Not Bar Harbor, with Rockefeller homes. That would come later. Twenty years ago, those happy days in rented white sloops, he with whatever woman he was seeing at the time, sometimes even alone, Gordy with Helen, maybe even Ginger, but she was new then, shy, and Gordy was uncertain about bringing her, what Sam would say, and Liz. Liz always with Sam. Mike thought of how it had all changed, how many places they had seen since, yachts they had owned, sloops they had flown to in private jets, urging life into grander and more complicated patterns as time went on, as lines were crossed, as doors that led back into safe childhood rooms of rights and wrongs were slammed shut behind them. Mike smiled, remembering the summer the lady psychiatrist on the island was prowling around his door at four in the morning until he let her in. What a crowd. What fun they all had sitting on screened porches after dinner, chairs hung back on nails pounded into cedar log walls, looking across the water in the pond, watching the fireflies.

Mike looked up and saw not Sam, Liz, or the lady psychiatrist, but the grand jury. It was now nine-thirty, and even though he had a pretty good sensitivity for elapsed time, he found it hard to believe that they had been playing Edgar Bergen and Charlie McCarthy for close to an hour. Mike had no idea of how many transcript pages one hour turned into. Maybe enough. He had no idea.

Spencer must have caught Mike's clandestine look at his watch, because he moved away from his position directly in front of the witness stand and headed toward the windows, drawing attention to himself, away from Mike. He glanced outside for a moment at the bricks on the other side of the air shaft, then crossed the room and sat down at his table, signaling to Mike that they were almost through.

"And none of these activities you have described involved overseas accounts anywhere?" Spencer said, knowing he had asked a question that he could take out of context, tying a bow that wrapped an empty package.

"No, sir," Mike said. Once the words were out, he knew he hadn't spoken his last answer loudly enough. He cleared his throat, but before he could repeat his answer while the room was silent, while there was no noise from Lillian's transcribing machine, no shuffling of feet or papers, he heard the sound of the doorknob turning as if it were amplified.

There was only one person who could waltz into the grand jury room like that, unannounced, without the prior approval of a judge, without checking with Spencer first or without being the fire department. Mike looked at the man from the thirty-eighth floor who stood in the portal. Mike knew his luck had just turned around. Standing in the doorway was Byron Varner.

Gordy's story of the warring Sicilian Mafiosi flashed through his mind: Death could be attributed to neither side, and must therefore be the work of an outsider.

One hand began perspiring ice into the other, so much so that Mike allowed his hand to fall on his trouser leg, which he used as a napkin.

41

"GOOD MORNING, LADIES AND GENTLEMEN," BYRON SAID, the timing of his smile just a fraction of a second late.

The door behind him was still open. Mike looked out into the waiting room and saw Arlo, quietly reading a magazine, pretending that Byron was not standing in an open doorway to the grand jury room, and that Mike was not on display alone in the center of the room, on the witness stand.

"I'm sorry to intrude," Byron said, closing the door behind him, cutting Arlo off from view. "I'll just take a seat . . ."

As he spoke, he walked to the back of the room, heading toward one of the side chairs near the window.

". . . back here." He took some papers off one chair and put them on the other one. "Please, Mr. Pelcheck. Continue."

"Well . . ." Spencer said.

"Well . . ." he said again.

Mike turned to the front of the room and wanted for all he was worth to yell stage directions to Spencer. The action. Dominate it with your eyes, your hands, your voice. Eyes first.

Spencer forced a smile, and he wished he could teach himself, fast, how to breathe deeply without anyone knowing it. Byron would scuttle all of it for all of them. Spencer felt his back to the wall. He did not want to come out slugging. Not that response. Do something else, not that.

"We were just beginning our discussion of . . . Lillian . . ." Spencer turned to his court reporter.

". . . will you read my last question?"

Dumb luck, Spencer thought. Talk about dumb luck. He knew damn well what his last question was. When Byron hears it he'll think Mike Anker had been raked over the coals for hours.

The room was quiet, the only sound being the catch-up clicks of the court reporter's steno machine as she keyed in Spencer's last words. Lillian tried to contain her smile as she pulled at the spool of narrow white paper. She found her place among the square holes punched in her tape. She looked up and read in a flat voice.

MR. PELCHECK: And none of these activities you have described involved any overseas accounts anywhere?

For the second time this morning, Mike saw that disheveled look, Spencer's eyes bouncing because bees seemed to be circling around his head. His papers were still sticking out of his notebooks. As Mike looked down, he saw that one of Spencer's shoes was untied.

Now, with luck, Byron would think they had spent the whole morning talking about nothing else but overseas accounts. Mike looked to the back of the room and saw that Byron Varner looked puzzled, unsure of himself.

"Mr. Pelcheck?" Byron said.

Spencer looked up.

"Thank you for having your last question read to me," Byron said. "I did not hear the answer. I assume your witness's answer was no, he does not have any overseas accounts. Is that correct?"

"Yes."

"That's fine," Byron said. "Proceed, Counsel."

Now what? Proceed where? Spencer thought. He looked at the sign with his name on it and the stacks of papers covering his counsel's table, and his eyes fell on the thick, bound document with the symbol of a green pine tree embossed on the cover.

"Have you ever seen any offering memoranda relating to Minneapolis Timber partnerships?" Spencer asked, suppressing triumph. "Those distributed to banks, pension funds, private investors."

Court reporting machines do not pick up widened eyes, exaggerated brow movements, or other such gestures synchronized with certain words, designed to emphasize them. Nor, Mike thought, do Byron Varners catch such cues, especially if they sit in the back of a room unable to see the face of one Spencer Pelcheck, who was, carefully, like a prompter at the opera, visible only to the performer.

"Yes, public documents. I've seen them."

Now everything Mike had to say, if he was careful, would be something that could be traced to publicly available filings, and nothing could be traced to him, to his own personal knowledge. They were back on track, putting their private, negotiated, custom-built legal system back into play.

Spencer, bright as a polished bugle, pulled open the thick printed document and handed it to Mike, Mike reading,

Spencer asking questions, Mike answering. Five minutes, ten minutes. More.

Mike turned pages, played for time, but carefully, knowing Byron wouldn't sit there all day. Mike checked the chair Byron was using. Uncomfortable as it could be. Good. It wouldn't be long. Mike went back to the offering memorandum. He would finger through it, not flip but not read word by word. He'd spend maybe five to eight seconds per page. He would count: one thousand and one. One thousand and two.

After more questions which he answered by reading or paraphrasing from the offering memoranda, giving what he regarded as safe answers, Mike sensed a stir in the room. Byron had left his chair and was walking forward. Mike watched as Byron marched to the front of the room and handed Spencer a note. He returned to his seat in the back of the room, folded his arms across his chest, and waited.

Spencer sat back and put some papers on his lap. Using them as a screen, he opened the note.

It read: *I gave that man immunity. Get something out of him.*

There was no sweat to wipe, but Spencer didn't check to make sure. He knew he had to respond.

"Tell me, sir," Spencer said, rising as he spoke, "did *you personally* notice anything unusual in the offering documents?"

"No, Mr. Pelcheck," Byron called out. "Not at all." The room was dead quiet.

"Ladies and gentlemen," Byron said, rising. "If you will permit me, please." He walked to the front of the room again, smiling this time.

"I am Byron Varner, the United States Attorney." He paused, waiting for Lillian to punch his name into her machine. She did not need to ask him how to spell it. "I have a few questions I would like to ask the witness." Byron stopped, as if waiting for a judge to give him permission.

Mike curled his toes inside his shoes, invisible to others, but tight enough to hurt, to keep him alert.

"Mr. Witness, I am aware of the special arrangements

governing your appearance in this grand jury hearing, and in order to protect that, I will not state your name even though it is written on this document I am about to show you. Nor, in order to protect your identity before this grand jury, will I introduce this document into evidence, also because of the fact that your name is on it. I do not want to prejudice the arrangement by which you have agreed to help us in any way."

So many words. What was he getting at? Mike wondered.

"Instead," Byron said, smiling again, "I will merely show this document to you and ask you if it is your name that appears at the top of it."

Byron handed the document over to Mike. "Is this your name at the top of this bank statement?"

Mike looked to Spencer, who in his next move was to breach centuries of legal precedent. He nodded, signaling Mike that it was okay to answer, providing a witness in a grand jury with a lawyer.

"Yes, that is my name," Mike said, following Spencer's signal.

Mike, who had all his life wished for an expressionless face, hoped God had given him one at that moment.

"Is this a bank statement of the Standard-British Bank of the Grand Caymans?"

Spencer nodded his okay signal to Mike again.

Mike stared back at him, then at Byron, feeling as up for grabs as any tree Sam had ever gone after. What would happen to him turned on the whimsy of others. He had fallen on hard times. For the first time in his life, people could look at him and say "Here's one on the way down."

"Yes, that is what it appears to be."

"Will you read to us, loud enough for the grand jury to hear, the amount set forth in that statement purporting to be the balance in your account."

Spencer nodded again, but Mike tried to hold back.

No more than an instant's delay could he allow himself. Anything more would make any rehabilitation impossible.

"Your answer, sir?"

"The amount is one million eight hundred thousand dollars."

Mike looked across the room, sweeping the surprised, suddenly unfriendly faces of the jury. Then it hit him. His next words had to be: "I only wish it were true!"

Spencer didn't laugh until he was sure it would be lost in the applause of Beethoven, Raoul, Estelle, Fats, and the two men in Sunday suits. When Byron held up his hand for silence, Spencer's smile disappeared.

"Mr. U.S. Attorney," Spencer said, holding out his hand, "may I see the document?"

Byron made a fist again, as if the pressure in his fingers alone could keep the document in his own possession, away from Spencer forever. Spencer weighed the six years he had worked with grand juries versus making war on Byron. He ran his eyes left across the back row and then right along the front row. No seats swiveled and no pencils took notes on the flip-up desks. They looked like ten-year-olds, fascinated but somehow frightened.

"Do we really think this is real?" Spencer said, canvassing his people, hoping they were still his people. He smiled, trying to pick up where Mike had left off, trying to sustain his mood. But it fell flat. Spencer looked at their faces. The jury had shifted from trusting Mike to doubting him, as often happens with a witness, in seconds. A million eight is a million eight.

Byron was the one smiling broadly now, flashing his campaign-for-office grin. "I guess we all dream about it, having the bank credit a huge amount like that to our account by mistake." Spencer saw their faces. More skeptical by the minute. Byron stood not too far from Spencer, who refused to sit down.

Finally, Spencer lowered himself into his chair, beaten. Why did he ever think he could pick Byron off with a joke? He should have known it would never work. Spencer looked at Byron's tight smile. All he had accomplished was to get Byron's anger level up to nine.

"I think, Mr. Witness, you may have avoided a direct

answer to my question about your Standard-British account," Byron said.

"No, sir. I don't think I have. That is not my account."

Mike touched his jacket pocket again to feel the fax that Liz had sent him.

Then there was mumbling among the grand jurors, and for a moment Spencer thought of reinforcing Mike's answer but decided to keep his mouth shut. You put too fine a point on the pencil and it breaks.

Lillian looked across the room at Spencer, and he gave her the subtlest signal that if Byron was through, he was through. She nodded just slightly.

Byron didn't mention perjury because he knew Spencer would have stopped him dead in his tracks. He wanted to back off. He needed Spencer, but he also wanted to move his offices two floors up and call them chambers.

"But you know people who have opened and maintained secret overseas accounts, do you not?" Byron said. "You know I can require you to answer."

At that moment, both Byron and Spencer, who had, unconsciously, found himself on his feet, were standing at the same time, the only two in the room so doing. Byron turned to Spencer and was about to speak, but then decided not to.

The grand jurors sat in their swivel chairs, nine of them with hands folded, looking like third graders waiting.

Mike's shirt was now sticking to his skin. He knew immunity would compel him to say Sam's name. Or lie to Byron and go to jail.

Mike looked at Spencer, standing there in the middle of the room, Byron Varner standing as well, the two of them squared off. Mike thought about Sam Yones, key chains and change jingling in pockets.

"Madame Court Reporter," Byron said, "strike that question."

The record would be blank. There would be no evidence of Spencer rising to his feet. It would look as if Byron had merely changed his mind.

"Ladies and gentlemen," Byron continued. "If you will

excuse me, please." He smiled and crossed the room, not stopping to say anything to Spencer or shake hands with anyone. However, for the second time he left a small note on Spencer's desk. Byron opened the door but didn't close it. Mike saw Arlo look up from a magazine, and then, out of the corner of his eye he saw Spencer head for the door to close it. But as Spencer reached the door, Byron put his hand against it, holding it open, making sure it stayed that way.

Byron held the door ajar for no more than twenty seconds, but it seemed longer to everyone in the room, especially to Raoul Novaes, who, as foreman, had read the rules carefully, including the part that required the hearings to be confidential and the doors to remain closed at all times "except for purposes of ingress and egress."

Members of the grand jury, especially those in the back row, craned their necks to see and hear what was going on. They could hear nothing, even though the grand jury room was silent. The only sounds from outside were whispers. All the time Byron's hand remained on the door, holding it ajar.

Byron finally released his grip on the door, but only as he poked his nose back into the room. Mike felt his eyes on him.

"Sir, I believe your counsel would like to consult with you," he said to Mike.

The timing of Byron's smile was once again off just a second, just as it was when he first appeared in the grand jury room an hour before. Mike looked at his watch. It was just after eleven. Whatever game Byron and Spencer were now playing, it was not with him but with each other.

"You may step outside if you wish, Mr. Witness," Byron said, his tone implying more than suggestion.

"One moment, please," Spencer said.

Mike watched as Spencer opened the note Byron had left for him, and nodded his head. He gathered up some of his files, walked toward the witness stand, and placed the files on the edge of the table near the witness stand to allow easy access when he needed to refer to them. With the files he left Byron's note where only Mike could see it.

The handwriting was small, but Spencer held the paper just between the long distance and the reading focus points of Mike's bifocals. He couldn't read the words. Too fast a tilt of his head or bobbing it back and forth would make him look like a chicken. It didn't take long, and eventually Byron's handwriting came into focus.

Byron had written, *You can't protect him. He's not yours. He's mine.*

People were pulling too many invisible strings that he felt were attached to him. He hadn't thought of Pinocchio in years, but somehow that image popped into his mind, and all he wanted now was what Pinocchio wanted. He didn't want to be a puppet. All he wanted to be was a real boy.

"Come back," Spencer said to Mike, "if you need anything." His words were full of meaning for the two of them, a reminder of the private testimony Mike owed Spencer as well as a promise of help if he needed it.

42

MIKE PULLED HIMSELF UP, LEFT THE WITNESS STAND, AND walked to the waiting room. He watched Arlo cover an old *People* magazine with legal papers and then put the stack down on the lamp table. Byron stood off in one corner and waited for the door to close.

"Why don't I leave you alone with your counsel," Byron said to Mike. "It's been good to see you, Mike." He offered his hand and left. No explanations, no excuses, no nothing.

Mike watched him go. Still standing, not quite sure where

his strength was coming from, he shook hands with Arlo. Tired as he was, he decided to remain standing to see if Arlo would rise, but he did not. Mike finally sat down, moved closer to Arlo, and swung one leg over the other. There was no stenographer here. He could speak freely again.

"To what do I owe this miracle?" he asked.

"We have to get this mess in order," Arlo said. Mike took out a set of keys and started to play with them. Then he thought of Sam Yones and the loose change in his pockets and put the keys away.

"What mess?" Mike asked sarcastically.

"Byron Varner likes you," Arlo said.

"I'm delighted."

"That's why he stopped in there this morning."

"Is it? I thought he stopped in to see what Spencer was getting out of me."

"That would happen only if you had immunity."

Mike wanted to feel new again, without a past, and he wanted to be rid of all these people.

"I'm not being abused," he said quietly, knowing better than to say more. He had probably said too much already. "I'm telling stories. I'm doing what I do as a Yones lecturer. That's what Sam wants me to do, isn't it?"

"So you've told stories, that's all? You're sure that's all?"

Mike took a deep breath. "It's not a bad enough thing that you do, Arlo, to do it just for money."

Mike stared directly at the lawyer, then quickly dropped his eyes.

"Sam gave me a special account too. Years ago," Arlo said.

"Too?"

Then Mike said nothing. He looked steadily at Arlo. He could tell Arlo had wanted to finish the story, but decided not to.

"What bothers me most is conscience," Arlo said. The words came slowly, and somehow Arlo seemed older.

"That's what bothers all of us," Mike answered.

"He was something back then," Arlo said, his eyes unfocused, "wasn't he?"

"Yes, he was," Mike said.

"You remember the laundry route? Running up and down Langdon Street in the old Studebaker? The starter was under the clutch. That's how you'd start the thing." Arlo smiled. "He'd let anybody use it who wanted to. That's the kind of guy Sam was." Mike sat back. "He used to buy his oil in bulk from Sears, Roebuck." The little lines around Mike's eyes crinkled in a smile and he looked far away. "That thing wouldn't go sixty miles an hour in free fall. He had a pet name for that car, didn't he?" Arlo said.

"Josephine," Mike answered.

"He let anybody borrow it who wanted to," Arlo said again. "Even me."

Mike looked surprised. "Why *even* you?"

"He was jealous. I dated girls he couldn't date. The Kappas, KKGs, on Langdon and Carol."

"No," Mike said, "the Kappa house was a block up from there."

"Liz was a Kappa," Arlo said. "She broke the rule for him." Mike let loose of the memories of yellow Studebakers. "And the speeches he used to give; he couldn't let go of a microphone. I remember Campus Carnival in the armory, that voice bellowing . . ."

Mike thought of Sam's speech for Matt's bar mitzvah, his arm on his son's shoulder, the Jewish Federation speeches, Israel Bond drives. "To a captain are you a captain?" That story and the speech at his own investiture at Columbia, "bending the street to make a corner, not waiting to be standing on one." Sam changing, remaking the world so he could do more of what he liked.

"He never came back to Madison to visit," Arlo said. "When he was gone, he was gone."

Mike remembered Sam saying "If you're going to move up, you've got to learn how to say good-bye."

"He didn't like New York when we first got there," Mike said, almost as if he were talking to himself. "It had only one level, you had to be on it, and Sam wasn't there.

We'd talk in the bookstore on West Fourth Street on Sundays, sit on a bench in Washington Square Park, maybe, look up at the Goodyear blimp when it went over in the afternoon. He liked that. It was the only slow, graceful thing in town, he used to say. In those days, his social quest meant big-time Jewish poker games on Saturday afternoons with guys like Modie Weinstock and Bunny Samuels.''

"He'd come down here for poker games," Arlo said, "years later, and then I'd meet him in Palm Beach. He thought he was going to play with the Kennedys. I did better than that for him, got him into games even the Kennedys couldn't get into. Games where they had a private servant stand in the card room all day to get drinks and empty ashtrays. ''Stanley, I dropped a chip. Please pick it up.''

"He must have been around forty then," Mike said, "but I didn't know you were the one who got him into that crowd."

"In Palm Beach, the third time, that's when he told me about the account overseas. It was a gift."

"That was one gift horse you should have looked in the mouth."

"Did you?"

Mike looked at Arlo, hard.

"I remember what Sam used to say about poker," Mike said. " 'Six is best at the table. Lets you know who they are, lets you give them a false sense of who you are.' " Then, abruptly, Mike stopped talking.

"You can go back in there now," Arlo said, coming back to the present. "I think you'll be all right."

"Do you?"

"Yes. I think you'll be given a pass."

"Who'll see to that?"

"Spencer was a student of mine. He came from shit. He'll never go back."

Today Arlo was dressed for class. His green corduroy jacket was twenty years old if it was a day, his olive pants had no cuffs, and his brown tie was knotted so that the bottom protruded about an inch below the top. Today, Mike thought, Arlo did not concentrate on his looks.

"What do you recommend I do when I come out of there?" Mike could hear the sadness in his own voice. He didn't want to hurt this man.

"Get on the first plane and go home."

"Will I leave all of this here?"

"None of this will follow you."

"Do you want me to talk with you before I head for the airport?" Mike asked.

"I doubt it. I think we've said it all."

"You don't believe that, Arlo. Do you?"

"No, not really."

"Are both of us such puppets?" Mike asked.

"You're not. You never were." Arlo went back to his stack of legal documents again, turning pages aimlessly with his thumb.

Mike sat perfectly still, barely breathing.

"Arlo, what do you think they would think if Spencer came out here to talk to me?"

Arlo didn't open his mouth farther or make any other voluntary response. A hurt look around Arlo's eyes made Mike want to hesitate again.

"Will you call him out for me?"

Arlo looked at Mike, and then his eyes went flat.

"I'll be doing both of you a favor if I don't. See him, but see him somewhere else."

Mike looked at him, wondering if his own eyes looked as tired as Arlo's. Arlo gathered his papers.

" 'Among other evils which being unarmed brings you, it causes you to be despised.' "

Arlo walked toward the door leading away from the grand jury room and opened it, cutting off further conversation, but not before he turned to Mike and concluded, "Thus Machiavelli."

Mike followed Arlo out but only after he had made sure Arlo had turned the corner. He would come back to Spencer, not now, but later, as Arlo had suggested. On that point, he gave good counsel.

43

SAM YONES, NOT HAVING DONE SO IN TWENTY YEARS, WENT downstairs from his tower to his bedroom in the middle of the day, opened the collar button of his shirt, took off his summer slacks, and took a nap in his boxer shorts. He had a nightmare of his mother embracing him for the last time, her face white, her eyes closed, falling lifeless against the hospital pillow. Then her face became Matt's face. Tubes this time, putting fluid in, taking life out. He kept yelling and screaming in his dream, but no sounds came out. He wanted both his mother and son to return to him, but they would not.

With some things in life, like right now, he was as ineffectual as he was in his dream, unable to work his will on the world, impotent. At such times he saw himself as he was: ugly, short, greedy, without the confidence of a loved child, without the luck of the male who was handsome and tall. This was one reason Liz was so precious to him. She was his guarantee of safe passage. And Matt his heritage and his legacy with his smarts and her looks.

There are places where a life goes wrong. He had put himself in the middle of one of them. It hadn't happened all at once. It had happened in baby steps. Mike's phrase, Sam thought. He remembered the times he used to call Mike up each fall, at the beginning of the High Holidays, wishing for him to be inscribed in the Book of Life, and feeling so warm inside when Mike wished him the same in return. "You and your family," Mike always added. For most of their adult years they did that, from the time they were twenty. It was the year before, Sam remembered,

312

back-dating the mortgage documents so he could buy the Nicollet Avenue warehouse. That was the first step. A baby step. Then Gordy's father's hints for payoffs, "a little green," and him slipping cash in among copies of sale documents when they sold Nicollet Avenue at a profit. Another baby step. But one that covered more ground. He walked to the temple, never riding, on Yom Kippur until he was thirty-eight, when his mother died. He admired the Rothschilds, who refused to do business on Saturdays, much less the High Holidays, the Reichmanns from Toronto, who followed the same rules. Then he had visions of Palm Beach card games, tall, elegant drunks seeing him as their passport to money that exceeded their public power, of him seeing himself in their company, tall and fit at last. The lines he had crossed, the steps he had taken to be there, inside. It's never one line, it's never just one step.

He had slept without the air-conditioning, and the flat dull heat went to his head. When he tried to sit up he felt dizzy. His vision seemed to blur, but then he steadied again.

He dressed and went downstairs to find Liz. She was not at the pool. She was not in the living room. He walked outside again and headed for the Chris-Craft at the end of the pier. She was not there either, and when he headed back toward the house, he happened to look up at the tower, and she was standing there, the windows open, looking down at him.

And then she looked at Billy, who had been outside all the time, not noticed by his father.

Seeing Sam as he looked from the top down was something new to Liz. The same for Billy. Sam looked strong, maybe because of the breadth of his shoulders. When Sam turned and father and son looked at each other, Liz, high above, was certain Billy's shoulders had fallen slightly and that his profile had changed.

She continued to watch them, her son who had quickly given up everything he thought he had talent for, and a father who encouraged him to expand the list until he was left with little except being a ladies' man. Did she know

313

what he excelled in? Of course. Was it dangerous, exciting, freedom for him? Yes. Did they ever talk about it? Of course not.

She should have told her son more often that she loved him. But the deed of love is more important than the words. She hoped. Love for a son is easy to sustain, easier than love for a husband. It is a different kind of prize, it is shattered by different things. She thought of Sam, with his slipshod standards, wondering just when he had become that way, when the steps had been taken, the lines crossed. It must have happened when his friends changed, when he no longer played poker with Modie and Bunny; when he began feigning an interest in horse racing, when he changed his tailor, when women she had read about sought her out, invited her to lunch, sometimes even both of them to dinner, but only for large parties. It was a process, not a single event. Had it only been as easy as finding a wad of cash rolled in his sock drawer. Then she could have said "What the hell is this?" and he would have had to answer. Instead, it was the glitter of his rise to power, the shimmer of it, that allowed no time for reflection, no hint of a dark side, just excitement, dazzle, for him and, she had to admit it, for her. Being out of his business world gave her no access to the gossip in it, and when she did catch hints of the tarnish there, it was not from someone who had benefited, for they would never speak. It was from Cheryl.

Maybe Cheryl had been right in saying something, maybe not. It was at the end of Sam's affair with her. Maybe it was a slip. Unlikely. Maybe it was anger. Whatever it was, Liz knew at the time there was no way it was not true. "He's a brilliant man," Cheryl had said, all smiles. "They dip in the till because he shows them where the till is. He's Faust."

Sam looked up, Liz was gone. He focused on his son standing on the other side of the pool dressed in his blazer, cream slacks, and a tie.

A tie.

At this time of day? Sam wondered. Why?

He didn't know what to make of his son standing across the pool, too dressed up for this hour of the day.

Instead of turning away, Billy looked straight back at his father.

"Uncle Mike's still with them, you know," Billy called across the diving board.

Liz couldn't hear what they were saying. She was waiting for the elevator. It was at the first floor landing and seemed to take forever, but she could hear the motor going. No stairs. No way down other than the elevator. "Do my deal or out the window." That was the purpose behind Carl Graham Fisher's tower. Finally, the double doors spread open and she was on the way down.

"What is that supposed to mean?" Sam asked.

"That he's still with them, Dad. He's on their side. That's what it means."

Billy reached into the side pocket of his jacket, trying not to smile too much. He felt the matchbook with some girl's number he had written inside.

Indulge him, Sam decided.

"That's okay, son. We'll figure it out together."

"Figure out what?"

"Together. We'll figure it out."

"Together?" Billy looked away.

Sam crossed to Billy's side of the pool. Sam had wanted to order Billy to come to him. Sometimes you did that, even in deals you wanted, made people come to you. But when you wanted someone relaxed, you let them stay where they were and you came to them. But he'd take his sweet time. He was still a father. He didn't come running.

"Billy," Sam said sweetly, as if he were talking to an eight-year-old, "where did you see Mike?"

Sam sat down on the end of a powder-blue chaise longue.

Billy sat as well, not next to his father, which is how Sam would have stage-managed him, but across from him, on the end of another powder-blue chaise longue, also in the sun. For a moment they avoided each other's eyes, looking out at the water, blue like the chaises.

"He was walking across the street with Cheryl. I guess

315

they were leaving," Billy said, not so cocky anymore. "I was supposed to be called again, don't you remember? But they let me go. Mike seemed happy to see me."

Sam began to nod. "Good, Billy," Sam said. "What else?"

Billy slid back on the chaise. "I don't know that there was much else," he said.

Sam looked out at the water again, wondering if he had the patience, the control.

"Did they say anything?"

"To each other?" Billy asked. Suddenly Billy was afraid again, feeling himself the dummy, just as he used to feel, hating Sam but still longing for him, remembering the stories Uncle Mike used to tell about his not having the father he wanted either. He wanted to say "Dad, I'm sorry I'm so dumb." But all that would get him is kicked more. "You want to know what they were saying to each other?" Billy's hand went into his jacket pocket again. He thought of the day Matt became the great one and he, Billy, was nowhere to be seen. Between that day and this, Sam totally missed the pain in his son's eyes.

"Yes, what were they saying to each other?" Sam asked. "Let's start there." Baby talk, that's how he had to do it.

"They didn't say anything to each other," Billy answered. "They just looked."

"How did they look?" Sam asked.

"How did they look?" Billy said.

"Yes, how did they look? Happy? Sad?"

"Happy? Sad?"

"What are you, a parrot?"

"They looked the way you and mother used to look at each other when I was a kid. Is that what you mean?"

"Your father and I still look at each other that way," Liz said, stepping forward. She hated the teasing, the baiting, the wild swings of a son who wasn't smart enough to suit his father, but wanted his love all the more. Liz walked across the tile toward Sam's lounge chair, wondering why she was trying to hold on to whatever little was left. She forced herself to sit down next to Sam and put her arm around his shoulder.

Sam, at this moment, couldn't care less about where her arm was.

Some of the men in his business had big focusing faces that never let loose of you until they got what they wanted. Sam was like that. Liz had decided that years before, even when his eyes told her he was frightened, as they did now.

"How *did* they look, Billy?" Sam asked, turning to Liz, his eyes narrowing. "Mike and Cheryl together."

Liz closed her eyes, full of so many regrets.

"Happy? Worried? Relieved?"

"Relieved." Billy already had his mother in his corner. He was looking straight into his father's eyes.

"Good boy." Sam saw his son smile. Exactly what he wanted. "That tells me something."

"What?" Billy asked.

"It tells me what I don't want to hear, but something I need to know. If he's relieved, they've released him. Mike's off. He must be." Liz turned away.

"Yeah," Billy said, excited. "You're right, Dad."

"You bet I am."

"Why the hell else would he be relieved?" Billy asked, agreeing for all he was worth.

"Only one reason," Liz said.

Sam turned his attention to Liz, but only for a second. Then he refocused on Billy.

"Who else was with him?"

"I thought I told you," Billy said, becoming nervous again. "Spencer Pelcheck."

Sam cleared his throat, trying to control himself. "What did Mike look like?" he asked.

"I told you." Billy felt himself a child, being bounced up and down, harshly, on Father's knee.

"No, you didn't."

"Yes, I did." The hurt and the anger together rose in his voice.

"Tell me again."

"Nothing special. He didn't look like anything special. Just relieved, nothing else."

"Try once more."

"Dad, I told you. There was nothing there."

"There had to be."

"Dad . . ." Now he was begging, the hope in him gone, so easily snatched away, that someday the torture would end.

"They were outside of the grand jury room, god-dammit!" Sam yelled. "Walking from one place to another. Where were they coming from? Where were they going? Back to the grand jury? With all those people waiting for them? Think, you dummy!"

"I can't think anymore, Dad." Billy hung his head. "I'm not equipped."

"Oh, Sam . . ." Liz said, turning away.

Sam stared at Billy, trying to get his breathing under control. Billy stood up, but Sam stayed where he was, on the chaise beside Liz. Then, before he left, Billy bent down and kissed his father on the forehead.

"I'll see you later, Mom," he said in a quiet voice.

Sam sat there, breathing more heavily than he could remember. He stood up and walked slowly back into the house. Was poker with Arlo at the Everglades Club worth it? Was having lunch in a room that wouldn't seat Leonard Bernstein worth it all? But he owned them. He owned all of them. Sam sat on the dark oak bench inside his elevator until the anger subsided. Liz walked in and they waited for the double doors to close.

"I haven't been very good company for you today," he said as they rose upward. "I'm sorry."

"I didn't marry you for your sense of fun."

He became aware of the makeup on her face, the colors of the clothes, her body. Maybe, he thought, she was beginning to look her age. Why was nothing or no one ever enough for him? Why did he always have to have more?

She seemed to stare at him.

"You were handsome once," she said.

"Me? I've never been good-looking."

318

"To me you were."

"That's because you saw other things," he said, wondering if all he was doing was trying to regain the upper hand. The elevator doors opened and they went into his office. They both turned and listened to the buzz of an airboat that went by.

"I used to wonder about that," Liz answered, "what other things I saw in you."

He didn't like the sound of her voice. She had become too quiet.

"Look," he said to her, his anger rising again, "I'll make you a deal. Don't take out on me what's going on with me and Mike and I won't take out on you what's going on with you and Mike."

Liz looked at him, stunned.

Sam gave her as hard a look as he could, a look with drilling eyes he usually reserved for lawyers trying to kill his deals. But he couldn't hold his stare as long as he wanted to. She returned it, and Sam looked elsewhere, anywhere. That he was in his tower, his throne room reachable by others only at his whim, didn't help the defeats.

"I've got to go to them," Sam said, his voice subdued. "Sometimes you get tired of trying to make it, to survive, but I suppose if I do nothing else, that's what I'll do. Survive. I'll have to go back and get immunity now. Do you know what that will mean? To me? To you? We'll survive, but it will never be the same."

"I don't know that I care."

"That's why your people aren't survivors. Mine are."

Blood drummed in her ears. "I knew this day would come. For you to throw that at me. Remember, I'm one of yours."

Her heart was thudding.

"I guess Rabbi Aaron did half a job."

"Yes, I suppose that's all he did."

44

MIKE, KNOWING HE OWED SPENCER PLENTY, SAT OPPOSITE him at a table on the outdoor deck of The Bay Side, within sight of Sam's tower in Miami Beach. The Bay Side was a faded clapboard fish restaurant hidden just behind the Rickenbacker Causeway, patronized more by men who worked on freighters than men who wore ties. The menu was chalked on a blackboard, and their table was made of planks not quite joining each other so you could see the sand underfoot when you picked up the napkin. The water wasn't more than fifty feet away, a back channel of Biscayne Bay, but big enough to allow some guy to roar back and forth in an air boat, propeller whirring, taking tight turns to the point where Mike, unfamiliar with such craft, wondered if it would capsize. Spencer never looked at it, but couldn't wait for it to race away or run out of gas because the noise was too much. Neither of them needed any additional irritation.

Mike's attention was wandering. Twisting and turning, up and down, back and forth in its own wake, that air boat was more annoying than he had imagined. It, not Spencer, took primacy. Over the noise, Mike caught words like "warm weather," "mending their nets," and "noise pollution."

Like an artist's vanity, maybe a vanity common to all men who stand beyond the pale, Sam had needed someone, a witness, an accomplice who, as the work went on, might admire him, the original creator of a great work of art. No one liked to paint a picture that would hang in the closet. Someone needed to know. Maybe that was why Sam had made Mike a witness, conferred upon him the role of marveling observer. Yet Sam was to him an *alito,* a Sicilian word Gordy had taught him, a breath of life, a human presence that softens loneliness and despair, as Gordy's father had softened his life that Christmas long ago with a cap gun. Mike wished, at that moment, as he had before, that he had been blessed with a slack memory. He had not.

"I know what you're going to tell me," Mike said to Spencer. "That by now I should know who my friends are."

"I was going to say something like that." Mike nodded, trying to envision a quiet word, if ever there could be one, with Sam the next time he saw him. "You look tired," Spencer said.

Mike didn't say a word. He looked out at the water, then at the Bay Side restaurant sign, then at the air boat, finally tied up and silent.

"Forget the Grand Caymans," Mike said. "It's just a transfer point. Convenient because of the time zone. Any list of names you get out of them can be doctored. You know that yourself." Spencer started to pull out notepaper. "Put that away."

No please. No request. An order. The pen was halfway out of Spencer's pocket, but he put it back.

"I've been thinking about this for two days, and this is all you will get. 'Lucky Strike Two.' That's the code. The Phaelzer Banque, Geneva. That's it. No more."

"That's not what I bargained for."

"Yes, it is. It's more than you bargained for. You just don't know it yet." Mike stretched out his arms, ten fingers locked together, and cracked his knuckles, something he hadn't done since they were kids together, as if he were bringing those times back one last time and saying goodbye to them forever. "Now I would like to order lunch." He signaled and the waitress was there. "I'll have the snapper and a cold lite beer. Spencer, how about you?" Spencer kept his eyes on Mike. Not looking anywhere else, he said, "The same."

"I suppose you'll tell me to go to the Swiss authorities and get them to open up the account."

"I'm not telling you to do anything. You do what you want."

The air-boat motor started up again, and its pot-bellied pilot pushed it out into the brackish water, gunned it, and sped away from the shore, but spun around, heading again across their range of vision, keeping the noise nearby, as if that were the purpose of the whole exercise. This time Mike didn't mind. He didn't want to argue with Spencer. If he couldn't figure out what he had just been fed, that was his problem. And on his own side, feeling more than sad, if he couldn't realize what he had delivered, that was his tragedy. You give away an anthill. You give away a mountain. You still give away something.

Mike knew he was too hard on himself. He hadn't given anything away. He had bargained it away. Bargained it for the right to sit outside, order red snapper and a beer, and listen to an air-boat motor drum in his ears. A bargain he never would have had to make if Sam hadn't set the trap. That's what pushed him over; the kindness of a friend convinced him to make the bargain.

Spencer, with his finger and thumb, made a gun that he pointed at the air boat, made a soft popping sound with his lips, and then sat back and started to drink his beer.

"You did the only thing you could do," Spencer said.

"It's not your place to make that judgment."

Spencer went back to his beer and Mike took some of his.

"If we had two cars, one of us could leave without stranding the other," Spencer said.

"The cabs work. You can go if you want," Mike said.

"No. I'll stay."

The snapper wasn't bad was about all each said to the other during the next fifteen minutes. The bay had become quiet again, the air-boat maniac had piled into his pickup and left, and, hopefully, there would be no other distraction to take his place. The sky was nice, blue, with clouds, and all that, although each looked up several times, neither said a word about it.

"Do you mind if I pick at your onion rings?" Spencer asked.

"We could have asked for two orders."

Spencer started with a fork, but finally gave way to his fingers, the breading falling off as he tried to break each onion ring in half before eating it.

"Do you always eat onions like that?"

"Like what?"

"With your fingers."

"Tastes better."

Spencer pushed the plate to the center of the table, and Mike put his hand in the middle and speared off a ring, a full one, with his index finger. He broke it in half with his knife, and ate the half moon of onion ring with his right hand, the breading flaking off too.

"Not bad," Mike said.

"You know, you're through now. You can go home if you want."

"Are you satisfied?"

"You're telling me I should be. Should I be?"

Mike reached for an onion ring but didn't say anything.

"I suppose I don't need to know anything about Lucky Strike One."

Mike laughed.

"I don't even know if there is a Lucky Strike One," he said, lying.

"Well, then we're even."

Spencer pulled a folded paper from the pocket inside his jacket draped over an extra chair. The paper, in a blue legal backing, had been sitting there in full view of both of them since they had taken off their jackets.

"This is your subpoena marked Satisfied. Cheryl's too. Technically, they can be renewed, but the odds are a judge will quash it if Arlo makes the right arguments."

"Are you recommending I go back to Arlo?"

"I'm not recommending anything."

"Yes, you are."

"Put this in your pocket and and don't lose it."

"Do you want me to tie it to a string pulled through my sleeves, like they do with children's gloves?"

"It's too hot down here. We don't wear gloves."

"No, Spencer, you don't."

Spencer puffed out his cheeks like the god of winds in a nautical map and then sat back in his chair. Mike and Spencer eyed each other for a moment, each taking the measure of the other and of his game as if they had been seated at a poker table, cards in hand, about to raise.

"Merely a precaution," Spencer said. "If the thieves were to take it into their heads to pay us another visit, it would prevent them from carrying off anything else of value."

Mike ignored the sadness in Spencer's face. He felt for him, but he was thinking of Cheryl. "You think there's anything left to carry off?"

"You know. I don't."

Mike thought of Liz's fax still in his pocket and looked at a black man fishing, his rod curved over and his line cutting around the water, this way and that.

"I've felt like I've had a gun in my mouth all morning," Mike said. "Not just all morning. For the past two days, and if the truth be known, for the past two months."

"I didn't put the gun there," Spencer said.

"It doesn't matter how a man got into a position of weakness. There's always somebody there to turn it to his own advantage," Mike said, thinking of Sam Yones.

Mike looked left and right, casually, then briefly over his shoulder, glad that no one had seen them together.

"Will you teach that to your classes . . . now that you've maneuvered yourself into a safe corner?" Spencer asked, staring hard at the canceled subpoenas that sat on the table between them.

"Do you think my position is safe?"

"It depends on what I find in Lucky Strike Two. The accounts could be canceled by the time I get there, but the records will go back and I'll get them. You know, Mike,

I'm glad you told me Switzerland. Their accounts don't disappear."

"Spencer, I want something else."

"There's nothing else in the bargain."

"I know. But I want it as a favor."

"Yes?"

"That kid has never had a chance, Spencer. His father treated him like an outsider all his life." Spencer's heart opened. "I don't know what he'll make of what's left."

Spencer saw the expression of God's pleader in Mike's eyes, and he thought of Potsy Pelcheck screwing him to the ground and wondered what his own life would have been like if he had had an advocate like Mike Anker.

"Don't worry, Mike," Spencer said, controlling his voice. "Billy's out."

"There're so many scars, so much evil left over." Mike cut his eyes away, looking at the water.

" 'My kingdom stands on brittle glass,' " Spencer said. "That's Shakespeare."

Mike picked up the blue-backed canceled subpoena and put it into his jacket pocket, the jacket hanging loosely across the fourth chair, with, he realized, Liz's fax falling out of it.

"Men don't have many good role models," Spencer said. "It's hard to learn how to be a man." Spencer swallowed hard, but now he was out with it. "It's even harder to learn how to be an older man. Our role models always stand for control, the bus driver who drives the bus, the general who leads the army, the president who, we hope, controls the country he loves. So, when you get older, if you ever want to turn your life around, it's got to be control that you give up, not get more of. And you can't make giving it up an empty gift. Whether you give up control, or something or someone takes it from you, you've got to get some reward out of it, and maybe that's being a little freer. Maybe that's what will come out of all this for you." Spencer thought hard, looking at Mike—freer, if he tried. "I'm not sure. I'm never sure about those things."

Mike shook his head and stared off distractedly for a

moment. He realized his temples weren't gray, they were turning white, and he felt as old as he would look someday.

"If you stand in the middle of the road," he said quietly, "you get knocked down by traffic going in both directions."

There's no point in thinking about people you'll never see again, Mike decided, noticing for the first time that Spencer's eyes were light blue. It only hurts.

PART SEVEN

45

THERE WAS NO PORTICOED HALL OF JUSTICE FOR SAM, JUST a driveway cut in front of a sleek marble office building two blocks from Burdine's. They had promised him that at this late hour in the afternoon there would be no reporters, no TV cameras, but he could see them clustered just ahead. He wanted the car to move, speed away, but it was not his car; it was theirs, a black Ford with a U.S. government license plate, and Byron Varner sat in the right front seat while Spencer Pelcheck drove.

Spencer was in his own world; his sadness was deeper than he could remember. Bryon had finally defeated him, but not in the way he had planned. Spencer wondered how much would show. Then he wondered about something else. Whether he was going from one father figure to another. Whether he was too old to be looking for a father. Or whether you're never too old.

Sam sat in the backseat with Arlo. His other lawyers followed in their own car, hastily assembled so they could all appear before Judge Hall on Thursday before he went home early for his poker game.

"He's only getting immunity, for Christ's sake," Arlo yelled out, spotting the reporters. "He's not pleading guilty. Who tipped 'em?'' Arlo leaned across the front seat and tapped Byron on the shoulder. Then he tapped him again.

"I haven't the slightest idea," Byron answered, his voice flat.

Byron had not turned around. He sat staring through the windshield, focused on the six, seven, and eleven P.M. TV reporters he knew well, plus a few new faces.

"All this leakage isn't going to help, Byron," Arlo said as hard as he could. "We'll go after your sources."

"No you won't."

"We'll be entitled to that."

Byron turned slightly toward Sam's corner of the backseat. "His immunity covers past offenses and present offenses, if Judge Hall agrees." Then he stopped talking across Sam as if he weren't there and looked straight at him. "If your lawyer keeps talking, you'll get less."

"Leave him alone," Arlo said, touching Sam's sleeve. He would change the names but use this as an illustration in his next book of how the tables can turn.

Spencer waited for the light to change. He looked into the rearview mirror, trying to decide if Sam looked sullen. All it had taken to move the process this fast was one call to Arlo. "Tell Sam, 'Lucky Strike Two.' Then Sam will tell you what to do." "I'm not his lawyer," Arlo had said. "Something tells me you will be" was Spencer's answer. He had been hitting below the belt, like they all were, the way everyone did at the end. No good-sport we-all-did-our-best. It never worked like that.

Abner Parks, Byron's chief U.S. Marshal, waited for them at the curb with Raoul Novaes, foreman of the grand jury. Abner shoved carefully, gently, several of the waiting TV people off to one side as he simultaneously opened both the front and the rear doors. An hour earlier, Byron would have begged for the attention, laid a cloak across a mud puddle for Sam to step across to get coverage, and it was an automatic gesture on his part to smile at the reporters, seek their notice, their audience, their by-line, his future. Not now.

The reporters, including a young man checking out Sam's features against a picture to make sure, clustered around the small man with the beady eyes and the key chain.

"Who're you going to name?"

"Who's on your list?"

"There'll be no comment," Byron said.

"Oh, yes, there will," Arlo said, pushing his way in front, standing next to Sam. "This gentleman is no longer a target of the grand jury. We have received written notification of that status."

"When?" a reporter asked.

"Now, there's a smart boy," Arlo answered. "Twenty minutes ago."

"Federal Express?" the young reporter asked.

"No, by hand," Sam Yones answered, surprising himself, still able to be cocky, giving them the same smile that had reassured and seduced for years.

"Please, gentlemen" . . . Byron then noticed two women in the group, "and ladies." He looked at his watch. Spencer, who had found himself with little to say, touched the huge arm of Abner Parks, who cleared the way once again and led the parade through the revolving doors. They passed the security desk, and Abner herded them into the special elevator that stopped only on forty, the chambers of the judges of the United States District Court for the Southern District of Florida at Miami.

It was Spencer Pelcheck who dominated the meeting. "You're new to this development, Judge Hall, so there's no reason why you should know the situation." The old man was putting his robe on. Maybe it was for Sam. Maybe it was something you did automatically when you've been a judge for so long, or maybe it was for the benefit of all of them. Spencer saw the initialed cigar box on the desk, regarded the man with white hair, rimless glasses, the bushy white eyebrows. Maybe, Spencer thought, that's what judges were all about. They were supposed to look like your father.

"Go ahead, Mr. Pelcheck," Judge Hall said, sitting down.

"Yes, sir."

Sam had been in a lot of offices in his day, including the Oval Office, but never in a judge's chambers. It looked like any other office of any important man, but despite all the windows it was darker, full of dull red and brown and with a lot more books lining the walls.

The eight of them, Byron, Spencer, Sam, Arlo, Abner Parks and Raoul Novaes, and the two New York lawyers, silent for a change, sat in front of Judge Hall's desk.

"I'm honored," the judge said, "that the U.S. Attorney himself is here, but if this is that important, we'll do it tomorrow."

"No, it's not really that important," Byron said, ready to leave, but scheming how to stay.

"Well . . ." Judge Selmer Hall smiled, the first smile Spencer had seen with sparkling eyes in a long time.

"Judge," Arlo said. "We have no objection."

The judge took off his glasses and started to polish them. "Apparently, the U.S. Attorney doesn't see any particular need to be here, but if you want him, you can have him." The judge put on his glasses again and refocused his old wise eyes.

"As you wish, Your Honor," Spencer said as Byron resumed his seat.

"Well, son," Judge Hall said, "if His Honor has one wish, he would like to go home to dinner." He smiled again, an honest smile, as Spencer was starting to think of it, but then the corners of his mouth turned down again. "How long is this going to take, Counsel?"

"Not long, Your Honor."

"Okay, let's do it." He pressed a button and his court reporter came in and set up his machine. It didn't take more than thirty seconds.

"You all set, Harry?"

"Yes, Your Honor."

"Okay. Let the record show that this is an *in camera* but transcribed hearing before . . . oh, hell, Harry, you know what to put in there."

"Yes, Your Honor."

"Any objections, Counsel?"

"No, Your Honor."

"Okay, Counsel, who are these people?"

"This is Mr. Raoul Novaes, the foreman of the grand jury. And this is Arlo . . ."

"Yes, I know the professor."

"Thank you, Your Honor," Arlo said.

Spencer introduced the New York members of Sam's team, Jenifer Heatwole, who gave him big eyes, and a Stanley something. Neither of them spoke.

"And, sir," the judge turned to Sam, "who are you?"

"Well, Your Honor," they all heard him, his voice filling the room, "my name is Sam Yones."

Judge Hall cleared his throat. "All right." He looked at his watch and then glared at Spencer while Sam pondered the collapse of his world as his name got out.

"I'll make it fast, Judge," Spencer said.

"Strike that, Harry."

"Yes, Your Honor."

Spencer started to say "Sorry, Judge," but took one look at those eyebrows and thought better of it.

"Judge, at my recommendation, this grand jury convened . . ."

"Is this a special or a regular grand jury?"

"A special, Your Honor."

"Which one?"

"Angel Fish, Your Honor."

"I thought so."

Sam wanted to know why Judge Hall thought so, but kept his mouth shut.

"Okay. Go on."

"Well, Judge, when we convened, the grand jury, at my recommendation . . ."

"I heard that."

". . . decided to allow a certain witness anonymity."

"Is that true, Mr. ah . . . Mr. . . ."—the judge fumbled through his papers—"Mr. Novatias."

"Novaes, Your Honor," Spencer said.

"That's what I said."

"Yes, Your Honor."

"Well, Mr. Foreman," the judge said, "did you agree to anonymity? For who? For this man here?"

"Yes, Your Honor, sir."

"One will be enough."

"Yes, Your Honor, sir."

"For this man here?"

"No, Your Honor," Spencer said. "This man is here for immunity."

"Then make your deal with him. He seems to be adequately represented. What do you want me for?"

"Our agreement, Your Honor, includes a requirement of your approval."

"Let's do this tomorrow."

"We have agreed, with Your Honor's consent, that it be done today."

"Have you now." Judge Hall looked mad. His clerk gave him a cautioning look. "Don't worry, Harry, I'm fine."

"Judge," Spencer said carefully, "there are very few documents we are going to be able to use in this case. Witnesses will be crucial."

"What's wrong with your documents? Did you forget a search warrant? Is there some entrapment here?"

"Well, Your Honor." Byron began to speak.

"I thought you didn't have to be here."

"I'm here because I knew you would ask this, and you need my assurance that there is nothing wrong with the documents that we have obtained." Byron didn't even chance a glance at Spencer. "However, it is likely that some counsel representing other persons, who may not be in this room, may seek to challenge the documents we do have, and I . . ."

"Okay, okay. I get it. So you want witnesses, huh?"

"Specifically," Spencer said. "We want this witness."

"You are or were a target, sir, weren't you?"

"Yes, he was," Spencer said.

"I'm asking him."

"Yes, Your Honor. I was a target."

"And you don't want to be a target, is that right?"

332

Sam started to smile, and then he shut his face down. "Yes, Your Honor. I don't want to be a target anymore."

"What changed your mind?"

"What changes anybody's mind, Judge?"

"You're a famous man, aren't you?"

"I suppose so, Judge, I'm not sure. I suppose I will be."

"Do you have that much to say?"

"Your Honor," Spencer said, "he will testify to . . ."

"I don't want to hear you. I want to hear him."

"I have partners, Your Honor. I think the U.S. Attorney is more interested in them than he is in me."

"What kind of partners do you have?" Judge Hall asked. "Let me see that immunity agreement."

"Yes, Your Honor," Spencer said, handing over the document.

Judge Hall read the immunity letter. There was nothing secret about this letter, nothing stand-by. It took effect immediately, for testimony now, to begin tomorrow and to go on and on and on until Spencer Pelcheck was through with the witness.

Harry thought he saw a slight tremor as Judge Hall held the letter.

"You realize, Mr. Yones, that this immunity covers you for just about everything in the world . . ."

". . .Yes, Your Honor."

Judge Hall's eyes narrowed, not liking to be interrupted.

". . .Except lying, misrepresenting, telling a fib. Got it?"

"Yes, Your Honor."

"One slip on that stand, in front of this man's grand jury, Mr. Novitian, and I'll have you in here for perjury so fast it'll make your head swim. Immunity for everything except future lying. Got it?"

Sam Yones nodded, bristling.

"No conviction? No fine for this man?"

"No, Your Honor."

"He must have done something or you wouldn't be giving him immunity. What did you get him on? And why isn't he going to jail?"

Without any warning the room seemed to close in on

Sam. First he thought the room was too small. No, that wasn't it. He felt as if he were watching an egg roll toward the edge of a table. From his seat, there was no window to look out of.

"And why aren't you giving him immunity in exchange for less time in the hoosegow? Seems to me like he's got a pretty good deal. Too good a deal. Who is this guy? Tell me, sir, who are you going to point the finger at? The president of the United States?"

"Close," Spencer Pelcheck answered, and when the court reporter stopped typing, he sensed all eyes in the room were focusing first on him and then on Sam Yones. He realized what he had said and he was angry with himself. Dummy. Maybe he was the dummy his father always said he was.

"Close, huh?" the judge said. "Close counts only in horseshoes," the judge said, taking off his glasses. "Tell me, Mr. Varner, isn't this a much better deal than you usually give? What are you going to get out of it?" Judge Hall said "you" to Byron Varner in a personal way, emphasizing it so that his meaning was unmistakable.

"That's why we're here, Judge," Arlo said. "We just don't want to . . ."

"No go, Professor. You can't have it both ways. You go plea-bargain this man. You get him to agree to a conviction and recommend reduction in his sentence. *Then* you come to me in exchange for immunity. No freebies."

"Judge?"

"Yes, Harry."

"Will you hold up a minute. I have to change my tape."

"For God's sake. How many times have I told you to do that before you come in?"

"Sorry, Judge." Harry fussed with his machine. "I don't want to give you another stroke."

"Then don't."

Please don't, Spencer thought. Keep this man with us. Please, no more sickness for him. It was almost like a prayer.

Harry pulled off the paper guide and yanked the side

plate back as fast as he could. Then he could remove the take-up spool filled with his strip of white paper punched with holes and reload.

"Off the record, Your Honor . . ." Spencer said, getting ready to help his boss. Why, he didn't know.

"Off the record, yourself, Mr. Assistant U.S. Attorney. You're giving away too much, Mr. Varner. I don't quite know why."

Sam, angry, looked directly at Judge Hall. They were talking over and across him again. He was not a nobody, not an animal, not a serf any longer. He would not stand for it.

"This man isn't in your hands," Judge Hall said, watching. "He's in mine. You gave him to me. That's your mistake."

"He asked for your approval, Judge," Byron said, defending himself.

"Then that's his mistake."

Sam Yones, until an hour ago, secure and inviolate, saw much of his life slipping miserably from his control. With every word he was drawing further and further into himself, thinking of his list, each name he remembered bringing back, like a trophy, favors he did, markers he received in return, each invitation to become a member of their various clubs, the first, or at least the third, offered to one of his race, as they put it. All so many years ago, all so fulfilling. The Beta house on Langdon Street in Madison, as clear as yesterday; Arlo Shields, head of the Badger party, seeking his advice, inviting him in for a 3.2 beer, illegal, but the Betas had it. Sam told Arlo how to win, two tries, but he'd done it. And the introduction to Liz in exchange. The dances Mike Anker couldn't come to, the places in life only he could be with her and the place in life he could make for himself and for her. But he never won her on his own. He won her by default because Mike didn't have the balls to take a chance. He didn't win. He succeeded, but he didn't win.

"Okay, Harry. Are you ready yet?"

Sam's memories were interrupted by Judge Hall's voice.

"One more minute, Judge."

The judge swayed back in his chair. "I feel sorry for you, Mr. Yones, but it's back to the drawing boards."

Sam had no smiles left. He felt like a beaten man.

"All right, gentlemen. On the record, Mr. Pelcheck, I want you to assure our witness that each and every agreement that has been made with him will be honored when and only when I approve it."

Sam tried to rock in his chair, but it was stone solid. Then he looked at Byron Varner as if he meant never to forget him under that light, at that instant, in that chair, having made his promises, having told his lies.

"Mr. Yones, do you understand that?"

It looked as if Sam were mustering his last bit of strength to suppress his fury. "Yes, Your Honor."

Judge Hall looked around the room. "Any questions?" He stood and so did Sam and Spencer and Arlo and Byron and everyone else present.

"All right, Harry," the judge said as he took off his robe. "Pack it up. I'm going to go home, have dinner, and play poker."

"Judge," Harry said, "you're not supposed to."

"Don't worry about me."

"He should live to be a hundred," Spencer mumbled.

Abner Parks led them back to the elevator, and they rode down forty floors in silence as the cab sped to street level. They could have talked. The elevator had only their party in it. Sam's aftershave invaded the elevator. Spencer hadn't noticed it before.

"Is there a back way out of here?" Sam Yones asked.

"Through the basement," Abner answered.

"Use it," Sam ordered. The elevator ride had given him time. He had recovered.

Outside, Sam looked up and down the street, but the government cars were not in sight. Abner took a phone from his pocket. "Bring 'em around." Spencer heard a crackled "Yes, sir," and he watched Sam. Not a muscle in his face stirred. As the black Ford approached, Sam said, "Arlo, you stay with me. Byron, you stay with me. Mr. Pelcheck. You too. The rest of you," he turned to his other lawyers, Jenifer and Stanley Whatever, "do what you goddamn please."

As the car pulled up, Abner opened the front and back doors as he had done when they arrived. Spencer took over the wheel and the car moved away.

Byron said to Sam, "You're not in charge now." He jerked his head toward the tower they had just left. "Neither are we. He is."

Spencer drove the two blocks to the old Post Office.

"Leave him off here," Byron said.

"You're talking past me like I'm a horse. I've had enough of that," Sam said.

"His car's parked here," Byron said. "Let him get in his car and go home."

"What will the judge trade me off for, Byron? At least I knew what you wanted."

"Mr. Yones . . ."

"Now he's got me. Once he's put me in a box, what will *he* want to take me out?"

"It's too late to do anything now," Byron said. "We'll deal with this tomorrow."

"You will? You think you have any brain power left to deal with it?" Sam asked, and Arlo's slow southern laugh filled the car. Sam pushed himself as far back in the seat as he could. He straightened his shoulders and stood his ground as best he could in a seated position.

Spencer stopped the car in front of the Post Office building. It was quiet. For the first time you could hear the cold air rushing out of the dashboard.

"How did you get Lucky Strike Two?" Sam said.

"You really want to know?" Byron asked.

Spencer looked in the rearview mirror and saw Sam nod.

"Tell him, Spencer," Byron said. "Tell him about Mike Anker."

"What difference does it make," Spencer said. Cars pulled around them and continued down Flagler Street. Sam sat perfectly still, barely breathing, not even moving his head. His skin was almost transparent, as if there were something wrong with his red blood count. Spencer looked across the street at the small park across from the old Post Office building, the benches with old men sitting in whatever sun was left for that day, the refreshment truck long gone.

"You all tried to hold him hostage," Spencer said, "and you all failed. Maybe failure is what the times should serve on your plate. None of you guys are going to get what you want. None of you."

Byron didn't move a muscle, but Sam raised his head. "Don't tell me that," Sam said. "Don't you dare tell me that. That's bullshit."

Sam, walking alone, headed for the basement of the old Post Office building, where his car was parked in the underground garage. He heard his footsteps echo as he crossed the now almost empty visitor's level, and standing next to his Lincoln, unexpectedly, he saw Billy, smiling, waiting.

"I thought I'd come and drive you home," Billy said, his voice echoing in the emptiness as Sam approached. Sam didn't answer. He walked to Billy's side of the car.

"Got off, huh, Dad?"

It was as if his father's hand reached Billy's face in slow motion. He felt the air whoosh before he felt the slap. Then he felt the sting, and in the silence of the garage, he heard his father yell, "You goddamn dummy."

PART
EIGHT

46

SILENTLY, NOT LOOKING AT HIS FATHER, TAKING CHANCES
as he changed lanes, Billy drove north up Biscayne Boulevard. He moved toward the causeway on-ramps. They
passed the Venetian Causeway tollbooth, and Billy hoped
he had a token. He had one, and he went through, fast,
without rattling Sam. The for-charter fishing boats tied up
alongside the piers went by in a blur. Billy stepped on it,
but was careful not to speed over the low white highway
bridges. Both men stared straight ahead. The roadway continued due east; the MacArthur Causeway, white also, but
older, flaking, angled south, heading for lower Miami
Beach. Then Billy heard his father mumbling something.

"What did you say, Dad? I didn't hear you."

"We're in this so deep, what the hell's another pound of
flesh." Sam's voice, the kind that shook a room, reverber-
ated through the car; it made Billy want to fade away.
"Can you hear me now?" Sam shouted even louder.

"I didn't mean I wasn't listening," Billy explained
quickly. "I just meant . . ."

"Trouble is, I don't have another pound of flesh. I have
no one else to give them." Sam kept shouting. "You hear
that?"

Billy nodded.

"My cupboard is bare."

Scouting the road for any potholes, any bump that might jar his father, Billy drove carefully, but not daring to slow their speed. There was a dip at the east end of the first graceful bridge that took them across the chain of islands that led to Miami Beach, and somehow Billy piloted the big car over it without disruption. He couldn't wait to see his father's tower.

"Where do you think you're taking me?" Sam asked, his voice tight and full of fury, a tone Billy knew too well.

"I thought you'd want to go home."

"Get over to the MacArthur. Now."

"I either have to go all the way back to Miami or to the Beach. There's no way to get to it except those two ways."

"Your choice."

Billy could not think of two more ominous words coming from his father.

"Where do you want to go when we get there?"

"Palm Island."

"Uncle Gordy?"

Sam nodded, his face hard, empty.

Billy took a quiet deep breath and drove.

When Sam arrived at the home of the man he now thought of as owing him everything, he found the door open. He walked through the house and found Ginger outside, sunbathing. This house here in Miami, Gordy had because of Sam. Minneapolis, Los Angeles, Miami—all of it was due to Sam. Gordy's old man with his hand out, no fee for the mortgage, just the back-date, the lie, and twenty percent of the profits, cash, for not telling. Then more of the same, the percentage whittled down and finally disappearing in exchange for helping Gordy take over the union. The high gorum were easier. They took what you gave them, thankful to be in, thankful you told no one they were in. Greedy, but only for personal privacy, evading taxes, and keeping their own world pure. They didn't own you. Once they were in, you owned them. Sam saw Gordy working on the Pearson, and he walked out to the end of the pier, Billy following.

Gordy was climbing down the ladder to the rear cockpit. He had just left the flying bridge and gave Sam a big wave. There were two fighting chairs; Gordy offered Sam one, and he took the other. Sam swiveled for a moment, looking over the transom at the water. He could see his son hovering, with no idea where to settle, whether to stay or to go. Sam looked up at the outriggers, then across the bay back to the skyline of Miami.

"We've been coming down here a long time, you and me," Sam said.

Gordy nodded, and the two men settled into a long silence, broken when Gordy asked, "Sam, what do you need?"

"Dad, I'll be going."

"No, Billy. Stay," Sam said. Then he turned to Gordy. "I got a judge who wants me to go to jail." Sam left the fisherman's chair. He knew Gordy was uncomfortable, and not only because he had come closer. Sam was unsure how to set his face. He could smell an afternoon beer on Gordy's breath.

"I offered to give them the partners, Gordy. GM, Prudential, Defense, the Bishop, all of them. I'd even go that far."

"You never needed the partners anyway. They were there for decoration. Why you needed them when they shit all over you was beyond me. What did you get out of them, Sam?"

"What did you get out of the pictures of your politicians?"

"That was business. You never needed the High Gorum. You never needed those people. I'll say it again, Sam. They were there for decoration."

"No, they weren't," Sam said. "They were there for a day like today."

A large yacht sent waves rolling toward Gordy's pier.

"Dad doesn't have another pound of flesh to give them," Billy said, wanting them all to look at him. "That's why we're here."

"You're learning, Billy," Sam said against the sound of metal fittings ringing as the Pearson rocked.

"Is this what you want your son to learn? Is this what you want to hear from a son?"

"Dad wants you to help him." The boat stood quiet now.

"How?" Gordy asked. "How does your father want me to help him?"

Billy hung his head. "I don't know."

"Then don't ask, Billy," Gordy said, touching the boy's shoulder.

"Why shouldn't he ask?" Sam said. "He's my son."

"For this purpose you acknowledge him as your son?" Gordy asked, standing.

"Can you think of a better purpose? To help his father?"

"Sam, what do you want?"

"Get me my deal back," Sam Yones said, knowing he was pleading. "I'll give you anything you want. Just don't tease me."

At first Gordy did not reply, nor did he show any expression. Sam watched him, wondering if he should say more. Finally, he said, giving Gordy his famous smile, "Okay, tease me if you have to." In imitation, Gordy smiled back.

There was no triumph to celebrate yet, but Sam, for an instant, felt that way. He would win when all was said and done. He was not dead. This man in this boat owed him. For this house, for all the other houses, for this boat, for himself.

"Gordy, listen to me." Sam watched Gordy lift himself out of the fighting chair and move toward the cockpit freezer, open it, take a beer for himself, toss one to Billy, and hold one out. "No thanks," Sam said, trying to ignore the interruption, the break in mood, the sad look returning to Gordy's face.

"Gordy, you don't understand. This man, this judge, refused to approve immunity in exchange for the partner's list, their hidden Swiss accounts, the real ones. He wants more out of me. He wants them to trade immunity for a reduced sentence." Sam moved on Gordy once again, walking through Billy as if he were a ghost. "He insists that there be a sentence," Sam said, looking Gordy flush in the eye, hoping that his voice hadn't faltered.

The boat and all this motion, tuning into Gordy's swinging eyes, was beginning to oppress him. It was worse when he looked up at the outriggers. The horizon offered no relief. This sudden uneasiness stirred thirty-year-old memories of sailboats on Lake Mendota, yawing masts, sickness.

Gordy set down his beer and put his hands deep into the pockets of his shorts.

Sam knew that if he could not find the words to secure his needs, the defeat would be his and his alone. Rather than tolerate more silence, or run the risk that the seas would take their toll on him, Sam came out with it. "Kill him, Gordy. Have him killed."

For one second, no more, Sam felt fear, a kind of terror he had never felt before. And then it passed, leaving him cold and faint, conscious of the boat rocking, but perfectly clear-headed. He felt calm. There was nothing to fear. Everything would be taken care of. He would be invincible again, out of reach, protected. Would Gordy understand that there was no evil involved? It was survival. The cossacks were coming.

"Sam, stop. Think," Gordy said. "If you're giving the partners to them, don't you think the partners are pulling the strings, giving that particular judge to you? Sam, they are the government. They do what they want. No free walkaways for Sam Yones. They can't lose and watch you win. If they lose, you lose. That's the message."

Sam stopped cold. "Of course."

Then Sam started to nod.

"All the more reason," Sam said. "All the more reason to teach them a lesson."

"How?"

Sam's eyes became even smaller. "Kill him, Gordy. Have him killed. Get me my deal back."

The color drained from Gordy's face. "Billy," Gordy said, "will you leave us alone?"

"No," Sam shouted, his eyes now wide and his voice carrying across the water. "Let him hear."

"There's nothing to hear, Sam. That's not the way it's going to be."

Their eyes met, and for a moment held. Then, finally, Sam said, "I came to your father. Your father came to me. Now I'm coming to you. I need your help." The sun reflected a flash off the flybridge windshield, and Sam covered his eyes. Gordy began to move around the rear cockpit, closing the transom gate, checking the live-bait well, turning off switches, wrapping his hand around the ladder. Sam watched Gordy getting ready to leave. Sam feared his expression made him look like a terrified child, that his mouth was half open, that he was without words. He heard himself say "No, oh, no. Please!" He found himself holding his breath, letting it out slowly. He saw Billy's hand stretch toward him, and he waved his son away. Sam's quick eyes were following Gordy's movements. Sam wanted him seated again, to fall under his spell, be able to see his magic smile.

"I don't think you know what I'm trying to say," Sam called out, turning his head as Gordy moved about the rear deck. "I need you to help me." Gordy turned to look at him. "Gordy," Sam cried out, "I need a second chance." Sam caught the lower lip between his teeth, looking at Gordy carefully. He shifted his weight and in the silence heard the creak of a floorboard under him. His voice was so faint when he finally spoke that Gordy and Billy had to strain to hear him. "I light seven candles. One for each of the six million, and one for my son."

Gordy settled down.

"And you want to light another one?" Gordy asked. "For a judge you perceive as an enemy? Sam, survive. I want you to survive. But don't break God's rules to do it. Not that way."

Sam looked across the short space in the back of the boat, and he saw Billy watching him.

"I won't do it, Sam," Gordy said, looking his old friend in the eye.

"But you could if you wanted to," Sam said.

"Ask your son, Sam. Ask him if he wants me to do this for you."

"You can?" Billy asked, excited, joining in. "You can really do this for Dad?"

"God help the two of you," Gordy said.

"Gordy," Ginger was calling out. They turned to see her standing where the pier joined the grass. "It's Liz. There's been something on television about Sam and she wants to know . . ." Her voice faded away.

Gordy looked directly into Sam's eyes. "God help all of us," Gordy said.

The water movement caused the Pearson to move slightly away from the pier, and Sam had to wait until the boat moved closer so he could step on the white planking. Billy followed. Sam headed toward Ginger, who stood holding the phone out to him.

"Sorry, Liz," Sam said, trying to sound normal. "This was a stop I had to make. What's on TV?" Ginger looked away, down to the boat, where Gordy remained alone. Billy listened to his father say several "un-huhs."

"Okay, okay," Sam said, sounding as though he were cutting her off. "I'm on my way."

Sam kissed Ginger, as did Billy, and then Sam turned and waved good-bye to Gordy, whose nod in return was barely visible.

"Don't tell your mother," Sam said to Billy as they drove away from Gordy's house. "Don't tell her any of it."

"You mean like I never told her about Cheryl? Or anything about Matt?"

Billy was instantly sorry he said what he said. Every time he tried to get close to his father, thinking he was sharing something, it came out all wrong.

But Sam was too preoccupied to pay attention to Billy's words. "Billy, we're not going home yet. Go up Pine Tree Drive past Forty-first Street." Sam could never get used to calling it Arthur Godfrey Road.

"And then what?" Billy asked, relieved. At least his father was talking to him.

"It's a white stucco near Forty-seventh Street. The mail box has the name Varner on it."

Jump. How far? How high? What difference did it make, Billy thought. At least they were together.

47

BEFORE THEY REACHED THE DOOR, BYRON HAD IT OPEN. He stood in the entrance hall, looking casual in white slacks with reverse pleats, beautifully fitted, Armani shirt buttoned at the throat, the same outfit he had worn when Spencer and Arlo came over that Sunday two months before, when this all started.

"Can I come in, or do I talk here on your doorstep?" Sam asked, Billy standing behind him, thinking of himself now as riding shotgun. "I understand I'm not supposed to be here. I understand I have no lawyer with me, that you want your assistant who's on this case with you and you don't have him either, so we're even."

"If I didn't know that this was inevitable after Judge Hall's intervention this afternoon," Byron said, "I would have closed my door a long time ago."

Sam nodded respectfully.

"There's no one home," Byron said. "Why don't you both come in?"

Billy smiled, included, but he didn't move until Sam did.

They walked through Bryon's rooms with red tile floors, Indian rugs; blue water sparkled beyond the living room windows that faced Indian Creek. The windows, which were really doors, were rolled back, and the whole room was opened to the lawn of crinkly Florida grass and the polished mahogany speedboat that rode quietly at anchor at the dock in the twilight.

Byron sat down. Sam stood. Billy found a corner.

"That was quite a surprise this afternoon, Mr. Yones," Byron said. "Never had that before."

"I think he's got friends to protect," Sam said. "The partners, the names on that list. They're pretty important. I'll bet he knows them. I'll bet he owes them."

"Mr. Yones, do you see everything as a conspiracy?"

"Don't you?"

Billy folded his arms across his chest, proud of his father.

"I don't think that at all. I think the old man has decided no more free walkaways. No immunity for wrongdoers without a sentence. Some sentence. Some time in, as he would put it, the hoosegow. Old southerners, not the trash, not the Bible thumpers, are like Yankees. They see it as a matter of principle. You people protect your tribes. I protect mine."

Billy's arms fell to his sides. He thought of the three-page list Matt had carried out of the country and the letter with it, signed with the fake name, "Brown," and the admonition, "Please keep this list in the strictest confidence because I never want to see it in the United States." The list, the double-blind list that tied one secret bank account number to another, allowing the breakthrough to the real name of the real owner, the matrix that went along with the letter Matt had carried to Switzerland, had dropped there before he came back through Miami, not New York, screening the trip as if it were a semester-break vacation. Then he thought of his father in jail, the harm to his mother, and he saw himself, with her, taking over.

"If there's some time in jail" . . . they heard Byron saying this, ". . .then immunity. Otherwise nothing."

"You want to be a judge?" Sam asked, drilling into Byron's eyes. "Make your own opening. You create the vacancy. I'll see that you get it." A fish jumped and splashed in Indian Creek, and Byron sucked his lower lip in under his teeth. One thousand and one, Sam counted. He had taught all of them, Mike, Gordy, Matt, all of them, the same trick. One thousand and two. If you count, you won't talk. One thousand and three. Sam watched Byron's eyes. They told him Byron had come around a bend.

"How do I do that?" Byron asked.

Sam hoped Billy had noticed.

"In this town, a million things happen to a million people," Sam said. "And often overnight." He looked at a rug and said, "That's a nice Caucasian. My friend Gordy has several of those."

"I've never been in his home, but I know who he is," Byron said.

Sam smiled. Byron would have to be quiet about everything, even his being there. The embarrassment would be too great. By opening the door to him, Byron had made his real decision. Sam felt safe. "There are silences and there are silences," he had told them, Mike, Gordy, all of them. "But there is nothing like the silence of a Christian gentleman."

"In two months you should have what you want," Sam said. "No clubs without female members . . ."

"I took care of that before."

"Be southern in your birth, New England patrician in your outlook. That's what works now."

"You've done your homework."

"We're important to each other, Byron. By tomorrow would be nice."

"What's my guarantee?" Byron asked.

"I'll give you the list," Sam Yones answered. "The real one." Sam was as excited as a child pulling a rabbit from a hat.

Byron gazed out over the tops of the palm trees, the corners of his mouth turning skyward.

"Now," Sam turned to Billy, "we can go home."

In the car, traveling the mile between Byron's house on Pine Tree Drive and Sam's home on Bay Road, Billy drove in silence. Dad, finally, had let him in on so much. Eight blocks wasn't enough time to understand it all. He hoped he wouldn't make any mistakes, that he would be smart. He never wanted to feel clumsy and short of the right word again.

As they pulled into the driveway, Billy looked up at Sam's Renaissance tower high above the roofs of Miami Beach. He would be up there with his father, and his dad would be in no hoosegow. Never.

48

LIZ, EATING ALONE, HEARD THE CAR PULL UP AND THE FRONT door close. The sounds startled her, and she remembered the times when Sam would sneak in and she would look up, her heart racing, and say, "You frightened me." And he would smile and that would be more threatening than the shock of him suddenly standing over her. She had no one when he was with Cheryl. Her eyes were lonelier than the rest of her face, Liz remembered, having seen Cheryl once at the office. Make her twenty years older and she would have been the perfect match for Sam. The fact that he had chosen Cheryl, even for a short while, hurt Liz even now. People said Sam was in love with life, but in fact he was in love with only a certain sort of life, a tycoon's life. And a Cheryl went along with that. At times Liz wondered whether she, too, the tall, one-time blonde, went along with that life, a perk. They ate out more than they ate in, and not with friends, because they had few of them, but on display, at this public dinner or that, a microphone often in Sam's hand. She would escape from the house, take long walks, take long rides, see fewer men than he thought, and then only once or twice, never satisfactorily. Every time she left the house, her spirits already low, they would sink lower as she drove through the night trying to outrun the facts of Sam's life becoming known to her, hazy facts, without details, but facts of lines crossed, greed displayed, traps set, men owned. One son, too dumb. The other, too dead. Fifty was a hard age to let go. She was still young enough to have ambitions and desires, but fewer chances. Sometimes she thought she had only one chance, Mike, to satisfy either. She could not, despite it all, mourn the death of love for her husband because she was not sure there had been such a death. Her thoughts drifted to the years since he had turned forty, the years of his greatest pride, his power at its peak, his charity sought, microphones presented. These were times she shared completely with him, ignoring moral strategies. Even then, after loving, they would fall asleep like children, hand in hand, and at those times she thought they would never let go of each other and go out into the world alone.

Liz heard her name spoken from the door. Sam was beaming, his hand in his pocket, the change jingling.

"I'm not dead yet!"

He looked delirious with his own achievement, a look her life, to this date, had depended upon.

Disconnected memories crowded her senses: the birthmark on the right side of his chest, round, red, like a third nipple; the cracks through the night as he flexed his knee. He would spring erect when she touched the hair on his inner thigh, and at night, just before the morning, with his eyes closed, he looked so vulnerable. She heard her mother remind her of "this man you're seeing. You'll never be together forever. They go their own way. They're different than we are," and she realized she had not pried herself loose of her mother, even though she had long been dead.

She watched as Sam closed his eyes and breathed deeply, as if he were inhaling his Hermès cologne. She had not spoken yet, she had not moved. She was staring at him, waiting for whatever he had to say. Or do. She had seen this euphoria before, and she knew what it meant to her, her body.

To his credit, Sam began at the beginning. He always did when the end of the story was victory. First he told her about the judge. His feelings of being cowed, lost, "fucked," he said, pronouncing the word harshly, hard, mean as concrete on the street. And as he said it, "they fucked me, tried to fuck me," he smothered her hand, and led her into his elevator.

"Then Gordy," he said to her in the slowly ascending

cab, against the whine of the geared motor lifting them, "another fuck." The elevator door opened at the top, but he blocked her way.

"I'm tired, Sam," she said quietly. Liz went to take his hand. "They've hurt you. I'm sorry they've hurt you."

"No they didn't. They tried to fuck me and I fucked them back."

He moved his hand away from hers and rested it on her breast.

She closed her eyes. "Sam . . ."

"What Gordy wouldn't do, Byron will do."

She took his hand away. "You're talking about life." She looked down at his hand and couldn't imagine she had once held it.

He controlled his voice, making it soft, almost light. "Take off your clothes."

She started to sidestep him.

He held her shoulder. "Take your clothes off here."

"Sam, the U.S. Attorney won't kill anyone. You won't either. It's not you."

He raised his voice, and his words echoed across the tile foyer at the top of his tower. "Do as you're told. In here. Now."

The elevator door was still open, and she stepped back into the cab. Her stare was sufficient to stop him short, the light from the fixture overhead making his eyes sink deeper into his face. He stood still, frozen, as if her gaze had mummified him. She pressed the Ground button, but before the cab doors closed, he was inside the elevator with her.

"They all will do as I say and you will do as I say."

She had moved no more than a few inches and he pushed her back.

The elevator gears wound, and within Sam's Renaissance tower the cab began its descent.

She looked at him, but there was no power in her eyes any longer. Her jaw dropped and her lips parted as he pulled, with pressure on the back of her throat. With his free hand he pulled at her sweater, her slacks, and unbuttoned his fly, and he said to her, "No one fucks with me

351

or mine," as he entered her. Her eyes were shut hard and she pressed herself against the cab wall, shaking as it headed for ground level. It shook and she shook and she tried to find in herself, along with him, that part of her that for so long had loved him, responded to his heated power, freeing her. Her heart accelerated along with his, and, in spite of herself, unwanted by so much of her, she felt excitement. She took the thrusts of her triumphant man, and she saw, in her reflection of the silvered elevator, a widened stare in her eyes and she felt sweat under her arms, above her breasts, and heard, above the whine of the elevator gears, his groans and hers.

The elevator came to rest, and its doors opened, and it was only when, simultaneously, they saw the shadow of Billy leaving that Sam shrank to nothing inside her and she let him shield her body. "Please don't look at me," she said.

The elevator motor had come to rest and the house was quiet.

49

AFTER LEAVING BYRON AND GETTING HIS CAR, SPENCER drove, but where the hell was he driving to? Fuck.

Yes, it was nice out. Yes, it always was in the spring in Miami. Yes, the two clouds in the sky were borrowed from postcards, but maybe it was time for him to head back to Cleveland, where he came from. What seemed like a good idea, staying down here after law school, didn't seem to be the greatest idea in the world now. He liked himself better seven years ago, when he believed in things.

He sat in his car across from Burdine's at the traffic light, waiting for it to turn green. The top was down and he had the kind of fine hair that stands on end in the slightest breeze. His eyes looked a little popped and he had a faint smile on his face, so that, as he leaned just a little bit forward toward the steering wheel, focusing straight ahead through the windshield, the kid in the car next to him, also waiting for the light, thought he wanted to drag.

The kid moved out ahead and the light went green. Spencer was paying no attention, his car still stopped at the light, because he was thinking, wondering.

Why wouldn't he give up on Mike Anker? Why was that man worth it all? Why do men never stop needing a father?

Did the maid show up? Will the bed still be unmade when he got home? If he ever does?

Will Becky's clothes, her pictures, still be there? Did a day or two with her family mean she was gone? Away from him forever?

The light had gone yellow, and as Spencer looked up, it went red again. He looked in the rearview mirror and there was no one behind him. At least he didn't look like an airhead to anyone else. The light turned green again, and with the windows and the top down, the warm air streaming around him, his hair blowing in the wind, he crossed over the MacArthur to the south end of Miami Beach to their unit, such that it be.

He crossed Washington Avenue, continued past the Hotel Shepley (Pullmanettes—air-conditioning—open all year round), then Rayzelle Apts., Tropical Coin Laundry, Optika Lopez, the neighborhood where he had lived when he first moved there. "Never marry a rich woman," Spencer heard Potsy say, his father's voice carrying over all the others at the country club. "You can't give her money. You can't give her a name, and after a while, she gets tired of you." Fuck.

He put his car away in the garage and passed up the desire to park over the white line separating their two spaces so that if she ever showed up, she couldn't park without talking to him, even if it was only to ask him to move his car.

He walked into their hot apartment, the one he could afford on his own, the one with shutters on the windows on a lousy side street in Miami Beach. But they were good shutters and the side street was wide, with royal palms and a graceful broad sidewalk. He turned on the air-conditioning. It worked. Why shouldn't it work? It was their home. A nice home, a decent home.

Nothing like coming from a fine Cuban family these days. Nothing like being the first non-Spaniard to enter her life, the first man since Philip II who didn't macho his woman into cooking and constant childbirth. But she earned more from her job at the bank than he could earn practicing law his way in a lifetime.

As soon as he closed the door he put on his earphones. Her things were still there, her desk, her books by her side of the bed. He closed his eyes, but only for a moment.

He had an extra-long cord so he could hear Aretha Franklin, walk around and undress at the same time. The fucking jaw was driving him nuts. Two shots of Scotch would do it. No more smoking dope; not since he was an Assistant U.S. Attorney.

He lay on their bed for a moment wearing only his shorts and his earphones. Then he walked back into the living room, the wire trailing behind him.

Suddenly he went over to the stereo receiver and yanked the cord out of the front panel and the room was blasted with the Talking Heads punching out of four huge speakers. *Her stuff is here but she isn't. I can play this as loud as I want. Fuck.*

He didn't hear the key in the door. He didn't hear the door open. But he caught sight of her back and the tail end of her suitcase as she lifted it on a chair near the bed, opened it, and started to move first a blouse, then a pair of shorts, from the suitcase, back into her drawers.

"I didn't hear you come in."

She smiled. "You wouldn't have heard a dinosaur come in."

"You want me to put the earphones on again?"

"No. It's your house." His heart fell.

He turned the music off.

"It's so hard to let someone else be in charge," Spencer said.

"Don't you think it's hard for me too?" Becky asked, reaching for another blouse to hang back in the closet. He touched her hand as she moved her clothes back with his. He could feel her pull away. "Have you been busy?" she asked. He listened to her question, but concentrated on her transferring her clothes back home.

"Yes." He tried a smile. "You know me. I'm always busy." Spencer felt on edge and tried to stare at something across the room.

"What are you staring at? I'm back, aren't I?"

"I'm glad for that," Spencer said.

"But you're wondering if I'm going to disappear again?" Spencer shook his head stupidly. "I didn't disappear. It was just for a few days. I had family to attend to," she said.

"No you didn't." Spencer walked away from the bed, where her suitcase lay open, and went over to her desk with the earphones still in his hand. He picked up the newspaper once more. His name was there on an inside page along with Sam's name and Byron's and, for the first time, Operation Angel Fish.

"Did you mean what you said about someone else being in charge?"

"That it's hard to let that happen? Yes. I meant that."

"I want to resolve the condo issue," Becky said. Spencer didn't move.

"I know you do." He waited a minute. "But don't." He turned away and then he turned back to her. "My mother and father are married thirty-five years and they've moved twice." He tried to smile the lopsided smile he had learned from Sam Yones. "Can we spend a little more time here?" He could feel his voice going unsteady. Then he let out a breath and touched her arm. "I'm no better at letting go of people than I am of bricks." He scraped his fingers against his stubble of whiskers. He sat on the bed next to her, and she put her hand on top of his and gently touched his face. Becky was home. And suddenly, for at least a moment, it made no difference to him where home was.

PART NINE

50

Sam thought that the whole process of procuring immunity, finally, was something that would occur on paper. He thought it would happen without the need, once again, for him to be present in the room, any room. He did not want to go back to the Federal Building; he did not want to see his New York lawyers, Arlo, Judge Hall, or, after he heard the news, any other judge, until he was sure. He remembered the television cameras clustered in the waiting room that served the chambers of all the federal judges, and the tripods and lights that were in place almost as soon as the paramedics wheeled the gleaming metal trolley into the judges' private express elevator. There was a moment just after the elevator doors closed when there was complete silence, even though the waiting room was filled with men and women with horrified expressions on their faces, their eyes fixed on the elevator door that had just shut. For a moment, no one seemed to move. People stood in clusters, frozen, as if in a painting. Sam thought of his father, hauled out the same way, seeing images of him in yellowed old photographs with scalloped edges, certain that he had learned nothing of value from that sweet but weak man.

A young woman, who in the old days of print news would have been called a stringer but who was now "your Channel Two On-Site Reporter," was given a signal and the television lights came up. She waited, and when the red light went on, she turned decidedly sorrowful. "Yes, Bill. We're here at the Federal District Court Chambers, and as you can see . . ." She continued to talk as the camera panned around the room. Sam turned his back as it approached him. "Judge Hall's colleagues and friends are in shock. He is still alive, but should he die, colleagues will say that he went the way he would have wanted to go. Judge Selmer Hall, senior judge of the United States District Court, the last surviving appointee of President John F. Kennedy, the judge who presided over four of the most controversial trials in South Florida, stopped by a stroke at eighty-four. The doctors tell us he was stricken just as he was about to mount the bench for his ten o'clock motion call." The camera had long ago left Sam Yones.

Sam never read documents in public, even in a crowd when he was sure to be unnoticed, but when the secretaries, the clerks, the lawyers, all of them, were concentrating on the TV reporter, he wanted to break his rule. He held in his briefcase a list of bank accounts, the most important three pages of bank accounts anyone could imagine, account number or account code, name and balance, zeros eliminated, cross-referenced from the Grand Caymans to the real accounts in Switzerland, the key that broke through both sets of bank codes.

Matt had carried the list out of the country. There had never been a copy. None was needed. Sam had it all in his head. Where it would serve him and no one else.

Gurney. As he touched the briefcase, Sam thought of the correct word. Not a trolley, but a gurney, the cart Judge Hall was rolled out on, the piece of hospital equipment they used to wheel Matt into an operating room in an attempt to save his broken body. Sam hated crowds unless they were his crowds at his home. Strangers could hurt him. Those watching the judge carried out in particular. He did not want to be on this floor near any of these people. Then he smiled to himself. Judge Hall was out of it. The only man he wanted to see now was Byron Varner.

Arlo came up to him and nodded discreetly.

"Now what?" Sam said.

"Obviously, there will be a recess."

"I don't want that." Arlo looked around to make sure no one heard.

"Sam, this isn't any chief judge. This is Selmer Hall. The man's almost dead. Everybody's going home."

"I don't want that," Sam repeated. "He's not even dead yet." Sam looked around. "Where's Byron?"

"He's left the floor."

"Where'd he go?"

"Spencer tells me they're locating an emergency motion judge."

"Don't stand here with me. Help them find one."

Several minutes later they entered the chambers of another judge, a middle-aged woman who wore no robe, who had no court reporter present, who seemed eager to sign whatever order the parties had agreed upon, ready to do so from a standing position if it would save time.

"Sam," Byron called to him. The New York lawyers turned when Sam turned, but he waved them on. Sam waved Arlo on as well.

The chambers floor was empty, as if it were Christmas. When Sam turned around he saw absolutely no one except Byron, and out of the corner of his eye just the flash of a door closing and the profile of the judge who had countersigned his immunity agreement leaving.

They stood there, the two of them, in the midst of a huge open floor, silent now, filled with empty secretarial stations. Byron moved into one of them and hoisted himself up on a desktop. The divider reached only to chest height so he could see across the open floor, from one end of it to the other. Better than a private office even behind a closed door.

"There's no more papers to fill out and sign. It's all been done," Byron said.

Sam turned his eyes on Byron, but had the brains not to thank him.

Byron looked at the briefcase Sam carried and patted

the top of the desk next to his knee. Sam did poorly with commands, but he smiled his Sam Yones smile, and nodded. He hesitated for a moment. Sam did not want Byron to have the matrix, but there was no choice.

He opened the briefcase and set the sheets of paper on the desk. Only after what seemed to Sam to be a very long moment did Byron Varner look down at the three sheets of paper, pick them up one at a time, and read. Names with pedigrees, men with Christian names like Seward and Prosser and Phillips and Brooks.

One thousand and one. One thousand and two.

Sam counted to prevent himself from speaking.

He made it to one thousand and twenty before Byron had finished the two top sheets and had looked up for a moment.

Then Byron went back to reading the last sheet. One thousand and twenty-one. One thousand and twenty-two. Up to thirty-eight. Almost a full minute before Byron was done. He then gave Sam a look that made him feel he had "Christ Killer" written all over his forehead.

"I could have done it, but I didn't have to. If he dies, it's not because you wanted him to die," Byron said, "but because it was time."

Sam found himself confused for a moment, thinking it was Christ Byron was referring to, not Judge Hall. Sam looked around the open core of the building, eerie and monumental, a vast center surrounded by private judges chambers, some doors left ajar, the sun streaming in, the space suddenly vacated. Byron was not looking anywhere except at Sam, and since those first days when the Arlo Shieldses of this world began to befriend him, Sam Yones knew he had something to fear.

With Bryon perched up on that secretary's desk, looking down at him, Sam hated his own height more than he could ever remember. Byron gazed into the few inches of air directly in front of Sam's face. "We got Mike Anker. You didn't get him. We did. We freed your hostage, huh, Sam?" Byron's voice carried only to Sam, not a foot farther. "He gave us Lucky Strike Two, Phaelzer Banque, Geneva. And we gave him a pass. Also one for his girl. Also one for your son.''

"My son?"

"Actually, Spencer gave them the passes. All three of them."

Sam's eyes suddenly changed, no longer as hostile, but open, human.

"Spencer did good work," Byron said, lowering himself from the secretary's desk, still taller than Sam.

Byron started to walk through the maze of desks, and Sam had a choice. He could stand still and be left alone in the empty center of the enormous space or move. He moved. Byron waited for him to close the gap that had opened between them. Sam hated himself when he scampered. "Mike Anker's account was real. He set it up himself. I can prove it," Sam said, calling after Byron.

"Does it make any difference?" Byron said.

Sam's body did a slight tilt. Then he regained his balance, gracefully and quickly. "Since when did watching me get to be so entertaining?"

"We have a copy of a fax from your house to the Grand Bay Hotel. That's documentary proof showing that you funded the fake accounts two days ago, not eight years ago. Two days ago, Sam."

"From my house?"

"From your house."

"I assume," Sam said, his voice without tone, "it went to Mike Anker at the Grand Bay Hotel."

"It did, but he never gave it to us."

Sam looked at Byron, who stood now in front of an open door leading to Judge Hall's private chambers, the sunlight slanting in from the windows, and he held Bryon's gaze for only a second.

"No, don't worry, Sam," Byron said. "Your wife will not be called for authentication. Sam, remember, we don't care about you anymore. You've got your immunity."

"And you've got my list."

"That's right, but I'm not going to use it," Byron said to the deserted floor. "These three pieces of paper will disappear. You won't give me a seat on the bench." Byron tapped the list. "These people will. They're a better bet than you are. Sam, I hate to tell you this. They always have been."

"Take the immunity back, Byron. I don't want it." The swagger once in Sam's voice was gone.

"That's yours to have, Sam. It's a sign of the chosen."

On the empty floor of the deserted judges' chambers Byron was studying Sam carefully; Sam was acutely aware of him, his eyes.

"Oh, Sam, by the way," Byron said as they stood in front of the elevator, doors opened, that had taken the body of Judge Hall off the top floor, "one more bit of advice." Sam looked up at the tall man with the faded blue eyes, afraid. "Your partners made a big mistake and they're sorry for it. The bad fuse in the windshield wipers and the severed drive shaft on the Lincoln was for you, not your son."

An old man, quite an old man, with yellow skin and drugged, blank eyes, that was how Sam saw himself.

"If you have a weapon, Sam, don't tell too many people about it. They'll want to take it from you. They'll want to fuck you and yours."

The elevator doors closed, and Sam Yones found himself inside, alone with Byron. The floor numbers flashed as the car descended.

The sign in his office, GRAB THEM BY THE BALLS AND THEIR HEARTS AND MINDS WILL FOLLOW, did him no good now. Nor did buying his good name, the Jewish Federation, Jews out of Russia, the business school, the Guggenheim, the excavations. He was never in it for the dinner parties: Bologna sandwiches with Liz at either end of a long table was enough. He thought of his own father and himself, the son who did not want what his father wanted to give him. He thought that his dreams, the haunted, haunting nightmares of Matt, the tubes, the once-strong young body mangled on a gurney, were over. Now, never.

"Why are you taking such pleasure in this, Byron?" Sam asked.

"Because you never expected me, the outsider, to cause your downfall. I never expected it either. Nor did I ever expect to get so much out of it." Byron looked at the flashing floor lights. "It's always at the hand of the outsider, Sam, isn't it? The outsider, the gentile. I'm not a bad man, Sam. I just see my opportunities."

Ten more agonizing floors went by.

"I am not without friends," Sam said.

The door opened on the main floor.

"Yes, you are."

51

THE NEXT EVENING CHERYL DROVE MIKE THROUGH THE security gate on Palm Island, heading toward Gordy's house for one of Ginger's homemade dinners. Spaghetti on linen outside under palm trees didn't exactly match, but that was part of Ginger's charm. Cheryl had made up her mind. She was not going. There was no chance of that.

When they walked out of the hotel they saw that both Friday evening papers still carried the story of Judge Hall's stroke in his chambers that morning, just before the ten o'clock motion call. The *Miami Herald,* but not the *Miami News,* also carried a story featuring Byron Varner as Judge Hall's likely successor and his refusal to make any statement except to speak of Judge Hall's almost half century of service, that his successor might indeed be a Republican with a pro-life bias, but that any talk of a successor was inappropriate and self-serving at this time. There was nothing in either evening paper about Sam's immunity. That was prematurely on the news the night before, today over and done with, swamped by the other news. Mike was still looking for something to do with his hands, which was becoming an end in itself.

Mike tried to relax as they continued down the silent road to the cul-de-sac at the end of Palm Island. He realized he had picked up Arlo's South Florida native's habit of leaving the windows open. Cheryl had not complained. Of course, she had never been the type to use hair spray either.

"Mike, you'll be finished when you'll be finished, but try to make the plane."

"I'll be there." He wasn't going to fight with her about it anymore. He was going to dinner at Gordy's. She was not.

"Do we need a fail-safe?"

"No. I'll make it."

"I'll meet you at the gate. If you're not there when the plane goes, I'll go anyway and wait for you in New York. I don't want to wait around at the airport."

"You won't have to."

Gordy's house was private, like the other estates, hidden behind tall stucco walls, covered with growing plants of some crawling type. Dozens of royal palms lit from below lined each side of the driveway that began behind an iron gate and curved gently to the main house, barely visible from the street. The only indication that a visitor had reached the right place was the address on the wall near the gate, no name plate, just four numbers etched in smoked glass framed in a small box, lit from behind by an amber bulb.

"I don't have to wait for you at the plane," Cheryl said, her voice softer now that they were there. "I can come back and pick you up. Mike, I just don't want to go in there." She lowered her eyes. "I don't understand it. I never will. These men have turned your life inside out." Then she looked at him directly. "Sam was ready to push you over a cliff with Gordy holding his coat. I'm sick of him. I'm sick of all of it. But not of you." Her eyes didn't waver. "I just don't understand it. Maybe it's because women are different. If someone hurts us, we don't go back, make up, and start all over again. We don't grow up like little boys, playing baseball games in school yards, getting beaten but ending up buddies in the locker room."

"I'll be there," Mike said. "I'll be there on time."

Gordy gave Mike a backslap. Then Mike looked through the alcove into the huge living room. Sam was sitting in a wing chair covered with flowered fabric, smoking a cigar.

"I wanted to patch things up," Gordy said quietly.

"You shouldn't have done this," Mike said, walking quickly to the far end of the living room, toward Ginger, seated at the piano. She tried unsuccessfully to smile.

Sam's color was better than the night of his party, but Mike noticed that his tie and collar did not quite meet and that his shoes were not quite shined, that from there up things didn't seem to be in the right condition or the right place.

Sam stood up. He knew Gordy was watching him. He walked toward Mike, his hand extended, the gold bar mitzvah pictures on his key chain catching the light.

Then it was as if Ginger took control of herself. She rose from behind the piano, which she seemed to have been using as a barricade, and set her shoulders. "Well, now that we're all here, how about a drink?" Gordy smiled and Mike watched her go behind the bar.

"I guess you haven't heard," Sam said.

"Heard what?" Mike asked, turning his attention to Sam.

"Looks like I'll be down here for a while."

Mike recognized Ginger's act: Give the boys a drink, stay long enough to keep it social, be ready to disappear and ready to reappear with the food at the right time, but no sooner.

"It's good times, all of us together," Gordy said nervously.

Mike turned back to Sam, and Sam repeated himself. "I guess you haven't heard."

"I saw the news last night, if that's what you mean,"

Mike said, his hands behind his back. "Immunity's not so bad, Sam. People survive."

Sam sucked on his Davidoff as if he were charging himself. "Some do better than that."

Mike wondered, now, after all this time, was it to Sam's interest to still have Liz, the prize? Had the notion of what the prize was changed over the years? How different from each other are the women you choose at different points in your life? He could not allow thoughts of times gone by to get too tight a hold. Mike became conscious of the sound of water lapping outside through Gordy's open windows and the touch of a breeze on his forehead.

"Enough of staying inside," Ginger said, sounding like the cavalry. "We can be indoors anywhere." She beckoned them out and rather than lead the way, brought up the rear, as if she sensed everyone's need for a push.

She was glad Gordy had let her put the thick white cushions out on the garden furniture, glad she was Gordy's hostess in his home. She liked the way the lawn ended at the water, the waves of Biscayne Bay hitting the low retaining wall as boats went by in the night. Soft nights were her kind of nights in Miami. She liked herself in bare shoulders, and here she could dress for it.

Outdoors, as the four of them sat around looking at the water, smelling of seaweed and lemon, Gordy said, "We heard this guy, Michael Feinstein, at a birthday party at somebody's house. Ginger, isn't that his record you're playing?"

She nodded, smiling, knowing she had pleased him. He reached out and took her hand.

Sam remained silent, eating canapes on Gordy's crackers. Mike drank Scotch without ice, the rest champagne, as if they had something to celebrate, but with no one wanting to stand up and announce what it was. The big boat, Gordy's Pearson, was at the mooring, all white, with a change to blue at the waterline, a light on in the aft cabin, a welcoming light.

"Who's the extra chair for?" Mike asked, pointing to the table outside set for dinner.

"It was supposed to be for Liz," Sam answered him, but with a different tone. "But she's gone." Sam's eyes were large and empty, and for an instant he looked like a frightened child. His hand went to his cigar as if it were artificial and worked by wires.

They sat and watched each other, on and off, in the light of white candles protected in hurricane chimneys, several of them. Mike wondered whether Sam had called ahead with the news, whether Liz had called herself or whether Sam had made some off-the-cuff excuse as he walked in the door, handing Gordy his jacket, extending Liz's apologies to Ginger. Liz is gone, Mike thought. Sam's eyes were dark now, angry. Mike wondered what "gone" meant. He probably knew more about what "gone" meant than Sam did.

Sam had an undecided look on his face. It was a look Mike knew, a look Mike had taken for over forty years mistakenly to mean understanding of what he, Mike, down deep wanted, even if he wasn't sure himself. Mike wished he had Cheryl to look at across the candlelight. Sure, it was too romantic, and that kid singing Irving Berlin songs made it more so. "There ain't going to be no next time for me" was the line he heard. He didn't want any next time. There probably would never be any. "People like us shouldn't marry people like us," Liz had once said. "There isn't enough oxygen in the room." But that was at the beginning.

"You like it being like old times, don't you?" Gordy said. Mike avoided his eyes and Sam didn't respond. He was paler than before and his eyes were glassier.

There were a few clouds and on the horizon, flashes of lightning, silent, without the thunder.

Sam looked across the terrace, at the tables, chairs, and puffed-up white cushion loungers. Their drinks and the ice buckets with champagne sat on the green terrazzo, nearby. Sam looked around. Then he took a deep breath and looked at Mike.

"I hope you know that someone was trying to nail me yesterday." His voice was his old voice, too loud. It wasn't easy to come to a state of alert under the circumstances, but Mike knew he had no choice. "Someone was trying to sandbag me," Sam repeated. "Yesterday, Thursday. Late afternoon." There was a long ash on his cigar and three burned matches. Lighters ruined good cigars. Sam never used them.

"You got your immunity, didn't you?" Mike said, his voice softer than he wanted, but he did not clear his throat. "The papers said so."

"But it's all right now," Sam said. "It was only the fucking judge that was trying to crucify me."

Gordy put his glass down, moved close to Sam, and put his hand on Sam's knee. "No more in front of Ginger," Gordy said.

Mike stared at Sam, feeling like the little man in a paperweight with snow falling all around him and no way out.

"A judge had a stroke yesterday," Mike said. "Was he the one who was in your way?"

Sam's eyes glowed.

"I guess I got lucky."

Sam kept looking at Mike, and the wind chime made a noise in the night air.

Ginger rose and started to clear the empty glasses, the ashtray, and the round serving plates with the remains of her special antipasto, now drying. She fumbled trying to carry two dishes at once.

Gordy took a champagne bottle out of the ice and filled his glass. Sam held up his hand and shook his head. No, he didn't want any more to drink.

Sam took out his gold pen and started to tap it, cap down, on the glass table.

He stood up. The change jingled and he toyed with the gold bar mitzvah pictures.

"Mike, why didn't you tell us about your lunch yesterday? Outdoors, with your lawyer buddy from the grand jury."

Mike sat back. There was a soft white pillow to lean against, but he did not feel comfortable. He wanted to say something that would nail Sam against the wall, but nothing more came out.

"You're like my Billy, Mike. You give me nothing or you give me bullshit." Sam tapped his pen. "Gordy, you see what I'm saying? I was the one, me, who had to find out who he eats lunch with. At the Bay Side restaurant. On Rickenbacker Causeway. I find out. Gordy, where were you? Don't you think I tried to find out who that kid is? I couldn't find a Potsy Pelcheck. Don't you think I tried that angle?"

"Sam, Sam, Sam," Gordy said, knowing he would hurt, "Even if you did, do you think every kid in the world does what his father tells him?"

The blood drained from Sam's face, and then his chest and his arms. He sat down again.

"Sam, I'm sorry," Gordy said.

Sam held up a hand to silence him.

Sam leaned forward and then he leaned back. He realized that with one arm on the table, he was listing. That was the last position he wanted.

"I let the kid take me to lunch," Mike said quietly.

"You did more than that," Sam said.

"And so I did," Mike told Sam.

Mike looked first at Gordy, and then he turned in his seat and swung around to face Sam.

"How come there's a bank account with my name on it? With over a million dollars in it? With the entries meticulously segregated between an original deposit and subsequent interest to make it look like the money had been sitting there since the year one? Can somebody answer that for me?"

Something detonated inside Sam, giving him great pleasure.

"I can," he said. His smile was first closed, then open. "That account was real and that account was yours. You don't deny you owned that account, do you? Are you going to lie to everyone about that?" Sam stopped and looked around. "You were Lucky Strike One. I even let you take precedence. Why don't you tell Cheryl that? Or Liz, for that matter."

Mike didn't speak to him or look at him.

"It was for less than a year," Mike said.

"Until you had to fill out your tax return." Sam went at him again. "Until that moment, it was a great idea, wasn't it?"

"Yes, Sam, it was."

Mike answered truthfully for his own heart and for Cheryl, not for Sam.

"So you, like everyone else, make up your mind about right and wrong only when you get close to punishment."

Mike thought of Cheryl, ready to accept a piece of luck if it were handed to him.

"I don't even remember what timber deal it was," Mike said, looking at him, then away, staring out at the water, the lights of Miami across the bay. "I told you to do it. That's right. I also told you to undo it. I did have to come face-to-face with a consequence. That's how I know the difference between right and wrong. I wish it were instinctive. I wish I had let right and wrong stay a part of me, the way it started out, the way I was brought up. The way right and wrong started out for all of us." Mike had his jacket off. He had taken it off and handed it to Gordy at the front door. Sometimes he thought he wore the best-tailored jackets in the world, but only to make an entrance. He wore a blue dress shirt and he opened his collar and lowered his tie to half mast. "But we let the world take its bites out of us." Mike had a faraway look in his eye. "How did we sing the Lord's song in a strange land? Not well."

Mike studied Sam.

"You never closed the account, did you? You kept it there. A bomb to go off in my throat. You sent Billy to put cash there, to make it look real. Sam, your son."

"This is not about Liz," Sam said.

Gordy interrupted, taking his elbow. "Sam . . ."

"Of course not," Mike said. "It never was."

Sam moved his arm and Gordy let loose of it.

The candles were burning down, leaving residue on the

inside of the hurricane glass that protected them from the wind, the light dim. Sam stared off at a blank spot on the water. He bowed his head for a moment.

There was a sense of melancholy in his eyes when he looked up. The men sat still, ignoring any sound other than their own breathing. An old piece of newspaper that Gordy must have been reading blew up against the side of the house and flattened out. Sam was in pain, not physical, the other kind, as he tried to look Mike in the eye.

"Liz always loved you," Sam said, roaring no more. "That should have been enough."

Sam started to bring his cigar to his mouth, and then he changed his mind. He turned again in his chair, and tapped the ash against the side of one of Gordy's huge ashtrays.

"Maybe one of the slivers of magic that made it work over all these years," Mike said, "was that I never wanted anything out of you. Others rode on your back, went to your parties, worked your living room for their benefit, leeched your friends, used your contacts. It was never that way between us. Gordy and I were the only friends you ever had."

Mike realized he made few judgments, never yanked Sam back, never pulled him up short, even if he felt that Sam had lost himself now and then. That kind of uncritical friendship happens once, maybe twice in a lifetime, and it has a chance only if it starts when you're a kid. It's too bad when it changes. Then there's no choice.

"Did I fail you that much, Sam?" Mike asked.

Sam walked over to the water, picked up a small stone, threw it into deep water, where it hit with no splash and was gone in an instant. He came back. "You always had to be the smart one. You always had to be better than any of us. Your mind is too complex and too busy." Sam's voice grated with a bitterness Mike had never heard before. "None of this would ever have happened if it weren't for you. You were the dangerous one."

"No, he wasn't, Sam," Gordy said. "You are."

Sam looked at them, fussing with another match to relight his cigar. "Maybe I am the dangerous one," he said.

"Maybe I did start it all." The smoke curled up in the dead air. "We all came from a life where we believed everything was solid, our parents, our grandparents, their candles, and their prayers. But the truth was that nothing was rooted. We all wanted to move on." Sam stood up. "I was just the one who led the way." The change jingled and he toyed with the gold bar mitzvah pictures. The emptiness wouldn't go away, not for a long time.

Mike's lips moved, and for a while he fought the impulse to say anything. The three of them had shared much, but not this. It was hard for Mike to take his eyes off Sam's face.

No one would notice as the years went on if Sam became less interested in his work, if he lived in automatic drive. His inherent meticulousness and his sense of theater would cover for him. Maybe the results would be the same. Maybe they wouldn't.

"How many people would have let you see what I let you see? Let you get your nose in under the tent, hear the voices. What do you call it, Mike? 'Read a new novel every day.' Maybe I'm sorry it happened." That was all Sam said for a moment. "Maybe I'm sorry that each of us has to remember it."

Mike kept looking down. There were no erasers for forty years.

"You never won the battle, Sam, did you?" Mike asked.

Sam stared into Mike's eyes.

"I win all my battles."

Gordy, without another word, got up, touched Sam's shoulder, and went into the house.

Sam let him go.

Mike could tell from the angle of Sam's shoulders that he was devastated.

"The High Gorum. I always wanted their life," Sam said. "They were never judged up front. Only we were. In everything we ever tried. They're the ones who in their righteousness are greedy." Sam's eyes were blank and burning at the same time. "They're the ones who steal strangers' raincoats off airplanes. They use the company plane to fly the kid to summer camp. Pocketing advantages. They don't know how to stop taking. That's why they're on that list. More of them than us."

"If they're thieves, Sam," Mike asked, "do we have to be bigger thieves? Must our evil be equal to theirs? We want what we don't need and we lose what we have."

"What did we have? What did they let us have?" Sam asked, his eyes dead with anger. "They're an island and they'll always want to be an island."

"We had a heritage." Mike's voice rang out. "Of honor, of truth before a tough God, of headstrong parents who taught us that truth. How about us? Who will our sons and daughters look up to? Who, now, are the heroes of our people? Forty years in the desert. Are we finished? Or do we have forty more years to go?" Mike's voice carried to the water.

Mike's question came from nowhere. "Sam, what happened to you today?"

Sam tried to make a ceremony out of relighting his cigar, but it wouldn't work.

"Nothing I can't handle."

Mike knew better. He had heard it all.

"Are you sure?" Mike asked. "Nothing you can't handle?"

"Do any of us in life know what we're doing? Every single minute?" Sam took a breath, thinking of Matt, of Liz, Billy. "I came here and I wasn't going to cry."

"Sam . . ." In spite of himself, Mike held his arms out.

Sam held his cigar upside down so it wouldn't go out.

"Taut, topical and brutally authentic... a damned good read!" —Frederick Forsyth

DEVIL'S JUGGLER

MURRAY SMITH

JUST ONCE IN A WHILE A BLOCKBUSTER OF A STORY HITS THE STORES, A FIRST NOVEL BY A NEW AUTHOR. THIS SEASON IT IS *DEVIL'S JUGGLER*....IT COMES FROM THE PEN OF MURRAY SMITH, WHO HAS CERTAINLY BEEN INVOLVED IN A NUMBER OF REAL-LIFE SITUATIONS ANY GOVERNMENT WOULD LABEL <u>CLASSIFIED</u>.
—FREDERICK FORSYTH